Late Bloomer

Late Bloomer

A NOVEL

MAZEY EDDINGS

ST. MARTIN'S
GRIFFIN
NEW YORK

First published in the United States by St. Martin's Griffin, an imprint of St. Martin's Publishing Group

www.stmartins.com

Designed by Omar Chapa

Library of Congress Cataloging-in-Publication Data

Names: Eddings, Mazey, author.
Title: Late bloomer : a novel / Mazey Eddings.
Description: First edition. | New York : St. Martin's Griffin, 2024.
Identifiers: LCCN 2023036047 | ISBN 9781250847089
  (trade paperback) | ISBN 9781250847096 (ebook)
Subjects: LCGFT: Romance fiction. | Novels.
Classification: LCC PS3605.D35 L38 2024 | DDC 813/.6—dc23/
  eng/20230814
LC record available at https://lccn.loc.gov/2023036047

Our books may be purchased in bulk for promotional, educational, or business use. Please contact your local bookseller or the Macmillan Corporate and Premium Sales Department at 1-800-221-7945, extension 5442, or by email at MacmillanSpecialMarkets@macmillan.com.

First Edition: 2024

10 9 8 7 6 5 4 3 2 1

This one I wrote for me

Content Warnings

Hello, dear reader!

While the following romance is light and fluffy and will hopefully make you laugh, please be aware that the following are discussed throughout the novel:

- Grief after the loss of a loved one
- Complicated relationships with alcohol
- Parental neglect/abandonment

As always, I've done my best to handle the above with nuance and compassion. Please take care of yourself while reading!

All my love,
Mazey

Late Bloomer

Chapter 1

OPAL

I feel, to put it delicately, like a dickhead.

And said dickhead feeling is becoming far too familiar. Comfortable, even. Like rewearing the same pair of sweatpants for six days straight without washing them because if I don't leave my couch during that time, do they actually get dirty? (Yes, I know they do. Yes, I am mentally ill, thanks for asking.)

But life seems dead set on plopping me into situations that bring out my dickheadedness. I regularly and melodramatically flick through my memories in search of one specific moment I can point to as the start of the chaos.

Maybe it was the time I was trampled by a herd of alpacas at a farm when I was four, my sisters watching in silent horror as those giant furry caterpillars with legs created a lifetime fear of long necks.

Or perhaps it was at age ten when I saw *The Mummy* (1999) for the first time at a sleepover and had felt . . . felt a *lot* for both

Brendan Fraser and Rachel Weisz. I'd felt so much, in fact, that that same night I'd tried to kiss my best friend at the time. She had screamed and locked herself in the bathroom, then told everyone at school on Monday that I was a giant lesbo. Surprisingly, we didn't hang much after that.

A more obvious moment would be the time I drunkenly—albeit hopelessly romantically—got my first boyfriend's name, Sam, tattooed on my hip. Sam then dumped me two days later (on my birthday), and I sobbed while returning to the tattoo parlor—sisters Olivia and Ophelia holding my hands—and had the inky, cursive *Sam* changed to *Sandwich* ♥.

But, as I stand on the street corner outside my place of employment, Sprinkle, dressed in an inflatable ice-cream cone suit waving a sign that says TRY MY FRESH WAFFLE, I'm wondering if chaos is less a consequence of actions that sends a life careening off any discernible path and more a curse afforded to the unlucky at birth. And I am very, *very* unlucky.

Or just a dickhead.

As yet another pickup truck speeds by while blaring the horn, the driver leaning out his window to pick the exceptionally low-hanging fruit of a waffle joke (Urban Dictionary edition), my phone buzzes in my pocket. Poisonous butterflies erupt in my stomach, lodging into a dangerous clump of hope in my throat.

The last thing I should want is a text from my shitty ex, Miles. But knowing I shouldn't want that and stopping my stupid little heart from earnestly cracking with how badly I want to hear from him are two entirely separate things.

I sigh, awkwardly stooping to lean the sign against the base of my cone body. Pulling my arms into the suit, I wipe the sweat from the back of my neck and push strands of orange-creamsicle-colored hair off my forehead before fishing my cell out of my pocket.

My heart sinks as I realize it's the group chat with my sisters, confirming our weekly dinner plans.

Olivia

> Pizza or curry tonight?

Ophelia

> The answer is ALWAYS curry

I blow out a raspberry through my lips, then force my mouth into a smile, texting back my order. Pocketing my phone, I waddle to the entrance of Sprinkle, the scent of ice cream and waffle cones smacking me even through the suit.

It's not that I don't enjoy Thursday night dinners with my two favorite people, but the tradition had sprung up from being miserably dumped by Miles and the excessive wallowing I'd done afterward. While eating curry and binge-watching *The Real Housewives* certainly does some heavy lifting to fill the gaping hole in my life since he broke up with me, the recurring dinners are still a reminder of how much time has passed since we split up.

And how the chances of getting back together are slimmer and slimmer.

It doesn't help that I'm stuck in a nasty cycle of feeling depressed and alone, getting a text from Miles to "hang out" on a random weeknight, going over to his crappy apartment with his mattress on the floor and two drool-stained pillows (without a pillowcase in sight), giving him a blow job or some other form of lackluster sex, then leaving immediately after (read: getting kicked out because he has an *early morning*—I've never known the man to wake up before eleven), only for painful radio silence from him for the next week. The routine leaves me feeling even more miserable than before. *Shocking.*

Anytime I get mopey and weak—more often than I'd care to admit—and blubber to my sisters how badly I want to get back with him, they ask the super-fun question of what I even liked about the man to begin with.

It's embarrassing how quickly it shuts me up. But, honestly, I don't have an answer. How do I explain that he was physically *there* (except for all the times he wasn't) and his smile was *cute* (but he stopped smiling at me sometime around the second week of us dating) and I'd sort of rather *die* than be alone (even if I felt lonelier than I'd ever been while in a relationship with him).

I squeeze behind the shop's counter, then through the kitchen, trying not to run into any appliances as I navigate my way to the break room. The suit makes a *shwloooping* sound as the swirl at the top gets cut off by the doorframe, then pops back up as I force myself through. My friend Laney turns from where she's hunched near the tiny window in the corner.

"Hey," Laney says, taking a final drag on her joint and blowing the smoke through the open window.

"Hi," I say as cheerily as possible despite my less-than-sparkling mood. People don't like me if I'm not peppy and happy. "Power me down?" I ask, turning and waving toward my butt.

Laney's footsteps clomp across the small space, and she flicks off the battery pack near the base of my cone, then unties the drawstrings.

I sigh in relief as I shimmy out of the nylon monstrosity. Despite it only being the start of April, the humidity in Charlotte, North Carolina, is smothering the city with a vengeance.

"Got something for you." Laney tosses a folded envelope to me, and I fumble, then drop it.

"What's this for?" I ask, stooping to pick it up.

"Belated birthday present," Laney says with a bored smile.

"Aw, thanks." I grin at her as I take a seat at the rickety card table we use to eat. My birthday was five weeks ago and Laney (and everyone else who wasn't my sisters or parents) had forgotten . . . which wasn't a big deal at all and didn't hurt my feelings one bit.

"Course." Laney perches herself back in her spot by the window and lights another joint. "So, I have a tiny favor to ask," she says as I slide my finger under the envelope's seal.

Laney always has a tiny favor to ask.

"What's up?" I pull out the ripped piece of notebook paper from the envelope. It reads *happy birthday* in pencil.

"I know I'm the absolute *worst* to ask so last-minute but, like, I'm scheduled for a double today but it turns out the band playing at McNally's tonight canceled and they asked us to play and it's like, one of those things you don't want to say no to because you never know when there might be someone important in the audience, you know what I mean?" Laney says, taking a drag, then fixing her features into a puppy-dog look. "So, would you cover my shift?"

My shoulders curl, a heavy blanket of exhaustion wrapping around me as I stare at the two creased scratch-off lottery tickets that Laney had stuffed into the envelope.

Laney is the lead singer in a band with Miles. It never really feels all that great to cover a shift for her to go hang out with my ex. I'd never admit it—mainly because I prefer to avoid conflict by bottling my feelings up so tightly I'm at risk of exploding like a Coke stuffed with Mentos—but it kind of eats me to pieces that Laney still hangs out with him. Especially since they only know each other through me.

And while I'm probably being paranoid, I have this awful, nagging sense that Laney and Miles aren't just platonic bandmates either. It's the oh-so-subtle potential clues of finding Laney's thong in Miles's car or her lipstick in his bathroom while he and I had been dating.

But those things weren't hard proof, and Laney and Miles had laughed hysterically any time I had broached the subject.

"You'd be helping me *sooooo* much," she says, giving me her most saccharine smile.

"Okay," I say, forcing a smile back. "I could use the extra money anyway." I wish that were the main motivation, but my dominant personality trait is pleasing others. I have about as much backbone as a cooked spaghetti noodle.

"Thank you, thank you, thank you!" Laney squeals, putting down her joint to give me a hug. "You're the best friend *ever*."

This, at least, is true. I barrel through life like an overeager St. Bernard ready to rescue literally anyone by doing anything. Four a.m. ride to the airport? I'll bring you coffee. Help moving? I won't bat an eye if you take a three-hour break to scroll on your phone while I do the heavy lifting. Left your wallet at home by accident? Of course I'll grab the check, and seriously, it's fine, don't worry about Venmoing me back. It's all good.

Unfortunately, most of the people in my life have no shortage of things they need help with.

It could be worse. At least tonight I'll be behind the counter scooping ice cream instead of standing on the corner in the extremely large and mildly degrading costume. When the previous cone maestro had quit, my boss had asked me to step in. Just for the afternoon. The afternoon had turned into three months of me in that suit.

"Are you gonna see if you won anything?" Laney asks, tapping her chipped nail on the scratch-offs.

"Oh. Yeah. Thanks for these, by the way," I say, reaching in my locker and rummaging around for a coin. "So, uh, thoughtful."

"Oh my God, don't even mention it," Laney says in a tone that makes the tickets seem much more extravagant than they are.

I take a seat and start scratching.

"I have this super-hot look for tonight," Laney says. She's a pro at unprompted monologuing. "It's this mesh crop top that I'm going to pair with my checkered skirt."

"Cute," I say, scratching away the last corner of the first ticket and pushing it aside. No matches.

"I know! I showed it to Miles last night, and that boy's jaw was on the *floor*."

What a totally innocuous and not at all inappropriate thing for Laney to say about my ex!

"That's great." I keep my eyes fixed on the two adjacent squares filled with flowers and $500,000 I just uncovered on the other scratch-off.

"Mm-hmm. We've actually been throwing around the idea of touring a little bit this summer. Hit Durham. Asheville. Knoxville. Maybe even go for bigger cities like Atlanta."

"Oh wow," I say, my heart cracking a little. Miles and I had talked about doing a road trip this summer.

But I'm not going to think about that. Nope. Not going to let that hurt linger.

Not thinking about it would be a hell of a lot easier if I had anything else to preoccupy my brain with. But without some shiny stimulus, my thoughts stick on the hurt like an insect to fly paper, glued to the torture until it gives up in exhaustion, rotting away.

I stare at the freshly scratched square with a frowning rain cloud.

"I just think it could be so good for our sound for us to travel together. Explore the world more, you know?"

"Yeah, for sure," I reply, blinking against the odd pressure building behind my nose and eyes as I scratch off another square. Probably allergies and not at all a tragically broken heart.

"And, like, maybe you could house-sit for me while I'm gone? Like water my plants and feed my fish and stuff? It would let you get out of your parents' place for a bit."

I open my mouth to give Laney my auto-response that I'll help however she needs when my attention snags on the cleared card in front of me. I squeeze my eyes shut for a moment, then open them, my heavy heart suddenly beating a little faster. A little wilder.

This can't be right.

Laney is still talking, but it's an incoherent buzz with all the blood rushing in my ears. With shaking hands, I lift the piece of cardstock, almost pressing my nose to it as I scan the tiny print over and over again.

"Opal, did you hear what I said?" Laney asks, waving her hand in front of my face.

I blink at her, so rapidly little silver stars swim across my vision.

"I can't cover your shift tonight," I say, jolting up to stand.

"What?" Laney snaps. "Why?"

"Because I just won the fucking lottery."

Chapter 2

OPAL

"I won the fucking lottery!" I screech, busting through Olivia's door like the Kool-Aid Man on uppers.

Both Ophelia and Olivia scream. But in the terrified, home-invasion type of way and not the holy-shit-this-is-such-exciting-life-changing-news way I was hoping for.

"I think I'm having a heart attack," Ophelia says, clutching her chest.

"You and me both," Olivia responds, taking a generous gulp of wine.

"I'm sorry, but did you not hear me?" I say, shutting the door with my foot and bouncing into the apartment. "I. Won. The. Lottery."

My sisters slow-blink at me.

"Like the actual lottery?" Olivia asks.

"I won," I whisper, getting way too close to Olivia's face. "Five hundred *thousand* dollars."

I punch my fist into the air, brandishing the ticket.

The room is silent for a few seconds.

Then all three of us erupt into screams. The screaming goes on and on, amplified by our jumping, gasping, and crying as we take turns holding the ticket. Olivia's downstairs neighbor starts beating on their ceiling with a broom handle, but nothing can burst our bubble.

When we finally shout ourselves hoarse, I walk them through the wildest hour of my life.

"I can't believe this," Ophelia says, draping herself across the couch.

"I can't either," I echo, plopping down on the floor and grabbing my phone out of my pocket as it dings.

Yikes. I have a ton of missed texts from Laney.

> SO HAPPY FOR YOU!!! THIS IS AMAZING

> YOU SOOOOOO DESERVE THIS

> Don't forget who got you that ticket ;)

> But seriously, are you not coming back tonight? You promised to cover for me

> Do you want to get out of here for a girls weekend soon? Or maybe get dinner next week?

I purse my lips as I scroll through the messages, getting whiplash from the rapid jumps between supportive and not-so-subtly hinting at wanting some sort of reward for giving the ticket to me. For my birthday.

I'm about to show my sisters all the texts when a call lights up the screen.

My head jerks back as I read the name.

"What's wrong?" Olivia asks.

"It's Miles," I say, waving my phone.

"Don't answer it," my sisters say in unison as I swipe my finger across the screen and answer the call. I've never claimed to have self-respect when it comes to communication with an ex, so might as well stay on brand. Can't let money change me and all that.

"Hello?" I say, my voice breathy and eager. Like a total fool.

"Opal. My God. It's so good to hear your voice."

I all but melt. Objectively, I know hearts and tummies are dirty fucking traitors, but even with all the mental resolve in the world, the second I hear Miles's familiar voice purr in that tone he knows makes me a little wobbly, a tidal wave of hope roars through my system, poisoning my mind and heating my blood and beckoning at me with a seductive crooked finger.

"I've missed you," Miles says, sweet and tempting like honey.

"Do you need something, Miles?" I ask, trying to sound cool. I'm sure I'm not fooling anyone.

"Nah. Just wanted to check in on you. Been thinking about you."

My heart twirls then floats heavenward. He's been thinking about me? All I've ever wanted is for someone to think about me.

"I've been thinking about you too," I whisper, dipping my toes in emotional quicksand. But I swear I can hear him smile on the other end. Wicked. Wolfish. Softened with a dimple. And, this time, it's genuine.

I can also feel my sisters staring daggers at the back of my head, but I'm pretending not to notice. I scuttle across the room, tucking myself into a corner.

"Been thinking a lot about *us* too," he says, voice even lower, the words vibrating through my cracked chest.

Us. Who knew two little letters could create such an impact. Whenever I'm part of an *us* I pour all my energy into the *u* and make the *s* stand for sacrifice. It's not like it does much good, I always seem to end up alone. I have a tendency to get too attached to people too fast, finding even the tiniest thread of connection and plucking it to death.

Miles is the latest in my tapestry of frayed relationships.

"R-really?" I ask, a dangerous swoop of hope in my voice.

"Of course. I . . . I miss you, Opal. Wanna get coffee tomorrow? Maybe talk about things?"

At this point, my heart is fit to burst. Miles is apathetic by nature, excitement and interest too cringey to indulge in, but I spent the entirety of our relationship bending over backward to try to make him smile, regardless. I nearly tore in two twisting myself into different shapes in the hopes that he'd like one of them. And maybe now, he's finally seeing what he lost when he told me he needed to focus on his music.

"I'd . . . I'd really like that," I whisper, biting my lip as I smile.

"Amazing. Waffle House?"

Jesus, I'm a swoon risk. "Perfect."

There's a pause that stretches a beat too long. "So . . . anything new?" Miles asks, his tone the epitome of casual.

"Ummm?" It's not like Miles to ask about my day. Or ask any questions at all, to be honest. "Not really. Why?" I respond, for once choosing to have caution with this stupid boy who always has me wrapped around his finger.

"Just curious. Just curious. Like I said, been thinking about you."

Another pause.

"So, I talked to Laney a bit ago and—"

In a burst of movement, my phone is torn out of my hand and I'm gaping up at my sister.

"Snort glass, asshole," Ophelia says into the microphone before ending the call.

"What the hell was that?" I shout, pushing to stand and looking at my sister with righteous indignation.

Ophelia gives me a bland look. "I think you know."

My shoulders slump. Of course I know. Despite evidence to the contrary, I do possess some common sense and a painful amount of self-awareness. It's just that, despite those two things, I still make *awful* choices. Especially when it comes to Miles. Or most men, for that matter.

It sometimes feels like a curse to be attracted to men, seeing as I don't generally like them. Now, women? I love women.

They are creatures I genuinely want to talk to and also kindly ask to sit on my face.

"You need to block him," Ophelia says. "I know what he's doing."

"You couldn't even hear the conversation!"

Ophelia crosses her arms over her chest, cocking her hip. "Doesn't take a genius to figure it out. He spends your relationship using you and cheating on you, then dumps you and regularly booty-calls you, then a few hours after you win the *lottery* he misses you? Come on, Opal."

I rub my fist against my aching chest. Ophelia is the brutalist type of honest.

"I know," I whisper.

"Opal, sweetie, I know that's hard to hear," Olivia says, holding out her arms from the couch. I cross the room and collapse into her. "But whatever you do, don't give that talentless ass clown a cent. I'm begging you."

"I won't," I say, voice shaky and thoroughly unconvincing. I don't *want* to give Miles money, but I have this disastrous tendency to give in when people ask me for something often enough. And no one is quite as persuasive as Miles. "I think Laney expects something since she got me the ticket."

"Oh my God, that's another person that can fuck all the way off."

"She's my friend," I protest (rather weakly).

"She's really not, Opie," Ophelia says, pulling out my childhood nickname. "And you don't owe her a dime. You've gone above and beyond with favors for her over the years."

"She only calls you a friend because she knows it means she can get something out of you."

And that's my problem. I'm so hungry to connect with someone—anyone—I settle for crumbs and pretend like they're a full meal.

Ophelia folds her long limbs onto the couch behind me, hugging my back. My sisters are quiet for a moment, letting me silently stitch the latest tear in my already broken heart.

"What *do* you think you'll do with the money?" Olivia eventually asks, pulling back to smooth a hand over my hair.

The question catches me off guard. I've been so stunned at even the idea that I'd won, then tangled up in others trying to lay claim on this life-changing money, that I haven't processed it's *mine*. That I can do whatever I want with it.

But what *should* I do with it?

Believe it or not, I didn't grow up dreaming of becoming an ill-paid giant ice cream cone. I went to art school, getting my degree in fine art, which, in this capitalistic hellscape I was tragically born into, means that I spent a lot of money to be deemed unemployable by pretty much every job application algorithm out there.

Which is fine. Totally fine. Every artist has to struggle. After graduating with no plan, I tucked tail and moved back in with my parents, naively promising myself that I'd be staying six months, tops. Just long enough to save money and move to New York, where all real artists lived and suffered and thrived.

Sprinkle was temporary. A means to a (slightly degradingly

earned) paycheck. And I had been close—so close—to making the move.

And then I met Miles.

And I put the move off.

And kept putting it off.

And, holy shit, *kept* putting it off.

I deferred my dreams, months ticking by, until those dreams faded and complacency disguised itself as comfort. The idea of being with someone, even someone who never really cared, was less terrifying than taking a step that would drop me all alone in a great big city.

Because, really, why give up a job—despite the demotion from server to sidewalk cone—and why throw a wrench into (what I thought was) a perfectly fine relationship with Miles? Those tiny questions always stopped me if I thought too much about a change.

But somewhere between the shitty job and the shittier boyfriend, I lost sight of the fact that I wanted change to be . . . happy.

"I want to use it for a fresh start," I blurt out, eyes going wide as I look at my sisters.

"That's great," Olivia, the oldest and far maturest of the three of us, says. "What would that look like?"

I gnaw on my lip as I think. "I . . . I want to be an artist. I want to seriously do it. I want to paint my textiles and sell my designs."

I frolic and play in every medium from charcoals to clay,

but my hands are never happier than when I'm painting fabrics and materials and using them to craft something stunning and wearable.

My favorite is shoes. I have hundreds of notebooks filled with sketches of shoes, hand-painted with vivid designs. Mules and clogs and flats and boots. Concentric patterns, abstract swirls, vibrant scenes of birds-of-paradise like rainbows at the tips of someone's toes. An infinite canvas exists with each step someone takes.

"Opie, that's amazing," Ophelia says. "We want that for you. You should do it."

"Maybe I'll finally move to New York," I say, sitting up straighter—this idea, this new life, gaining momentum. "Get an apartment. Hell, maybe buy something? Use it as a studio? Sell my work?"

My sisters go silent at that.

"What?" I ask, catching a glance between them.

"Why does it have to be New York?" Olivia asks gently.

I shrug. "It's what artists do. They move to New York and are constantly and devastatingly inspired by the energy of the city."

"I mean . . . maybe some artists are. But aren't you more inspired by nature?"

"She has a point," Ophelia chimes in. "When Mom and Dad took us to New York when we were teenagers you complained the entire time about how much you missed trees, and your favorite thing we did was walk through the flower market."

They aren't wrong; I do tend to prefer nature. Something

about the colors and textures of the wild—the smell of summer heat on grass or the first gentle fall of snow—makes me feel peaceful. At ease. Like my brain can slow down and catch its breath.

But when I think of artists—the kind I admire, the kind I want to be—they're rebels and revolutionaries, their work small acts of protest, the emotion of art grinding against the cold anonymity of large cities.

And I want to belong to a group like that. I'm constantly trying to define myself, to fit nicely and neatly into the boxes and spaces I attempt to occupy.

All I've ever really wanted to do was belong.

Somewhere.

Anywhere.

"You don't have to make any decisions tonight," Olivia says, picking up on my runaway train of thoughts like she's always able to do. "Just something to think about. And that's the amazing thing about money, it gives you time to think. The space to plan."

I nod, trying to pull myself back into the moment. I know Olivia is right, but my restless brain loves latching onto an idea, turning it over and over and demanding a plan *right now*. It's hard to shut it up.

I steal my phone back from Ophelia, heart bottoming out when it buzzes with a new text from Laney:

I'm coming over! Wanna celebrate with you!

Then another:

Miles wants to come too! Let's party!

"Can I sleep here?" I ask Olivia, chewing on the inside of my cheek.

"Yeah, why?"

I toss my phone to the side and blow out a raspberry. "I feel too keyed up to drive home," I lie, not wanting to worry Olivia and Ophelia any further that I'll do something reckless with the money. Which, in all fairness, they have a right to worry about. My silly heart often works in cahoots with my people-pleasing brain, all common sense shooting out my ears when I need it.

Ophelia untangles herself from us and stretches, arching her long and graceful neck.

"I better get going," she says. "Teaching an advanced pointe class in the morning."

All three of us are artists in one form or another—Ophelia a ballet dancer and Olivia a writer—which holds a delightful bit of irony as our mom and dad—a statistician and environmental lawyer, respectively—don't have a creative bone in their bodies. We love dabbling and playing with different ways to express ourselves, often taking on some random project or another together to bond over.

"Love you."

"Text us when you get home."

After the door clicks shut behind Ophelia, Olivia makes up the couch for me, and I burrow into the soft sheets and pillows.

"Why are you hovering over me like Kathy Bates in *Misery*?" I ask, squinting one eye up at her.

She laughs through her nose. "I'm just that obsessed with you, love bug," she says, smoothing a hand over my orange hair. "And I'm also excited for you. I think a fresh start is exactly what you need. Find your spark again."

She bends down, placing a kiss on my head, then retreats into her room.

I blink at the dark ceiling.

My spark.

That's what I'm missing. That glow of joy, a candle in a winter window, warm and welcoming and a guide home.

I hope I can find it.

Chapter 3

OPAL

I wonder if I'll ever get a good night's sleep again.

Agonizing hours of endless tossing and turning isn't a particularly new phenomenon—I actually can't remember the last time I slept well. My parents never miss an opportunity to whine about how they didn't sleep through the night for the first ten years of my life—always waking up with a jolt from the force of my gaze as I hovered at the edge of their bed like a Victorian ghost child.

But it's been a week and a half since I won the lottery, and my sleep is worse than ever.

And damn is it frustrating. I wish I came with an off switch, a way to power down the pinging circuits of my hyper brain. But no, the second I put my head on a pillow, electricity surges through my veins, jump-starting my heart any time I even mildly drift off. My mind decides to make me relive every embarrassing moment of my life on loop or come up with endless worries, all of them bouncing around my skull like a jar of marbles spilled over a staircase.

I stare at the sharp green lines of the 4:00 a.m. glowing from my clock until my eyes go hazy, early morning darkness hovering in the room. With a sigh of defeat, I give up on the idea of sleep.

It doesn't help that my phone keeps buzzing—DMs and texts and tweets from people I haven't heard from since high school or earlier—that blue light adding fuel to my jitteriness. Apparently, Laney didn't stop with Miles when it came to sharing my good news.

The money was deposited into my previously laughable bank account a few days ago, creating a world of problems. I've spent most of my life desperately searching for friends and closeness and companionship—always serving as people's back-up plan, a good time in small doses, ready and eager like a puppy to jump at anything I was lucky enough to be included in, then doing everything possible to ensure the people around me had a good time, even if it left me feeling spent and empty.

So many moments of my life I wanted someone to text me to see how I was, break up the loneliness of chasing one-sided relationships.

Now, *everyone* wants to see how I'm doing. If I want to get drinks. Dinner. Coffee. Some of the messages are subtle. Most are downright demanding.

All of it hurts my feelings.

No one wanted anything to do with me until I had something

monetary to give them, and it's painful to realize how accurate my sisters' concerns were about people wanting to use me.

I know nothing about this will change unless I find the courage to make the next move. But stagnation is comfortable. Making a change takes bravery, a willingness to declare what I want then be swept into the unknown consequences of it. If I never move, nothing ever changes, but if nothing ever changes, I can't be crushed by the disappointment of it not working out.

I scroll through my messages, a particularly long one from Laney snagging my attention.

Another unanswered call. Cool. I just find it really funny that for someone that likes to pretend to be some fucking martyr all the time, you have no problem blowing everyone off the second something good happens. But you do you I guess. Not like any of us have any real problems, right? And like, I wouldn't even be mad or bother reaching out if i didn't care about you and shit. I guess that's what makes it so frustrating though . . . you're just looking out for number one. Fine. Don't crawl back to my DMs when you're sad and mopey in a week because someone hurt your precious feelings. Careful what bridges you burn, babe

Guilt roils through my stomach and up my throat. I'm not trying to be selfish, I'm . . . I'm . . .

I'm overwhelmed.

I'm overwhelmed and confused and have never felt so isolated as I do now with everyone blowing up my inbox.

I start typing out an apology text, but Olivia and Ophelia's voices swirl in my head.

She's not your friend, Opie. She's really not.

I won't take my own advice, but I will take theirs. With a sigh, I swipe out of the app and chuck my phone to the end of the bed. I smack the heels of my hands against my forehead, trying to jolt myself out of this slump. I hate the idea of being hated—it makes my skin itch and my stomach churn—but if I'm already being painted as a villain by my so-called friend, I might as well put my money toward finding a new place to ghost everyone.

I sit up, pulling the top half of my short (now bubblegum pink) hair into a little fountain at the crown of my head. After turning off all push notifications on my phone, I grab my ancient laptop and boot it up.

With a deep, shaky breath, I open the browser and begin to search.

I start basic and broad, my *New York apartments* googling offering too many options for my already crowded brain. Then I start researching neighborhoods. Brooklyn. Lower East Side. Hell's Kitchen. Chelsea.

Clicking through apartment listings on countless sites, zooming in on the grainy pictures of gray walls with tiny windows and stained plastic floors that seem to make up all of New York's property options . . . that are in my budget, at least.

It turns out hundreds of thousands of dollars does not actually get you that far when it comes to New York City real estate. An incredible revelation that's totally, utterly shocking for one of the most expensive cities in the world.

I drag my hand down my face and squeeze my chin, none of this feeling like I imagined it would.

Maybe Olivia and Ophelia were right. Again. Damn them.

Maybe New York isn't actually for me. Because the idea of moving to a giant city made of concrete and metal and glass without knowing a soul makes my aching heart crack even further with loneliness.

I'm about to give up on the entire thing and exit out of the search when an ad in the corner catches my eye.

Visit Asheville, stay weird! it reads, a picture of a small skyline and lush mountains in the background.

Like the flip of a switch, I'm flooded with happy memories.

I've always loved Asheville—my parents took us on countless trips to the mountains when we were kids. It's an incredible, eclectic mix of waterfalls and forests, hiking and art-filled streets, buskers and beauty.

It's a little bit of everything, nestled in the Appalachian Mountains.

I change my search terms.

The next thing I know, I have fifty-two tabs open and haven't blinked in hours, falling down a rabbit hole of hidden gems in the town that's now calling to me.

But one listing in particular, a Facebook Marketplace ad with a few grainy photos and endless loveliness, has grabbed me by the heart and won't let go.

Without thinking, I pick up my phone and dial the number.

"Hello?" a sugary-sweet voice with a southern accent answers after the third ring.

"Hi! So sorry to bother you. My name is Opal. Opal Devlin. I saw your Facebook Marketplace post for the farm."

There's a brief pause, then the woman says, "Oh right! Well, hello, darlin'. I'm Trish. Pleased to meet you."

"You too," I say, meaning it. I automatically like this woman and her sweet voice and dripping charm. "Is the listing still available? I had a few questions and I—"

"Now let me just interrupt you right there, sweetheart," Trish says. "I want you to know that the price isn't negotiable. The Thistle and Bloom is a fine piece of property and I'm already selling it for a song. I don't want either of us wasting our time."

"Sorry! Sorry!" I rush out. I'm incapable of having a conversation without profusely apologizing for, like, talking and whatnot. "That's not what I'm asking. The price is fine. Not an issue at all, actually."

Another pause. "Well, okay, then. What can I help you with?"

"Is it . . . Can you tell me about it?"

Trish takes a deep breath. "Oh, honey, it's the most beautiful place in the world."

She launches into an outrageously gorgeous description of the flower farm, painting a picture of rainbow sweetness, dewy leaves, and sun-dappled petals. An astonishingly cozy cabin perched in the center of the five acres. Gorgeous views and green grass and a scene so charming it might as well have a constant stream of folk music humming in the background.

"It sounds incredible," I say breathlessly, peony-pink hearts in my eyes.

"Sweetie, it's heaven on earth."

"And you haven't sold it yet?" I ask, knowing how desperate I sound. I don't even care. Suddenly, nothing in the world feels more monumentally important than getting myself to this perfect, flowery Eden, spending my days frolicking in fields of tulips, nights wrapped in a warm blanket next to a roaring fire in the stone fireplace Trish described, sipping chamomile tea as crickets sing through the windows.

Trish sighs. "You know, there's been offers. So many offers."

My heart sinks.

"But none have felt quite right. A place like this, somewhere so special, deserves a special person to own it. Keep it lovely. And I'm searching for that person."

"I can be that person," I basically yell. "I know I can." My jaw is tense, skin buzzing and muscles bunched with how much I want this to be my future.

"I don't know, honey. You sound so young. You sure you can take care of a place like this?"

"Yes. Absolutely yes." At this point, I'm willing to do just about anything to prove it to Trish. To myself.

Trish pauses again.

"I'm ready to write you a check for the asking price today," I blurt out, needing to hear this sweet older woman's voice tell me yes. Open the door to my new life with that one simple syllable.

"Oh, bless your heart. You are serious, aren't you? Where

do you live?" Trish asks slowly, and I cross all my fingers and toes.

"I'm in Charlotte."

"What a coincidence, so am I. If that isn't a sign from heaven that you're meant to have this place, I don't know what is!"

My entire body is flooded with warmth and excitement like the first time stepping out into the sunshine after a brutally long winter.

"Let's meet and do this in person. I'll hand over the deed and you can write me the check. We can meet at the Starbucks in the Blakeney Shopping Center. How about ten a.m.?"

I grin. "See you then."

. . .

"Hi, darlin'. Would you by chance be Opal?"

I turn around to the cheery drawl, smiling. Trish's appearance exactly matches her voice, sweet, bubbly, and exuberantly southern.

"I am! And you're Trish?"

"Guilty. Thanks for meeting so soon, sugar," she says, fluffing her poofy blonde hair, sparkly pink talons glinting in the sun. She looks like Dolly Parton but with more cheetah print. I can't stress enough how much I adore her.

"Thank *you*," I say, unable to fight the urge to reach out and give her arm a friendly squeeze. Comfort radiates out of her. "This is honestly just . . . so exciting."

"Sure seems like kismet, huh, dear?" Trish says, sitting

down and taking a long sip of her sweet tea. "You sure you're ready to take on a place like the Thistle and Bloom?"

This makes my heart trip. "What do you mean? Is it not in good shape?"

Trish's head jerks back and she stares at me, affronted. "Why, it's perfect. That's the whole point—if I'm going to let go of somewhere so wonderful, I need to know whoever takes it over will care for it properly."

I beam, emotion building in my chest at the passion and love in Trish's voice. She clearly cares deeply for the farm. "I will. I promise. I actually plan to use it as my fresh start. I'm an artist and I want to start working seriously at it. The Thistle and Bloom seems like a spot of endless inspiration."

"What kind of art, sugar?"

Heat curls up my cheeks, and I toy with the lid of my iced coffee. "Uh, well, it's kind of niche, I guess, but I really like, er, painting textiles?" I wonder if it will ever stop feeling uncomfortable to talk about the thing I love so much. Why does passion feel so embarrassing?

"How neat," Trish says, eyes glinting as she leans toward me. "Tell me more."

Damn, I *love* this woman. She makes me feel like the most interesting person in the world, like she genuinely cares about me.

"Shoes are my favorite to paint," I say, voice rising in excitement. "Creating unique designs on leather mules and clogs. I want to sell them."

Trish's smile never falters. "Honey, that sounds like the

greatest idea in the world. You're gonna make a fortune. And I can't tell you how happy it makes me to imagine you doing that at the Thistle and Bloom."

I can see it too, my hair undone, long, gauzy dress flowing in the soft summer breeze as I stand on the porch of that perfect cabin, the sun on my cheeks and the sweet scent of flowers in the air. I'll walk barefoot across the grass, set up a spot under a shady tree, working for hours on my tiny labors of love. Peace. Purpose. It's all about to be mine.

My eyes go a bit misty, and Trish reaches across the table, holding my hand.

"But, to be blunt about it, darlin'—and I hope you can forgive me because I truly hate talking about money, it's such a dirty thing—but are you sure you can afford it? Like I said on the phone, the price isn't negotiable. And I'm certainly sick of all these men calling me up and insulting me with low offers. I'm giving away a piece of my heart here, I'm not going to be steamrolled on the price on top of it all."

"Hell yeah. Know something's worth and hold your ground," I say, as if I've ever held my ground in my life. I'd give my soul away if someone asked for it nicely enough.

Trish winks at me. "Three hundred thousand ain't something to scoff at."

She riffles through her purse for a second, then pulls out a manila envelope, sliding the deed across the table to me. I pretend to look at it like someone who knows what they're doing would. Seems real enough. The seal on the bottom is raised and everything.

I swallow past my dry throat, the reality of that amount thumping at every pulse point. A queasy wave rolls through me, but I push it down. I *can* afford it. After taxes, it's most of what I made from the winning ticket, with just enough left over to buy supplies and live off as I try to get my business going, but everyone always says to invest in property . . . right?

"I can afford it," I say, lifting my chin and holding Trish's kind gaze.

Trish studies me closely for a moment, and I'm swamped with respect for how thoroughly she's vetting me, that she cares enough for this piece of land that she'll make sure whoever buys it is worthy.

"I believe you," she says at last, taking another sip of her tea. "But—and I know this is none of my business, darlin', so tell me to mind my beeswax if I make you uncomfortable here—how can a girl as young as you afford that kind of chunk of change? Have you been doing something besides art?" She leans forward, excitement glowing across her glossy pink smile. "Let me guess, you're one of those brilliant entrepreneur types, right? You are, I can tell. So smart and creative."

I giggle, fluffing my pink hair. "Eh, I'm not sure about that, but thank you."

Trish smiles expectantly at me, waiting for a viable answer. It's my turn to size her up. Her big blonde hair doesn't move with the breeze that passes by, and I can't help but respect a woman who commits to that kind of height. Her eyes are kind and bright, a thick smear of purple eyeshadow over each lid accompanied by spiky, black eyelashes. The whole thing somehow works with her skin-tight cheetah-print top and painted-on leather pants that hug her full curves that are similar to mine. I can smell the soft tang of cigarette smoke and vanilla on her skin, oddly comforting and sweet. She has an energy to her, a true exuberance like she's fully in the moment, thrilled to see what happens next.

I'd be a fool not to trust her.

"Well," I say, voice low as I lean forward, glancing around us. "I know this will sound completely fake, but I swear it's true. I sort of . . . won the *lottery*."

Trish's perfectly lined lips drop open in shock. "No you did not."

"I did!" I giggle at the absurdity of it all.

"Like, the Mega Millions?"

I shake my hands. "No. Not that extreme. But a pretty decent chunk on a scratch-off. I . . . I honestly still can't wrap my head around it."

Trish stares at me with her mouth hanging open for a moment longer, then she closes it into a radiant smile, eyes crinkled at the corners. "My heavens. Sugar, I know I don't know you, but good Lord am I happy for you. Unbelievably happy."

"Thank you. I . . . That truly means a lot to me. I've had some weird reactions from people in my life finding out about it. Many who never gave me the time of day suddenly want to 'catch up.'"

Trish slaps her palms on the table, making our drinks quake. "Pardon my French, sugar, but hell no. Don't give those no-good opportunists a dime. You're too kind of a person to be taken advantage of."

I suck in a breath, ready to back down, tell her it's not that serious, but she holds up a hand, cutting me off.

"And I'm sure you're about to tell me how you're okay and end up convincing yourself that what they're doing isn't really like that, but I want you to listen to me real good for just a minute now."

I'm frozen by the wisdom etched in the lines around her eyes, the knowing press of her lips. I hang on every word.

"Life has handed me so many bitter pills over the years," she says, gaze flicking to her lap for a forlorn moment. "And I've made some pretty darn big mistakes of my own, but my greatest sin is being too trusting of others. Not protecting myself when it's all said and done."

Her eyes fix back on me, steady and vulnerable. "I'd change a lot of things. Say no. Leave sooner. Put myself first for once. And it's hard not to be angry when I think back on it all."

I get that—the raw frustration of giving as much of yourself to others as you can in the hopes they accept you. Want you. Death by one thousand naive cuts.

"But what makes it all worth living"—Trish continues, reaching her hand across the table to take mine, her touch warm and comforting—"is seeing good things happen to good people. You're a giver, Opal. I can tell. One of those beautiful souls, like an angel walkin' around down here, spreading kindness to others, reminding us of the good in the world. That's why I'm so willing to hand over the Thistle and Bloom to you.

You're a good one, and that slice of heaven dressed up as a farm is a good place for a good person."

I'm so moved by her speech, the crack in her voice, that a rogue tear rolls down my cheek.

"Are you sure you shouldn't keep it for yourself?" I whisper. "You deserve something good too." I'd hand over the fantasy I've built of that place to see someone as kind as Trish happy.

"Ah, sugar, my time with it has more than passed. And while I'm devastated to part with this place that means so much to me, I have no other choice but to let it go."

My brows furrow, head tilting to the side in question.

Trish looks at me for a moment, then purses her lips, eyes flicking away, color creeping up her cheeks. "It ain't easy to admit—like I said, I hate money talk and whatnot—but I'm low on funds."

Trish pulls her hand away from me, leaning back in her chair. She scratches her nose, then tries to discreetly wipe it on her sleeve. "Running from a no-good boyfriend, you see. Find myself in a bind once again."

She watches a white plastic grocery bag roll across the parking lot, face cracking in hurt. I'm full-on crying now.

"But it'll be my fresh start," she says at last, taking in a shaky breath before fixing me with a wobbly but genuine smile. "No one believes in me, but I do. You're giving me my chance, Opal. A good person like you, buying this land, allowing me to pay off my debts, have enough to take care of *me* for once, is the greatest blessing I could have ever hoped for. I'm thankful for you, sugar."

I'm so overwhelmed by the resilience in Trish's voice, the determination etched on her features, that I'm tempted to hand over my winnings for nothing. Someone like her, someone who's always struggled even while doing good, deserves a windfall more than anyone.

But I want to honor her, learn from her lessons, get my fresh start right alongside her. I reach into my purse, pulling out my checkbook.

"What's your last name?" I ask, clicking my pen.

Trish's smile is watery, and she lets out a tiny hiccup as she speaks. "Boden."

I fill out the check (which I had to google how to do before I left home this morning). I hover over the amount box, gaze bouncing to Trish, who's delicately blotting her eyes with a napkin.

I add an extra ten grand to the total, signing my name and ripping it out of the booklet with a flourish.

"To our fresh starts," I say, sliding it across to her. She glances at the number, eyes bulging.

"Sugar, you sure about that?"

I wave away her question.

She gets up, rounding the table to wrap me in a bear hug, crying her thanks against my shoulder. As I hug her back, I see a small yellow balloon rapidly rising toward the clouds, my heart following a similar path. It's a sign. A tiny, perfect sign from the universe that I am doing the exact right thing.

Chapter 4

OPAL

"You did *what*?"

"I bought a farm!" I cheer, throwing my hands to the sky and jumping up and down in my parents' living room. "A flower farm!"

"What the fuck is a flower farm?" Ophelia asks.

"That sounds completely made-up," Olivia adds.

"Opal, angel, tell me this is a prank," my mom, Linda, says, as my sisters and dad continue to gape at me.

"It's not," I say in a singsong, twirling over to boop my mom on the nose. "I saw it on Facebook Marketplace and I called the number and then we met up and I signed the contract and—"

"*Facebook?*" Olivia shrieks. "*You bought land on Facebook? Is that even like, legally binding?*"

"I, uh, I have the deed?" I say, a twinge of worry starting in my chest. I glance at my dad, but he's still gaping at me, face ashen.

"Do you know literally anything about flower farming? Or any type of farming?" Ophelia asks, eyes wide like an owl.

"I'm not going to *actually* farm the flowers, silly," I say. At least this part of the plan I'm certain about.

"Then why, may I ask, in the ever-loving hell did you buy a farm?"

"For, uh, the vibes . . . I guess?"

My dad, Lloyd, groans, then drops his head in his hands, Olivia hovering behind him, the bulging vein in her forehead looking at risk to pop any second.

"You told me I like nature!" I add, pointing between my sisters.

"*So?* I like wine, that doesn't mean I impulsively buy a vineyard!" Olivia counters.

"That sounds like a super-fun idea!"

"Opal. No."

"I'm sorry, but there's no way this isn't a scam, right?" Ophelia says, turning to Dad.

He groans again, then lifts his head. "The likelihood of this being valid seems marginal at best."

My stomach plummets into a different dimension. Scam? No. It couldn't be. That's absolutely not possible. I mean, objectively, yes, I understand that internet scams happen. But they happen to elderly people still trying to fire up their Hotmail accounts or Gen X moms on Instagram after a few too many glasses of rosé. They aren't carried out by older southern ladies who only want the best for their property . . . right?

"Holy shit, was this a scam?" I screech, fisting my hands in my short pink hair.

"Let me look at the contract and deed," Dad says, pushing up from his ottoman and heading toward the kitchen island.

With an audible gulp of nerves, I search for the crumpled-up paperwork in my messy purse, trying to smooth it out as I meet Dad in the kitchen.

He sets himself up on one of the barstools, and I perch next to him, tucking my legs to my chest and dropping my chin to my knees. The rest of the family hovers behind us like an anxious cloud.

Dad reads.

And reads.

And *re*reads.

After what feels like an eternity of reading what honestly can't be more than four pages, he pulls off his glasses and sighs.

"Opal, my love," he says, massaging his wrinkled forehead. "You are incredibly, *incredibly* lucky that this does seem to be a legitimate contract and deed."

My mom gasps, and Olivia and Ophelia say something in the vein of *halle-fucking-lujah* in unison.

The instantaneous wave of relief crashing with my adrenaline makes me want to collapse on the kitchen tiles. So I do, crying out all the too-big emotions while clutching a hand to my chest.

"This is easily one of the most unhinged things you've ever done," Ophelia says, nudging my side with her toe.

"I know."

"Opal, sweetie, what is your plan?" Mom asks, staring down at me with big, worried eyes.

"What makes you think she has one, Mom?" Ophelia says, pinching the bridge of her nose.

I flick her off then turn to my mom. "I guess," I say, swallowing past the lump in my throat and trying to get my buzzing brain in order, "I'm moving to Asheville. To be an artist."

And as that fresh, exciting, beautiful idea dances through my mind, swirling down to my chest and ballooning my heart, I smile. This is it. This is the fresh start I need.

Things couldn't look better.

Chapter 5

PEPPER

"I'm not sure things could look much worse, Pepper."

I nod slowly at Diksha's words for a moment, then—very calmly and carefully as I do all things—stack my palms on the worn kitchen table.

And proceed to repeatedly slam my forehead against them.

"Thanks for telling me so delicately," I say to my accountant (and best friend). In all fairness, the friendship portion came first, but I'm actively and shamelessly exploiting said friendship to get a clearer picture on how the Thistle and Bloom, my recently deceased grandma Lou's flower farm, is doing financially.

Royally fucked seems an apt way to describe it.

"I'm sorry, but Lou didn't do you any favors with this bookkeeping," Diksha says as she rifles through a shoe box of papers and crumpled receipts. "She used the profit and loss sheets from two years ago as a gum wrapper."

I nod again, rubbing my temples. I truly wish I could feel

frustration at Grandma Lou's scatterbrained nature, annoyance that she never told me the farm was in financial sham-
bles. Those are easy emotions. Focused ones. But any time I let
myself think of her, all I picture is Lou's puff of white curls like
a cloud around her head, the year-round rosiness of her plump
cheeks like she'd spent her days with her face turned to the sun,
and the softness of her hugs, the safest place on earth. When
I think about Grandma Lou, I can't feel anything besides love
and gratitude that she'd existed at all.

"I'll figure it out," I say, straightening my shoulders and
taking a sip of tea.

And I will. I don't have any other choice.

There are only three things in this world I love:

1. Grandma Lou
2. The delicate scent of a freshly bloomed anemone
3. The Thistle and Bloom flower farm

I've lost the first, but I'll be damned if I fail and lose the
last. But with the summer season knocking at the cabin door
and five acres of flowers that need tremendous care, and very
little money to do anything about it, things aren't looking good.

"Have you found the will yet?" Diksha asks, closing up her
notebook and neatly sliding various papers into a folder.

I consider banging my head on the table again. That's
the other major issue: Grandma Lou had died suddenly, albeit peacefully, and a will (if she even had one) has yet to be
found.

"No," I say tersely, twisting my heavy chestnut-colored hair into a loose bun, then pushing back from the table, taking our mugs to the deep basin sink.

"Would she purposefully hide it? She was never one for games."

I shake my head, turning on the tap and letting the too-hot water flow over my fingers. Lou was the only person in my life who I never had to worry about manipulating a situation. She was honest to a fault.

But she also lacked any real form of organization.

Lou didn't do filing cabinets or folders or have any inclination toward running a business. Instead, she had her flowers and ready laughs and fingers lovingly stained with soil. Her mind was always so tangled up in the garden, thoughts about paperwork wouldn't even be a blip on her radar.

She was one of those special, rare people, so firmly rooted in the present—absorbing and radiating all the joy a second could hold—it wouldn't surprise me to find out she'd never even thought about what the future looked like without her in it, a will being the last thing she'd realize she needed to make.

"You need to talk to a lawyer, Pepper. Like, yesterday," Diksha says, taking the hint and wrapping her pale pink scarf around herself before sliding on her windbreaker. Despite it being spring, the Western North Carolina nights release any daytime heat, a cool sharpness in the air as soon as the sun sets.

I huff in response, giving all my attention to the soap bubbles on the sponge as I scrub the dishes. I know I need to talk to a lawyer. But knowing I need to do it and actually getting my brain to cooperate are two dramatically different things.

I need control of every situation—which is likely a manifestation of my autism—and even the thought of the probable bad news talking to a lawyer would bring is enough to send a sharp and bright burst of anxiety straight up my spine and jolting down my limbs. There are too many uncertainties to face.

So I won't face them at all.

All very healthy coping mechanisms, et cetera, et cetera.

"It's going to be okay, love," Diksha says, rubbing her hand in a gentle circle around my back before leaning in to give me a hug from behind. My knees almost buckle from the comfort of the contact, but I hold myself rigid, not leaning in. If I lean in, I'll crumble, and that won't do anyone any good.

"Maybe you can do another round of bulb and tuber sales?" she asks, voice gentle, but I know her well enough to feel the pushiness in the suggestion. "You made a little extra money doing that over the winter, right? Or try and court more wholesale buyers?"

I shake my head. "It's too late in the season to sell any bulbs. And I already spent all winter trying to get more accounts with little to show for it. My to-do list is a mile long with spring here."

Winters are seasons of rest. But this past one was my first without Grandma Lou. My first time living without her.

Rest was never an option.

I took on any and every task, keeping my hands moving and my brain ferociously focused on anything to avoid being alone with my thoughts, and my grief, for even a minute. I supplemented the farm's revenue by spending the winter digging in the frozen ground, harvesting (way too late, as any YouTube video will scold you) bulbs and tubers of our flowers and selling them online. It didn't rake in much money, but it did leave me cold and exhausted enough each day that it was well worth it.

But with the spring sun digging its warm fingers into the soil, the season of searching for ways to be busy is done, and harvesting is here. It's early mornings and sore knees and cramped muscles as I move through row after row of flowers, cutting the stems deep so they'll bloom again. And I love it. I love the ache in my neck after a long day bent over the blossoms, the crescents of dirt perpetually under my fingernails despite wearing gloves.

Diksha sighs through pursed lips. "Well, Tal and I are here to help you. However you need," she says, pulling away.

"I know," I respond, meaning it. Diksha and her partner, Tal, are probably the only two people left on the planet that I can rely on. But just because I *can* doesn't mean I *will*. Trusting others—hell, even trusting myself—feels as unnatural as driving in reverse on a highway. It can only lead to disaster.

I grew up around people so disturbingly toxic, there's no way I'm not equally as damaging. If I allow myself to get too close to someone, I'll hurt them. It's in my DNA.

"I'll figure it out," I add, giving Diksha a tense smile.

Diksha rolls her eyes and pats my cheek. "What a stunningly convincing performance of bravado."

"Don't make me kick you off my property," I say, snapping my tea towel at Diksha, a more genuine smile tugging at my lips.

"Tsk, tsk. So much grumpiness from someone that looks like they stepped out of a cottagecore Pinterest board. Pick a lane, Pepper." Diksha grabs the sprig of chamomile from the front pocket of my dungarees and twirls it between her fingers.

"I don't know what any of that means," I say, snatching the small flowers from her and gingerly placing them back in my pocket. I shoo her toward the door.

Diksha cackles. "You're getting way too out of touch with lesbian subtypes. You need to brush up."

"I'll make sure to prioritize that right between brushing my teeth and saving the farm from bankruptcy."

"Atta babe," Diksha says, bouncing down the porch steps and getting into her truck. "There's hope for you yet."

I wave as Diksha peels out of the long dirt driveway, disappearing into the wall of pines that protects the property from the road.

And then there's nothing but perfect spring silence curling around me. The crisp scent of cold air and warm earth soothes my clouded brain, letting peacefulness weave its way in.

Wrapping my arms around myself, I move down the porch steps and into a row of ranunculi, the swollen pink and yellow and orange buds flirting with the potential to bloom any day now. A sharp gust of wind nips at my cheeks, and I nestle my chin into the warmth of my thin, loose turtleneck. I love this time of day, the mottled lilac of dusk dancing over the hopeful green growth of the flowers, the way nature seems to settle in, ready to face the night ahead.

I spent most of my childhood whisked from one place to the next. Motel rooms and beat-up cars and countless couches of my mom's revolving-door boyfriends all condensed into a blurry streak of unpredictability and confusion.

But none of that disastrous uncertainty ever touched the Thistle and Bloom. Spring, summer, autumn, or winter, it was the first place I ever found comfort. As a teenager, I'd walk for hours across the fields, sometimes untangling a thorny thought or losing myself to the beauty of this place and thinking of nothing at all. And, even now, the perfect hush that falls among the rows of baby sprouts and full-grown flowers always recharges me.

How long will it take before I stop expecting a tight hug from Grandma Lou after one of these walks?

I scrub away a silly stray tear. I'm fine. I don't need one of those hugs to survive. I don't need anything from anyone.

The sudden grinding of an engine breaks through the peaceful silence . . . probably Diksha returning for some forgotten item. With a sigh, I walk back toward the cabin, the grass—in desperate need of mowing—whispering against my shoes with each step.

But it isn't Diksha's truck parked in front of the cabin.

It's a dinged-up silver car.

With a short, pink-haired woman standing beside it, her arms full of . . . shoes?

I squint at her.

Those are definitely shoes . . . Like, an absolutely ridiculous amount of white shoes in a giant mesh bag clutched to her chest?

The woman sighs wistfully as she looks at my home, something like longing falling across her features as she smiles.

I don't like that look one bit.

"We're closed," I say briskly, striding toward her. "In fact, we aren't open to visitors in general."

Pink Hair screeches, throwing her bundle of (now confirmed) shoes in the air, which land with a dull thud on the dirt.

"Oh shit, you scared me," she says, gripping her hand to her chest but managing to give me a wobbly smile. "Sorry. I'm Opal."

Opal holds out her hand. I stare at it with narrowed eyes, my lip curling a bit. Opal eventually lets it flop to her side.

"Do you live nearby?" she asks, tugging at her bubblegum bob.

"You could say that."

"Oh. Awesome. That's great. We'll be neighbors!"

"That so?" I ask, crossing my arms over my chest, apprehension snaking through me.

"Yeah! I think so. I just bought this place." Opal sweeps her arm grandly toward my squat cabin. "I'm so excited."

The words echo in my head, each syllable feeling like a blunt strike to my skull. As they sink in, my heart plummets out of my chest, worry dissolving into my bloodstream, making my muscles tense and prickle. "You . . . what?"

"Bought this farm!" she says, gathering up her (absurd

amount of) dropped shoes. "I'm going to convert parts of it to an art studio. Have a sort of working-living space."

"Like hell you are," I say, taking a step toward her.

"Um, what?" Opal's eyes—an unnerving pale blue—shoot wide with fear.

"This is my home. The Thistle and Bloom is *mine*," I say, pointing between the cabin and my chest.

You haven't found the will, an awful, honest voice whispers in my ear. I shove the thought away. Will or not, I would know if someone bought the place I'm *living in* . . . right?

"I . . . uh . . . This kind of maybe feels like the most uncomfortable moment of my life," Opal stammers out. "But it's . . . it's actually mine."

I'm silent, face hot with anger and confusion and, more than anything, dread.

Opal adjusts her sack of shoes to one arm, riffling through the giant purse at her hip before pulling out a handful of papers. Staring down at the dirt like a guilty child, she holds them out to me.

I snatch them up, eyes scouring over words, too anxious to actually read them. With a shaky breath, I try to steady my hands, the text still blurring in and out of focus as blackness creeps into the edges of my vision.

It doesn't take long to get the gist of what they signify.

I flip to the final page, looking at the signatures, the familiar swirl of a gratuitously large *T* telling me everything I need to know.

My heart sinks so low, it's melting into the earth's molten core.

Of course that name is on these papers.

The worst person I know.

My fucking mother.

Chapter 6

PEPPER

"Explain it to me again," I demand, leaning forward to rest my forearms on my knees. It's all too much to process, words jamming up in my head as I make Opal repeat them over and over. I pull out the sprig of chamomile from my front pocket, nervously twirling the stem between my thumb and forefinger.

Opal sighs and pushes her bangs off her forehead, swaying a few times in the creaky rocking chair on my porch. She repeats the story for the third time.

". . . and then Trish asked me to meet up and we talked about the farm a bit more and then she said there was a notary in the FedEx next door and we walked over, I signed the papers, and she told me where to find the key." Opal's eyes flick to the tiny ceramic snowman by the door, which Grandma Lou had left out year-round to hide the spare key for as long as I can remember. "I packed up all my stuff, bought a ton of supplies for my shoe business I'm starting and . . . yeah. You know the rest."

I groan, dropping my head into my hands, my spine curling up into a protective shell. I want to cry. Scream. Throw a tantrum. Get this pink-haired stranger off my porch.

But I can't do any of those things, the last one for apparent legal reasons, which makes me even more upset.

Opal sucks in a breath, getting ready to say something else, but I can't take any more information. Bolting up, I take a few paces away from the porch then spin around.

"I have to call Trish."

"You know Trish?" Opal asks, a bright smile pulling across her lips.

"Unfortunately," I grumble. "Can you give me her number?"

My mother cycles through at least a dozen phone numbers a year, and it's been a long time since I've initiated contact with the woman.

Opal hesitates for a moment, and I fix her with a sharp look, daring her to say no. With a sigh, she pulls out her phone and scrolls.

"I wish you'd tell me what's going on. I feel like I'm an intruder or something," Opal says, holding out her cell.

"You are," I reply, pounding the number into my own phone. Marching away with what little dignity I have left, I turn down a nearby row of narcissus flowers.

I pace among the plants for a few moments, trying to get my breathing under control.

Okay, deep breath. In and out. Find Zen or whatever.

Doesn't help.

I try again, tilting my head up to the inky night sky.

Then three more times.

It's useless. No amount of deep breathing can dislodge the block of concrete clogging my chest.

I stop pacing and plop down to sit on the cool ground, branches and leaves enveloping my curved back like a safety net. A hug.

I hold my phone in one hand, the tiny bundle of chamomile in the other. I gently drag the pad of my thumb across the delicate white petals, young and soft and comforting. I do this so often—any time I feel nervous or overwhelmed or oversensitized, which is almost all the time—that the sweet and gentle smell of flowers is forever embedded in my skin.

After pushing a frizzy lock of hair out of my eyes, I call the number.

It rings. And rings. And rings some more. I should be used to my mom not being reachable when I need her. This isn't anything new. This isn't anything new, poking at an old wound between my ribs.

"Hello?" a cheery voice answers, making my skin prickle and shoulders hunch up to my ears.

"Hello, Trish," I say, hoping using her first name will sound cool and unattached instead of moronically immature. "It's me."

There's a pause. "Sorry, sugar," Trish responds, voice still disgustingly sweet. "Me who?"

"Your daughter." There's a heavy beat of silence. "Pepper."

The line is silent. I hope Trish feels shame. Fear. Regret. Discomfort.

But, adding to the list of endless disappointments, the woman has the audacity to let out a tinkling laugh of glee. "Well, bless my heart. Yours was the last voice I expected to hear when I answered this call. How are you, sweetie? Where ya living these days?"

"Right where you left me," I respond through clenched teeth.

Another long pause. "The Thistle and Bloom?"

I let out a loud scoff in response. The last time I saw my mom was nine years ago, when I was a terrified seventeen-year-old who had been forced to grow up way too fast and dropped on Grandma Lou's doorstep.

Don't worry, Pep. I'll be back in two days. Three, tops, Trish had told me, as she left me with a woman I'd never met. *You have a nice long weekend with Grandma Lou, and by the time I come back, I'll have us a brand-new apartment to live in. Just ours. And you can finish out senior year in the same spot. Then college. Everything's gonna be better. I promise.*

I had sat stone-still on that porch for hours, eyes wide as I stared at Trish's tire marks, my entire body numb, like all my senses, my very soul, had curled up into a tiny ball in the corner of my stomach and left the rest of my cells empty to fend for themselves. I don't have a fight-or-flight response. I always freeze, and the fear of this unknown place with the unknown person made me feel like I'd never move again.

But Grandma Lou, with her voice soft as morning dew and her smile bright as a sunflower, eventually coaxed me inside, wrapping a warm blanket around my shoulders. She'd explained she was actually my great-aunt, and I quietly explained that, seeing as I don't know my dad, Grandma Lou was the only relative I had left. Grandma Lou had shown me to the guest bedroom on the second floor, and it was the first time I'd ever been offered a space entirely my own.

It had taken four months for me to accept that my mom wasn't coming back for me, and five months to find out how much damage Trish had caused.

"I was sorry to hear about Lou," Trish says, voice full of supposed remorse.

"That's funny. I don't remember seeing you at the funeral."

"Well, sweetheart, I didn't receive an invite. Lost in the mail, I'm sure."

"Kind of hard to send an invitation to someone constantly on the lam," I snap. I hate how calm, how unbothered, my mom sounds. The woman abandoned me. She could at least sound a little sorry.

"Now, I don't think it's very fair for you to talk to me like that. Especially after how long it's been since I even heard from you, baby," Trish says, her voice soft like a wilted southern belle. It makes my stomach churn.

"You want to talk about fair? Was it very *fair* of you to sell my *home* right out from under me?"

"How was I s'posed to know you were living there?" Trish whines. "Not like you ever call me."

While I hadn't heard from Trish the entire first year I was abandoned here, she did start trying every six months or so to manipulate me into fixing our broken relationship, every time leaving me feeling more robbed than before. I finally stopped picking up phone calls from strangers when I turned twenty-one.

"Maybe you shouldn't be selling property you haven't set foot on in almost a decade," I counter. "How did you even manage this great con, by the way?"

"Oh hush. It's not a con. The house was given to me when Lou died."

My throat goes painfully dry, and I'm unable to swallow past it. Did some attorney have the will all this time? Did Grandma Lou actually hand my safe haven to the one person with the power to destroy it?

"W-what? How?"

"Well, darlin', you know I don't know all the technicalities when it comes to legal jargon and whatnot . . ."

This is patently false. Trish Boden knows the law well, and how to bend it even better.

"But it's something called intestate succession. If no will is found, property and the like are given to the next of kin. It's all very official, I'll have you know."

My world tips, its axis spinning out of control like it's been yanked by an overeager *Wheel of Fortune* participant.

"And you just . . . *sold* it? Just like that? Knowing how much Grandma Lou loved this place?" *Knowing how much I loved this place*, I want to add. But that isn't really fair. My mom doesn't know. Trish only concerns herself with her own interests.

"I was in a bind, Pep, and it's not like I have the know-how to run the dang place."

"Yeah, well, I do." I hate the way my voice cracks. "You have to give this Opal girl her money back. Undo this." I mean for it to sound like a demand, but it comes out far closer to a desperate beg.

Trish has the decency to sigh. "Wish I could, darlin', but I can't. I've already made plans for the money. And even if that weren't the case, I still wouldn't change it. This was a good business move."

"Business move? Or some first step in yet another one of your scams?" There's no way this is aboveboard no matter what Trish says.

"I'm on the straight and narrow now, I'll have you know."

"Yeah? Does the straight and narrow include paying me back the money you owe me?"

"Good Lord, Pepper, are you ever going to let that go?"

"No." The betrayal was too personal. Too acute. I'll go to my grave with that grudge.

"I can't talk to you when you're like this," Trish says, voice watery and hurt. It's like a siren song, luring me in to feel guilty for being honest. For speaking my feelings. Trish has always deployed it with the skill of a sniper. "I won't let you use me as your punching bag. You're so ungrateful for everything I've given you."

My hand curls into a fist, the soft, vulnerable plant crushed to a pulp in my palm. Which part am I supposed to be grateful for? The instability of never having a consistent home address? The constant fleeing in the night for a fresh start? The parade of my mom's boyfriends I would either hate or get just close enough to care for only to never see them again? What a plethora of blessings Trish Boden has rained down upon me.

"Thank you so much for selling both my place of employment and my lodgings to a total stranger with some sort of shoe obsession. I'm eternally grateful." Anger is easier than acknowledging the acute hurt that lives just under my skin.

"I've always known you were selfish, Pepper, but I didn't know you were cruel." The exaggerated southern accent takes some of the sting out of the words, but not much. "One day you'll have to thaw that frozen heart of yours, and when you do, I hope you call me. I want a relationship with you."

Trish hangs up, and I sit there, staring at the tiny sprouts of weeds at the base of my narcissus plants, hitting the corner of my phone against my forehead.

Do. Not. Cry, I will with every tap. That woman doesn't deserve my tears. Trish has never done anything to stop them before; she certainly isn't going to do anything about them now.

Eventually, I move on hands and knees to the weeds, plucking them out, scanning the bed for any other intruders before I pull myself up and make my way down the row in the inky darkness toward the cabin. I'm shocked absolutely shitless to find the world's most unwelcome bearer of bad news standing at the end.

"I . . . I demand you tell me what's happening." Opal says,

putting her hands on her softly curved hips and squaring her shoulders, standing her full height of what couldn't be more than five foot two. I loom over her by a solid nine inches.

It's a bit difficult to take Opal's demand seriously, with her big scared eyes and messy hair and full, rosy cheeks. The woman is, unfortunately, rather cute. Which makes the massive upheaval she's caused in my life all the more disarming. And annoying.

So very fucking annoying.

"Fine," I say, slipping around her and trudging toward the porch. "You want to know what's happening? I'll tell you. Trish—the nice lady who sold you this place for a song?—she's my mother. And a massive con artist. Tragically for me, this is apparently the one time she's done something with the law on her side, which puts me in the super-fun position of being homeless. And I guess jobless since you want to turn this flower farm into some sort of shoe factory like a pink-haired Keebler elf. Does that paint a clear enough picture for you?" I turn on Opal, towering over her. I know I'm not supposed to shoot the messenger, but I'm certainly not above yelling at one.

Opal is silent for a moment, then swallows. "Don't Keebler elves make cookies?" she whispers.

The anger that floods through me is hot enough to send this entire farm up in flames.

"Sorry. Sorry," Opal rushes out. "I imagine now isn't the right time for elf semantics."

"How much did you pay for it?" I know—from endless studying of interactions between neurotypicals—that talking about money is rude. But I'm beyond forcing myself into social niceties when my entire world is falling apart.

Opal blinks those wide blue eyes. "I . . . uh . . . th-three. Three hundred. Thousand. Three hundred thousand dollars."

That amount of money is so inconceivably large that I, not for the first time that evening, feel like I might collapse. My knees give out, and I plop down onto the top step of the porch.

"Let me get this straight," I say through a rough throat. "You paid three hundred *thousand* dollars, in cash, for a flower farm on the verge of bankruptcy that you've never even set foot on before?"

"I . . . I paid with a check," Opal whispers, like it makes any fucking difference to how absolutely bonkers the whole thing is.

"What am I going to do?" I mumble to myself, voice cracking as overwhelming thoughts clog up my brain. "Like, seriously. If I lose this place, I have . . ."

Nothing.

If I lose the Thistle and Bloom, I have nothing. No purpose. No safe space. No shelter filled with the happiest moments of my life. I'd once again be a lost buoy in the endless ocean of life. Directionless. Untethered. Alone.

"Stay with me." Opal's words are loud. A bit startling. I'm coming to realize that everything about her is startling, though.

"What?" I say, turning to look at her.

Opal clears her throat, eyes fixed on my face. "Stay here with me. Or, uh, I stay with you. Or, um, I guess we stay together? In the cabin?" Opal's hand flaps wildly toward the front door.

My mind goes blank. There is no way I can live with this strange woman with wild hair and an alarming amount of shoes who bought property off Facebook Marketplace without some sort of homicide situation.

"Inconceivable," I eventually press out.

Opal giggles. *Giggles*. At a time like this? The woman is nothing but a compact, pink-haired monster.

"I've never heard someone say that word without doing the *Princess Bride* voice." Opal giggles even harder. The homicide might come sooner than I anticipated. "But seriously," Opal continues, trying and failing to gulp down her remaining laughs. "I think it's the best solution to our problem."

"Does it really solve anything?" I snap, looking at Opal, tracing the sincerity of her eyes, the kind softness to her dimpled smile.

She chews on the question, full lips puckering and a small furrow forming between her eyebrows. "I think . . ." she says slowly, carefully, "it solves enough for tonight. And tomorrow we can figure out the rest."

I continue to stare at her, heart wary and exhausted, everything in me screaming that Opal can't be trusted. No one can be trusted. Especially someone associated with Trish. But my oversaturated brain isn't able to come up with any alternatives, and all I really want is to put on my softest pajamas, curl up under my quilts, and wake up tomorrow morning to find this was all an awful dream.

"Okay," I say at last, standing up. "We'll leave the rest for the morning." I walk to the door, Opal's boots clunking up the porch steps behind me. I hold open the screen door for her, but she hesitates.

"And, uh, just to like, confirm and stuff . . . you aren't a serial killer or anything, right?"

My head jerks back. "Excuse me?"

"I'm not saying you give off that vibe," Opal says, waving her hands frantically in front of her. "I just thought I should double-check. Since we'll be like . . . in the same house and stuff. And like . . . I mean I guess I just don't want to get . . . well. Murdered. Or anything."

I scan this bizarre woman from the top of her head to the bottom of her cuffed jeans. Was she sent from my personal seventh circle of hell just to torture me here on earth?

"I'm not murdering anyone tonight," I say with a sigh. "But now you have me super freaked out so I'll be sleeping with my door locked and pepper spray close if it turns out you're the actual murderer."

"Let's just agree on a mutual no-murder situation," Opal says, stepping through the door and into the cabin's warm kitchen. "See, another problem solved. We're on a roll."

"Right. I'm sure everything else we have to figure out will be as easily handled as agreeing not to kill each other." I maneuver around Opal in the small kitchen, blowing out the candles on the table as I go.

"We'll find a happy ending to all of this. Just you wait."

Today has been filled with so many curveballs and upheavals, there's one thing I know, beyond reasonable doubt, to be true: there is no happy ending that could ever, *ever,* come from this nightmare.

Chapter 7

PEPPER

"Good morning!"

I need to make something very clear: I am, above all else, a creature of habit. A stage-five clinger to my routine. Every morning at six thirty I wake up, roll out of bed, brush my teeth, wiggle into my slippers, and am downstairs by six thirty-five sipping coffee and staring out the window over the kitchen sink as I run through a mental checklist of my tasks for the day.

I do not willingly talk to anyone before eight thirty (at the very earliest), and when I am eventually forced to make human contact, it's usually Diksha calling to check on me.

My world revolves around this routine. It's sacred. Special. And any disruptions to it set my entire day spinning off course.

Which is why my bloodcurdling scream of surprise and the sloshing of hot coffee onto the counter at the sound of Opal's far too cheerful and startling greeting is a totally reasonable reaction.

"Fuck, you scared me," I say, running my burned hand under the tap, then wiping off the counters. I'd convinced myself it had all been a nightmare, that there wasn't a cotton-candy-haired stranger sleeping in the spare room across from mine claiming to own this place. That the stress of Grandma Lou's passing was wearing on my psyche and the whole thing had been an awful hallucination.

"Someone's a morning person," Opal croons, shooting me a tragically lovely smile as she moves farther into the kitchen.

"This is the world's most prolonged home invasion," I mumble.

Opal's smile falters, her wide eyes looking down at the floor with something close to regret. "I'm sorry," she whispers, cracking her fingers. "I didn't mean to . . ." She gestures vaguely with her hand.

And, damn her, she does sound sincere. Which makes it so much harder to be mad at her, that barely there wobble in her voice tugging at my heartstrings.

"Would you like some coffee?" I begrudgingly offer, refilling my own cup.

"In an IV drip if you have it."

I attempt a brief courtesy laugh.

"I'm serious," Opal says, leaning toward me with a glint in her eyes. "More than once after an all-nighter in school, I took like seven shots of espresso through a beer bong."

I blink. "That sounds . . . disastrously hot."

"I've been known to turn a head or two." She shoots me a gratuitous wink, her face back in that unfettered smile that seems to be her default setting, those round cheeks and full lips creating a feeling in my chest that's bizarrely . . . comforting.

A gentle tickle of awareness travels down the back of my neck, and I clear my throat, looking away before offering Opal a steaming mug, taking a scorching gulp from my own. I don't need comfort from this chaos demon. What I need is my routine to be restored and this whole thing to turn out to be a sick joke.

"Ah, nothing like that first sip," Opal says, bringing the rim of the mug to her mouth, the corners still ticked up in that decadent smile. She lets out a soft groan of pleasure as she takes a swig of coffee, and something about that noise coupled with Opal's eyes closed and lips parted in bliss sends a violent rush of heat to my cheeks.

Bewildered, I whip back around to the counter, spilling even more coffee as I go. I bite back a string of curse words as I slam the mug down.

Everything about Opal is disruptive and invasive and . . . and . . . and just so *much*. I've only known her for twelve hours and she's already driven me half-mad. What am I supposed to do?

"Here, let me help," Opal says, moving to my side.

"I've got it." I try to nudge her back as she reaches for a sponge.

"Seriously, no biggie," Opal says in her cheery voice.

She grabs a towel from the edge of the sink, then crouches down to wipe the floor, the movement swift and in sync with my next step, sending my ass torpedoing straight for Opal's face.

In a moment of sheer awkward panic, I twist, catching

my hip on the counter and knotting my legs under me. Balance off-kilter, I topple to the ground, knocking Opal over in the process. She lets out a sharp yelp as we bounce across the kitchen, then land in a heap. My immediate impulse is to try to roll away, but it tangles us further together until we're both lying on the cold wood floors in stunned silence, panting slightly from the commotion.

After a few seconds a slight tremor runs through Opal's frame.

"Are you okay?" I ask, blinking at the ceiling as I try to collect myself.

Opal's shaking continues. "Fine," she eventually wheezes out, her entire body vibrating.

It's the choked, snorting sound that comes next that makes me realize Opal isn't holding back tears. The heretic is *laughing*. It's also the moment I realize just how closely our bodies are pressed together.

I feel the heat of Opal's laugh on my neck, how tightly our legs are notched together in the tangle, Opal's knuckles brushing mine as she brings her hand up and pushes back her pink bangs.

I jolt up, crab-walking backward until I bump into the cabinets, using the counter to hoist myself up.

"I told you to leave it," I snap, looking down at Opal's flushed face, her nose crinkled with laughter. How could this woman find anything funny about any of this?

Opal's laughter dies, and she blinks up at me with those big blue eyes. "Are you . . . are you mad at me or something?"

I fist my hands in my hair, pulling until I nearly wince. "I can't say you're my favorite person at the moment."

Opal sits up, gaze fixed on me, and I have to look away from her tiny frown filled with worry. That frown has no right being as cute as it is.

"I'm sorry." Her voice is soft. Gentle. It rips through me. "I was just trying to be helpful."

"What would help me is if you left." I lean into my anger, gripping it with both hands. Anger is easy. Justified. Who is this woman to barge into my life and mess everything up?

The owner of the property, you numbskull.

"I . . ." Opal bites down on her lip, giving me a look so tragic, the anger whooshes out of me. "I don't know what to do," she whispers. "I'm sorry I've caused you so many problems, but I . . . I really have no idea what to do."

I squeeze my eyes shut, dragging a hand across my forehead as I try to think of any solution.

"I could reach out to Trish. See if she'd be willing to reverse the sale," Opal offers, that lilt of optimism always present.

"She won't."

"Maybe she will. I could—"

"She *won't*," I say with too much force. Too much bite. But Trish won't do anything that helps anyone but herself.

Opal gives me another wounded look, filling me with so much guilt I might as well be yelling at Bambi. After a moment, she stands up, dusting herself off and straightening her shoulders.

She lifts her chin with something close to defiance . . . she doesn't look wholly comfortable with the sensation.

"Stop talking to me like I'm your enemy," she says, jaw set and voice more serious than I thought she was capable of. "I'm not. I swear I'm not. I'm trying to be your partner in finding a solution to this mess, but you're making that really hard with the way you speak to me."

I blink in surprise, a ripple of guilt trailing down my spine. "I'm sorry. I don't mean to be an asshole. This is just . . ." I wave my hand in a jerky movement.

"This isn't ideal for me either," Opal says, her voice softening at the edges but her eyes still holding a determined glint. "I had plans for this place. For my future. I put most of the money I have into buying it and the rest into getting supplies for my business. I can't walk away from this investment. I'd have nothing left."

"One of us is going to end up with nothing," I whisper, the truth of this situation twisting my stomach into knots. I reach into my pocket, grabbing a small, wilted lavender sprig and rolling it between my fingers. Opal watches the movement.

"What if I buy it from you?" I say, unable to hide the desperation threatening to crack my chest in two. But desperate is all I am. I will do anything—absolutely *anything*—to hold on to the only home I've ever known.

Opal lifts one shoulder in a loose shrug. "That would certainly solve some of our biggest problems."

My stimming increases in speed as anxiety and ideas

tumble around my gut. "It's just . . . I'd need to do it over time. I don't have money like that sitting around. We could arrange something where I work off payments? Like proceeds from the farm's sales?" Considering the bad shape Thistle and Bloom's finances are in, this would likely take a lifetime. But maybe there's some hope? Somewhere money could be squeezed, operations made even leaner? "Or I could try to take out a loan?"

Opal shrugs again. "I'm okay with that."

My brain trips over itself as endless what-ifs vie for attention. "We could come up with a deal? After this season, I give you what I earn, and maybe it will be enough to put a dent in the total? Enough that you could, uh, find somewhere else to do your shoe . . . business . . . thing?"

Opal gives me a sad smile. "And until then?"

"I . . ."

I'm hit with a visceral type of fear as I realize I might not have a place to stay through summer and early fall. Memories of the loneliness—the helplessness—of being that little girl who didn't know where her next shelter would be slap at my cheeks and singe my nerves. My lips start tingling, palms sweating, as anxiety hums through me, hope disappearing like smoke.

"I think we could manage being roommates for a few months, if you're open to it."

It takes me a moment to process what Opal said.

"You mean"—my voice is rough—"we both stay here?"

"If you're open to it," Opal repeats, taking a step toward me. "I know I've massively intruded into your life, but if you don't mind sharing the space . . . I'm not generally the best at living alone anyway. And things can't exactly get worse for us, right?"

I try to swallow past the lump in my throat. "I think you should knock on wood or something."

Opal's smile returns with full force, her entire face glowing. I'm filled with this odd sensation that I kind of . . . *missed* Opal's smile in the moments it was gone. Which is bizarre. And likely just because I'm being bombarded with so many emotions I can't think straight.

Slowly, she leans toward me, and my heart pounds so violently in my chest that my head swims. Is she . . . It almost seems like she's going to press that smile to my mouth. Teach me how it tastes. She's a whisper away, the warmth of her skin tickling mine, and I can't do anything but stand there as she closes the distance and . . .

Sways at the last second, rapping her knuckles against the wooden cupboard.

She straightens up, smile still radiant. "Do we have a deal?" Opal nudges my foot with hers.

I nod, licking my lips, trying to catch my breath as it leaves me in sharp bursts.

"Okay," I eventually manage, my voice half defeat, half hope. "Yeah. Okay."

Opal lets out a tiny squeal, then claps her hands, her energy like a bolt of lightning through the cabin. "Can we hug it out, roomie?"

In a daze, I feel myself give a tiny nod.

Opal's arms are around my neck in an instant, pulling me close. I'm quite a bit taller than her, so I have to stoop for her to rest on her flat feet, but she presses against me all the same.

It must be how tightly Opal holds me that makes all the air rush from my lungs. My heart beat in double time. My limbs flood with warmth.

"This will end up being great, I promise," Opal whispers into my shoulder, the soft glow of her voice skipping down my spine.

As a perpetual pessimist, I know it's far more likely that this will end in disaster, and neither of us should expect anything different.

Yet, for some unknown reason, I let Opal continue to hug me—even hugging back a bit—a teeny-tiny ember of hope glowing in my chest.

Chapter 8

OPAL

My fresh start is not going great by any account.

Which is fine. So totally fine. Because I can pivot. I can pivot the hell out of any situation. If anyone has experience finding the bright spot in a steaming pile of shit, it's me.

So what if this new situation means I'll have to move in about four months and likely won't see the majority of my investment in the property for the next several years? Minor details. The kind of things finance bros worry about. Not me. Because I have all those pivoting skills and whatnot.

The important thing is, I'm not going to defer my dreams for a single day more. Nope. I just need to morph said dreams a bit.

I've lived here a week now and spent most of it setting up my (sadly) temporary new room . . . and maybe finding as many excuses as possible to hide in here because Pepper scares me a bit.

The week hasn't been a particularly comfortable one. The first few days I tried desperately to connect with Pepper, inserting myself in her path, asking about her day. But the woman's monotone grunts in response withered up any bravery I had, and I've spent the rest of the time tucked away.

Standing on my bed, I hammer two tiny nails into the top of my window frame, draping a garland I fashioned from old handmade paper cut into shapes of birds. The sun streams through the window, catching the golden glint of fibers woven into the thick paper, and a light breeze makes the birds dance like they're preparing to take off.

I glance at the grass sprawled behind the house, my eyes making a quick sweep, then landing on the small smudge that is Pepper in the distance. My eyes always seem to land on her.

I've developed a sort of fascination with watching her work this week, which, objectively, sounds creepy. But it's a fascination in the way she moves. The clockwork of her tasks. The precise tenderness with which she cares for the thousands of blooms around her. She moves among the flowers like someone moves around the house they're born in, with an intuitive sense, one of purpose and belonging—knowing exactly where she's needed and what to do. I catch myself sketching her—the arch of her back and the bend of her head as she bows to the flowers— more often than I care to admit.

It's captivating to see someone so comfortable in nature.

And this is also pretty much the only opportunity I have to get to know my new roommate. As soft and gentle as Pepper is out on her land, she's prickly and harsh any time we interact in the house . . . when she's not avoiding me and vice versa.

She doesn't trust or like me, which, fair, but it doesn't feel good to live with so much tension. I genuinely like people, and an achy sense of loneliness keeps burrowing deeper into my bones with each silent day.

With a sigh, I dust my hands off on my thighs and hop to the floor, appraising the room and my handiwork.

I really freaking love it.

I'm tucked into the back of the second floor, fairy lights strung across the slanted ceiling and framing a round window that looks out onto a grove of trees. Various trinkets and pieces of art I brought with me are propped on every open inch of shelves and cabinets, and a tapestry I hand-painted a few years ago—depicting a posy of violets and their delicate, intertwined roots laced with dirt—hangs behind the head of my bed. No matter how temporary my stay is, I'm determined to make this room a snug little sanctuary.

Out of things to putz around with, I scrounge up my courage and decide to explore the rest of the house.

The upstairs has two bedrooms—my room on the right of the staircase, Pepper's on the left—with a shared bathroom at the end. The ceiling is tall and lofted with a seam running down the center, the roof slanting from either side of the A-frame structure.

I pad down the creaky wooden stairs to the spacious ground floor. The kitchen, which connects to the cabin's wide porch, is lined with open cabinets, a dusky rainbow of mismatched plates and mugs and cast-iron skillets filling the cubbies. A large window over the farmhouse sink lets in a golden beam of light that lands right on the circular wood dining table off to the side.

The space transitions into the family room, a stone fireplace the center of the cozy scene, an overstuffed couch packed with blankets and pillows facing it with plush recliners flanking either side. Large windows look out on rows of flowers, the red barn—where it seems most pickups from florists are conducted—standing proudly in the distance. I'm not brave enough to plop myself down on that couch like I'm so deeply tempted to, but I at least let myself linger for a few minutes, running my hands over the different textures with a soft exploration I haven't allowed myself yet.

It all sends a tingle of unfettered comfort down my spine. This house feels like entering a small alternate universe where everything smells like lavender and none of the world's problems can touch you while you're snuggled up in the warm, gentle space.

With a deep breath and quick glance toward the back door, I make my way down the long hallway attached to the living room, finding an additional bathroom, and a shut door at the end.

I am, rather unfortunately, nosy by nature, and closed doors call to me with a siren song so strong, I generally barrel right on through them. Without much thought, I turn the handle of the pine door, letting it swing open to reveal a fully furnished bedroom.

This third bedroom is slightly larger than the ones upstairs, flooded with light from the two wide windows that look out on the back of the property. A neatly made bed sits in one corner, a vanity and mirror in the opposite—small jars of lotions and powders lined up in a neat row, a vase of dried flowers on the other side.

While the room is airy and bright, a thin layer of dust sits on the furniture, a certain sadness lingering in the space, like its usual source of light has been snuffed out, and it's lying in wait for a new one.

My heart twirls in excitement. It would be the absolute perfect studio to start working on my shoes.

A series of photos are hung along the wall, a young brunette who looks suspiciously like Pepper in each of them. Unable to resist the shiny frames and bright smiles, I move to get a closer look when a low, angry voice sounds near my ear.

"Don't go in there."

I jump, then turn, looking up at the sharp angles of Pepper's face.

"Why?" I whisper. "Is it cursed? Radioactive? Haunted?"

Pepper flinches. "It's none of your business. Just stay out."

My heart sinks, welts of embarrassment swelling along my skin. I hate being this chronically sensitive, hurting with a deep and aching type of pain from just a few choice words.

"I need somewhere to work," I declare, steeling my spine

and hoping I look stronger than I feel. This situation is as familiar as a hug and sharp as a slap. It would be so easy to yield to Pepper's icy tone and scurry back to my room; mold myself into the smallest possible form until I melt into the background to make everyone around me more comfortable.

But that was the old me. New me is tough and implacable . . . or at least new me is *pretending* to be those things.

Unfortunately, soft-launching this new me on a person like Pepper—i.e., intimidatingly hot with sharp and regal features, a tall frame, and gingerbread eyes that hint at a hidden hurt—is turning out to be rather challenging. How am I supposed to be assertive when what I'd rather do is kindly ask this beautiful woman to choke me with those endlessly long legs?

"Well, it won't be in here," Pepper says, closing the door with a definitive thud, then shoving her hands in her overall pockets.

My heart sinks even deeper, making itself comfortable on the floorboards, but I make a show of looking around dramatically. "Guess the living room will have to do?"

Pepper lets out a noise that can only be described as a growl. "I hate change," she murmurs, dragging a hand down her face.

She does look genuinely distressed, and any resolve I have whooshes out of me. There's literally nothing I hate more than causing other people to hurt.

"I'll figure something out," I say with a wave, hoping the big mess of feelings in my chest won't knot up my voice.

Pepper looks at me, eyes trailing up and down. I know the

look isn't supposed to be an appraising one, but dammit if I don't flush hot all over just the same.

"Come with me," Pepper says, voice sure and determined as she turns and marches down the hall.

Something about Pepper's stern voice and the soft sway of her hips as she moves so assuredly makes the thought that I'd pretty much do anything and everything she asks flash through my head. An unnecessary confirmation that I am, in short, an absolute sucker for beautiful people with even a hint of authority.

I trail behind her, trying my best to corral my runaway thoughts into horny jail.

At the front door, Pepper slides on her clogs, hardly breaking her stride while I fumble around like Bambi on ice trying to get my tennis shoes on. With an awkward little walk-jog, I catch up to Pepper, who's already made it halfway down a row of tall, brilliantly pink flowers. The entire farm seems like a perfect little Eden, endless beds of blooms draped across the land like a quilt. Some stand tall and proud, their petaled faces lifted to the sun, others are short, spreading wide as they hug the earth.

"Did you plant all these yourself?" I ask, dragging my fingertips lightly along the emerald leaves as we walk.

Pepper glances at me, the look somehow both earnest and distrusting. "No."

She opens her mouth like she's going to say more, but shakes her head instead, shoving her hands in her pockets and ducking against the sharp rays of midday sun.

Cool. Too fun. I really, really, *really* love this whole painfully awkward small-talk thing.

"I don't do small talk. I'm autistic. My psychology basically rejects the entire concept of it."

It takes me a moment to process what Pepper said and that, apparently, I spoke my last thought out loud.

"Shit. I . . . uh. I'm sorry," I bumble out.

Pepper stops in her tracks, pinning me with a look that could kill—eyes narrowed and lips pursed. "Don't be. Not like it's terminal."

I slow-blink a few times, trying to figure out how things are derailing so disastrously fast. I replay the conversation a few times.

"Fuck. No. I didn't mean I'm sorry you're autistic." My tongue trips over my teeth as I speak. "I meant I'm sorry what I said was rude. Shit. I didn't mean it like that *at all*. I—" I gesture around wildly, trying to figure out what to say.

Pepper arches one perfect, dark slash of an eyebrow as I start to choke on air.

"I really didn't mean it like that," I eventually squeak out.

Pepper's face softens a bit. "I believe you. I can be . . ." She tilts her head up to the sky like the words she's searching for are written in the clouds. "Defensive about it. People often have a really ridiculously apologetic response when I mention I'm autistic like it's something I should feel bad about or whatever."

"I don't think that at all," I whisper, taking a tiny step toward her.

Pepper looks at me for a moment, eyes trailing over my face. Something about her look feels close. Intimate. Like a delicate thread is weaving its way between us. Then with a flippant shrug, she turns and starts walking again.

"I'm pretty sure I'm neurodivergent," I blurt out, almost yelling the words as I trail behind her again.

She glances at me, then focuses back on the grass.

"It wasn't until I was in art school that a doctor even suggested it," I continue, words tumbling out of me, ones I've wanted to share with someone for so long, they've grown to be a heavy knot in my chest. "The big thing was impulse control. Because, apparently, I have none." I let out a sharp, self-deprecating snort that earns me a second glance from Pepper.

I'm starting to feel a bit better about those glances, like they aren't pleading looks telling me to shut up, but an unspoken invitation to say more.

My gaze locks with hers and holds. After a moment, Pepper's eyes widen a bit, like she's nervous. I clear my throat, reminding myself to blink away. I've gotten better at not staring at people with the laser focus that feels most natural—learning from Olivia and Ophelia when I was younger that the intensity of it can make people uncomfortable—but something about Pepper's face is so dynamic, so captivating, I can't help it.

"And while Savannah, Georgia, doesn't immediately sound like a place to hard-core party," I continue, "I definitely found groups that would provide as much while I was there for school. After visiting student health for the third time in a month because of dehydration and/or to get the morning-after pill, I started seeing a counselor there about it."

"Having to see a counselor over your sex life seems a bit puritanical," Pepper says, pursing her lips as she brushes her hair over her shoulder.

I grin. "I think it was more the heavy alcohol and frequent drugs that accompanied the sex that warranted it."

Pepper opens and closes her mouth a few times. "Ah," she finally lands on.

My grin grows. I'm not ashamed of my wilder past. If anything, all the reckless choices launched me to rock bottom—the depression that followed benders leaving me at risk of failing more than one class due to unfinished projects. It was at rock bottom that I learned to actually face myself and my clanging brain instead of trying to numb it all away.

Life definitely feels easier at the end of a blunt with a fourth drink in hand or tangled in the sheets with a random person. Ever since I was a borderline feral child, I've been searching for something to drown out my thoughts, make my heart race, slow my brain down. It was sugar highs and new best friends and endless crushes and the rush of a new hobby. It was bummed cigarettes in my high school parking lot and stolen sips from my parents' liquor cabinet.

It's a basic, primal need for *more*. Stimulus. Numbness. Adrenaline. Blackouts. My brain wants it all.

But *more* has its limits and reaching them doesn't feel very nice.

Eventually, with gritted teeth and a particularly helpful

counselor, I learned to stop trying to feed the numbness and instead channel every painfully intense emotion I have onto whatever canvas is on hand.

"Anyway, after I told the school counselor about my hyperfocus and this kind of . . . *desperate* need for stimulation, they suggested I might have ADHD or autism. We talked about it a bunch, then I did some of my own research, and both overlapped and fit in different ways. I looked into taking formal exams for both but they were repulsively expensive and the wait was something like eleven months so I basically said fuck it. Neurodivergent feels right and that's all I kind of need. I know how I feel and experience the world."

Pepper has stopped walking at this point, her mouth pressed into a firm line. Anxiety and embarrassment braid together in my chest.

"Sorry. I'm sure that was like, way too much of an overshare," I say, digging my nails into my palms as I stare at the dirt, wishing I could bury myself under it.

Pepper clears her throat. "I can promise you," she says, voice soft like a rose petal, "as someone with little to no natural instinct on what's socially acceptable in conversations, nothing feels like an overshare."

A small hiccup of happiness floats through my chest. "Guess we have something in common after all," I say, reaching out my foot to nudge hers.

Pepper's eyes flick to my face, and a whisper of a smile touches her lips. "Saying I'm stunned is an understatement."

I let out a bark of a laugh, clapping a hand over my mouth when I catch Pepper's startled jump.

"Come on," Pepper says, leading the way again.

We walk a bit farther through the rows of flowers, some patches fully in bloom, others vibrant green with swollen buds ready to burst.

"Will this work?" Pepper asks with a gruff flick of her wrist, stopping at a shed a few yards from the barn.

"For what?"

Pepper lets out a sigh like I am exceptionally dense. "Your shoe factory."

I snort, giving the shed a closer look.

The structure is on the kinder side of shabby, extensively chipped green paint exposing the weather-worn wood beneath. A small door with iron hinges sits crookedly in the frame. I push it open and take a hesitant step in.

It's dirty but dry, smears of soil decorating the floors. Large windows are centered on three of the walls, letting in bright slices of light that turn the dust motes into sparkles. I test the panes, confirming I can open them to let out paint fumes. Besides a few rogue shovels, the space is empty, and I can already picture my worktable in one corner, a drying area in another. A spot for supplies on the shelves already lining parts of the walls.

A quick loop around the outside of the shed reveals ivy climbing the back while flowers and overgrown grass hug the base. I lean closer to a white flower, its petals delicate and flung wide to the sun, and watch a bumblebee lazily tumble around the center, collecting pollen.

"So?" Pepper says, voice sharp at the edges.

I look over my shoulder to find her watching me closely, eyebrows scrunched and mouth tipped down in a nervous frown. I grin at her, and her shoulders release a bit of tension.

"It'll do," I reply primly, my smile still growing as I stand and face her.

"Yeah?" Pepper takes a stilted half step closer.

Something about her hesitant movement and the genuine concern in her voice propels me forward, and I laugh as I wrap her in a hug.

"It's perfect," I say, holding tight. "Thank you."

Pepper is stiff in my arms, and I'm about to pull away, worried that I made her uncomfortable touching her so suddenly. But she shocks me by giving me a quick squeeze, then clears her throat as she steps away.

"Well . . . one problem we can cross off our never-ending list, then."

"I'm surprised you don't use this for farming stuff," I say, poking my head back in the shed.

Pepper brushes past me. "We've never really needed it." She bundles up the shovels and heads back out the door toward the barn. "A farmer down the road gave it to Lou after he decided to retire and move closer to his kids a few years back, and she was never one to turn down free resources. It's a nice building but somewhat poorly sealed. Lou worried it would let bugs in for any seeds or tubers we'd try to keep in there, and she already had the tools organized how she liked them in the barn. It's just sat here, waiting for a purpose."

"Who's Lou?" I ask, skipping after Pepper as she enters the barn, the sweet smell of shaded earth filling my lungs. I tilt my head up, looking at the beams crisscrossing above.

Pepper stops short, and I plow right into her, my forehead smacking into her shoulder blade and her elbow lodging into my ribs.

"Ah, damn." I stumble back, rubbing at the spot above my nose. "We need to put a bell on you or something, or I'm not gonna make it out of this alive."

"Sorry," Pepper says, voice rough and low.

"You okay?" I ask, her face ashen.

Pepper is still, gaze fixed straight ahead, intense, but gone, lips parted and ticked down in the corners. After a moment, she gives her head a shake, twisting her features into something a bit more neutral.

"Lou is—*was*—my grandma. She started the Thistle and Bloom," Pepper says, dropping the load in her arms and rubbing vicious circles around her temples. "She passed away last November."

My throat is sharp as a knife's edge as emotions flood through. I hate seeing people upset, and something about the quiet, contained way Pepper holds her hurt makes me wish I could pull it all out of her and swallow it away, let it chew me up instead.

"My grandma planted a lot of these flowers," Pepper blurts out, then cringes. "I mean, that's rather obvious, I guess. She basically tilled the entire farm, so of course she planted the flowers." She lets out a choked laugh that slices through my stomach.

"Sorry," Pepper continues, waving at her face, her cheeks sparking red as she continues to hold back emotion that clearly wants to boil to the surface. "I just really miss her and sometimes it catches me out of nowhere."

Without thinking, I press forward, wrapping her in another hug. It seems to melt Pepper, her arms circling around me as she curls against my embrace.

She sucks in a deep breath, holds it at the top of her throat until the strength of it is pressing on us both. With all the gentleness I can muster, I reach my hand through her hair, tracing it to where it ends on her middle back, then rubbing small circles up and down her spine.

Something in her releases, a rattling sob shaking her frame, arms squeezing me tighter. I have the bizarre and disarming thought that I wish I could hold her forever. Hold this quiet, prickly woman while she cries and while she's happy. I want—

"Pepper? You okay?"

Pepper wrenches away from me, turning toward a new voice, and I feel achingly . . . empty, my arms dropping to my sides with a slap.

"I'm fine," Pepper says, dragging her hands over her face. "Allergies," she says, voice wobbly and wet.

The woman rolls her eyes and lets out a huff before closing the distance and pulling Pepper into an embrace, cradling the back of her head and rubbing her hand up and down Pepper's spine. "Of course it is, love."

Pepper lets out a choked sound, then nuzzles closer into the woman, finding comfort in her touch. It's intimate and beautiful and it has no right to gnaw so sharply at my too-sensitive heart.

It's obvious these two are close, and whatever tangled, *ridiculous* feelings I conjured up a minute ago from nothing make me feel like a total fool. I need to get out of here. Leave them be. Paint away these sharp emotions that are leaving brands on my skin.

I try to back away quietly toward the door but, being a chronic dumb-ass, I naturally collide into what I can only describe as the loudest gardening tools known to man, all of them clanging together as I trip over them, sending me tumbling backward until I knock an entire toolbox over.

The two women untangle from each other, both looking at me with alarm as shovels and hoes and other outrageously loud metal objects continue to hit the ground.

Eventually, silence falls, the endless tools circling around me so I'm an embarrassed bull's-eye at the center. The woman blinks at me, eyebrows furrowing.

"Pepper," she says, voice guarded. "Who the hell is this?"

Chapter 9

PEPPER

"I'm nobody," Opal says before I can take a breath. "Swear. Nothing to worry about."

My eyebrows pinch. "What a truly bizarre thing to say."

Opal turns to me, flapping her hands in front of her, a deep pink crawling up her neck and across her cheeks. There's something a bit . . . captivating about that blush.

"I mean . . . um, I didn't want your girlfriend to think anything weird was happening."

My gaze clashes with Diksha's, and we stare at each other like we're racing to solve an extremely complex math equation.

Then we burst out laughing.

Diksha leans toward me, one hand resting on my shoulder as she sucks in a deep breath, her entire body shaking. I bury my head in my hands when a small snort escapes.

A high-pitched, sort of hysterical sound peals through the

barn, and I look at Opal. She's pretending to . . . laugh? I guess?
Eyes wide and mouth in a broad and terrifying smile.

"We're not together," I say, gesturing between my body and
Diksha's.

"Pepper wishes," Diksha says. I give her a tiny shove at
her additional round of incredulous giggles. "I'm a married
woman," Diksha adds, proffering her ring finger like she's flipping Opal off.

"Oh," Opal says, her mouth pinching into the word's shape.
She nods a few times, the blush still staining her cheeks and the
bridge of her nose.

"So the question still stands: Who the hell are you?" Diksha says, eyebrows quirked up as she takes a step toward her.
Opal jerks back, stepping again on a rake and causing more
clanging of my tools. I see Diksha's lips twitch in satisfaction.

Although Diksha barely reaches my shoulder, she has a tendency to turn into a towering mama bear whenever someone
new is around. She's ruthless and quick and can read people
like every motive is written on their skin. And she's always on
extra high alert when it comes to me.

It's mildly embarrassing to admit that, as an adult woman,
I kind of need her protection. But I've trusted the wrong people
enough times to rely on her gut instinct more than my own.

"This is Opal," I say, since Opal seems to be too flustered
to talk. "She . . . well, I guess she technically owns the farm."

"You found the will?" Diksha whips to me, eyes blown
wide, lines of worry scouring her face.

I let out the world's longest sigh, sharp tension building behind my eyes and down my neck. I haven't told Diksha anything about the past week, unable to force myself to talk about it, listen to her tell me all the things I have to do to fix this situation. "Not exactly."

There's a pause, then Diksha makes an exasperated gesture, swirling her wrists in large circles like she can conjure the details from thin air.

"It's . . ." I glance at Opal. Her mouth is pinched and brow furrowed. Something about her guilty look makes me feel . . . I'm not sure exactly how it makes me feel, but I know it's a tiny bit soft and tender and totally ridiculous. "It's a long story that, of course, involves Trish."

Diksha doesn't miss a beat, launching into an exceptionally graphic yet clever monologue of curses for Trish that starts with *neglectful crusty washcloth* and ends with *delinquent twat stain*.

"That was amazing," Opal whispers when Diksha pauses long enough to suck in a breath.

Diksha gives her a double take. "And are you in cahoots with Trish?" she asks, moving toward Opal again.

Opal's eyes widen, and she trips backward, landing squarely against the wall of the barn, head jolting forward from the impact and making me wince in sympathy. "No. I mean, kind of. But not really. I don't . . . I'm not . . ." Opal looks at me with pure desperation as she rubs the back of her skull.

I rest a hand on Diksha's shoulder, tugging her back and inserting myself between the two. "Opal's an innocent component of Trish's latest scheme." I give Diksha the broad strokes of this twisted situation, and the fact that she looks as worried as I feel is not much help.

"This is unbelievable," Diksha says, still eyeing Opal with distrust.

I give a helpless shrug. *Unbelievable* about sums it up.

"So, what? You're just letting this stranger stay here? Are you nuts?" Diksha says, turning on me.

"We did come up with a pretty rock-solid no-murder rule on the first night," Opal says from her corner. "It's sticking so far."

Diksha doesn't laugh, but some demented part of me does, and Opal's lips part in surprise, then kick up in a soft smile.

"Please tell me you have a plan, Pepper. I'm begging you."

I sigh, rubbing my head again, the sharp tension from before building a bridge between my temples. "The plan is . . . The plan is . . ."

"Nonexistent?" Diksha offers with a snarl.

"Not great," I admit, throwing my hands up. "But it's the best we've got. I'm going to slowly buy Opal out. Make a lump-sum payment at the end of this season—"

"Enough that I can find somewhere else to paint my shoes," Opal chimes in.

Diksha blinks at her. ". . . Paint shoes?"

"And then I'll look into getting a loan or something. Get on some sort of payment plan," I finish. It sounds weak even to my own ears, and the resulting silence in the barn is its own presence, large and intimidating.

"This is absurd," Diksha eventually says, rubbing the heels of her hands against her eyes. "And you need to call a lawyer."

"Can't really afford one," I mumble.

Diksha's shoulders fall at that, and some of the harshness melts around her edges. "I actually stopped by to tell you about something that might help the farm," she says, dragging a hand through her hair. "Seems more pertinent than ever."

My heart leaps. Please, all goddesses above and below, let it be some sort of massive, easy-to-secure grant that solves all my problems. "What is it?"

"Have you heard of the Living Art Festival?"

I cringe. "Can't say I'm big on festivals, Dee." Any type of festival—or event, or gathering, or damn farmers market for that matter—usually ends up being an absolute sensory nightmare. There are just so many *noises* and *smells* and . . . I don't know, *people* that my battery drains immediately and I spend the entire time white-knuckling it to avoid a public meltdown.

"This is different," Diksha says, flicking her wrist. "High-brow artsy shit. It's a nationwide flower show where florists and farmers create these amazing art pieces. Tal travels to attend it every year."

Tal is a brilliant florist who's cornered the Western North Carolina wedding market with their innovative arrangements and bold choices on color and composition. Tal is also one of my biggest wholesale buyers and a bit of a financial lifeline for the farm.

"Okay. What about it?"

Diksha shoots me a crafty grin. "The Grove Park Inn is this year's host."

I blink. "Oh. That's cool. Tal won't have to travel too far." The Grove Park Inn is an Asheville landmark, providing lodgings for everyone from Fitzgerald to Obama.

Diksha rolls her eyes. "The whole point of the festival is the big competition," she says. "There's like, a million small categories for Best in Bloom or whatever, but for the big showcase, entrants design a piece out of flowers that matches the theme, and the winner gets, wait for it, one hundred thousand dollars and a spread in *Something Blue*, one of the biggest bridal magazines out there."

I stare at her blankly. "Again, still trying to figure out what this has to do with the Thistle and Bloom."

Diksha clasps both hands on my shoulders, leveling me with a stern look. "You need to enter the competition."

I stare at her, waiting for her to laugh. For the punch line of whatever joke this is that I'm not getting. I'm not an artist. I'm not creative or innovative. I don't do grand ideas or enter competitions. I stay on my farm, keep my hands in the warm soil, and help flowers grow until they're ready to be harvested and admired by people with much more exciting lives than mine. And that's how I like my life. Small and safe and simple.

"This year's theme is Love in Bloom," Diksha says, ignoring my silence. "I'm sure you can think of something clever for that."

"Wow. *Bloom* for flowers. How groundbreaking."

"Why don't you rein it in there, Meryl Streep. With a grand prize like that, they could call it Pee-Pee-Poo-Poo-Petal-People and it would still be worth doing. One hundred *thousand* dollars? A spread in *Something Blue*? That exposure alone would get you enough business to keep this place going for years. This could be huge for you."

"Nooo," I say slowly, drawing out the word. "It could be huge for someone that knows how to do any of that artistic stuff. Someone like Tal."

Diksha clicks her tongue against her teeth. "Tal's been featured in *Something Blue* at least three times. Any more praise and their head won't fit through the door. Plus, Tal likes to go and observe. Soak up inspiration from others or whatever. Working under a strict theme, quote, *disrupts their creative flow*, unquote. You, on the other hand, need this. Pretty desperately, if I'm being honest."

"I'd rather you not be honest," I whisper. I truly don't need the reminder of how screwed I am.

Diksha cocks her hip, arms crossed over her chest as she glares at me.

I try to hold her stare, but end up blinking away. "I guess I could think about entering one of the smaller ones? But I've never tried to grow an, er, award-winning dahlia, or whatever."

"The smaller categories have a prize of less than a hundred bucks. It wouldn't be worth it. You need to go for the big one."

I throw my hands up in defeat. "I wouldn't have a clue where to start."

"I could help."

Diksha and I both whip our heads over to look at Opal. Her shoulders curl forward as she worries her bottom lip between her teeth, eyes wide with a spark of excitement.

"If you want, I mean. No pressure. I don't want to, uh, insert myself where I'm not—" She waves her hand as she searches for a word. "Wanted," she says at last, the syllables dancing on a defeated sigh.

"Say more," Diksha commands, fixing her with a skeptical squint.

"Please don't," I counter. I don't have room in my brain for more.

Opal smiles a bit. "I'm an artist," she explains to Diksha, that damn smile growing. "I work in tons of mediums. I'm sure I could figure out how to wrangle some flowers into a structure. I honestly think it could be amazing. The possibilities are endless, especially with flowers like this to work with," she says, waving toward the open barn door, my flowers spreading across the horizon. "I actually did some pretty intricate installation pieces a few years ago that took a lot of building and structuring, so this could be really cool. I think playing with height would be super eye-catching? What do you think?"

It takes me a moment to realize she's directed that question at me.

"About what?" I say, a tinge of exasperation in my voice. Opal's brain seems to whirl ideas around and out of her mouth at one hundred miles an hour, while I process at a more glacial pace.

"Doing the damn thing!" she says, spreading her arms wide. She's backlit by sunshine streaming through the doors, but somehow her smile is the brightest. I grimace.

"It sounds like an incredibly expensive investment with virtually zero percent chance of reward when I already have to pay you three hundred thousand dollars," I say, rubbing my temples.

The deranged woman actually laughs. "Are you always such a pessimist?"

"Yes. It makes disappointment *much* easier to take."

Opal has the audacity to tut. "What part will be expensive, exactly?"

"Um, let's see. You want to build a giant monument which will require . . . I don't know, wood? Netting? Nails? General building bullshit? Then you want me to set most of my *product*, my literal source of income, aside during peak selling season to cover said statue thing? That doesn't sound expensive to you?"

"I'm sure we could figure out a way to do it on the cheap," she says, tapping her full lips with her finger as she slowly turns in a circle. I shoot a sideways glance at Diksha, hoping we're sharing the same thought about this ridiculous idea, but she's staring at Opal with steady interest.

After a moment, Opal snaps her fingers and twirls back to face me. "Why don't we collect a smaller portion with each, er, cutting . . . session? Thing? And use any that don't sell too. That way we can build up a stock?"

Hopefulness is a barbed seed in the center of my chest, aching as it puts down roots. I shake my head, ripping out the small sprout and tossing it away. "It's pointless. Even with that, I wouldn't be much help in making it, and it sounds like too big of a project for one person to take on."

"You do have two months to work on it," Diksha says, as if this isn't a monumental task that would require way more time than that.

Opal apparently has an answer for everything. "My sisters are artists!" she all but squeals. "I'm sure I could get them to come down and help. Bring supplies they already have too. It's amazing what you can do with scrap materials."

"There's more of you?" I splutter out, eyes bulging.

"Two more," Opal says with a wave. "They're brilliant. You'll love them. I'll text them right now."

My brain is short-circuiting just thinking about the force of three Opal-esque women running around my farm. I march across the space, gripping Opal's wrist as her thumbs dart across her phone.

I meant for the touch to stop the spiraling situation, pause the runaway sensations zipping through my body. Instead, it focuses all of them, a jolt shooting from where I touch Opal, up my arm and through my chest, radiating out to every inch of my body. I quickly pull my hand away.

"I can't afford to pay you for labor when the winnings would end up going toward buying you out anyway." I can feel Diksha's eyes on me, but I ignore the look.

"You don't have to pay us. We love doing stuff like this. And you can use the earnings how you need to. If it goes toward buying me out, great. If you need to put it toward something different to help the farm, I get that too."

My head jerks back like she slapped me. Honestly, that would probably be easier to process than what she said. "Why would you do that?"

Opal gives me a one-shoulder shrug. "Because I thought it would be helpful?"

"But why would you . . . *help* me?" I ask, voice rising in confusion. "Why wouldn't you want the money for yourself as soon as possible?"

That shrug again, Opal tilting her head as she looks at me like I'm some complex riddle she can't solve. "Because it's the kind thing to do?"

I back away from her, my heart skipping beats and pounding in my ears.

Kindness? She's actually trying to convince me this is kindness? The concept is so outlandish, my skin crawls with distrust. I think of Trish, how the woman manipulates every situation until she's squeezed the very last cent from someone and pocketed it for herself. How she did that to me. If my own mother could pick pennies over me, how could it ever make sense that a virtual stranger would forgo immediate profits to . . . *help* me?

She's playing me. Or trying to. Or . . . or . . . *something*. People don't just help other people without something being in it for them.

"No," I say at last, my throat rough as a serrated knife's edge.

"But—"

"No," I repeat, voice rising in volume. "And I'm done talking about it."

I stalk toward the barn door, shooting a look at Diksha that I hope conveys I'll contact her later, when I'm ready, then nearly break into a run toward my flowers and my plots and the soil that lets this beauty grow.

The only place that ever feels wholly safe.

Chapter 10

PEPPER

Disrupting my usual routine, I set my alarm for an hour earlier this morning, and I'm now making my way into the fields as the sun's rays curl up the horizon, my pruners tucked in my belt and a large bucket of cool water in tow, head aching with that damn pressure that won't leave me be.

I tell myself the early start is necessary to beat the day's sweltering forecast, a sticky early summer heat wave flirting with my flowers, threatening to scorch them to dust. And I wish that was the whole truth. I wish Opal wasn't part of the reason, her smile popping into my thoughts all night as the pad of her footsteps through the cabin kept time with my insomnia.

But I can't face her. I don't want to hear more of her excited words and see that vibrant flush on her full cheeks. I don't want to slip into the trap of believing in whatever it is she's ultimately selling. Everyone has a hidden motive, and I'd be smart to re-member that.

Early morning mist slips like smoke between the moun-tains on the horizon, the sky a hazy blue as I walk down my rows to the first plot for picking.

May is my favorite month, the earth swollen with new blooms worshiping the sun after a long winter. The heavenly sweet scent of lilacs makes my head swim, daffodils raising their trumpets to the sky while snapdragons and sweet peas sway with the breeze.

But today, not even the explosion of Technicolor, the softness of the blossoms' sweet start, can hold my attention.

I make my way to the peonies, picking blooms in a me-chanical, detached way, my thoughts drifting far from the flowers as I work and move between beds, getting stuck in a vicious loop of financial spreadsheets and scary numbers and memories I don't want to relive with a return point of a girl with bubblegum-pink hair and a too-earnest smile.

I don't know why she distracts me so much. She's a person. Just a person. Historically, I don't like people. So why does this one have me tangled up like this?

I move to the plot of roses, wiping sweat off my forehead before diving into the thorny thicket.

Why am I wasting my time thinking about her—I mean, the competition? It's a nonstarter, a silly little fantasy that I have no business entertaining.

With a careless slip of my hand, I nick my finger on a thorn.

I whip my arm back, the point snagging my skin in a sharp line with the motion. I drop my shears in the process.

I stare into the knot of thorns dotted with pale pink roses and want to scream at the pressure building through my body. This unknown swirl of feelings and fear and confusion . . . and . . . and . . . It's all too much. Why can't things be simple?

Carefully, I weave my arm into a small opening, gritting my teeth at the bite of prickers as I grapple for the tool. Angry pink slashes score my forearm, but I finally grab the shears and pull them out.

Fire swells through me, and I'm tempted to rip the rosebushes out from the earth, toss them in the woods out back, and let them decay into the soil.

While I generally love all flowers, I've come to hate roses. I hate their uncomplicated beauty. Their cliché symbolism of love. Their built-in protection. Their delicate scent that becomes pungent and oppressive if enough are shoved into a room.

They're a challenge, Grandma Lou used to say, gently pinching a stem between her fingers before snipping the flower free. *The thorns are what really make a rose beautiful. Their blooms are made all the sweeter for the care and tenderness it takes to reach them.*

I hate that they remind me of Lou every time I look at them, making a deep and empty hurt open up in my chest, swallowing me whole like I'm collapsing in on myself.

Roses were her favorite, and everyone who loved Lou—which was pretty much every person she ever met—sent them for her funeral, the parlor stuffed to bursting with a rainbow of them. After the memorial was over and trite condolences were offered, it was just me, her casket, and an endless sea of roses and their awful thorns.

I screw my eyes shut, cramming the memory into the smallest box I can find and kicking it to a dark corner of my brain.

Pushing to stand, I fight off a lurch of nausea, then make my way to an anemone plot toward the back of the farm, nearly running to escape the whispers of feelings trying to seep into me. I start harvesting again, the late-morning sun sharp on my neck as I bend over the stems.

These are flowers I adore. Delicate. Complicated. Pale petals hiding a dark center. Just the tiniest bit fussy when it comes to keeping them alive. They're flowers that need me. My care. My support. My protection from drought and frost and wind.

My vision blurs as I look at them and, with a whip's quickness, emotions slam into me. I plop to the ground, grinding the heels of my hands against my eye sockets, pushing the tears back in. I don't want to cry. I don't want to feel sadness and confusion and this scary, overwhelming loneliness that always sits like a lion at my doorstep, ready to rip me apart.

I take two deep breaths. Then two more.

I finally push the feelings down until they poke and prod at my gut but can't do any significant damage. I stare at the anemones in front of me, their moon-colored petals and midnight-purple centers all fragile anticipation and hope. A small universe in this plot of dirt.

They don't actually need me, these blooms. They grew long before I was here, and will grow long after I'm gone. But it's nice to pretend something needs me. That something *wants* my attention. Wants the care I'm capable of giving.

I try to pull myself together, getting to my knees to start clipping stems, but something isn't right.

I've been feeling off since yesterday, words heavy and hard to form, a bone-deep type of exhaustion making every movement leaden. But the sensation of *wrong* strikes me like a slap. Jolts of electricity bloom across my brain, sending a wave like a fun-house mirror across my vision and making the world distort and bend as I struggle to get to my feet. It makes me sway, and I've endured enough migraines to know I need to get inside before the oncoming storm lays me out on the ground, but invisible hands reach from the soil and clamp around my ankles, tripping my every step.

The wrongness is familiar, but pumps panic through me nonetheless. It's like the flip of a switch, and I go from human to animal, desperate to escape the pain that always comes close on the heels of the aura.

The tingling comes next, the right sides of my lips feeling like they're swelling. The pinpricks travel from my mouth up the bridge of my nose to cluster at the corner of one eye—a swarm of hornets searching for a nest—before shooting down my neck.

I have five minutes, maybe ten, and then I'll be out for hours, if not a few days. The only thing I can think about as I stumble home is my flowers. All the beds I didn't get to. All the ways I've failed them like I fail everything else.

The nausea almost takes me to my knees, but I keep pushing

toward the cabin in the distance. If I stop, I'll have to endure the slicing of pain through my brain under the heat of the sun, and nothing sounds worse than that.

By some miracle, I make it to the porch, wincing at the whine of the screen door as I push it open, every squeak of the staircase like a stab to the temple as I desperately climb the steps to my room.

I collapse onto my bed as another white-hot prod of pain traces across my brain. My teeth grind together so hard I'm scared they might shatter, but at least that would be a distraction from my skull.

I burrow under the covers and get ready for the long, painful hours ahead.

Chapter 11

PEPPER

Shh. It's okay. I'm right here.

The dream is blurry but the pain is sharp, my bones aching as I shiver from the hurt. I'll never feel good again.

I dip in and out, whipping between reality and nightmare land—a place of darkness and panic and never, ever being enough.

Sharp.

It hurts.

So sharp.

It . . .

If my entire body weren't locked up with pain, I'd cry out at the sudden comfort curling around my back.

I'm here.

And she is. With the smell of outside and paint and coffee, lovely, soft Opal has me. Soothes my sharp aches and bone-deep chills

cool hand on my forehead
    warm words in the shell of my ear
        soft thighs, tangled legs, arm wrapped tight
          around my middle

The darkness of nightmare land clears with a gentle glow of sunlight breaking over the horizon.

And I sleep.

Chapter 12

OPAL

It's another restless night for me but, for once, I'm not bothered. I had a purpose in those wide-awake hours. A reason to keep watch: Pepper and whatever made her sharp whimpers cut through the cabin around midnight.

I'd anxiously loitered outside her room for close to an hour, her grunts of pain coming frequently through the door, but it was when I heard her start to cry—tiny, choked sobs that were equal parts frustration and fear—that I opened the door and kneeled at the side of her bed.

What's wrong? Are you okay?

She'd grabbed my hand instead of answering, squeezing tight.

My head, she'd eventually said through gritted teeth. *Migraines. Happen sometimes.*

What can I do?

She held my hand even harder, a small pull toward her.

Now, Pepper's arm is looped around my waist, her forehead and cheek resting on my shoulder, each breath she takes a deep, gentle puff against my neck that sends small electric sparks across my skin. I'd started the night sitting on top of the sheets, back resting on the headboard, but at some point, I must have dozed off, tucking myself under the well-loved quilt with Pepper.

She's loose-limbed and pliant against me, my hand splayed wide across her back as I keep her pressed close. I have an odd, gnawing type of panic building up in my chest at the knowledge that any moment she'll wake up. Pull away. Tense all those relaxed muscles as she looks at me. Whatever delicate comfort I deluded myself with in the gauzy hours of night where emotions feel rounded and approachable will disappear like the smoke of a snuffed-out candle.

Pepper stirs in her sleep, burrowing closer to me in the process, her cheek nuzzling against my breast, my pulse kicking up, pounding in a heavy rhythm. She lets out a small sigh, and it's like I can see the delicate curve of the noise travel through her parted lips.

She's so warm and so damn pretty and as much as I want to resist the impulse, I hug her tighter, squeeze her to me like I can keep her there for hours, this new bubble of comfort my favorite place in the world.

But, because I can never do anything right, the movements rustle her too much, and her breathing changes, becoming shallower. She stiffens with alertness as she surfaces from sleep and feels me next to her.

Her arm retreats to her side, her head pulling back as she looks at me with those wide brown eyes.

The bubble is popped.

"How are you feeling?" I ask, keeping my voice low. "I was so worried about you."

Pepper stares at me, sizing me up like she's ready to fight. She's always ready to fight.

She sucks in a deep breath, and I can tell she's shoring up the energy to tell me just how fine she is. How nothing is wrong. But her eyes are pinched at the corners, her frown taut as she tries to hide a wince. After another heavy moment of her looking at me—gaze searching and almost desperate—her eyes flick away, and she deflates a little.

"Kind of shitty, to be honest." She says it with a sigh of defeat, like she just let the gate down on a stronghold and I'm about to lay siege.

It takes everything in my power to hold back a laugh at the melodrama.

"I'm not surprised. Last night seemed rough. You said it was a migraine?"

Pepper gives me a curt nod, then pulls further away, sitting up and digging the heels of her hands into her eyes. Her legs knock mine in the process.

"Sorry, I'm all knees and elbows," she says, staring down at the mattress.

"I don't mind at all." I sit up too. "Is there anything I can get you?"

"No." The word comes out clipped, automatic, that denial of help always sitting like a loaded spring at the tip of her tongue.

I know I should leave, but I hesitate. A kind, considerate me would swing my legs off the bed, tell Pepper I'm around if she needs me, and leave her to her peace and quiet and aloneness. But I'm a selfish creature—a needy one—and the soft, subtle ache for more of this closeness expands through my chest.

"Thanks for, um—" Pepper waves her hand at me, a deep red creeping up her neck and cheeks as she continues to stare at the comforter. "I'm sorry I woke you."

I shake my head, ducking to get in her line of sight. "Please don't apologize," I say, finally catching her gaze. She looks skeptical. "I'm serious. I rarely sleep most nights anyway, so I was already up. I . . . Well, like I said, I was really worried about you."

Her blush intensifies and I watch the way her diverted eyes roam around the room, trying to find somewhere safe to land.

"Do you get migraines like that a lot?"

Pepper lets out a humorless laugh, rolling her neck. "I used to get them all the time as a teenager. At one point, it was happening almost every week. I was doing a lot better the past five years or so, only getting a few a year, but they've picked back up in frequency since . . . Been getting them a lot more the past few months."

The quiet, almost imperceptible tremble in Pepper's voice slices me to ribbons. She keeps so many emotions dammed up in there, threatening to crack her open. I want to pull her into a hug tight enough that she feels safe to open the floodgates and let it all out.

"Anyway," she says, voice back to a smooth, detached timbre, "I have to get to work."

"A day off won't kill you," I say in what I hope is a coaxing tone when, really, I want to command her to lie down and rest until she can look at the window without wincing. But I've never commanded anyone to do anything, and starting with Pepper doesn't seem like a wise move.

"Financially it might," she mumbles, hoisting herself up to sit on the edge of the bed. She sways for a moment, one shaky hand moving to her temple, the other gripping the sheets.

I scurry around to her side, resting my palms on her shoulders. I smooth out their slight hunch before gently pushing her back against the pillows.

"Tell me what to do," I say, pulling the blanket up to her chin. "I can take care of the flowers today."

Pepper's eyes shoot wide like I just asked for nuclear codes. "Absolutely not."

"Ever the charmer," I say, pressing my lips together despite the smile tugging at the corners. "But I'm not letting you leave this room, so you might as well tell me what needs to get done."

Pepper shakes her head, a slight sheen of sweat on her forehead despite the clattering of her teeth. She tries to get up again, but my fingertips pressed to the center of her chest keep her down.

"You might have about nine inches of height on me but, in this state, I think I'd win any fight you can muster."

Pepper lets out an exasperated sigh, looking stunningly put out at my offer of help. I don't even attempt to hold back my grin this time.

"Trust me, Pepper," I say, reaching out and giving her hand a quick squeeze. She stares at where I touch her, eyebrows notched low. After a moment, she lets out a deep, shaky breath, pulling her hand away and repositioning herself to sit up.

"It's important to harvest the blooms before the afternoon heat," she says, still staring at our hands. "Anything cut after eleven will wilt quicker than normal. Evening—like six or seven—is a bit better, but that doesn't give you as many hours to work."

"Avoid high heat. Check."

"And make sure you have buckets of water with you to put the stems in as soon as they're cut, otherwise you're just wasting your time. They'll shrivel up and die before we can deliver them to our florists."

"Flowers are thirsty little sluts. Got it."

"Don't call the flowers sluts," Pepper says, brow still furrowed but a soft curl of a smile trying to pull through.

"Respect the flowers' delicate constitutions and fear of profanity. Understood."

"Maybe call Tal and Diksha. See if they can come out." Pepper grabs her phone, opening up her friends' numbers and showing me the screen. "Tal is a florist and one of my biggest buyers, so they'll know how to tell what's ready to be picked. Diksha's helped around here a bunch too."

"Bring in the troops. Consider it done."

Pepper's gaze snaps up to mine, brown eyes sharp and searching, flicking across my face, cataloging every inch. "Why are you doing this?" she says at last, guarded and slow.

"Doing what?"

"H-helping . . . me."

I let out a confused huff of a laugh. "Because it's a nice thing to do? Because you spent the night crying in pain over a migraine and it's objectively shitty to wave you out the door the next morning to do manual labor in the sun? Despite what you very vocally believe, I'm not trying to make your life any harder."

"But that's . . ."

"What?"

"Selfless." Pepper spits out the word like it's a curse.

I laugh with a bit more conviction this time, a small smile curving my lips. "Oh my God, you distrustful little goose, it's really not. Helping you ultimately helps me, right? Anything you make goes back to buying me out. If anything, I feel kind of guilty about it."

Pepper stares at me like she literally cannot process this. Like no one had ever offered a helping hand before.

"Pepper," I say, widening my eyes and leaning toward her until we're almost nose to nose. There's a small catch in her breath, so quiet I wonder if I imagined it.

"Yeah?" she whispers back.

"Overthink it tomorrow. For now, rest that head." I reach between us, lightly booping her nose with my finger. You'd think I'd just body-slammed her to the ground with how heavily she falls back, blinking at me with a stunned expression.

I take advantage of the momentary lull in her protests, and slide off the bed, shooting her a wide grin before I leave the room and shut the door behind me.

• • •

Diksha's car rumbles up the gravel drive thirty minutes later, two other people hopping out with her as soon as she cuts the engine.

"How is she?" Diksha asks in greeting, looking up toward the second floor of the cabin like she wants to plow past me and march straight to Pepper's bedside. It strikes me then how deeply Diksha cares for Pepper, how all her snap and bite is a defense mechanism to protect her friend.

"After I threatened to tie her to the bed if she didn't stop trying to escape to take care of the flowers, she begrudgingly agreed to rest. Room is nice and dark and quiet."

Diksha nods, eyes still fixed on Pepper's window. "Good."

One of the people with Diksha clears their throat, snapping her out of her trance. "Shit, sorry. Opal, this is my partner, Tal." Tal gives me a small wave and stilted smile. "And this is our friend, Alfie. We thought another set of hands wouldn't hurt since it's already so late in the morning."

I throw up a peace sign in greeting.

"I brought provisions too," Alfie says, his British accent brightening each word. He gives me a broad grin as he lifts a woven basket overflowing with baked goods. "Some of Pepper's favorites."

"He owns one of the best cafes in Asheville," Diksha says, snagging a ridiculously large biscuit from the top of the pile and taking a bite.

Alfie rolls his eyes in feigned modesty, waving away her words. He plucks a lemon poppy seed muffin from the mountain of pastries, handing it to me. I'm not sure if I'm PMSing or just emotionally frazzled from seeing Pepper hurting so badly, but the gesture and the smile attached has me getting a bit misty-eyed.

"Thank you all so much for coming to help on such short notice."

"No ask is too big when it comes to Pepper," Alfie says.

"We should probably get to it," Tal says, bundling up their shoulder-length black hair into a sleek ponytail as they march toward the barn, Diksha close behind. Alfie darts into the house to deposit the pastries, and then we both jog to the others.

"Alfie and I can take the snapdragons," Tal says, nodding to a plot of flowers blooming in a cone shape down the stalks, their bell faces smiling in the sun. "You two want to handle the lilacs?"

Diksha gives Tal an incredulous look, eliciting a sigh from Tal. "We're the only two that know what to do. It would waste more time to leave them to their own devices," Tal adds, nodding at me and Alfie.

"Fine," Diksha says through tight lips, stalking toward the tall lilac trees.

"Love when you talk about me like I'm a toddler," Alfie

says with a teasing wink, following Tal as they move to their designated plot.

Feeling like more of a nuisance than a help, I follow Diksha to the pale purple blooms. The smell is heavenly, rich and heavy and undeniably sweet. I press my face against the cluster of small flower heads that bow the branches under their magnificent weight.

"Make sure the stem has at least half its buds open," Diksha says without preamble, gripping a cluster and unpocketing her shears. "And cut pretty far down. You don't want any of the flower heads to be touching the water in the bucket."

I watch as she pinches a spot about six inches from the base of the blooms, cutting at a sharp angle. She deposits the stem into a bucket of water, moving quickly and efficiently to the next waiting branch.

It doesn't exactly seem like rocket science, so I give it a go, grabbing a branch and moving to cut.

"No," Diksha says, her tone harsh as she grips my wrist. "That's way too low. You won't get any regrowth this season if you cut like that."

She shakes her head, then moves my hands out of the way, cutting the stem and putting it in the bucket.

"Honestly, I can handle this myself," she says, maneuvering around me as she continues to harvest. "You can go back to the cabin. We've got it covered."

"Why do you dislike me so much?" I blurt out. A deep and sharp type of fear pumps through me at the look Diksha turns my way.

"Excuse me?"

I want to stand down. I want to swallow my words, sprint back to the cabin. Avoid any and all confrontation because, in the end, isn't that always easier than having rough conversations?

But this is supposed to be the new me or whatever, so I stand still, swallowing before I repeat myself. "Why do you dislike me as much as you do?"

Diksha stares at me, her mouth a tight line, eyes sharp and assessing. After a moment, she lets out a breath, turning back to the lilacs. "I don't trust anyone to treat Pepper like she deserves," she says at last. "She doesn't have a stellar track record of people treating her well, and I can't say this little situation you've tied her up in with Trish gives you any brownie points."

"I'm not looking to hurt Pepper," I say, the words far more defensive than I intend. But it's true. I kind of . . . *like* the woman. "I'm not looking to hurt anyone. All I wanted to do was . . . was . . ."

"What?" Diksha says, tone clipped.

"Start over," I say, hanging my head. "My life was kind of a mess before this and I—" I wave my hand, trying to find the right words. "I don't know. I feel like I make a mess of most things. Or I let people in my life make messes of things because I'm too afraid to stand up for myself. But then for the first time I had actual money and this dream of painting shoes—"

"Shoes? Who are you, Mother Goose?"

"—and I thought this would be my fresh start. But apparently, I can't even do that right." A knot of suppressed frustration unravels in my throat, words and tears pouring out of me. How mortifying. "I'm trying my best. I'm always trying my best and I don't really know what I'm supposed to actually do, and I'm sick of making even more problems for people wherever I go but I—*Oof.*"

Diksha pulls me to her with so much force, all the air sweeps out of my lungs, more of those silly tears continuing to fall. For a moment, I'm scared she's trying to wrestle me into shutting up but she's actually . . . *hugging* me. It feels so damn good to be touched, I melt into her.

"You're okay," she whispers, one hand drawing motherly circles up and down my spine, the other cradling the back of my neck, her chin resting on the crown of my head. "I promise, you're okay."

"Wait, why are you being nice to me now?" I mumble into Diksha's shoulder, getting whiplash from her moods. But I'm so comfortable in this tight hug, I'm not sure I even care about the answer.

"I can be wary you're going to screw over my best friend and still offer comfort to someone who needs it. I'm a woman of multitudes," she says, a tiny smile in her voice.

"I'm not going to screw Pepper over," I say again, a tiny bit of fight coming back to my voice.

Diksha lets out a long sigh, giving me one more squeeze, then pushing me to arm's length. "I believe you," she says at last, eyes meeting mine. "Now, enough of the dramatics. Let's pick some damn flowers or whatever."

"Now who's acting like Mother Goose?" I say with a smile as I drag my hands across my tear-streaked cheeks.

Diksha rolls her eyes and makes a big show of grabbing her shears and cutting another bough of lilacs, but I don't miss the tick of a smile at the corner of her mouth.

We work in friendly quietness for the next few hours, filling up bucket after bucket with blooms.

Diksha shows me the converted cooler attached to the barn that keeps the cut flowers from wilting as quickly, explaining Pepper's organization system—grouped first by color, then by type. It feels like standing in the center of a color wheel.

"They're all so beautiful," I say, pressing my nose to a pale pink peony, inhaling the softly sweet scent.

"And Pepper knows everything about all of them," Diksha says with a nod. "When they like to bloom. What pH level they prefer for the soil. How much sun. Water. She keeps it all stored up in that brain of hers like an encyclopedia."

I grin. "I love it. Not everyone can make careers out of a special interest like that."

"She'd do anything for this place."

"Truer words, darling," Alfie says, bursting into the cooler, arms filled with daffodils, Tal close behind. "You'd think she sprouted from the soil like her flowers for how connected she is to it."

"The Grandma Lou effect," Diksha says softly, a gentle sadness ghosting through the space.

"It's going to be her first birthday without her," Tal says from the corner as they evaluate a bundle of pale blue puffballs of flowers.

"Is her birthday coming up?" I ask.

"End of the month. May twenty-ninth," Alfie says. "She's a Gemini. Try not to judge her too harshly for that."

Diksha slaps his shoulder. "We'll have to make this the best FriendsBitching yet."

"Friends . . . bitching?"

Alfie giggles. "It's our tradition of sorts. Pepper has always hated celebrating her birthday so, naturally, we make a really big deal out of it, but she refuses to acknowledge our efforts. It was, what, probably four years ago now that she renamed it FriendsBitching?" Alfie looks to Diksha, who nods.

"Yeah, just about. None of us celebrate Thanksgiving because, well, fuck Thanksgiving, but we were always trying to do something for her birthday so, instead, Pepper dedicated the day to us all ordering a bunch of food from local restaurants, drinking way too much cheap wine, and bitching about the atrocious injustices in American politics."

"How cliché," I say with a giggle. Alfie grins at me again.

"You'll join us this year, right?" he says, throwing an arm around my shoulders. "I'm bringing my new boyfriend, and it would be wonderful for him to not be the only fresh meat among the vultures." He shoots a pointed look at Diksha.

"I won't say anything to him I wouldn't say to you," Diksha says, fists perched on her hips.

"That's what scares me, darling," Alfie says, Tal letting out a rough laugh from the corner.

"I'd love to go," I say, little stars in my eyes at the idea of hanging out with this mildly intimidating but undoubtedly charming group. "Can I— Wait, never mind."

"Can you what, love?" Alfie asks.

I wave his question away. "I was about to be really rude and ask if my sisters can come too. I think they were planning on visiting me that weekend, but I'll reschedule with them for—"

"The more, the merrier," Alfie cheers. "So long as they bring either gifts or interesting stories."

"I'm sure Pepper wouldn't want my siblings crashing her birthday."

"On the contrary, she'd love anyone that can divert attention away from her."

"That's, unfortunately, very true," Diksha says.

"It's settled, then," Alfie says, steering us out of the cooler and into the bright sunlight. "No doubt it will be a night to remember."

Chapter 13

OPAL

I spent the rest of the day setting up my little art shed. Diksha and Tal showed me the storage unit toward the back of the farm, saying that anything in there was fair game to make the space more usable.

Pepper is just like Grandma Lou, never getting rid of anything, Diksha had said, eyes skimming the organized chaos of dusty tools and supplies.

They both believe everything has a purpose, it just takes time to figure out what that is, Tal added.

I found a scarred table toward the back that we were able to squeeze into the shed, and I'll use it as a place to paint. I hung a few work lights from hooks already in the walls, and Tal showed me the easiest way to set up some basic shelves from the beat-up planks forgotten in the corner. None of it can be described as aesthetically pleasing, but it certainly does the job.

Inspiration dug its claws into my brain shortly after I got

things set up. I don't remember saying goodbye to everyone, my thoughts fully focused on the delicate pattern that was unraveling itself in my mind. I sketched it on paper a few times— the swoops and lines untangling until it felt like I could reach out and touch the scene—then ran back to the cabin, hauling my giant sack of shoes to my studio and getting to work on a pair of mules.

Now, I have four completed sets of leather shoes in front of me, each covered in a unique design meant to mimic classic blue-and-white china patterns.

I tend to create art in a bit of a trance, my brain blurring at the edges as my hands work, chasing a shimmer of an idea while the rest of the world melts away. As my eyes trace the delicate path painted across the top of one shoe, winding to the steps of a sweet-looking home, I realize I've painted Pepper's cabin. My cabin? Ours? Regardless, the cozy A-frame is immortalized in a brilliant blue, the sagging porch a center point to the design.

I study the rest of the finished shoes, recognizing other areas of the Thistle and Bloom that have apparently planted themselves in my memory in the short time I've been here.

Stretching out my stiff neck and shoulders, I glance at my phone, having to blink a few times as I realize how late it is, inky midnight framing the small windows, the bright yellow glow of the work lights reflecting back like enlarged stars. I groan as a string of texts from Laney and Miles pop up on the screen.

Laney

Hey

Oh wow, another unanswered text

Cool

You know, you used to pretend to be so fucking chill or whatever

But you get a little bit of money and the rest of the world can fuck off right?

Do you not see how boring and cliche that is?

Like you haven't even checked in on me in weeks

And I'm sorry but it's pretty fucking rude to ghost your best friend like this

I've been going through a lot of shit with Miles and I could really use your advice

But you only ever have time for yourself so i'm not sure why i'm surprised . . . fuck my feelings, right?

I didn't tell Laney, or anyone outside of my family, that I was moving here, and I have about fifty unanswered texts from her over the past week, ranging from heartfelt to downright shitty. I even got a call from my mom saying Laney had been ringing the house phone, asking where I was. My far-too-honest mom, God love her, told Laney I'd moved, which apparently resulted in quite the hysterical declaration of how devastated she was.

I've been ignoring her. Or, not ignoring as much as just . . . forgetting she exists? Which is an objectively shitty thing to do to someone, and guilt froths up in my stomach every time I linger on the truth of it. But coming here, to this farm and the flowers and the complications with Pepper, was a Laney detox.

My brain has always functioned on the out of sight, out of mind philosophy, something a counselor once told me is part of neurodivergency. If I don't leave vegetables at the front of the fridge, I forget I bought them, only to remember when they're rotted and smelly. If I don't leave my markers out on my desk, I'll forget I have a certain color and end up buying three more. Apparently, the same applies to people I cared about who never really treated me well.

My fingers hover over the keyboard, trying to decide how to respond. But it all makes me feel so . . . so *tired*. It's exhausting to be regularly reminded how I come up short with a friend I've given everything I can to.

I swipe to Miles's messages instead. It's like he's writing a fuckboi textbook.

Miles

heyy

been thinking about you lol

wanna hang?

This last one makes me genuinely snort.

you know I moved out of Charlotte, right?

I watch the text bubble bounce in and out of the screen. Poor Miles, he's probably going to strain something from thinking too hard.

you did?? When

a couple weeks ago

where?

Right. Not about to run the risk of him passing the info on to Laney and her showing up here to tell me what a shit friend I am in person.

the hundred acre wood

bro you moved all the way to california??

I pocket my phone with a shudder. I can't believe I ever let that person penetrate my body.

Gently, I move the completed shoe sets to a shelf so they can dry, then do a cursory cleanup before switching off the lights and trudging back to the cabin. I stop in the kitchen, ears pricked for any noises from Pepper. I slip off my shoes and tiptoe up the stairs, holding my breath as I press my ear to her door. A rush of relief like a retreating tide flows through me at the peaceful silence. Good. She deserves all the rest after what she went through.

Slipping back downstairs—cursing every squeaky step along the way—I grab some water, then look around the living room. I'm tired, but I know it's not the type of tired that will actually let me sleep. It's a worn-out brain tired from a creative afternoon, but with buzzing limbs that are still running on the high-stimulus frequency. I eye the overstuffed couch, imagining how good it would feel to collapse on top of it. Allow myself to relax just a notch and let this place feel like the home I'd hoped it would be.

Oh fuck it, it's just a couch. With a zealous leap, I launch onto the cushions and burrow into the throw blankets.

Heaven. Pure, upholstered heaven.

Maybe I'll be able to sleep after all, a gentle weight tugging at my eyelids.

But a creak on the stairs jolts me upright, guilt zipping through me like I've just been caught with my hand down my pants.

Pepper's rumpled form appears in the archway, dark circles ringing her eyes despite her being in bed most of the day.

"Hey," I say softly, my gaze trailing a circuit from her head to her toes.

"H-hi," she says, eyebrows furrowing as she looks at me like she can't quite place me. "What are you doing up?"

"I'm a bad sleeper," I respond, waving away the concern in her voice. "How are you feeling?" I scooch off the couch and stand in front of her.

"A lot better." Pepper's smile is sheepish, like she's been avoiding work and lazing around on a beach for months instead of taking a single day to battle a migraine. She looks away from me, that frown fixing back on her lovely face as she stares at the ground. She clears her throat a few times.

"Diksha texted me and told me all you got done today and I, uh, I wanted to say thank you for, um, you know . . ." She swats at the air in front of her like she's impatient for the right words to appear. After a deep breath, she lifts her chin, fixing me with those gingerbread eyes. "For taking care of me. And the flowers. Particularly the flowers. It means . . . it means a lot. And I appreciate it."

I tilt my head as I look at Pepper, wishing more than anything I could understand this woman, see the tangle of thoughts that constantly sits at the tip of her tongue. She talks like she's not used to help. I wonder what someone would have to do to earn her trust.

"Don't mention it," I say at last, breaking the heavy tension that's settled around the room. "It was honestly really fun. My back is going to hate me for the next week for all the stooping I did, but I had a great time. I'm just glad you're feeling better."

"Do you want to get food with me?" Pepper blurts out, voice loud and vibrant in the quiet stillness of the night. She clutches a hand to the base of her throat like she can't believe the sound came from her.

I blink a few times. "Right now?"

Pepper nods, the movement jerky. "If you want. I'm starving and haven't been to the grocery store in a hot minute. But I know it's late and you're probably tired and we'd have to go somewhere crappy because, again, time and all that late-hour stuff, but if you want I'm sure we could find somewhere but absolutely no pressure, in fact, I don't need to eat, I think I'll just shove some of Alfie's pastries in my mouth and go lie down and—"

"I'd love to," I say, leaning toward her. "Let's go."

• • •

We pull into the Waffle House parking lot, a guy in a chef smock and backward baseball cap sitting on a wheel stop smoking a cigarette out front. Pepper maneuvers into a spot and cuts the engine, eliciting a bored look from the guy.

After a moment, he closes his eyes, takes a final (impressively long) drag, then flicks the butt away and pushes to stand, slinking back into the restaurant and behind the counter.

"See that," I say, tapping on the dash as we watch through the windows as he slips on an apron and plants his hands on the counter, head hanging low like he'd rather be anywhere in the world than this Waffle House at one a.m. "That's how you know it's going to be good. If your chef isn't smoking in the parking lot five minutes before ordering, you might as well take your business elsewhere."

Pepper snorts. "You aren't supposed to verbalize the reality. It ruins the magic."

We make our way inside and grab a booth near the counter, the pleather seats cracked with tufts of stuffing poking out. We get about thirty seconds to settle ourselves and pick up a menu before our server appears.

"What'll it be, dolls?" an older woman asks in a scratchy voice as she plunks herself in front of our table, her chipped name tag showing MAUDE in big, messy letters. Her hair is tangled like a bird's nest on the top of her head, smears of mascara rimming her eyes while a not-so-subtle perfume of weed wraps around us. She's giving zero fucks and I absolutely love her for it.

"Your nails are amazing," I say, transfixed by the hot-pink manicure with rhinestones on each finger.

"Not on the menu, honey," Maude says with a cheeky half smile before fixing her face back into a bored expression.

"Can I get the All-Star?" Pepper asks, eyes skimming over the menu. "With bacon, rye toast, and the hash browns smothered, covered, and capped?"

"To drink?" Maude asks, not bothering to write anything down.

"Hot tea, please." Pepper gives Maude a small, brilliant smile as she tucks her menu behind the napkin dispenser, her chestnut hair slipping over her shoulder. She wraps her long fingers around the strands, playing with them for a moment before pushing her hair away.

There's something so disarming about the simplicity of her smile—the crooked corners creating deep brackets in her cheeks, the tiny chip on the corner of her front tooth. She's filled with a sort of steady softness—a certain confidence in each movement but awareness of every ripple it will create—that even watching her tuck a lock of hair behind her ear seems like witnessing art in motion.

"And you?" Maude's voice cuts through my thoughts and pulls me out of my (not at all creepy, I'm sure) staring. The tone indicates she's already asked me for my order more than once.

And, in classic restaurant-anxiety form, I panic and forget any meal I've ever enjoyed ever. "I'll have . . ." My eyes scour over the menu, everything fuzzy as I fumble for an answer. Maude sighs and it does absolutely nothing to help my frazzled state.

"T-bone," I blurt out, a picture of a grayish steak the first thing I can focus on. "And, uh, eggs. I guess."

Maude and Pepper fix me with similar looks of disbelief.

"Do you actually want that?" Maude asks, slanting me a look.

No. "Yes, please."

"How do you want it prepared?" she asks.

"As good as possible," I mumble, pushing my menu to the side.

"And the eggs?"

"Scrambled. Bacon instead of sausage if you can."

Maude clucks her tongue as she walks away, yelling our order to the guy from the parking lot as he heats up the grill.

"Did you really just order a steak from a Waffle House at one a.m.?" Pepper asks, her face pure horror.

"Of course," I say dryly. "Best beef in town."

We sit in awkward silence, accidentally catching each other's gazes every few minutes before darting away.

"Is your neck okay?"

The question catches me off-guard, and it isn't until Pepper nods toward my right shoulder that I realize I'd been rubbing at a knot.

"Just a little stiff," I say. "That's what she said," I add. Because, apparently, I'm twelve.

Pepper lets out a small snort, her eyes crinkling as she smiles. My own mouth mirrors the grin. "You just triggered some of my worst middle-school memories."

I slap my hands to my chest. "Ouch, Pepper. Going straight for the jugular. I'm not sure there's an insult that can cut deeper."

"Serves you right, talking like it's 2009."

"That joke is a timeless classic and you know it."

"You need some serious help if that's what you consider a classic," Pepper says, arching one of those perfectly sharp eyebrows at me.

"I'll bring it up in therapy. Which I'll go to as soon as I can afford some cute little health insurance."

Pepper laughs again. "A daunting five-year plan."

I tut. "Let's be realistic. In this economy? Ten-year minimum."

Pepper's smile notches higher before she groans and drops her head to her hands. "This whole *life* thing is pretty hard for you too, then?"

A laugh is pulled out of me so violent it sounds like a hog squeal, making us both jump. Our eyes lock for a moment, Pepper's wide with surprise, and then we burst into giggles.

"I'll take that as a yes?" she asks, cheeks brilliantly red and eyes glassy. She's so cute, and laughing with her feels so damn *good* that my heart swells like a balloon, about to lift me to the clouds. I have the irrational urge to ask her to hold on to me.

"I might be the worst adult on the planet," I say, leaning toward her. "Like, deadass. I can't handle anything. I'm not sure I've ever actually paid taxes correctly or what taxes even are, I'm always hungry and never have any food, I can't hunt or gather, and I lose my phone at least nine times a day."

"How old are you?" Pepper asks, pulling her hot-chocolate-colored hair up and into a ponytail. I trace the lines of her long neck with my eyes.

"Twenty-four."

"I wish I could say it gets better, but it only gets worse."

"Lovely."

"Well, if by the time you turn twenty-six you wake up and don't have a flower farm on the brink of financial collapse with a random pink-haired woman with a giant sack of shoes excitedly announcing your sudden eviction notice, you'll be in a more put-together spot than me."

I giggle again. "Oh please. I'm not going to evict you. Not

when torturing you by being your housemate is so much more rewarding. It's only been two weeks and I'm already telling time by your various sighs of disappointment."

Pepper rolls her eyes, but a tiny smile inches up the corners of her mouth.

"Here, honey," Maude says, clanging our plates onto the table. "Need anything else?" she asks, already walking away.

"What more could one ask for?" I say, jamming my fork through the thin "steak" and holding it next to my face with a goofy smile. A steady drizzle of grease falls to the plate.

Pepper grimaces. "This situation would be a lot funnier if we didn't have to share a bathroom."

Another booming laugh. Damn, Pepper has some jokes. It's rather unfair that she's both hot and funny.

"Alfie would wring my neck if he found out I passed over his biscuits and scones for a soggy waffle," Pepper says, pouring a generous helping of syrup over her plate before digging in.

I frown at her, placing both fists on the table with a sturdy thump. "Waffle House waffles are the perfect level of limp. Put some respect on the name."

Pepper blinks at me for a moment like she's worried she actually offended me. My frown cracks, and I give her a playful wink. A giddy electricity hums between us—something about the late night and shitty food and slumber-party giggles that has my heart thrumming in my chest.

"Thank you again for helping out today," Pepper says, taking a sip of tea. "You really did me a huge favor. I promise I won't dump my problems on you like that again."

"I didn't mind it at all," I say, cheeks stuffed with hash browns. Pepper gives me a disbelieving look. I swallow down my food. "Seriously, I'll help out whenever you need. I had a lot of fun."

"*Fun?*" Pepper says the word like it's profanity.

"It was cool to get a glimpse of what you do during the day. And I liked spending time with Diksha. She's really nice."

"*Nice?* I don't think anyone's ever described Diksha as nice before."

"Well, I love her," I say, stealing a piece of Pepper's toast. She lets me get away with it. "I love all of them. So, fair warning, I'm not-so-subtly going to insert myself into your friend group and annoy them until they like me."

Pepper tilts her head, brow furrowed as she looks at me. Studies me. "Why?" she says at last.

"Because being obnoxious is my natural state."

"No, I mean why them? I'd be surprised if someone like you didn't have a million friends."

Something about the question opens up a small crack in my chest, pressing on a dull, quiet ache that's always there. "Well, um. I'm not actually sure I really have any friends. Besides my sisters, I guess. And I'm, um . . ." I clear my throat. "Really fucking lonely? Like, all the time?"

I glance at Pepper, then stare back down at the table. This kind of honesty is bare-bones and gratuitous and mortifying to share, but I can't seem to hold it back. "A lot of the time it feels like I don't have a place I fit. Or one where I'm not having to work double time to be enough for the people around me. It . . .

I . . . I'm not making any sense," I say, blowing out a raspberry in defeat. I twist my face into a goofy look. "Ignore me."

She stills my fidgeting with that piercing gaze of hers, eyes tracing across my face as a beat of silence grows between us.

"You're rather impossible to ignore," Pepper says at last, the words soft as a lullaby. "The pink hair pretty much ensures that." She reaches across the table, giving one of the short strands a gentle tug. "I'll pass along the warning to everyone else that you've infiltrated the group."

Heat rushes to my cheeks and floods through my body, a big buffoon grin stretching from ear to ear. Pepper smiles too, brief and dazzling, before averting her eyes and focusing on her food.

My ridiculous smile is stuck like that through the rest of the meal.

And the drive home.

And the next few hours lying in bed, staring up at the ceiling with that warmth still pressing through me, every cell in my body alive and vibrating. And one thing becomes rather obvious:

I'm so undeniably fucked.

Chapter 14

OPAL

Pepper's birthday-celebration-FriendsBitching-thing is tonight and I'm ever so slightly shitting my pants with nerves. Well, not like, *fully* shitting, but like, at *risk* of shitting because there's a greater-than-zero chance I might have a fat crush on Pepper and a raging need to integrate into her group of friends.

I study Pepper's birthday gift, then compare it to the tiny photo propped on the corner of my desk in the shed, one I found a few days ago, taped to the wall of the storage unit, while I was searching for materials to use for a flower press. The snapshot has become the touchstone for my eyes to land on in the short time it's been there, an endless well of inspiration.

Teenage Pepper, her crooked smile tentative but brave, small creases lining the corners of her eyes, her long, gangly arms thrown around Grandma Lou's shoulders, their cheeks pressed together in a hug. Norman Rockwell himself couldn't have conjured a scene that embodied joy so fully.

It wasn't necessarily hard to render the gist of the photo in my painting, but knowing it's going to Pepper makes me feel like it could never possibly be good enough of a gift.

I tilt my head back and forth, analyzing how the different angles change the watercolor portrait. I don't use watercolors that often, and I have to fight the urge to crumple the damn thing to a pulp and chuck it in the trash.

"It's okay," I whisper to myself, dragging the pad of my index finger over the background, giving the damp mix of colors one last loving smudge. "You're allowed to play. You're allowed to try."

I used to feel this heavy knot of guilt that I flit from one medium to the next—like I'm not a real artist because I can't settle into a niche. But there's so much beauty to be created, whether in clay or ink or charcoal, that it feels impossible to focus on only one. For the most part, I've come to terms with being flighty, but there's still a gentle hum at the base of my skull that likes to tell me I'm an imposter every time I trade one form of art for another, playacting and perverting the dedication it takes to be a "real artist."

I usually render my landscapes and still lifes with acrylics or ink, leaning into the pristine lines. Mother Nature has already done such a breathtaking job with her artwork, all I can hope is to capture it as closely to the original as possible. But portraits are different. The human body begs for watercolors. The soft lines. The ebbs and flows. The whims of the water and pigment spreading across the paper in a chase of the constant, subtle changes of people.

Faces in particular are hard to do justice. Someone's expression in a moment is never just one emotion. There are layers and edges and hidden feelings all merging into a single instant. Watercolors capture that aching nuance.

I pick up my brush, swirling it in water, trying to pinpoint the spot I can tweak to make the entire thing perfect. I gave up perfection in any other aspect of my life long ago. It's simply not possible with a brain like mine. But my art is different; it's the better version of me, the one I wish people could know me by.

With a light swipe through a soft copper pigment, I touch the tip of the brush to the ends of Pepper's hair, hoping to give it a bit more dimension.

Then everything falls apart.

The color spreads, bleeding from Pepper's hair into the burgundy sweater she was wearing, the water tracking a path across the entire scene until it slams into Grandma Lou, small veins tracing toward her face.

All I can do is stare as the painting dissolves into a mess in front of my eyes.

It's when the copper reaches toward Lou's perfect white hair that I finally get enough sense to move my limbs, grabbing a paper towel and blotting at the watery surface.

I look at the absolute mess, my heart collapsing in on itself, the jagged edges slicing me fresh open. Every detail is ruined. Their faces are still recognizable, the majority of their features unsullied, but the rest is a maroon mess.

"Shit!" The tears are hot and quick when they spring up, a few landing on the damn painting, messing it up even further.

I push away from my desk with an angry shriek, pacing as I tear my hands through my hair.

Shit, shit, *shit*. I've been here so many times, it's actually silly that it keeps happening. Being so close to something good. Something great. Then tinkering with it to death, killing the bright beautiful thing before it reaches its fullest potential.

I press my back to the wall, sliding to the floor. My shirt snags on the unfinished wood, the soft sound of the fabric ripping echoing around me.

Of course.

I sit there for a moment, the white-hot frustration diffusing out of me until I'm wrung out, every cell drained of the ability to care.

An unhinged burst of laughter peals from my throat as the tears continue to fall. This is typical. So typical. All I wanted was to create something nice for Pepper—an olive branch, something, *anything* that makes her see me as someone other than a total mess—but all I have is another failure.

My phone buzzes, and I pull it from my back pocket, using the heel of my free hand to scrub at my tears.

It's a text from Ophelia.

We'll be there in about an hour!!!!

Followed up by:

we're so excited to see you we haven't
stopped screaming

That, at least, tugs a smile from me. I may be a chronic screwup, but at least my sisters will always love me.

I check the clock, then sigh. The party starts in two hours, and I don't have enough time to make a fresh painting for Pepper or even come up with something semi-decent to give her. I'm in desperate need of a shower and like to allot for at least fifty minutes of stressing over what to wear before I end up throwing on a pair of shorts and my emotional support sweatshirt.

Pushing to stand, I walk over to my desk, grab a thick paintbrush, and dip it in the water.

I can't look directly at the painting, the monster of failure sitting on it, threatening to bite me if I gaze too close. I swipe the wet brush around the perimeter of the paper, then swirl it through my golden pigment, touching it to the edges of the ruined portrait.

If I'm going to give Pepper something ruined, at least it will have some shimmer to it.

I still don't look at it as I set the brush down and clean up my palette, shutting off the lights and trudging back to the house. I'll let it dry and grab it once the party starts.

Diksha's truck is parked on the gravel drive, and I hear her laugh as I let myself into the kitchen. Pepper's low voice travels from the living room, and I take the stairs up to my room in a dead sprint, still feeling far too emotional to see her yet. When

I've shut myself in, I glance at the mirror. My mascara has streaked down my cheeks, splotches of paint on my forehead and jaw looking like poorly healed bruises, eyes watery and red-rimmed.

At least my outsides reflect my insides.

Stepping closer, I look at my hair. The bubblegum pink has faded to a grayish hue, the roots growing in as a mousy dark blonde. Stone-cold fox right here.

An idea, one that always makes me feel good and fresh and excited, grips me tight, and for the first time in hours, I feel a small swell of relief. At least there's one thing I can control.

I slide across my messy bedroom floor, fishing out my duffel bag of goodies from under the bed. I rip it open, flicking through the various neon packages until I find one that feels right. With a triumphant yip, I yank off my T-shirt, throw on an old white one covered in paint stains, and dart across the hall to the bathroom.

I tear open the box, flicking away the directions. I know the deal.

With the care of a chemist, I mix the hair bleach into my trusty plastic bowl, stirring and scraping until it's a consistency I'm familiar with. Giving myself a mischievous grin in the mirror, I start to paint it on, lathering the goop from root to tip until every strand is covered.

I want to bleach the stupid from my head, but my hair is an okay starting point. Setting a timer, I play the waiting game, the anticipation growing as I sit on the closed toilet and scroll through my phone, leg bouncing.

I always keep a decent supply of hair dyes on hand, the sudden need for a change not one that's particularly patient with trips to Sally Beauty Supply.

I love the smell of the chemicals—sharp and vibrant—a fresh start in a bottle. I love changing my hair, using it as a canvas when other ones are uncooperative. In almost every avenue of my life, I don't feel fully myself. Not in relationships or friendships or online or jobs. It's like there's some part I'm supposed to play, but no one bothered to give me a description, yet they're disappointed when I show up as someone else.

My hair and its changing colors are my little act of rebellion. The thing I do fully for me.

When my timer dings, I turn on the shower, giving my hair a thorough scrub. I watch the dirty, faded pink circle the drain, being replaced by an icy, platinum blonde. I can't wait to see the result. Cool. Aloof. Tough and impenetrable. Sleek light strands showing the new me. Or, rather, the me I wish I could be.

Stepping out of the shower, I rub a towel over my head, then grab my brush and plug in my hair dryer, flipping my head upside down and getting to work. The mirror is fogged but it doesn't matter—I could do my hair with my eyes closed, I've tortured the strands so frequently.

When it's dry, I drag my fingers through it. It feels . . . Well, honestly, it feels a bit crunchy. But that's okay. Nothing I can't deal with. I wipe down the mirror, smiling as my face comes into view.

My cheeks are bright red from the heat and excitement, eyes scrubbed free of makeup.

And my hair . . .

I lunge at the mirror, one hand slapping the glass, the other knotting in my hair.

No.

  No no no no.

    No.

      No.

        Please God No.

My hair. My *hair*.

It's . . . it's . . .

Bright. Fucking. White.

I look like a dandelion with half the fluff blown off. A tiny howl of agony tears from me, and I hear the stairs creak below.

"Opal? You okay?" Pepper hollers.

I shriek again in response, then clear my throat. "Fine," I yell back. I hear another step creak.

"You sure? You keep, er, screaming . . ."

Instead of answering, I spring open the door and tear across the hall to my room.

I start pacing, towel clenched around me, wet footprints marking my chaotic path. What do I do, what do I *do*? I can't just go to this party looking like Gene Wilder in *Young Frankenstein*.

The thud of feet running up the stairs has enough bass to be a soundtrack to a horror movie.

Pepper's voice calls over the noise, "Uh, Opal? I think—"

The door bursts open, likely from the force of the screech following it. "Opal!" my sisters scream in unison.

Their excitement is short-lived, their faces falling from massive grins to looks of alarm as they register my hair and my tears and my towel and my patheticness.

Ophelia's shriek cuts through the silence.

"Jesus, are you sure you're okay?" Pepper says. I hear the squeak of one of the bottom stairs as she mounts them.

"Leave me alone, Pepper!" Squaring my bare shoulders with nonexistent dignity, I march toward my sisters, grabbing each by the wrist and jerking them inside, slamming the door behind them. "And, uh, happy birthday," I add with a yell. I can feel Pepper's annoyance from here.

"What the hell happened?" Olivia asks, grabbing me by the cheeks and tilting my head from left to right.

"Hair like that only results from extreme emotional crisis," Ophelia whispers, looking at Olivia. "It's giving Albert Einstein."

I rip out from her grip and collapse against the wall, letting out a small whimper as I slide down to the floor. "Yeah, well, clearly I'm a genius."

All Olivia can manage is a soft "Oh, Opal."

"Please go away thank you," I say, flapping my hand as I bury my face in my knees.

"Oh, Opal," Olivia repeats, coming to wrap me in a big hug.

"Fifty bucks says it's girl problems," Ophelia says, plunking herself down on the edge of my bed.

"Shut up, Ophelia," Olivia and I say in unison.

Ophelia flicks us off lazily before collapsing against my pillows and scrolling on her phone.

Olivia continues to hold me, rubbing up and down my arms. After a moment, she clears her throat. "But, uh, is it?"

Ophelia's laugh grates against my groan of outrage.

"Yes," I say, untangling from her and scooching to my closet, searching for anything to put over this monstrosity on top of my head. "And the girls are *you two*. So, kindly, fuck off."

I dig around for a few minutes, panic starting to spike as I can't find a hat. "Or help me figure out how to hide this situation," I say, pointing at my hair.

My sisters—wonderful, awful humans that they are— laugh at my misery but help in my search, asking me a billion questions in the process.

Chapter 15

OPAL

Despite summer being in full swing and the humidity at purgatory levels, I have a beanie shoved low around my ears as I hover awkwardly on the outskirts of the party. It doesn't really do me any favors that the hat has SLUT with a *Shrek* "S" embroidered on it, but at this point I'm picking and choosing my battles.

My sisters finally dragged me out of my room, swearing on their lives that the bits of my hair sticking out from the hat didn't look *that horrific* in low light. The second we stepped off the stairs, Alfie materialized at our side, introducing himself, wrapping each of my sisters in a giant hug, announcing that the tall gorgeous man next to him was his new boyfriend, Evens, then swooping my sisters into the thick of the group crammed into the living room.

"How did you and Alfie meet?" I ask Evens, who's stayed with me, watching with a soft smile as Alfie makes everyone laugh across the room.

His grin grows, his dark skin crinkling at his eyes and the bridge of his nose as he looks at me. "I'm a modern dancer," he says, eyes flicking back to Alfie for a beat like he can't quite keep his gaze off him. "Alfie was at one of my shows, and afterward, he snuck in through the back of the theater and into the dressing rooms. He walked right up to me, stuck out his hand, and said: 'Hello, I'm Alfie. And you're the most beautiful thing I've ever seen. I think we should know each other.'"

My marshmallow heart melts into a gooey mess at the obvious adoration in Evens's voice. "He kept it subtle, huh?"

Evens chuckles, deep and rumbly. "He's the epitome of subtle, can't you tell?"

With perfect timing, Alfie's voice travels through the room, followed by another wave of laughter.

"What did you say back?"

He looks at Alfie again, catching his eye. With a smile that's equal parts impish and innocent, Alfie makes his way toward us.

"I told him he clearly had good taste and wasn't too difficult to look at either, and that I thought, just maybe, I'd like to know him too."

"You're talking about me," Alfie says, looping his arm around Evens's waist and planting a kiss on the swell of his shoulder. "I can tell."

"How can you tell?"

"Because you look all lovesick and dopey," Alfie says with a bored shrug.

Evens chuckles, bending to give him a light kiss.

"Wow," I say, staring at both their glowing smiles as I blink back little pokes of tears. "You're so into each other it's almost disgusting."

"I know!" Alfie cheers, plopping a hand on my shoulder. "Isn't it marvelous?"

"Can I get you a drink, Opal?" Evens asks, giving his own full wineglass a quick swirl. I watch the deep red liquid slosh around the sides.

I open my mouth, almost saying yes. Damn that looks good.

But instead, I bite my tongue, then shake my head, grabbing a can of sparkling water from the open cooler by the wall near us. I crack it open and chug down half of it in a second, letting the ticklish burn bubble up my head and down my throat. "I'm good with this, thanks."

"Easy, wild one, we'll be scraping you up off the floor if you keep that up," Alfie says with a smirk. "Come on, darling," he adds, tugging on Evens's arm. "I'm so close to convincing Diksha to tell you about the time she nearly ran me over with her truck."

"I have no doubt you deserved it," Evens says, shooting me a brief wave as they head into the center of the fold. I watch from my safe corner, chugging down more of my drink and wishing it were, in fact, wine.

Wine would help so much right now.

Wine would make my hair less hideous, my attempts at conversation less awkward. It would make me funnier and cuter and interesting and brave enough to walk over to where Pepper sits on the couch, a smile plastered on her face while Alfie entertains her and the others with another delightful story.

But, as I chug down the rest of my sparkling water and grab another, I know wine would be a bad choice . . . and I'm trying to make less of those.

Like most labels in my life, I'm not sure if the term *alcoholic* fits, but my relationship to drinking is certainly messy. Whatever I may be—autistic or ADHD or some tangled swirl of both—moving through the world often feels like a sensory assault, and blunting the impact with a bunch of drinks is a lovely temptation.

Alcohol isn't something I crave, necessarily—I don't even like the taste, and I can go months without thinking about it. A glass of wine here or there at a movie night with my sisters usually is nothing more than that. But a drink at a party like this—with lots of voices and people and energy and this frenetic need in my body to act the right way and connect and make people like me—most often turns into three drinks. Then five. And next thing I know, it's morning and I hate myself more than ever.

It's like some amorphous, blobby creature is plopped on top of my brain after the first sip, growing and snuggling between the lobes and dimming the stimuli around me, making the world a little less sharp and the people a little less scary. Like I can't be hurt if I give the bacchanalian beast enough.

"You're being very 2011 emo sulking in the corner with your beanie pulled low," Ophelia says, leaning against the wall next to me, Olivia hovering in front of us with a fresh drink.

"Yeah, well . . . I peaked in my Tumblr era, what can I say?"

"Something a little less sad, maybe?" Olivia says with a shrug.

"Come on, Opie. Join the party!" Ophelia tugs on my arm, but I stay rooted.

"I'm really embarrassed about my hair," I squeak out, mortification pinching my voice. "I feel really uncomfortable."

"No one will notice your hair," Olivia says, wrapping an arm around my waist.

"Or, if they do, it will make a really funny story."

Olivia punches Ophelia for me.

"Do you ever get so swamped by the irrational devastation that you're the ugliest person in the room? And it's so startling it makes you feel like you're going to cry?"

"Yes."

"All the time."

I glance at my sisters with incredulity. They're two of the most beautiful people I've ever seen.

"Seriously," Ophelia says, leveling me with a look. "Everyone has those crushing moments of insecurity. We're all human." She nudges Olivia out of the way, cupping my cheeks in her hands. "But you, my sweet sister, are one of the coolest, funniest, hottest pieces of ass to ever walk the planet. So I'm gonna need you to snap out of this pity party and go be the bad bitch you are, okay?"

I laugh in spite of myself, then nod.

"Good. Now, let's go."

They lead me to the center of the room, easily transitioning into Diksha and Alfie's conversation while I scramble onto the arm of the couch, sitting like a gremlin. I smile and laugh along, missing half of what everyone is saying as I continue to fidget with my hat, eyes regularly swerving to land on Pepper. She doesn't look my way once.

With a sigh, I force myself to watch my sisters, the smooth ways they interact with these virtual strangers they so quickly turned into friends, the easy flow of their conversations. It all feels foreign to me. When I talk at parties, I feel like a golden retriever puppy desperate for attention, my brain bouncing around from idea to idea, voice too loud, comments unrelated.

After a while, Diksha stands, clapping her hands together.

"Cake time!" she calls, marching to the kitchen. She reappears a few moments later, arms stretched under a platter carrying a . . . a . . .

"Oh my God, what is *that*?" Ophelia asks from her spot on the couch.

"It's a foot cake," Diksha says with a cackle, propping up the, uh, thing for us all to see.

I shoot a glance at Pepper for a bit more detailed explanation, but she has her head buried in her hands. "Feel free to elaborate," I say to Diksha.

"Pepper has a foot thing," Alfie says.

". . . As in an eating-them type of thing?" Olivia asks.

Diksha laughs even harder.

"No," Pepper groans, dragging her hands through her hair. "I literally don't even know where this rumor started—"

"I do," Alfie says with glee.

Pepper shoots him a look that's equal parts scathing and teasing.

"A while back Pepper was picking our brains for a get-rich-quick scheme," Alfie says, tilting his head conspiratorially toward Ophelia and Olivia. "I tried to talk her into selling foot pics online."

"She ended up doing a bit too thorough of research," Diksha cuts in. "Found her shell-shocked on the couch a few days later, way too many tabs of questionable websites open on her computer and a few viruses to go along with it."

"And now I'm officially the 'foot friend,'" Pepper concludes, twisting her face into the most exaggerated frown I've ever seen. It's so cute I let out a tiny laugh. Pepper's gaze flicks to me, and that deep frown curves into an almost smile.

"Where do you even find a cake like this?" Evens asks, viewing it from multiple angles with a mix of horror and artistic appreciation.

The level of detail is exceptional, somehow making a severed foot look . . . well . . . kind of beautiful. The toenails are painted aqua, a few delicate toe rings and an anklet adorning the structure.

"This amazing bakery in Philadelphia, actually," Diksha says, pulling out plates. "It's called Bernadette's Bakery and they specialize in erotic goods. The owner, I think her name is Lizzie, started shipping specialty cakes when the business took off online. She usually does vulvas and stuff, but I called, and she was super excited to dip a toe—buh dum cha—into other body parts for our sweet Pepper's party."

"You really, truly, seriously shouldn't have," Pepper grumbles, the tips of her ears bright pink.

"No need to thank me!" Diksha says.

"I absolutely will not."

"All right, birthday boo, you get the first slice. What'll it be?"

"Anything but the toes," Pepper says, scrunching up her nose.

"Gonna have to agree there," Tal says, Ophelia nodding beside them.

"I'll take the toes," I say. Everyone's eyes whip to me in horror. "I . . . It looks like it has the most icing . . ."

"Get your freak on, Opal. We aren't here to judge," Alfie says, passing me the lumpy slice Diksha cut. I splutter in protest, but a rough laugh cuts through, drawing my attention.

Pepper is looking at me, smile broad and cheeks rosy, one hand cupping the back of her neck as she continues to laugh.

And damn if that look doesn't undo me, my heart bottoming out to my knees, then bouncing up to my throat. With a cheeky glare, I hold her eyes, leaning into the morbid and digging my fork into the cake, bringing the big toe to my mouth. I pause, lips parted, staring at her for a beat longer, then pop the whole thing in my mouth and lick my lips.

Like I'd hoped, Pepper laughs again, that smile growing.

And I realize I'll play any type of fool to make her laugh.

Chapter 16

PEPPER

Stuffed full of cake, we're sprawled around the living room, Tal and Diksha cuddled together on the plush love seat while Olivia and Ophelia lean against the coffee table, their feet outstretched toward the blazing fire Tal started as the cool mountain evening curled around the cabin. Alfie and Evens sit cross-legged facing each other near the small Bluetooth speaker, quietly arguing about what song to cue up next. Alfie's voice rises a notch, a stern and serious look on his face as he points at Evens, who lets out a deep rumble of laughter before leaning close and giving Alfie a kiss.

And Opal . . .

Well, I can't seem to take my eyes off Opal.

Right now, she's sitting on the arm at the opposite end of the couch as me, back curved and knees pulled up to her chin as her attention flits around the room.

There's been endless movement in the cabin all evening, but

my brain is only capable of registering her. The twitch of the corner of her mouth in that hesitant smile she has, the pattern she taps out on the soda can clutched close to her chest as she watches the party from the corner, the way she regularly pulls her bizarre hat down her ears and bites her bottom lip as she listens to other people talk. The sway of her full hips when she moves.

Which is all truly ludicrous because I'm still not even sure if I like the damn woman. It's probably the wine going to my head.

It's funny; Opal always seems like a live wire to me, this electric current of uncontrollable energy. But in the group she's . . . quiet. Reserved. Trying to sink into herself.

It makes me want to ask her why.

Again, ridiculous.

"All right." Alfie's voice cuts through the room. "Since Evens has decided to die on the hill of bad music choices, let's get to know each other a bit better, shall we?" he says, crawling toward the center of the room.

"So, I can tell Opal is bi, but what about you two?" Alfie says, looking at Ophelia and Olivia. "Are you—" He dangles a limp wrist at shoulder height, making the sisters laugh.

Opal rolls her eyes, her lips twitching at the corners. "I call bullshit."

"Tell me I'm wrong," Alfie says with a sniff.

"It's a lucky guess at best," Opal says, narrowing her eyes as her smile wins out. "How can you *tell*? You hardly know me."

"I have an excellent sense of the sapphics," Alfie says with a level of righteous indignation.

"He saw your bi flag bumper sticker on the way in," Evens says, smacking Alfie on the shoulder.

"Dirty liar," Opal gasps, pointing at Alfie. Her smile grows, and the hesitancy of the last few hours slowly disappears. She opens up like a flower unfurling its petals to the sun.

Ah. There's the you I missed.

Wait . . . where the hell did *that* come from?

It's Alfie's turn to roll his eyes. "Fine. Yes. But the alarming amount of dents on your car, your cuffed jeans, and the fact that you greet me with a peace sign every time I see you are all pretty good confirmations of your leaning."

"I'd argue bisexuality is more a straddling," Ophelia says, bobbing her head from side to side. "But yeah, the three of us are the Devlin family bi-trifecta. Such a novelty we're mentioned during hometown tours."

"A statue is being erected in our honor," Olivia adds. "The three of us, not sitting straight."

Opal giggles. "The artist is rendering us at our most iconic moment in high school when we all had the Timothée Chalamet haircut."

"It looked best on me," the sisters say in unison. I choke on a sip of wine.

"Are any of you seeing someone?" Alfie asks. Only he can make nosiness seem endearing.

"Fuck no," Olivia spits, mouth twisting.

"I don't have time," Ophelia says.

"Opal?" Alfie reaches over, giving her calf a friendly jiggle.

She shakes her head. "Definitely not. I've given up on that pipe dream."

"The pipe dream being . . . ?" Diksha prompts.

"Finding someone who isn't a dickhead, I guess?" Opal's face scrunches up. "My past few relationships lead me to believe I've dated some of the world's worst offerings of men, but Miles, my most recent ex, might take the cake." She lets out a scratchy laugh, the sound both hard and soft, like a violet growing through the cracks in the sidewalk.

I've never dated a man. I've never dated anyone, if I'm being honest. I think I like men. Or, at least, I find some of them attractive. I *know* I like women—their curves and angles and soft skin and beautiful smiles . . .

I used to stress over finding a label that fit me. Lesbian. Bisexual. Pan. Demi . . . I've filtered through them all many times over, none ever feeling quite right.

Just say queer and move on with your life, Diksha finally told me late one night after what was probably my sixth sexual identity crisis of my early twenties.

But what does that mean? I'd wailed, draining more boxed wine into my plastic cup. My brain loves order and labels and concise frameworks to understand things, and not knowing where I fit feels unbearable.

It means you're you, and only you get to decide who you like and when you like them, Tal had said from their chair in the corner. *The name of your feelings isn't anyone's business but yours.*

"Miles cheated on Opal with her 'best friend,' Laney," Ophelia says, using air quotes.

"What a totally appropriate and not at all highly personal detail of your sister's life to tell the room at large," Olivia says, smacking Ophelia on the shoulder.

"What? Opal's the one who said he was the worst! I was offering proof."

"Your conspiracy theories are not synonymous with proof, Ophelia," Opal says, squeezing her fingers into her sparkling water can.

"Oh, Opie, honey," Olivia says, confirming that Ophelia's admission was spot-on.

"Let's do presents!" Evens says, diverting the conversation from the rising voices of the Devlin sisters.

"Great idea," Tal says. They have very little tolerance for dramatics of any sort, which makes their marriage to Diksha quite the anomaly.

"Here, open ours first," Diksha says, popping up from the love seat and grabbing a gift bag from the corner, depositing it in my lap.

I pull out the wonky lump at the bottom and rip off the tissue paper. I let out a chirp of laughter as I unroll a pale pink T-shirt. My eyes skim across it as my smile grows, then I turn it around for everyone else to see.

ASK ME ABOUT MY SPECIAL INTEREST is written across the front in a font made of twisting vines and vibrant flowers.

"Oh my God, it's perfect," I say, reaching over to wrap Diksha in a hug. "Thank you so much."

"Tal had it custom made," Diksha says, waving at them as they beam from their seat.

"We're about to see her in that every day for the next eight months," Alfie says. He's honestly not wrong. "Ours next," he adds, handing me a bundle of carefully wrapped cylinders.

I tear away the lilac wrapping paper, revealing three large prayer candles—Phoebe Bridgers, Taylor Swift, and Fleabag staring at me front and center in saintlike glory.

"The holy trinity of twenty-twenties emo-ism," Alfie says, offering his own version of a pious bow.

"I feel blessed already," I say with a snort, placing the candles in the middle of the coffee table. Out of habit, my eyes flick to Grandma Lou's leather ottoman, expecting to see her happy, curious smile, a litany of questions about if the three people on the candles are personal friends of mine on the tip of her tongue.

But Grandma Lou isn't there. The chair is empty in its dark corner, a hollowness carving through me at the reminder.

"Okay, so, sorry in advance if this totally isn't your vibe," Ophelia says, breaking me out of the dark thought and placing a heavy gift bag on my lap. "But we decided to take our chances."

"We assumed that owning a flower farm, you probably like having potted plants around," Olivia adds as I grab the tissue paper. "Hope you don't mind housing them in rather, um, revealing pots."

"You seriously didn't have to get me anything," I say.

"Yes they did," Diksha says with finality. "Presents are mandatory, Pep. It's the law."

"I've only known her for a few hours and I'd rather walk on broken glass than go against her rules," Ophelia says with admiration, jutting her thumb toward Diksha.

"Don't encourage her," I plead, pulling out a ceramic pot, wider than it is tall. I turn it around and let out a gasp suitable for a middle schooler as I take in the voluptuous ass carved into the side and a few centimeters of full thigh at the base. The top of the pot is tapered slightly for a waist. A huge giggle erupts from me, my cheeks heating. I have the bizarre impulse to look at Opal.

Which would be *weird* and *inappropriate,* so I focus on unwrapping the second piece of pottery in the gift bag. It's somehow even better than the first, a big pair of asymmetrical boobies front and center.

"Absolutely amazing," I say, my face on fire and even more giggles tumbling out of me. "No notes."

I can't fight the urge any longer, and risk a glance at Opal through my lashes. She's staring at the pots, her mouth slightly ajar and brow furrowed, then she slants an accusing look at her sisters.

"We have a confession to make," Ophelia says, giving Opal an arch look. "Our dear sister here didn't tell us this was a birthday party until we were five minutes from leaving the house. So we didn't have time to go out and buy these."

"But, we figured every home needs some Opal Devlin originals," Olivia says, fixing me with a bright smile.

My throat goes dry, and I'm worried that if any more heat

floods my face, I'll start glowing like a spotlight. "You made these?" I ask, looking again at Opal. I don't know why I picture her hands, caked in clay, moving and shaping the curves of the pot. Leaning close as she studies her intimate work from multiple angles. Fingers tracing over—

Absolutely not. I refuse to get hot and bothered from thoughts of ceramic pots.

Opal takes a deep breath, tilting her head up to the ceiling. "During school, yeah. They're . . . Well, I've made better since."

"Nonsense, Opie," Ophelia says, giving her sister's knee a squeeze. "These are some of your best works."

"I don't think that's the compliment you think it is," Opal murmurs, giving a death glare to Ophelia.

"They're amazing," I whisper, eyes locked on Opal.

She looks at me, brows furrowed over those big blue eyes, a gentle blush creeping up her round cheeks. She scratches her nose, then tugs at her hat as I continue to stare.

And then I sort of . . . short-circuit, I guess. I jolt forward across the couch, pots tumbling off my lap and against the cushions as I get closer. I throw my arms around her neck, pulling her into a hug that's way too aggressive. Way too ferocious.

A hug that means way too much.

I feel Opal jump, and I pull away immediately, garbling out something that sounds vaguely like *Thank you*.

There's an awkward pause in the room, and then, in perfect unison, Olivia and Ophelia chirp out, "You're welcome."

I don't miss the devious glance they share.

"Clean up!" I squawk, bolting upright and grabbing everything within reach. I trip my way to the kitchen, plates clanging as I drop them in the sink.

"Smooth," Diksha says right behind me. I whip around.

"Excuse me?" I say, staring at the ground and tucking my hair behind my ear.

"I said, *smooooth*." She draws out the vowels, ducking to make sure I see every ounce of humor in her gaze.

Embarrassment churns through every inch of my body.

"Not sure what you're talking about," I grumble, turning to the sink and flicking on the water.

Diksha lets out a wistful sigh. "Sure ya don't, babe." She grabs some of the plates, scraping off scraps of food into the garbage can.

I try to focus on washing the dishes, but I can't shake the image, the fantasy, of Opal creating those pots. Her hands tracing over the curves, touching every inch. Pinching the nipples to sharp points, dragging the pads of her thumbs across the underside of the breasts. And then it isn't clay. It's Opal's hands on skin, trailing down, my body shivering below the touch. Then it's her mouth, following the path, rewiring circuits. What would it be like to have those beautiful hands touch me?

"So are you going to do it?" Diksha asks, nudging me aside to deposit more dishes in the sudsy sink.

I jolt, wondering how in the world she knew my runaway brain had latched onto Opal and taken a bizarre turn to the smutty.

"The flower competition," she says, spinning her hand in a way that tells me I need to keep up.

My shoulders drop in relief, and I shoo out all thoughts of Opal and the fantasy of her body against mine and the warmth of her and how that might feel pressed against me if we were both—

"Uh, no." I give my head a violent shake for emphasis.

"Give me one good reason why not." Diksha plants her hands on her hips, arching an eyebrow.

"Because I don't even know where to start? I grow flowers, I don't . . . make *art* with them. It's not in my wheelhouse."

"Oh, what a pity you don't have someone hanging around that would be perfect to help you," she says, glaring at me.

I give her a few more confused blinks.

Diksha fixes me with a bland look before dramatically sweeping her gaze to the living room, a loud peal of familiar laughter careening through.

"Opal?" For some reason, saying her name makes my hands shaky and my voice wobbly. "Yeah, right. That would be a disaster."

"More of a disaster than living on a property that North Carolina courts have apparently decided belongs to your mother who in turn sold it to a pink-haired pixie who wants to turn it into a shoe mill?"

"I think something happened to her hair," I say, craning my neck to see around the corner. She usually wears the pink with so much pride.

"Focus, horny Pepper," Diksha says, snapping her fingers in my face.

I choke on air. "I'm not horny!" I say. Way too loudly. Like, it will be a miracle if my neighbors a few acres away didn't hear me.

It's Diksha's turn to blink. "Delusion doesn't really suit you, love."

"Okay, party's over," I say, pushing Diksha toward the door as she cackles.

"Thank you for coming," I say as enthusiastically as possible, interrupting the hum of conversation in the living room. "And, uh, bye!"

There's a two-second pause, then my friends get moving. They're used to quickly recalibrating to my abrupt ends to social events.

"Bye, darling. See you soon," Alfie says, kissing me on the cheek.

"Happy birthday," Evens adds, giving my shoulder a quick squeeze.

"Need help with cleanup?" Tal asks, surveying the cups still littering the living room.

"Just need you to get that one out of here," I say, jerking my thumb at Diksha, who is giving Opal a far too thorough goodbye for my liking. The pair laugh. That can't be good.

"Ha. As if I have any more control over her than you do," Tal says, voice low and a glint in their eye as they watch Diksha make her way toward us.

"Used an entire birthday wish on exactly that," I say, glaring at Diksha's shit-eating smile.

"Bye, Pep," she says, finally—*finally*—getting to the door. "I'll bother you tomorrow."

"Would rather you didn't."

"That's cute but I don't really care," she says, pinching my cheek before heading out, Tal following close behind.

"Thanks for having us!" Olivia says, she and Ophelia popping up in front of me. "Sorry to crash your birthday, but we had such a blast."

"You aren't driving back to Charlotte, are you?"

"We got a hotel closer to downtown Asheville," Ophelia says. "For some reason, Opal wasn't jumping at the chance to share her full-sized mattress with both of us."

"The youngest are always the most selfish," Olivia says with a mournful sigh.

"The least she could do is go hiking with us tomorrow," Ophelia adds. "But no, the delicate princess is too good for such physical exertions."

"She said, and I quote, *I would rather put my foot in a meat grinder than subject myself to hiking.* Unquote." Olivia laughs, and my eyes flick to Opal, but she's no longer in the living room. I have to check the urge to go searching for her.

Ophelia and Olivia give me a quick hug, then duck into the inky night.

I shut the door, pressing my forehead against it with a sigh of relief.

But energy still thumps through the house like a plucked harp string, soft and subtle but vibrant nonetheless. It's all very . . . Opal.

I turn around, half expecting her to be staring at me with those big eyes, unnerving and disorienting.

But she's not.

I do another sweep of the living room, then around the kitchen.

She's gone.

And I'm a chump.

Still not horny, though.

With a sigh, I grab an armful of glasses, then walk into the kitchen, taking my spot in front of the sink. I let the hot water run, squeezing out dish soap and watching the bubbles form.

I need to get a grip. I grab my sponge and get to work, trying in vain to shut my brain off with the automatic cleaning motions as I stare out the window, my bewildered reflection going fuzzy at the edges, mixing with the sprawl of land beyond. My conversation with Diksha loops around my head.

Lust? Is that what this is? Can you even lust after someone you aren't sure you like?

Lust would be horribly inconvenient right now with the ridiculous living situation we find ourselves in. And I can't help but wonder if Diksha has a point (outside of her depraved comments on desires I'm definitely not feeling). Opal *would* be a good person to recruit to help me with the competition.

I've . . . Well, I wouldn't call it spying, exactly, but I've peeped into her shed a few times. The small space has morphed into a galaxy of color; controlled chaos with shoes propped on shelves, canvases half-filled with paint up on the easel or leaning against the wall. It's . . . it's a lot. But even my untrained eye can recognize that it's good.

I could ask her. Despite her sporadic nature, it's pretty obvious Opal would jump at the opportunity to help anyone with anything. But it doesn't seem like a good idea. Our lives are already far more intertwined than I ever wanted to be with another person. Entering a competition with the financial resuscitation of my farm on the line doesn't seem like the best move in establishing distance with the woman.

But part of me feels kind of . . . God, what *is* this feeling? A bizarre sort of poppy, punchy energy at the idea of working on it with her. A kind of . . . giddiness.

Very ridiculous considering what a terrible idea it is.

"Hey."

Opal's voice cuts through the kitchen, scaring the life out of me. I let out a mortifying little scream, hands shooting up and bubbles flying everywhere.

I spin around, looking at the short little menace standing in the archway.

Her lips are pursed, half a smile tugging at the corners— the look entirely too affecting.

"Do I scare you, Pepper?" she asks, the smile winning out.

"Yes," I answer honestly, my heart flip-flopping around my chest. "Why are you wearing that hat?" I ask, desperate to change the subject.

She leans against the archway, head tilting back as she

groans. She opens and closes her mouth a few times, shakes her head, and then reaches up, ripping off the hat.

I suck in a startled breath. "Oh my. That's, er, a change."

Opal rolls her neck, glare locked on me. But it's like getting a dirty look from a crested duck, those white strands puffed up at odd angles. I bite hard against my lower lip to hold back a laugh.

"Oh fuck off, Pepper," she says, a grin growing on her own face. There's no holding my belly laugh back when she lets out a soft chuckle. "It was an accident," she says, raking her hands through her hair.

"I'd certainly hope so." I laugh so hard they turn into obnoxious goose honks. Opal, for her part, snorts at that.

"God, we sound like a barnyard," she says, wrapping her arms around her middle as she continues to giggle.

"We should go roll in the hay," I say. Without thinking. Obviously. Because *why the hell would I say* that *of all things.*

Opal's laughter stops, her eyes going wide. Our gazes hold for a second, before she blinks away, color creeping up her throat.

"As in, like, uh, farm animals," I weakly offer. Another moment of painful silence.

"I . . ." Opal coughs, then clears her throat, staring down at the ground. "I have a present for you," she whispers. I lean forward, not wanting to miss a word. "But it's kind of silly yet not at all funny and I think I totally missed the mark on the gift-giving theme tonight . . . Hard to believe that's not the first time that's happened to me, right?" Her laugh is sharp and loud, like it hurts her to make the sound. Nothing like the usual playful tinkle of it.

"Anyway." She thrusts her arms out, eyes averted, a small brown rectangle clutched between her hands.

I look at her for a moment, an odd mask of worry on her features. After a beat, her gaze sweeps to me, earnest and vulnerable, making my pulse trip over itself.

She's cute in the most inconvenient type of way. Round and rosy cheeks that look devastatingly soft. Full lips quirked at the ends as if constantly desperate to jump into a smile. Even her absurd hair has an effect, something a bit wild, a bit feral. Just like her.

And her eyes. Well, her eyes are *majorly* inconvenient because I can't stop feeling like I'll drown in that pale ocean blue.

Which is an incredibly dumb idea to have.

She proffers the gift again, this time holding my stare. With a shaky hand, I take the board. It's about the size of my palm and, turning it over, a small hiccup catches in my throat, making my eyes burn.

The other side is a canvas, covered in the most beautiful watercolor painting I've ever seen. A moment I'll never forget.

I don't hold on to a lot of memories—my autistic brain has left a lot of holes in my mental film reel—but I could never forget that day.

It was my first Christmas Eve with Grandma Lou—her sixty-eighth birthday. She used to joke that being born on Christmas Eve was proof she was the greatest gift to the world

Santa could have conjured. After those first few months of living with her, I knew in the deepest parts of my bones it was true.

It was the first holiday I'd ever had where the focus was on comfortable, quality moments. It wasn't at one of Mom's random boyfriends' houses, sitting on the edge of the couch while one or the other screamed at the top of their lungs about a gift coming up short or being forgotten altogether. It wasn't Mom snipping the tags off a Walmart dress in the store, stuffing me into the itchy stolen garment in the parking lot while filling me in on what long-lost relation we were pretending to be to whoever her latest target was.

That Christmas, it was me, Lou, and our plump evergreen from a farm up the road, a roaring fire in the living room and a steady snowfall out the window. We'd made three different varieties of hot chocolate, the sugar fueling our dances around the living room as her record player cranked out Ella Fitzgerald's Christmas songs.

I'd been snuggled up close to Lou on the couch when she'd snapped the photo, grabbing an old Kodak from the junk bowl on the coffee table, blinding us both with the flash.

And Opal somehow captured the magic of it perfectly. Our faces pressed close, cheeks rosy, hair tangled together. The background is illuminated with a gauzy swirl of gold and copper, our smiles shimmering just as brightly.

"What do you think?" Opal's voice is small. Hesitant. It rips through me and my eyes jerk away from the painting to look at her.

"You . . . you painted Grandma Lou," I say, swallowing past my rough throat.

"And you," Opal whispers, taking a step forward and tapping lightly on teenage me. "I love your smile in this picture so much."

The soft and subtle smell of her curls around me—ink and paper and something sunny. My hand dives into my pocket, pulling out the sprig of chamomile in there as my fingers twirl it around and around.

Opal's eyes trickle away from my face to my hand.

"Do you play with those when you're nervous?" she asks, nodding at the flowers as she watches me.

"Yes."

"Are you nervous right now?" She takes a step closer. It seems impossible that I can *feel* her without actually touching her. So much warmth and energy circling my waist. Pulling me a step closer too.

My words trip out over a humorless laugh. "Yes, and I don't know why."

Oops. Too honest. I can tell by the way Opal's eyes widen, her eyebrows arching up.

"But I'm also happy," I bumble out. "I'm feeling a lot of things, I guess."

A comfortable beat of silence passes between us as we both stare at the delicate white petals as they spin in a blur, the portrait clutched to my chest. "I play with them when I'm feeling anything . . . *big*. Or hard to understand. Nature's little stim toys."

Opal laughs at that, her eyes creased at the corners as she looks up at me.

And, because I apparently am dead set on embarrassing myself tonight, I find my body lurching forward once again, closing the few inches of space remaining between us and holding her snugly against me. She stills, and I'm screaming at myself in embarrassment. But in half a heartbeat, she's hugging me back, pressing that cute button nose against the spot where my shoulder meets my neck. Breathing me in.

Her hands move slowly, lazily. One grazing low on my spine, the other tracing around my ribs to my back, her palm splayed between my shoulder blades.

Want slices through me with a breathtaking ache. Sudden and sharp. A need for closer. For more. For that intoxicating smell of hers to embed itself in my skin.

And that want takes over.

One hand curls around the swell of her hip, the fingers of the other tangling in her hair, tilting her face so her lips are centimeters from mine. I release my grip to drag my touch across her cheek, down her throat.

She sucks in a breath, stealing all the air from my lungs, eyes fixed on my mouth. I feel her pulse pick up speed under my fingertips. Then, she licks her lips.

And I'm gone.

I press my mouth to hers. She presses back. Little sparks jolt through my chest and down my limbs, making me gasp. Opal swallows the sound.

We're a mess—fumbling lips and clashing teeth and hands

fisting clothing—pressing closer and closer together until there's no space between us. Finally, we collide into a rhythm, kisses searing hot and desperate. I trace my tongue along the seam of her lips and she moans as she opens to me and it's madness and mayhem and I can't get enough.

Opal presses up onto her tiptoes—closer, harder—tongue tangling with mine in some wordless battle to conquer this pleasure blooming around us. Her hands travel all over me. Down my hips, up my rib cage, across the sides of my breasts until both cradle the angle of my jaw. The nudge of her nose against mine as she shifts her head, kissing me deeper. Rougher. Lovelier.

The world stops spinning. I'm the one orbiting the sun.

Opal presses her teeth into my lip, and the effect is sharp and vibrant—an effervescent bite that shoots to my stomach and fizzes through my veins like champagne. My knees start to wobble, and I take a step forward, pushing her along with me until she's up against the wall and I'm pressed against her soft curves.

The painful press of the doorjamb into my knuckles—my hand tangled in Opal's hair—brings reality crashing into me.

Wait.

Oh no.

I'm kissing Opal.

I should absolutely not be kissing Opal. I can't exactly think of reasons *why* I shouldn't be kissing Opal when kissing her has quickly become one of my favorite things in the world to do, but facts are facts, and I jump away from her.

We stare at each other, chests heaving. Opal's eyes are perfect circles, pupils blown wide, her lips swollen and red, and I try really hard to tamp down the swell of excitement that surges through me seeing her wrecked like this.

"You kissed me!" Her voice cracks like a whip.

"No I didn't."

"I'm pretty sure you did."

I gape at her like a fish for a moment, then violently shake my head, my pulse sawing at my chest in a jagged, painful rhythm. I can't suck in a breath past the top of my throat, and I start to feel light-headed, everything going fuzzy, the press of Opal's mouth against mine still so fresh my lips tingle with the memory.

Opal starts to say something else, but I cut her off.

"I'm sorry. I have to go." I spin away, desperately searching for an escape. The back door seems reasonable.

"Where are you going?" Opal's pitch is high, dripping with disbelief.

"For a run," I say, forgoing shoes and pushing open the screen door, bolting down the steps.

"You run?"

"I'm a track star," I yell over my shoulder, taking off into the pitch-black night.

The grass is cool and damp under my bare feet as I continue to sprint across the farm. Maybe if I run far enough and fast enough, I can hurtle myself into a different dimension. One where I don't make an absolute fool out of myself.

I know that's wishful thinking. Every alternate universe version of me is probably a massive fool too.

My toe catches on something, and the world tips. I tumble down the small hill until a small apple tree catches me, knocking the wind from my lungs. I roll to my back, head spinning as I try to catch my breath, floating among the stars.

Holy shit.

Holy fucking shit.

I kissed Opal. My nightmare sprite of a landlord/roommate. This is not good. That should have never happened. And it certainly can never happen again.

Never.

Ever.

Seriously. Never.

. . . The problem is, I kind of want it to.

Chapter 17

PEPPER

I've discovered the cure to, erm, indecent thoughts about one's, uh . . . roommate: spreadsheets.

Pages and pages of spreadsheets.

Ones with lots of confusing columns and formulas and pie charts that all paint a lovely picture of how financially screwed you are.

It turns out it's very hard to think of anything in the sexual realm when you realize your livelihood is on a spectacularly negative slope.

Diksha had sent over a workbook of information that I printed, which is now scattered across my kitchen table. Lots of menacing lines and red numbers. I read over Diksha's email for the twenty-seventh time. The last sentence holding my attention:

. . . The competition won't solve all your problems,

*but it sure as hell will make a dent. Stop being so
stubborn and ask her, Pepper.*

I slam my laptop shut and stack my hands on top before banging my head against them a few times. None of what Diksha sent over is new information, but it's all organized in a way that really drives home what a mess this place is in.

We haven't broken even in years. Grandma Lou, damn perfect, altruistic saint that she was, apparently lacked an understanding of just how high our operating expenses were and had been buying excess tubers and seeds instead of cultivating our own from previous crops.

Small farms support small farms, she'd told me a few years back when I'd brought up us investing in a greenhouse and growing our own seedlings during the winter months instead of purchasing from a grower up the mountain. *No reason we can't help someone else while helping ourselves.*

Well, apparently, we'd been actually fucking ourselves, Lou.

The anger burns white hot for a moment, then snuffs out. I can't be mad at the woman for trying to do good in the way she was able. It was her nature, and I'd rather suffer debt a thousand times over than wish for change in the woman who saved me.

But I do need to get a plan.

I'd already started implementing some leaner methods around the farm at the start of the season and secured new wholesale accounts to local florists and hotels, even before I knew the gravity of the situation, in fear that if I wasn't careful, I'd lose the place in a month. The problem is, with almost everything in farming, it takes years to see the fruits of your labor.

And I don't have years.

Not with Opal owning the damn place.

It's fine. Everything is fine. All I need to do is ask the white-haired hellcat to help me win the flower competition and accept a third of what she paid for the place as an act of good faith to get the hell off my farm, then pay her the remainder of the balance for the rest of my miserable life. All while ignoring some very bizarre and unprecedented . . . *urgings* for the woman.

Easy.

A tap on the doorframe snags my focus, and my head whips up to see her standing there. My gaze gets stuck on that full mouth of hers, pulse hammering as she slowly licks her lips.

Fucking hell.

Opal clears her throat. "There you are. I was starting to think you were avoiding me."

"That's correct, yes," I say hoarsely. Because it's true.

After the . . . shenanigans of last night, my head has been a muddled knot. The only way I could think straight for a second was to avoid her. I got an early start this morning, skipping lunch and only dragging myself back here when I was about to pass out from hunger (and also confirming her car wasn't in the driveway).

Color floods her cheeks. "Well . . . I appreciate the honesty . . . I guess."

"I didn't hear you come in," I say, scrubbing my eyes. My brain feels gritty, full of sand from the laser focus of the past few hours.

"Slipped in through the front," she says with a soft smile, tilting her head toward the opposite end of the house. "I had dinner with my sisters downtown."

I nod because, honestly, I'm not sure what else to do. I have this bizarre urge to ask her a thousand questions. Where did she go? What did she get? Did she like it? Did she have fun? Would she want to go back? Maybe with me?

All nonsensical and ridiculous.

There's a long pause, and a rush of adrenaline floods my system as I look at her, memories of last night trying to bust out of the boxes I've shoved them into.

With a few hesitant steps, she moves to the table, pulling out a chair and sitting next to me. She picks up one of the papers. "What's all this?"

"A giant mess."

Her eyes skim over one of the pie charts, brow furrowing as she nods. My urge is to hide it, sweep all the awful papers to my chest and pretend it's not real. This is how people scam you. They figure out your biggest problems and leverage them to their advantage. But I don't have the energy for that. Opal is my only chance at making a dent in this disaster; I might as well let her look her fill.

"I take it business isn't . . . *blooming*," she says, pressing her lips together against a smile. There's a pause. "Get it?"

"Please don't make me kick you out of here."

She laughs at that. We sit in tense silence for a moment before she clears her throat.

"I've been thinking—"

"That can't lead anywhere good," I mumble.

Opal rolls her eyes, sticks her tongue out at me. The movement holds the entirety of my attention.

"I personally believe you'll like my idea," she says with a prissy flick of her hair.

I shrug, casting my gaze to the floor. Here it comes. She's probably figured it out. Not only does she own the only place I've ever been able to call home, but she also knows how she can help me. And, tragically, the damn woman seems to actually want to help people. The only thing I hate more than asking for help is accepting it. Looks like I'm about to do both.

But I will humble myself and do what I can to hold on to this farm. For Grandma Lou.

I take a deep breath, trying to untangle the words at the tip of my tongue. Say it. Just say it. I'm gonna do it. Here it goes. Any second now . . .

"I know what you're going to say," I finally bumble out, right as Opal sucks in a breath. I find the courage to look at her.

Deep crimson floods her face and neck. "You do?" she whispers.

I nod, licking my lips as my gaze travels over her face. "It could go horribly. I shouldn't even broach the subject but it's probably obvious how desperate I am. Very real chance it would be a total disaster."

Opal's mouth flaps open and closed a few times, eyes narrowing at me. "Ye of little faith," she eventually says, an odd, self-deprecating laugh punctuating the words. "I know a thing or two."

My eyebrows knit. "With all due respect, not all skills are transferable." From what I've seen of her studio, she works primarily with paint and ink, a few sculptures in the mix. Creating something from flowers seems like a totally different ball game. "You might be clueless with this, and I don't want to pressure you into anything."

Opal's face twists, and she pushes away from the table, the legs of the chair screeching as she plants both hands on her hips. "Well, with all due respect, yours would hardly be the first clitoris I encounter."

My mouth absolutely plummets to the floor. "Um . . . what?"

Opal's face is full of anger as she leans toward me. "That's what you're implying, isn't it? That I wouldn't be good in bed? Just because my last relationship was with a man doesn't mean I don't know what I'm doing."

I reel back, eyes wide and frantic. I think there's a very real chance I've totally misread this.

"I was about to beg you to help me do the flower competition," I push out. "But I'm, uh, sorry I kissed you last night." I am so lost in the direction this conversation took, and I have no idea where to go from here.

Opal's jaw hangs open. "You're *sorry*?"

"Yes. I mean . . . Yes, I'm sorry. I'm sorry I kissed you without, erm, asking."

Opal is silent, staring at me with those big blue eyes.

I blow out a deep breath through my mouth, making my lips flap as I scan the ceiling for words. "I'm sorry I, er, threw myself at you. I don't usually make a habit of . . . randomly . . ." I wave my hand around.

"Sticking your tongue down a girl's throat?" Opal offers.

My eyes bulge out of my head like a cartoon character. "Well . . . shit."

This is truly my waking nightmare.

I stand too, doing an embarrassed twirl around the room before planting myself in front of her. Her anger is replaced with a skeptical look, a sharp glint in her wary eyes.

"Sounds like my technique was lacking," I say, twisting the hem of my shirt. "Guess I need to apologize for that too."

Which is rather devastating seeing as Opal's technique left my stomach swooping all night as whispers of her lips against my mouth invaded any dreams I managed to have.

"So, I guess I'm sorry for pretty much everything," I say. "For randomly kissing you and not asking first and also apparently slobbering on you and I want you to know it didn't mean anything and I don't want to make you uncomfortable because I'm aware of all the—"

"Pepper?" Opal steps forward, pressing the index finger of one hand to my lips, and using the other hand to grab mine.

My eyes fix on where I'm touching her, unable to fully process what's happening.

Opal slowly pulls away her finger from my mouth, hand ghosting down my body. She reaches out, gently plucking the sprig of flowers poking out of my jeans pocket. Her fingers brush against the bare skin above my waistband, and we both suck in a breath. Body tingling, she presses the flowers into my palm, closing our fingers around it.

"Pepper," she repeats. She's staring at our hands too.

I lick my lips. "Y-yeah?"

"Did you like kissing me?" she asks. Quietly. So quietly, it could be a fantasy of her asking.

I move my head with a jerky movement, eyes finally pulling away from our hands to her face. Is it my imagination, or does she sway a millimeter closer?

"Yes," I whisper. Then, "Did you like kissing me?" just as softly.

A massive grin breaks across Opal's mouth, and I realize how sick I am of talking. I want her. I want to learn the sweetness of that smile. Make it a core memory.

I step forward, closing the space between us, our clutched hands pressing between our chests, my free hand darting out to grab her belt loop, tugging her closer still, hips flush against mine. With a smile still on her face and enough slowness she could pull back, I press my lips to hers.

And Opal melts.

Her arm snakes around me, knotting her hand in my hair,

her tongue sliding out, licking my lips, electrocuting my blood. I feel the rise and fall of her chest as she breathes, the curves of her full and soft breasts pressed against me.

If our first kiss shocked me, this one rewires my entire system. She teeters between shy and frantic—angling the kiss so it deepens, rubbing her tongue against mine, dragging her fingers from my hair down my neck, pulling me against her as if we hadn't already obliterated the pretext of space.

This kiss runs like a fever through me, hot and dangerous, leaving me shaking.

We finally come up for air, untangling and taking a step away from each other. Opal's cheeks are crimson. I'm sure mine match.

"What is happening," I whisper, utterly dazed.

Opal shakes her head, chest heaving as she stares at me with wild eyes. She traces her fingers over her lips, and I feel an echoing tingle on my own as I watch the gesture.

She clears her throat, sucks in a deep breath. "This is what I was trying to tell you about," she says. "My idea."

I blink at her.

"I know things are kind of . . . tense . . . between us," she says.

I snort. I *wish* this was as simple as tension. This isn't tension. Tension is a sore spot, a defined point of stress that can be untangled. Worked through. This is a tornado, and I'm getting whiplash from the spectrum of feelings living with Opal is putting me through.

"But maybe they don't, uh, have to be?" she says, scrunching up her face as she says it.

More blinking. I've never pretended to be a particularly good conversationalist.

Opal huffs, squaring her shoulders. "Listen, our living situation isn't ideal. We don't really get along personality-wise, but, to be quite blunt about it, I'm really attracted to you and I think you might be attracted to me and I think we should—" She waves a hand between us. There's a long moment of silence as I dangle on her unfinished thought. "Jesus, throw me a lifeline here, Pepper."

"We should what?" I say, voice hoarse.

She groans, throwing her arms out. "Bang it out!"

My mind, my entire body, goes blank. I can see the words hanging there, but I can't process what she means by them, so I continue to gape at her.

"This silence is, quite possibly, the worst thing I've ever experienced. Including the time a stranger on the bus licked my neck," Opal says after a minute, eyes frantic and color still high.

I shake my head, trying to clear the pink fog of lust. "You mean . . . have sex?" I whisper.

Opal nods.

"With each other?" I don't recognize my own voice. It's low and breathy and dripping with want.

"I didn't start this conversation just to tell you I masturbate, Pepper," Opal says, throwing her head back. "Yes, sex with each other."

"Would that involve . . ." My eyes are stuck on her exposed neck. The soft, delicate skin. I have the alarming urge to sink my teeth into it.

Opal sighs, closing her eyes. "It can involve whatever you want. We both want. A mutually beneficial arrangement to blow off some steam and have some fun."

She looks at me again, and her face is so earnest and open and filled with a hunger that mirrors my own. I'm not sure I'll survive this.

"What about . . . *feelings*?" The last word comes out like a curse. I'm not sure how Opal can find anything funny while so much heat floods my body I'm scared my brain is going to melt, but she laughs.

"The less, the better," she says, biting her bottom lip and tugging at her snowy hair. "I'm not interested in a relationship or anything and I know you barely tolerate me . . ."

A silly chamber of my heart squeezes, and I want to cut her off. Laugh at the absurdity of that statement. Tolerate her? I can't stop thinking about the damn woman. And it scares the hell out of me.

But what she's offering . . . Well, maybe it's just what I need to stop obsessing. She's right, we're fundamental opposites. Any . . . *feelings* are purely motivated by lust, and lust alone.

And what better cure to totally platonic lust than—

"Just sex?" I say at last. Opal's eyes are so fiercely fixed on me, my skin prickles.

"Might as well get something out of this forced living situation," she says, a devilish smile curving those full lips.

"Frequent, emotion-free orgasms doesn't seem like the worst compromise, right?"

Right. Yes. Absolutely. An orgasm sounds great right about now.

Opal laughs again, and I realize I said all that out loud. My face fries with embarrassment.

"Easy, kitten, we should probably come up with some ground rules," she says, slinking toward me. She isn't touching me, but every cell in my body stands on alert, desperate and aching for the pressure of her that I already know feels so good.

"That's smart," I say. Rough. Low. Staring at her mouth. Rules would be very good right about now. "You start."

"Um." She bites that lip again, and I suck in a breath. "Well, we already established no feelings."

"Right. Yes. A core value. I hate feelings. Don't need them."

Opal grins, looking up at me through her long lashes, eyes glinting. "What else?"

"Uh . . ." I flick through memories of the constant stream of rom-coms Grandma Lou would have playing throughout the day. "No sleeping in the same bed? Keep our separate rooms?"

I've never shared a bed with someone as an adult, so I don't really know if this is a good one, but it seems like the kind of rule a woman like Sandra Bullock or Meg Ryan would come up with in a movie with a situation like this. Might as well follow expert advice.

"Definitely. Way too intimate." Opal bounces on her toes. "Maybe no dates and stuff?"

I snort. "In this economy? Absolutely not."

Opal giggles.

"Do we avoid, like, kissing on the mouth?"

Opal's eyes shoot wide. "Let's not get carried away there, Pretty Woman. You're rather good at the whole kissing thing." She takes another step to me, brushing her knuckles down my arm, braiding our fingers together as her hand slides into mine. "I'm not particularly interested in shutting any form of kissing down."

I gulp, wishing so badly I could tamp down the ridiculous, embarrassing, glee-ridden smile pulling at my cheeks.

"No need to look so damn smug about it," Opal says, watching my grin. She rolls her eyes but smiles back, lifting my hand to brush her lips against the back of it.

My heart bottoms out.

"Will you help me with the flower competition?" I yell. Because, clearly, I'm excellent at sexy talk.

Opal blinks a few times. "This escalated into a quid pro quo situation way quicker than I anticipated."

Ugh.

"I'm sorry. I didn't mean it in a transactional way. I just . . . well. I . . . I need your help." The words dangle in the air, repulsive and naked, like slabs of meat left to drain in a butcher's shop. But it's true. I need her. "I'd like us to work on it together. Win the damn thing. I know you offered before but I don't want you to feel pressured to do it but I also am sort of desperate but if we hook up I kind of wanted to talk about it first so there's no weird—"

"Of course I'll help you."

I release a huge breath, shoulders deflating. "Thank you."

"That whole thing will be separate from this thing," she says, gesturing between us. She reaches up, brushing my long hair behind my ear, then dragging her hand to cup my cheek. She's so warm and gentle, I let out a mortifying whimper.

"So when do we, er, um . . . start the whole, uh, sex . . . thing?" The last word is a squeak, and I cringe.

Opal presses her lips together, but there's no hiding her outrageous smile. "If you aren't busy, maybe . . . right now?"

Chapter 18

PEPPER

Sex with Opal as an elusive, gauzy idea seemed pretty great. Probably one of the best I've ever had.

But all the steps that lead up to that idea's realization—me guiding us up the stairs, hovering outside my bedroom door, the knowledge that she's going to see me naked and vulnerable and did I mention fucking *naked*—release a tidal wave of nerves through me, anticipation and worry cresting against my wrung-out heart.

Emotion-free orgasms, emotion-free orgasms. Opal's words loop around my head in a chant. That's all this is. A simple agreement that we'll both (hopefully) enjoy . . . If I can just get out of my own head long enough to do so.

"Where'd you go?" Opal whispers, tugging me back down to earth.

I look at her—that sinfully full mouth, those rosy cheeks,

eyelids heavy and hooded—and even more panic tangles with the sharp ache of want pressing into me.

"I'm nervous," I admit, voice small.

One brow flicks up, tugging the corner of her mouth with it, a look that I can only describe as hungry.

She takes a step toward me.

I trip backward.

She moves again.

I do too.

And then my back is against the wall and Opal is right there, the warmth of her body and the smell of ink on her skin hugging me tight.

I forget how to breathe.

"Pepper," she purrs, leaning in, closing the last millimeter of space between our breasts, our thighs.

"Y-yeah?"

"Open the door. Invite me in—" She presses her lips against the pulse point on my neck, my heartbeat stuttering, then kicking up into a frenzy. She must feel it because she laughs, nuzzles the spot with her nose before pulling back to look in my eyes. "—and let me fuck the nervousness out of you."

Like the strike of a match, my body is nothing but flames and heat. Gaze locked on her, I reach out beside me, palm slipping on the knob once . . . twice . . .

The door bangs open. I grab Opal with both hands, one to her hip, the other curling behind her neck, tugging her toward

me in a move that's desperate and clumsy and has us both tripping into the room and tumbling to the bed.

I've always loved following directions.

Opal groans then giggles, rolling so she's over me, pressing
me into the mattress as she devours my mouth, hands knotting
in my hair.

I'm so gone, I don't know if the clothes I'm tearing at are
hers or mine, but what I do know is I need more. I need more
of her sweet mouth against me. More vibrations of her moans
as I grab handfuls of her full ass. More of her hot skin finally
touching mine. She pulls away to lift her T-shirt over her head
and pull her shorts off so she's down to a bright-green bra and
blue boy shorts.

"Lie back and lift your hips for me," she says against my
neck, nipping the spot. The noise that's ripped from my throat
isn't even human.

I do as she says.

"Perfect," she whispers, moving down my body, her soft lips
everywhere at once. It's so much. Too much. Not enough. My
hands fist in the bedsheet.

She undoes the snaps of my jeans, pulling them down my
thighs and throwing them to the floor with what can only be
described as exuberant determination.

She pushes my knees apart, gaze tracing over me. Our eyes
lock for a moment, then she hooks her fingers around the edges
of my underwear and rips them down my legs.

"Fuck." Her usually soft and light voice is rough and low,

and the way she's looking at me sends a throb of desire up my center, my thighs trying to clamp shut.

She holds me open, laughing before biting her lip. I have no clue what could possibly be funny right now, seeing as I'm about to die from all the sensations running through me. She's hardly touched me, and I'm poised to detonate like a bomb.

We haven't even fully started, and yet I never imagined sex could feel like this.

A fresh pang of anxiety twists in my chest as her mouth meets the inside of my knee, dragging up my thigh.

It's sharp and scary and only grows as her mouth gets closer to my center. She adjusts herself, on her knees, back arched and her round ass high as she nudges closer. She presses forward . . .

And I jolt up, gripping her forearms and scooching away at the last second. Her eyes are huge as she looks up at me in confusion, lips parted, and then she tips forward, face-planting on the bed.

"I've never done this before," I blurt out, a wash of embarrassment heating my skin.

Opal twists her head, cheek still pressed to the sheet, to look at me. "Oral sex?"

I nod, trying to swallow past my dry throat.

Opal sits up and shrugs, shooting me a wicked smile. "No worries. We can try it if you want. Or do something different. I don't care."

She licks her lips and so much need floods my system, my

entire body jerks. Opal catches the response, her grin growing as she prowls up my body, gently pressing me back down to the mattress as her breasts drag against my skin, making me squirm.

I can't believe I ever thought she was timid. This woman is a force of nature.

"What do you want me to do to you, Pepper?" she whispers into my ear before lightly biting the lobe. "Do you *want* me to kiss you here?" she asks, her touch soft as butterfly wings as she traces over my slit.

I groan, pressing my head into the mattress.

Fuck. I want that. I really want that. But I want to *do* that too. I want to know the feel of Opal on my tongue, her thighs against my cheeks. Memorize the taste of her desire.

But the only sound I manage to press out is an inarticulate gargle.

"I could finger you," she says, tickling her way down to my knee then back up. "Find that spot deep inside you that makes you see stars."

Her fingernails press into the skin at my hip bone, the sensation like a shock, pulling another gasp from my throat, my vision going fuzzy.

Opal hums in response, and I feel her smile pressed into my neck. "Or focus on your clit? Find a rhythm that makes you wild?" Her touch curls up my side, skating across my ribs before reaching my breasts, tracing in teasing circles. "Maybe there's a toy you'd rather I use to fuck you?" she says, voice sweet innocence as the circles get tighter, my nipple aching for her touch, my heart beating erratically in my chest.

She stops suddenly, planting both hands on the sides of my head and staring down at me with that viciously beautiful smile.

"Or should I just grind your pretty pussy against mine until we both come?"

My body is a live wire and every syllable out of that gorgeous mouth shocks my system.

She kisses me again, her hands everywhere. All I can manage is to grab her waist and hold on for dear life.

"I need you to tell me what you want," Opal says, a sharp edge of desperation in her voice as she comes up for air. Her hips absentmindedly nudge against my thigh as she kisses me again. "Please, Pepper."

"I . . ." Words are way too hard with every sensation flooding me.

"Say it. Tell me what you want." She ducks her head, pulling my nipple into her mouth, swirling her tongue around the peak.

"I don't know what I want," I finally gasp as she gives my breast a sharp bite. "I've never done any of this before."

Opal stills, then tilts her face to look at me, my nipple dislodging from her mouth with an obnoxiously loud pop. If I wasn't absolutely dying from the combination of lust and nerves, I'd laugh.

"What did you say?" Opal's face is hard to read.

I clamp my jaw shut, sliding out from under her, pulling my legs up to my chest as I lean against my headboard.

What the fuck. Oh what the fuck. Why did I admit that?

Why did I ruin the moment? Plenty of people have sex without saying a word to the other person. Why did I make it a big *thing*? She's probably thinking that I'll be bad in bed, which, fair enough concern, but also, give a girl a chance.

It's not like I haven't *wanted* to have sex. But being inherently distrusting of every single human I've ever met, compounded with living with my grandma for most of my adult life on a flower farm in the Appalachian Mountains, hasn't exactly been a conducive setup for sex practice outside of my own hand.

Or maybe she thinks I'm too old to be a virgin—which it's like, screw anyone who thinks that because virginity is a social construct and I shouldn't be having sex with a person like that anyway blah blah blah but I'm also about to lose my mind from the tension she's teased into my body so I don't exactly want her to stop. Or maybe she's thinking I, like, *care* about virginity or whatever and I *don't*, but . . . UGH.

Opal's face morphs into a soft smile, and she leans forward, placing a soft kiss on each of my kneecaps. She sits up, and scoots closer, our noses almost touching. "I can almost hear you thinking," she says, dropping her forehead to mine. "Relax."

I let out a deep breath, some of the tension dropping from my shoulders, but a small tremble still vibrating through me.

"First and foremost," Opal says, bringing her hand up to cup the angle of my jaw, rubbing her lips against mine. "I don't care at all. I want to make that totally, one hundred percent clear. You could tell me you've been with a thousand people or none at all and as long as it was consensual, it doesn't matter to me one bit. Believe me?"

I swallow, then nod.

"Good," Opal says, giving me a soft peck on the tip of my nose. "Now, the important thing: you say you don't know what you want. Well, I'm at your total disposal to figure it out. Any. Way. You. Need." She separates each word with another kiss. On my cheek. My neck. My temple.

"Opal," I say, my voice fractured.

"Hmm?" she intones against my throat before biting softly.

I grab her face with both hands, this desperation in me something wild and uncontrollable. I devour her mouth, kissing her until I'm dizzy, then find the only words I'm capable of: "At this point, I don't care even a little bit how you go about it, just please. Please. *Please*. Make me come."

Opal's lips fall open, and my heart stops beating.

Then she smiles.

"As you wish."

Chapter 19

PEPPER

Opal is slow. Careful. Eyes sharp and vibrant as she looks over my body. It's a look I recognize, the same determined focus I've observed her give to her art, catching moments of her in the shed when she didn't know I was watching.

"Just tell me if I do something you don't like and I'll stop," she murmurs, slipping down the bed, hands dragging over me as she moves. I have a hard time imagining any touch from Opal that I wouldn't like.

She sits at the end of the mattress on her knees. In a flash of movement, she grabs my ankles, jerking me down the bed until I'm lying flat, my head spinning. I find a molecule of strength to prop myself up on my elbows, my breath wild and frantic at the heat in her gaze. She keeps touching me like she can't stop, and she pulls my legs apart, settling between my thighs.

Strands of her ridiculous white hair tickle my skin, and every nerve ending is so damn sensitive, a giggle bubbles up through me, my entire body shaking. The friction of my inner thighs rubbing against her arms pulls even more desperate laughter from me. If I don't laugh, I'll cry at the flood of sensation.

Opal grunts and drags her teeth over the spot where my thigh meets my sex. My voice fractures from the zap.

"You shouldn't be laughing, Pepper," she says, eyes glinting as she looks across my body at me.

I giggle again. "I'm sorry," I choke out.

Her smile is slow. Dangerous. Divine. Voice so low I barely hear what comes next: "You should be screaming."

She buries that full mouth against me, and I feel the long drag of her tongue from my entrance to my clit, where she lingers, swirling lightly.

My body jerks so hard my hips lift from the bed. I throw my arm over my face, biting hard into my forearm to muffle the sound clawing from my throat.

In a flash Opal's hand is gripping my wrist, pulling my arm away.

"Don't," she says, mouth red and glistening. "I want to fucking hear it."

All I can do is nod.

She looks at me for half a second, then licks her lips and moves back into position.

Thoughts and sensations thread through me into an incoherent knot, words and cries tumbling from me as she works me so good. She reaches beneath me, cupping my ass and pulling me closer to her mouth, moving my hips in a glorious rhythm as she slides her tongue in and out of me. There's no way my body can survive this kind of torture, every cell building. *Building. Building.* To the sharp peak of need I want to throw myself off.

But Opal doesn't push me over the edge.

She pulls back and I cry out, actual tears springing to my eyes. I blink them away.

She lets out a husky laugh when her gaze locks with mine. I'm sure I look rabid.

"You take it so good," she whispers, kissing my belly. My thighs. "So, so good."

"Opal, *please,*" I pant out, voice a fractured yell.

She hums in satisfaction. "I know you're going to look so pretty when you come."

I whimper, squeezing my eyes shut. She takes mercy on me, and I feel her tongue against me again, traveling in a circle around my clit. I feel so much, my body is beyond recognition. I'm not in control of it. Opal is. And she's going to make me wait.

I force my eyes open, watching her, wanting to memorize every movement. The way her tongue works against me, the flutter of her eyelashes against her cheek as she savors me, the almost frantic pace of her arm as she pushes her fingers in and out of me, her other hand snaking down her own body and dipping below her underwear.

All of it refracts through me until every feeling is stretched thin, poised between pleasure and pain and I feel like I'll die in this delicious hell, teeth gritted and every muscle taut.

Then her eyes flash open, watching me watch her. Both her hands move to my thighs, fingers digging into my skin as she pulls me even wider, fixing her mouth directly over my clit and destroying me as she sucks.

She gives me exactly what I need.

And it wrecks me.

I scream as I come, the noise sharp and primal, and I barely register the quiet laugh of satisfaction from Opal as she works me through it, riding the wave with me until I'm so sensitive, it hurts.

She pulls back, crawling up the bed and pulling me to her, our bodies slick with sweat as we tangle together. Her mouth on mine. More tiny teardrops bud in the corners of my eyes, but I force them away. I can't imagine anything quite as mortifying as crying after coming, but it was all so much I can barely control myself.

It could be seconds, it could be hours, but eventually, I come down from the high. Opal holds me through all of it.

I feel so comfortable that, for a moment, I wonder if she did kill me and this is heaven.

Something sharp and terrifying pokes at my chest, and my entire body jolts. I bottle up that dangerous sensation and shove it far, far away.

No feelings. No feelings. No feelings.

Action will definitely prevent feelings.

In a movement so sharp and assured I can't believe I'm the one doing it, I pull back, pushing Opal beneath me, kissing her so roughly I wonder if our lips will bruise. She kisses me back.

I hover there for only a moment, but when her hands whisper across my skin and cup my jaw, a hold that feels inescapably tender, more of those sharp sensations poke against my ribs.

I sit up, tugging her to the center of the bed, then shift so I'm kneeling between her hips.

"What are you doing?" she says, cheeks flushed and eyes glazed.

"Returning the favor."

Chapter 20

OPAL

I'm dead. Or dreaming. Or astral projected into an alternate universe where gorgeous, grumpy Pepper is naked and undone and offering to eat me out.

Probably dead.

I twist against Pepper as she hovers over me, kissing her hard and deep, knotting my fingers in that long, chocolate hair. I swallow the gasp she lets out against my lips. Pepper's hands wrap around my wrists, giving them a quick warning squeeze before pinning them to the mattress.

My skin erupts in heat as my stomach tightens with the thrill that shoots through me. I've always preferred taking control during sex; it's the one thing I'm pretty confident I'm actually good at. I've always felt so shitty in every other aspect of a relationship, a good lay is the least I can offer. Plus, I *like* making my partner come. I live for that rush of finding what pushes them to the edge, how to hold them there, being the reason they finally tip over. It makes it easier for me to find release knowing they've enjoyed it.

But, as Pepper presses me down, biting my lip, then licking the spot, I wonder if maybe giving up control has some allure after all.

I've never fucked like this before, slow and unhurried—like each touch is just as important as the big finish. Pepper's kisses alone are turning me inside out, the hungry yet careful way she explores, how she's soft and gentle one second, deep and dirty the next. She told me she's never done this before, and I wonder if that extends to kissing. It feels like she's trying every variation of kiss possible—discovering what feels best. I hope that's true.

She moves from my lips to the edge of my jaw, then down my neck, and I feel almost high from the subtle scent of chamomile on her skin. The pleasure builds slowly, languidly winding through my veins and wrapping around my bones until I'm weightless from it.

Pepper moves down my body. Palms skimming over the soft curves of my belly, framing the swell of my hips.

"Fuck, you're soaked," she whispers as she looks between my legs, dragging her knuckles across her lips. A small blip of embarrassment pulses through me.

"Umm, Pepper?" My voice sounds far away even to my own ears, like noise can't properly travel through my lust-crazed brain. I squirm as the anxiety grows, but it does nothing to shift Pepper's focus from between my thighs.

"Yeah?" Pepper finally says, glancing up at me.

"I feel like there's something I should tell you first."

"I'm listening," she mumbles, hooking her fingers in the elastic band of my boy shorts.

"I should probably warn you I'm not shaved." The last word comes out as a squeak, punctuating the exact moment Pepper tears my underwear down my legs.

I instinctively cover my less than perfectly manicured vulva with both hands, squeezing my eyes shut in mortification.

I used to drag myself to waxing appointments with religious devotion, making sure every hair was ripped out. It was the only way Miles would go down on me, and him going down on me was the only way I could ever get off with him.

I haven't been since we broke up. I like to tell myself it's out of protest, reclaiming my body hair. When, really, it's just from a lack of need.

The silence in the room grows, and I squint one eye open to find Pepper staring at me.

"So?" Pepper says, head tilted to the side and brows knitted in confusion. She drags her nails down my forearms, then across my knuckles before skating down my thighs.

"I . . . er . . . well, it's not, uh, as nice-looking?"

"Why would I care about how you groom yourself?" Pepper looks at me with such pure confusion I almost laugh. Or cry. Damn woman really makes me spell things out for her.

"I . . . I don't know. You're shaved, so I'm assuming it's what you'd prefer."

Pepper absentmindedly traces circles around my ankle bones as she studies me. "I shave my body hair because it's a sensory processing thing. I don't like the way it feels against my clothes and the sensation is enough to send me into a melt-down. Why is it any of my business what you do with yours?"

Fucking hell, she's looking at me like she wants an answer. "People always care," I say, an edge of frustration in my voice. The echoes of so many small cutting comments filling up the room.

Pepper manages to pull one of my hands away from my pussy, but the other immediately replaces it.

"People meaning Miles?"

I shrug. "Not only him, but yeah, he was pretty vocal about wanting me to be as smooth as a Barbie down there. Wouldn't . . . It . . . I don't know. It made me feel like people wouldn't find me sexy or desirable if I wasn't waxed."

Pepper sits back on her heels, face pinched in thought. She tucks her hair behind her ears, then glances at me through her lashes with a look of raw vulnerability. "Did you consider me less sexy when you found out I hadn't slept with anyone before?"

"God. No, Pepper. Of course not."

"Have I done something that makes you think I don't find you desirable?"

"No! It's just—"

"Because I found you pretty damn desirable the entire time your head was between my legs. That was kind of what the whole screaming thing was about."

I can't help it, I giggle like a loon. "Pepper, the screaming thing had a lot to do with what I was doing *to* you. You might not feel the same way doing it to me once you see . . . everything."

Pepper blows out a sharp breath through her nose. "Do you not want me to do this?"

"I do! I just—"

"So the way I see it, we have three options." She ticks them off on her fingers. "You either tell me you don't want me to fuck you with my mouth. You go shave as fast as humanly possible, then get back in this bed. Or you get over it, move your hands, and let me taste you. What'll it be?"

My jaw falls open. And, without another moment's thought, my hands drop to my sides.

"Good girl," Pepper says, a devilish smile tugging up the corners of her mouth. Her eyes slowly leave my face, trace down my body.

Pepper licks her lips as she gently pulls my knees apart, staring at my center, eyes nothing but heat and smoke and want.

"Sweetheart," she said quietly, gaze darting up to lock with mine. "You couldn't be prettier."

Her touch is gentle, almost timid, gaze sharp with focus as she watches her hand. Watches herself touch me. She starts at my hips, tracing the crease along my thigh, then between my legs.

I'm so keyed up, my entire body bucks, a tremble running through me. Pepper blinks rapidly, then meets my eyes. My breaths are so sharp and short, I worry I might pass out.

But then, a slow, delicious, delighted smile curves Pepper's stern mouth. And I worry I might die.

I open my mouth, ready to beg for relief, but all that comes out is a broken whimper.

And that smile glows.

Still as gentle, but one hundred times surer, Pepper traces

across my slit, parting my folds. I'm so wet—aching and ready—her fingers slip between me, gliding to my opening. A sharp gasp is tugged from the center of my chest, my head rolling back. Pepper hums in satisfaction.

"This okay?" she whispers, circling around me. My muscles clamp, desperate for her to fill me, to fuck me.

"Please," I whine.

Pepper doesn't tease, doesn't wait. She gives me what I need.

Two fingers pushed inside, her own breathing stutters. We're still for a moment, maybe two, our ragged breaths and my pounding heartbeat the only noise.

And it's all so much. Too much. I'm breathing but oxygen is no longer working, my head floating and my muscles tense as Pepper looks at me with those big brown eyes and those red parted lips and that flush of her skin and it's all so painfully intense and raw and real and I—

I clench around her fingers, and it's like the crack of a whip, spurring Pepper into action. Her fingers pump in and out of me in a sure rhythm, working me until I'm gritting my teeth, groaning.

She adds another finger, using her other hand to spread me, rubbing my clit with her thumb. Sensation shoots through me that's so vibrant, it's almost painful.

I grind against her, begging for more, my own hands pulling out my hair because I can't fucking take it.

This kind of wanting is sharp. It has teeth and demands to be satisfied. Indulged. And just as I think I'll never come back from this, never recover, Pepper removes the hand spreading me.

And replaces it with her mouth, tongue darting out and lapping at my clit.

Pepper doesn't have a rhythm or technique or any finesse. She's a little sloppy and wild and it's somehow all the better for it. She devours me like she was starving and I'm the sweetest thing she's ever tasted.

I hope she becomes addicted.

My hands leave my hair and travel to hers, stroking, grabbing, pulling. I need her. I need to touch her as she fucks me with her tongue, feel her there, an anchor in the madness she's creating.

Pepper pulls her mouth away, fingers still moving in and out as she looks up at me, expression wrecked, lips swollen and glossy.

"Teach me how to make you come." She says it like it's suddenly the most important thing in the world, like her sole purpose is to pleasure me until I'm twisting under her, begging for it all. Something about the way she looks at me, so desperate and eager to please, nearly tips me over the edge.

"Don't stop what you're doing," I manage to groan. Which, with how equally wrecked I am, is quite the miracle. "You're fucking perfect."

I catch another flash of that smile before her mouth is pressed back against me, lips and tongue working in tandem with her fingers.

I let out a moan that's equal parts relief and agony as I teeter on that precipice, every nerve stretched taut, every touch rocketing vibrations of pleasure through me.

Pepper curls her fingers, and my head lolls to the side. My eyes land on the mirror in the corner, angled so the setting sun hits the top corner, sending a golden glow through the room, across Pepper. I watch her reflection, her chestnut hair tumbling across her back and by my thighs, long body curled between my legs, eyes closed as she works me, her own hand between her legs, every muscle tense as she pushes me closer and closer to the peak.

And that look of hers, one of divine reverence, delicious devastation, as she pleasures herself while pleasing me, tips my world upside down.

"I'm coming," I gasp out, like it's much of a secret to anyone in the room. "Fuck. I'm coming. I'm—"

Please.

Right there.

So good.

Don't stop.

And she doesn't. She laughs triumphantly as I shake against her mouth, my toes curling and back arching.

She carries me through every last shudder, until I beg her with a gasp to take mercy on me and my shattered nerves.

She laughs at that too.

Pepper collapses next to me on the pillows, and both our chests heave and work in disjointed rhythm as we stare up at the ceiling, our ragged breaths the only sound in the room.

Awkwardness tickles at my sides, threatening to wedge between me and Pepper's warm, relaxed body. And that's the last thing I want. I want to say something, do something, that will confirm that this was a good idea. A brilliant idea. An idea we should have a million iterations of over the next few weeks.

But I'm scared that if I say anything—move even a muscle—I'll pop this bubble. I'll wake up from this dream and Pepper will disappear and that . . .

Well, that simply cannot happen.

Because the sex was so great. Obviously. No, like, emotional reason. Or whatever.

But a misplaced ooze of panic seeps through me at the idea that this won't happen again and it's just that Pepper's breathing has started to even out and she no longer feels like a boneless mass next to me but kind of tense and like maybe she's realizing this was a mistake and—

"Do you still want to do the competition?"

I turn my head, blinking at Pepper. Her eyebrows are furrowed in question as she continues staring up at the ceiling, lost to some completely other phase of reality.

"Is post-nut clarity giving you second thoughts?"

Pepper's gaze flicks to me, eyes tracing over my face. "Sorry, I have a feeling that was a totally inappropriate question to ask after . . ."

"Fucking each other senseless?"

Pepper's face scrunches up. "How poetic."

I laugh, deep and throaty, a laugh that can push away all

the other odd feelings trying to clamber up my throat. Then I lean in and kiss Pepper. Soft and light.

"I'll do the competition with you," I whisper against her lips. In a way that is totally devoid of feeling and intimacy. Obviously.

I pull back, then sit up, tucking my knees to my chest as I search for my clothes, feeling oddly modest after what just happened, another slosh of panic filling my chest. But it won't do me any good to lie in bed with Pepper, collecting those smiles of hers while the sun frames her head like a goddamn halo.

Pepper sits up too, nodding. "Great."

"Great."

"And this was . . ."

"Great." A long pause as I gather the nerve to look at her. "And for you?"

Pepper's face wrecks me. Earnest, hesitant smile. Glowing cheeks. Hair mussed from where I fisted it. "Really great," she whispers. Soft and sweet and rather devastating. "Already looking forward to next time."

And I nod.

Slip out of bed.

Grab my clothes.

And dart from the room.

Leaving every almost-feeling that threatened to consume me in that moment on the bed next to her.

Chapter 21

OPAL

"The weekend went by too fast." Olivia pouts before popping the last bite of biscuit in her mouth. "I'm tempted to move here myself." She waves her arm around toward the main strip of West Asheville where I met her and Ophelia for brunch before they head home this afternoon.

"You *should*," I say, leaning forward. "It's not like work is keeping you tied to Charlotte." Olivia is a journalist and can pretty much do her job wherever.

"No way I could afford it. Not all of us win the lottery."

"Not to get all Elton John, but I'll buy a big house where we all can live." I waggle my eyebrows at my sisters.

"Opal, have you ever heard of savings and money management? Just curious."

I stick my tongue out at Ophelia. "You should be nicer to me, I might be your last hope at property ownership in this lifetime."

"Might? I gave up on the idea of owning a home when I was ten," she shoots back. "You, my dear, are my *only* hope. And that's a rather terrifying idea."

"So it's settled. You'll both move down here and I'll buy us a mountain mansion and we'll live out our days listening to *folklore* and lying in fields of overgrown grass reading June Jordan poems."

"Sounds pretty gay. I'm in," Ophelia says.

"Think you're forgetting the tiny little problem of already having invested most of your winnings into a flower farm being run by a ridiculously gorgeous woman with a penchant for dungarees who is going to take years to buy you out. But yeah, let's go be forest nymphs with no income flow."

"Party pooper," I say, crumpling up my napkin and tossing it at Olivia. I hate that she's right. I'm as lost as ever and in a hole so deep, I'm having trouble tracking the light. But even in this tangled disaster I feel . . . content.

I know I should want to have a plan and a checklist and know exactly when and how I'm going to actually get my fresh start. But, I find it kind of hard to care. I *like* living on the farm. I like my tiny room and my even tinier shed. I like my crabby roommate and her group of friends I'm trying to force to be my own. For once, I don't have that nagging itch in the back of my mind that there's something else I should be doing, somewhere else I should be, a different person living a better life.

This one I have is a mess, but it makes me happy.

Or a chump.

I guess time will tell.

"And to stay on brand, we better hit the road," Olivia says with a glance at her watch and an exaggerated frown.

My lip wobbles a bit as I smile at them. "Thank you for coming down. I miss you two so much."

"Don't get sappy, Opie," Ophelia says, blinking rapidly as she looks up at the ceiling. I kick her under the table.

We draw out our goodbyes for another five minutes before Olivia steps fully into big sister mode, pushing Ophelia into the passenger seat and revving the engine. I wave as they pull away.

I drag my feet to my own car. I stare out the windshield as the engine idles, pulled by conflicting urges to zip home as fast as possible or putz around here for the rest of the day. I haven't seen Pepper since I left her bed last night, and I feel almost feverish with the anticipation of our paths crossing.

I didn't sleep at all, staring up at the ceiling, ears pricked for the tiniest squeak of a sound in the cabin, some desperate knot of hope that maybe Pepper couldn't sleep either. That maybe she was kept up thinking of me. Of what we'd done.

Bitch apparently slept like a rock.

She woke up with the sunrise like usual, and I watched from my window as she loaded up her van with buckets of flowers to sell at the farmers market she had a booth at every Sunday.

I was tempted to meet her on the lawn, walk across the dewy grass with the golden sun poised behind me à la Matthew Macfadyen sluttily strutting in *Pride & Prejudice* (2005). But fear that I'd be bothering her, disrupting her flow by inserting myself and probably saying something stupid, kept me trapped on my bed until the dirt of the driveway settled after she pulled away.

Which is all so ridiculous and melodramatic and very much the old Opal and not the new and improved Opal.

Because I can do this. I can have sex without emotions. Just because I've never been able to successfully separate feelings from hooking up with somebody before doesn't mean I can't now. I can have a no-strings-attached arrangement and thoroughly enjoy myself and ignore that jagged, achy void in my chest every time I need to feel close to someone. It's called growth, dammit.

I need to get over myself. I can't avoid Pepper forever— we have a lot of work ahead of us with the competition, and helping her win brings me one step closer to her buying me out. And then I'll be able to have my fresh start for real. Plus, avoiding her throws a wrench in the whole us-having-sex thing, which I'm really, *really* looking forward to.

With a sigh, I throw the car in drive and wind my way through the mountains back to the house.

•   •   •

"This was a mistake," Pepper says, appearing in my shed doorway out of thin air a few hours later. I jump so hard I tip over an ink bottle, all of it oozing across a leather bag I was working on.

I groan, tossing it aside. I'll try to fix it later, but my creative well is so bone dry I can't be bothered to deal with it right now. I've actually had a pretty great response to posting my first few listings on my Etsy shop, but something about people actually *wanting* my work has my brain shriveling up the second I sit down and try to create. It's times like this that a drink sounds its best; something to blur out that booming voice of doubt and give me enough false confidence that I can make something clever and important.

"A massive mistake," Pepper repeats, now pacing the length of the shed.

Not the nicest way to be greeted by the woman you recently agreed to hook up with, I'll admit it.

She digs her hands in her pockets as she moves, puffs of white flowers spinning like tops between her active fingers when she pulls them out. My entire body sears hot as the wind pushes the scent of chamomile toward me.

"Good to see you too, Pepper. How's the freak-out?" I ask, blotting up the rest of the ink that landed on my desk.

She shoots me a dirty look. "Great, thanks. I love a good Sunday spiral."

I huff. "Listen. If this is about last night, let's just talk it through. Get on the same page."

Pepper stops in her tracks, tilting her head as she looks at me. "Last night?"

She continues to stare at me, that blank look causing mortification to pierce through me. Awesome. Amazing. Love that I've spent the past twenty hours thinking about nothing but our mind-blowing hookup and she's already forgotten it.

I point an accusatory finger in the general direction of the cabin's second floor, and she follows the gesture.

"Us having sex?" she says, turning back to me. "What's there to talk about? We set up our rules and the first trial was a success. Are we not on the same page about that?"

Right. Of course. Pepper hasn't been thinking about it because she's not tied up into knots fist-fighting feelings like me. Because we agreed not to have any.

"No, yeah. Of course we're on the same page," I mumble, digging the toe of my sandal into the rough floor.

"I'm talking about the competition. I sent in our application to participate today. And the second I did, I realized what an absolute shit show it's going to be."

"And why's that again?" I ask, unable to bite back my smile. I didn't know pessimism could be so endearing.

"Oh, let's see. As far as I know, neither of us have done something like this before, my yield won't be nearly big enough to put it all together, and I have absolutely no idea what we'd make even if we *did* have enough resources to pull it off. I'm stretched thin enough as it is, I shouldn't be adding more to my plate."

"I can help you pick the flowers," I offer meekly.

"It's not just about picking them," she says, raking her hands through her long hair. "It's about having enough bloom at the right time to keep them fresh for the day of the event while still fulfilling orders. My plots are staggered to try and cut back waste." She hangs her head, sucking in a deep breath. "What it boils down to is I'm not prepared to take on something like this. I'm not sure I'm even prepared to be running this damn farm."

Her lips twist with anxiety as she continues to fidget, and my heart cracks in half at how hopeless she looks. I'd give anything to snap my fingers and take that worry away.

"Do you want to hang out with me?" I ask, the words crawling out before I can think better of them.

My question stops her in her tracks, head whipping to me. "What do you mean?"

I tug on my hair. A few strands break off. Love my life so much.

"I don't know. Like . . . go somewhere? Into town, maybe? Or just . . . anything? My brain is getting itchy and I need a change of scenery."

"Itchy?"

I wave away the question. "Do you want to come or not?"

"Opal, I'm slowly suffocating under an avalanche of a to-do list and problems to figure out. Were you even listening?"

I slide off my stool and pad toward her. Her eyes grow wide as an owl's as I pop into her personal space. She makes a move like she wants to step back, but I grab her before she can.

And wrap her in a big hug.

"Of course I was listening to you," I say, arms cinched around her waist, my cheek landing in the center of her sternum. "And what I heard is you need to get out and clear your head. So let's go. We can brainstorm ideas for the piece if it will help."

Pepper's breathing is short and sharp for a moment. I hug her tighter. Nestle closer.

She sighs and every muscle melts as the tension eases.

Slowly, she wraps her arms around my shoulders. Hugging me back.

"Okay," she whispers, chin resting on the top of my head.

My smile presses into the front of her overalls. "Great. I'll drive."

Chapter 22

PEPPER

It's a bit of a shame I let Opal drive, since this trip into town is apparently how I'm going to die.

This woman is either an adrenaline junkie or has no concept of how fast she's hurtling us down a mountain in the tin can she calls a car. She's so close to the guardrails I'd be surprised if her speed isn't whipping off the reflectors. She takes a hairpin turn on the parkway and my stomach is left behind, free-falling into the valley below.

I'd say something—yell at her to slow down—but my skull is plastered to the headrest from the sheer g-force she's generating, and opening my mouth isn't particularly feasible at this point.

I'm not even sure why I agreed to this.

I don't like going anywhere—everything I need is right there in the safety of my sweet little home—but there's this

awful . . . *pull* in the center of my chest whenever Opal talks
to me, and it tugs me toward her.

Clearly a fatal mistake.

"Oooh, look! Antique shop! Let's check it out."

Opal makes the sharpest turn known to automotive history,
crossing three lanes of traffic to skid into the gravel driveway of
Aunt Gertie's Goods & Antiques. It's a miracle she didn't ram
straight through the front door. I swear, Opal bounces out of
the car before it's even come to a complete stop.

"Don't dawdle, Pepper. We're on a mission."

Proving Newton's first law of motion, she bolts into the
store before I can blink.

"Fucking nutter," I mumble, unbuckling my seat belt and
uncurling my fear-stiffened limbs from the tiny death trap.

I half expect the shop to be in ruins when I step inside,
Opal spinning around like the Tasmanian Devil, but there's a
hushed peace to the place, tinny bluegrass music playing from
distant speakers and a few older people browsing nearby glass
displays of jewelry.

It takes me a few minutes, but I finally find her, kneeling
as she quietly digs through a box of old tools in a far corner of
the shop. Next to her is a small pile of old iron nails, a pair of
pliers with exaggeratedly curved teeth, and a few woodworking
tools lined next to it.

"Opal?"

Her face lifts, a wide smile breaking across her full cheeks.
"Hiya! Find anything good yet?"

"Um . . . what are we looking for exactly?" I ask, eyeing the wall of hammers behind her.

"Nothing in particular," she says, attention fixed back on the box.

"What's all this?" I gesture at the random crap she has laid out.

She frowns as she looks at it, then up at me. "It's tools, Pepper."

"I know that," I say. "What are you going to do with them?"

Opal shrugs, smiles again. "Don't quite know yet. But they're too pretty to leave behind, that's for sure."

It's my turn to frown, trying to find anything pretty in the sharp-looking metal. "I thought you said we're on a mission."

"We are," Opal answers, finally shelving the box she was working on and grabbing another.

"Doesn't a mission need a purpose?" I say, throwing my arms out.

"This mission's purpose is to get my Silly Putty brain to stop being so apathetic and instead light up with creativity and endless amazing ideas to paint on shoes and also make flower art." She says all of this like it should be perfectly obvious.

"And those rusty nails are doing it for you?"

"A good nail always does it for me," she says, eyes darting up to meet mine as she gives me a lecherous grin.

It makes me furious that I laugh at such a dumb joke. But I do.

I laugh so hard, my eyes start to water, sides aching with it.

I'm still laughing as I sit down on the dusty floor next to this bizarre fiend, resting my shaking shoulders on the shelf behind me.

"Damn. That really landed. I'm proud of myself."

"Trust me, I don't mean to encourage you here," I choke out between giggles, trying to pull myself together.

Opal bites her lip as she looks at me, that sinfully full mouth kicking up at the sides. "It's working anyway."

That half smile of hers drains all the laughter out of me, and I'm left wanting nothing more than to press my lips against hers in the vain hope that some of her light will flood into me.

But before the thought can get any more ridiculous, she turns away, scuttling down the aisle to a row of shoe boxes overflowing with papers.

Like the sucker I am, I follow after her.

She flicks through a box of postcards, eyes darting like lightning as she scans worn drawings and scribbled cursive.

"I always hope I'll find a love letter in one of these," she says, switching to a new shoe box. "Something achy and hopeful and a tiny bit desperate to express how much the recipient means to the writer."

Something hot glows through me, making my skin prickle and chest stretch. I realize, after a moment, it's longing. For what, I don't know.

Whatever it is, it's ridiculous and pointless. I don't have anything to long for. I push the feeling far away, knotting it all up into a ball in my stomach, then kicking it out. I'm granite. Marble. A statue. Solid and unfeeling, no emotions cracking through me. Exactly as I should be to stay safe and whole.

"Or find one that's super dirty. Someone really putting their whole heart and pussy into a four-by-six rectangle of cardstock."

"Charming," I say, that scary hot feeling snuffed out. Unfortunately, it's replaced by something like glee at this ridiculous woman's ramblings—equally as brilliant and distracting.

"It's honestly such a power move to raw dog the mail system like that. Put it all out there with nary an envelope to protect your horniest thoughts."

"You're extremely weird," I blurt out. I realize this is probably a bit harsh, but it's also true.

Opal grins. "Took you this long to realize, Pep? Little slow on the uptake, I see."

"No. I've known that since you pulled up like a pink-haired monster and told me you wanted to paint shoes for a living. I guess I'm just now realizing that I kind of like it." My hand darts to my throat like I can clamp around it and stop those disastrous words that tumbled out of me.

Too honest. Too scary. Too dangerous. When you share soft spots like that with people, they'll only take advantage of them. And something about Opal is making me nothing but soft spots.

Opal studies me, her face open and curious. I turn away, squirming under the intensity of her focus. Out of the corner of my eye, I see her lean closer.

"That might be the nicest thing you've ever said to me," she whispers.

I snort. "Tell me I'm an asshole without telling me I'm an asshole."

Opal chuckles, then falls silent.

I hear her suck in a breath, and I brace myself for her to say something more, to poke and prod at my confession until I'm bruised from it, finding all the ways she can break me down with it.

But instead, she reaches out to me—opening her hand like a flower unfurling its petals to the sun.

I stare at it. The ink stains and calluses and chipped nails and bitten cuticles.

For a moment, that hand looks like a second chance. A lifeline.

Then I blink.

And her hand is just her hand and I'm a fool.

I pat my palm against hers in a weak attempt at a high five, then move down the aisle.

After a moment, Opal follows, discovering a box of old photos to rummage through.

Thankfully, she lets the silence linger until the tension of the previous moment evaporates, cooling us down.

"Do you ever wonder if you'll end up in one of these boxes?" I ask, watching her pull out a grainy black-and-white picture of a solemn-faced woman standing in her front yard, studying it close. I used to love silence more than oxygen, but for some unhinged reason, I like noise when it's coming from Opal. "A photo of you crammed into a shoe box with hundreds of others, random people flicking through?"

Opal tilts her head, putting the picture back into the stack and dragging the pad of her thumb over the softened edges of the others. "I don't know. I kind of hope so."

"Really?" I purse my lips, bringing a faded snapshot of two little kids holding hands and grimacing at the camera close to my face. "Doesn't it seem sad? All these memories given away for strangers to gawk at."

Opal scrunches up her nose. "Nah. I hope photos of me end up scattered in ratty boxes all over the place. And I hope I look ridiculously happy in every single one. I hope they make people stop their flipping to look closer. To wonder what I had to be so happy about."

"What *do* you have to be so happy about?" I ask, staring at that magnetic smile of hers that always draws me in. It's pure sunshine, warmth radiating from the crooked corners.

She shakes her head and shrugs. "Nothing in particular, I guess. Happy for happiness's sake."

Air whooshes out of me, and I feel light-headed, my stomach twisting as I continue to look at her smile. I really need her to stop saying such lovely things with that full and gorgeous mouth if I'm going to refrain from kissing her in public. We don't have an explicit rule against that, but the choppy sea of emotions in my chest leads me to believe it would be just as bad as breaking the others.

Opal is oblivious, thumbing through more photos, pulling out a few and adding them to her growing pile of crap.

"Come along, Pepper," she says, moving to the next aisle. "There's an entire acre of junk to explore."

Chapter 23

OPAL

"You're Marie Kondo's worst nightmare," Pepper tells me after we finally Tetris all the stuff I bought into my tiny car.

"Au contraire, Pepper," I say with the world's cringiest French accent. "That bitch—affectionate—loves mess. I'd be her dream come true."

We get into the car and I start the engine. Since my legs are so short, my seat is always set far forward, but we had to move the passenger seat all the way up to accommodate my treasures, and Pepper's long legs are folded into her chest, shins pressing against the glove box.

"Don't forget your seat belt," I say, throwing the car in reverse. I can't see out my rear window so I'm relying on hope and a prayer for a few seconds.

"I feel like I need full body armor when it comes to your driving," she mumbles, securing the strap across her chest.

I click my tongue against my teeth. "So dramatic. I'm an excellent driver."

"I saw my life pass before my eyes at least six times on the drive here."

"Yeah? Any good memories sticking out?"

"Getting my appendix out when I was seven really left a mark, I guess."

"Ugh, Pepper, I set you up so perfectly there and you completely squandered it."

"Excuse me?"

"That was a prime segue for a suave and sexy *last night left quite the impression* line that would then flow oh so casually to you asking me to rock your world again this evening, but instead you go with *appendicitis*? We need to work on your flirting skills."

I risk a glance at Pepper as she squirms in her seat, splotches of red climbing up her neck and cheeks to the tips of her ears. "Don't hold your breath on that. I don't have a suave or sexy cell in my body, trust me."

"Last night certainly left a different impression. See? See how easy that was? You try now."

"New subject, please."

"Would you like me to transition into the art of dirty talk? Would that be satisfactory?"

"What are you going to do with all this stuff anyway?" she says, ignoring me while her face glows red. She scowls at the one-eyed doll perched on my lap. I stroke its hair.

"I'm going to look at these treasures and smile as I remember what a great time I had messing with you," I answer honestly, pulling off the parkway to one of the long dirt roads that winds toward the cabin.

Pepper snorts. "You're incorrigible."

"Ooh, so close," I coo. "But flirting tends to lean more toward compliments and less toward insults."

"Not the way I do it."

I slam on the brakes, and Pepper jerks forward, hands slapping against the dash.

"What the hell happened?" she shrieks.

I throw the car in park, then launch my torso over the divider, grabbing her cheeks in both my hands and placing a thorough kiss on her parted lips. It takes her a moment, but she softens, leaning into my touch. Kissing me back.

I continue to sip at her lips until her breath comes short, hands curling and uncurling from where they're fisted on her thighs. With a tiny laugh, I pull my mouth away, resting my forehead to hers.

"What was that for?" she asks, eyes closed and breathing still jagged.

"For your first decent flirting line," I say, dragging my lips against hers again. "I'm very impressed. Quick learners get rewarded."

Pepper laughs, opening her eyes just so I can watch her roll them.

"You're the worst," she says, pulling away and pressing her cheek to the fogged window.

"An absolute *monster*," I agree with a grin, putting the car in drive and continuing along the road.

A few minutes later, I pull into the gravel driveway, following the end of the path until we reach the squat cabin, golden light glowing from a few windows.

Night has firmly settled in for the evening, cool and inky black, thousands of stars visible in this slice of the mountains. I cut the engine, the sound of cicadas humming in the darkness.

The moment tiptoes from comfortable to awkward as we continue to sit there, both suddenly shy as the possibilities of what can happen inside crook a finger and beckon us in. I'm about to say something to break the growing tension, but Pepper steals all words from my mouth, reaching out and taking my hand, braiding our fingers together.

The gesture is so soft and comfortable, my throat constricts and something sharp pokes at my eyes.

"Tonight was really fun," she whispers, eyes fixed on our hands. "Thank you for getting me off the farm to clear my head. I needed it."

"My pleasure," I murmur, leaning over the center console and brushing my lips against her cheek, her jaw. She turns, seeking out a kiss, mouth sure and strong as she leans into me.

We continue kissing, squirming until we're pressed together, fingers tangled in each other's hair. I send up a silent prayer that none of mine breaks off in her hands.

Pepper kisses me in a way I never knew I needed to be kissed. She's a little clumsy, a lot enthusiastic, lips silky smooth and tongue hot as she explores my mouth.

She kisses like she needs me.

It rewires my circuits, every nerve sparking at her touch, every pulse point beating in a rhythm of want.

And I kiss her back like I need her.

"Should we go inside?" I ask, nipping at her lip. "The night doesn't have to be over."

I feel her smile stretch against mine. "Yeah. Okay," she whispers. "I can afford to stop stressing for a few more hours. But come morning, it'll be full force. I'm giving you fair warning."

I chuckle, but something twinges in my chest. I look into her gingerbread eyes, tucking a strand of her hair behind her ear. "Right. Why worry today when you can bottle it up until tomorrow?"

"Maybe I could avoid worrying altogether if we forget the competition idea," she whispers, scrunching up her nose.

I pull back. "What?"

Pepper shrugs. "I don't know. I've been thinking about it, and while it's a nice idea in theory, maybe I was too rash with deciding to do it."

"Rash? You sat on the idea forever. I've never seen someone less rash."

Pepper's eyebrows furrow, but she waves a flippant hand at me. "I don't think you get what a huge commitment this will be. Resources, product, time, investment in materials—"

"I get it, Pepper. It's going to be a lot. That's why I offered to help you."

"Why are you getting so mad?" she says, color rising on her

cheeks. It's not the soft, rosy color of desire from before. This is deep red. Angry.

"You're just being so wishy-washy," I yell, throwing my hands in the air. "It's frustrating."

"Why do you even care?" she yells back. "It's not like any of this really impacts you in the long run, does it? You'll get your money or you'll kick me to the curb. It's not like you're invested, so who are you to question my decisions?"

Embarrassment slices through me like a knife. I open and close my mouth a few times, trying to find something— anything—to say. But she's right. I don't necessarily have skin in the game. It shouldn't bother me one fucking bit if Pepper goes back and forth on the decision for the rest of her life. But this thing—us working together, trying together—it's something I can *offer* her. My art is one of the few things I'm good at. I've disrupted and destabilized her entire life with my impulsive decision to buy this place; the least I can do is try to help her. But she's taking that chance away.

"What are you so afraid of, Pepper?" I ask, crossing my arms over my chest, pinning her with my glare.

Her eyebrows lift. "What do you mean?"

"With the farm. And the competition. Everything. You're terrified of trying. I want to understand why."

"You don't know me," she spits, face twisting in anger. She holds my gaze for a moment longer, then drops her eyes.

"Excuse me?"

"You don't know me," she repeats, face stony and stare fixed out the windshield. "And what I do is none of your damn business. You don't get to spend a few weeks with me and pretend like you care. Like you want to fix me. I'm not broken."

A fist of guilt clenches around my gut, and I wish I could take every word back, erase the past few minutes. "I never said you are. That's not what I meant. I—"

"Why don't you focus on your shoes and your bags and your mountain of antique crap and stop trying to psychoanalyze me, okay? We don't mean anything to each other so let's not pretend."

Pepper undoes her seat belt, tumbling out of the car and storming into the house. The bang of the door as she slams it behind her echoes around me.

And I stay sitting in my shitty car with my shitty stuff and my shittier mouth, regret pulling me down from the inside out.

Chapter 24

OPAL

I can tell I'm in a bad mental place because, instead of making eye contact with myself in the bathroom mirror this morning, I grab a pair of scissors.

And proceed to annihilate any remaining shreds of dignity I have left.

I let out a groan of regret as the last broken clump of hair falls.

Okay. This is fine. This is so fine. I can be a person who pulls off bangs. Just because the past ten years of experimenting with them have ended in a mad spiral of self-loathing doesn't mean this time will be a problem.

With a shaky breath, I evaluate the damage.

It's . . . it's pretty bad. I can't say it's necessarily worse than White-Hair-Gate, but the fact that both are existing at the same moment has a rather horrifying effect.

I was aiming for a shaggy fringe look but went too short,

and the fried strands are stick straight and standing forward like they're held up with static from a balloon.

Okay. Again, totally fine. I can fix this. Maybe a color change will help . . . I don't know, round out this disaster of a look? I clomp to my room, digging through my boxes of dyes.

Because I learn from my mistakes, thank you very much, I grab a tub of Lime Crime *temporary* hair dye, which apparently won't damage my hair any further. Small mercies. I skim the directions, then glob it on, setting a timer for half an hour. I slump on the edge of my bed, staring at the wall, entering the worst mental place in the world: alone time with my thoughts.

Guilt chews me up, gnawing at my soft heart and hard head. I hate myself for being so mean to Pepper last night. Honestly, who am I to call someone wishy-washy? It takes me at least nine hours to decide on something to stream on Netflix.

I just . . . I want this thing with Pepper to *work*. I want to team up on this competition and show her I can do it. I want to live with her without driving her to an early grave. I want to be her . . .

I want to be her friend.

But like with everything else in my life, I overreacted. I latched onto an idea like a raccoon digging through trash and became rabid when even the smallest thing challenged it. And now I'm sitting here with fucked bangs and swollen eyes from crying in frustration all night, hating everything.

I wish I could lose myself in a distraction (other than my hair), but my brain is spinning and twirling and leaping from thought to thought, leaving me a queasy mess as I fail to keep up. I tried sketching last night and painting this morning, but my hands won't work, won't translate any of the feelings eating me whole into art, my mind wandering far and wide.

The harsh trill of my alarm cuts through my dissociation, and I stare at my phone for another minute before shoring up the energy to turn it off. With a sigh, I trudge back to the bathroom and rinse out my hair.

After drying it, I give it another look.

It's not much better. I was hoping for a Sailor Neptune vibe but ended up a mix between Cosmo from *The Fairly OddParents* and Greta the Gremlin.

Cute.

With a defeated sigh, I flick off the lights in the bathroom and head back to my room. I stare at my messy bed in the doorway for a while, tempted to fall face-first on the mattress, pull my sheets over my head, and lie there in my stale stench of self-pity until the cloud clears. Or until the next cloud replaces it.

Actually, what I'd rather do is drive to the store, buy a box of wine, and drink straight from the spigot while I lie in bed until my thoughts are fuzzy and ticklish and my tongue is heavy and unusable. The idea is a delicious itch, a vibrant need that permeates through my skin to grate against bone. It's the overwhelming, teeth-gritting confusion of wanting both stimulation and numbness, any source of oblivion that makes it easier to exist in my head. The need to flee my own unbearable thoughts, mute every feeling trying to bubble through me. Because it's all so sharp and real, and numbness is much easier to deal with.

The hunger of it hurts, shooting panic through me. And medicating myself with nicotine and weed and alcohol is the easiest way to satiate it.

I used to indulge it without a second thought—taking so much, enough, that I'd feel like I got to a very human baseline, everyone else's normal. But the problem with a quick fix like drinks or cigarettes is how fast the numbness wears off. The shitty taste in your mouth from your own disappointment, the achy shame that you can't regulate yourself like everyone around you can. The vicious loop of self-sabotage.

For the most part, I push all this buzzing, itching need through my hands. Into my art. My racing thoughts vibrating through me and out to the tip of my brush or my fingers molding clay. Little bits of me and all this chaos in my brain live in every piece I've created. Art is the vice I let myself chase.

But right now, the art isn't coming. I'm blocked and frustrated and want to pull my (atrocious) hair out.

Slowly, I slide my keys along the top of my dresser, playing with them, listening to their tinkle as I twirl the ring around my finger.

Maybe it wouldn't be the worst thing to run to the store. I'll pick up some junk food. Maybe even a block of good cheese. A dip and some pretzels.

And a bottle of wine . . . No more than two.

I'll spread them out. Totally acceptable.

I grip my keys firmly, the metal teeth digging into my

palm, ready to turn and head down the stairs, straight to my car before the shame can catch me.

But just as I move to take a step, the clouds outside the window shift, a rectangular shaft of sun slicing through the pane, straight to the mirror.

The room is dipped in gold, burnished light dripping down the walls.

And something about it locks my ankles in place and lifts my chin to the light. To the window. It's bright and shimmering and turns something over in my chest, dislodges a stone and lets the flood rush out.

Sometimes I hate myself. I hate my meekness and my boldness. I hate my fear and my audacity to try. Sometimes the hate digs its roots in so deep, it feels like it *is* me.

I hate that hate. I have endless grace for everyone in the world, but none for myself. Why am I not allowed to make mistakes? Why does my compassion stretch to strangers but stop at my own front door?

A few silly tears fall down my cheeks. And it's all so ridiculous because why am I crying? Why am I feeling so much and all at once? All I know is that life is hard and it's lonely and feelings are sharp and big and somehow we're supposed to spend every day of our life facing them.

With the sunlight streaming through my room, I decide, at least for this moment, to shed that self-loathing, lift its claws from around my throat.

I march to the window, throwing it open as far as it will go.

The warmth of the day curls around me, coaxing me outside with its softness.

I raise my face to the sun, drowning in the light seeping through my closed eyelids, letting the heat kiss my cheeks. After a few deep breaths, in and out, I smile, opening my eyes.

It takes me a few moments of blinking and adjusting to the brightness, but I eventually see Pepper in the distance, long limbs extended as she pulls a bag of soil toward a plot of flowers.

And my feet are no longer my own; they carry me down the stairs in a flurry of stomps and squeaks, across the lawn, until I'm running barefoot toward her.

By the time I make it to her, I'm out of breath, panting as she stares at me with a frightened expression.

It's probably for the best I can't breathe; in my rush to reach her, I didn't gather a plan of what I want to say.

"What did you do to your hair?" she finally asks, eyes wide and fixed on my forehead.

"Honestly, Pepper, I would think you'd be used to the synthetic colors by now," I wheeze.

"I mean . . . I am. Kind of. But this is . . ."

"Super cute and approachable?"

"I was going to say a bold choice." She takes a step closer to me. "It looks like a monstera leaf."

"Sweet of you. Thanks," I say with a grimace, fluffing up the chin-length strands.

"What prompted this . . . decision?" she asks, reaching out and following a green strand to its end.

"Doesn't matter." I catch her wrist. I grip her hand between both of mine, bringing it to the center of my chest.

Her lips fall open as she looks at our hands. I give her palm a squeeze, hoping she'll look at me. This would be so much easier if she'd look at me.

"I'm sorry," I say, my voice hoarse. "I'm sorry I hurt you."

Her eyes slowly trace up to meet mine, widening further. I'm at risk of falling into her stare, drowning in those light brown eyes. I was wrong; this is actually way harder with her looking at me.

"I don't have an excuse or an explanation or even a qualifier," I continue. "I'm just sorry. And I hope you can forgive me. Because I don't like you being mad at me, and I don't like making you mad at me even more." I swallow, the pad of my thumb tracing the knobs of her knuckles. I clear my throat. "So, um, can we talk?"

Pepper stares at me, face falling into something unreadable. And she slips her hand from mine.

She clears her throat, mouth a stern line and eyebrows furrowed. She's mad. And she has every right to be. But that doesn't stop it from breaking my heart into a million pieces anyway.

She takes a deep breath. Then another. "No one's ever said that to me before," she whispers. I watch her swallow. "That they're sorry they've hurt me."

"That seems . . . not right."

Pepper shakes her head like she's trying to shake off a jitter.

"Thank you," she says after a moment, voice rough. "I . . . That means a lot."

"Can I . . . Will you let me help you? Or at least help you figure out what to do?" I gesture vaguely at the flowers around us.

Pepper reaches into the pocket of her grass-stained jeans, pulling out a sprig of flowers. "Okay," she whispers, twirling the plant between her fingers. "Maybe you can start by helping me here?" She waves at the plot next to us, flowers of blue and pink and purple waving in the sun.

"Sure. Every garden needs a hoe, right?" I say back. "Tell me where to start."

Pepper's lips part as she looks at me, then they stretch into a smile. "Okay."

She hands me an extra pair of shears, explaining that I should keep the stem long and cut at an angle, removing any leaves that will be below the water before depositing them in one of the buckets sitting in the grass.

While it seems pretty self-explanatory and basically the same thing I did that day with Diksha, my hands still tremble as she watches me make my first few cuts. When I look at her, wide-eyed and desperate for approval, she smiles like I discovered buried treasure.

"Perfect," she says, grabbing her own shears and going to work next to me.

We trim in silence for a while, the sun stroking its fingers down my neck and across my shoulders. It's nice at first, but then I start sweating, back muscles cramping from my kneeling position in the dirt.

Despite the twinges of discomfort, I feel . . . happy. Good. My hands are comfortably busy as they play in the dirt, my mind still, and my heart—

My heart isn't a participant in this moment because feelings aren't a factor in harvesting flowers in peaceful silence with Pepper.

"I really do think we can do the competition," I tell Pepper as we fill another bucket with snapdragons. "I'm not bullshitting you when I say I want to help."

Pepper glances at me. "I believe you," she says, a drag of wind lifting a few loose strands of her hair. "It's just very overwhelming for me. Life in general kind of is. It takes me an obscene amount of time to wrap my head around a new idea, a change in routine. I don't even feel like it's indecision, when it comes down to it. It's more that I physically and mentally don't feel capable of starting something new."

I stare at Pepper, the way the sun creates a halo around her. "Maybe that's how I can help," I say, setting down my shears and wiping some sweat from my forehead. "I have no issues diving into something headfirst without a second thought. It's the seeing-things-through part that kills me."

Pepper snorts. "My polar opposite."

"Maybe we can use it to our advantage," I say, bouncing up and down on my heels from my kneeling position. "I'll bulldoze our way into it, and you create the refinement for us to finish it."

She eyes me from tip to toe, and my skin heats under her gaze.

"What the hell," she says, throwing her hands up and smiling at me. "Might as well go for it. I apologize for being a neurotic mess during it in advance."

"Right back atcha," I say, giggling.

"I still have concerns about how we'll get a big enough yield to make anything worthwhile," Pepper says, nibbling her bottom lip.

"I was thinking about it last night, actually. What if we spend these weeks leading up to it drying some flowers? I checked the rules and regulations, and dry flowers are permissible as long as fresh flowers make up the majority of the design."

"That's actually not a horrendous idea."

"Your shock does amazing things for my ego."

She ignores my sarcasm, eyes glazed over as she looks across the field, deep in thought.

"That could work," she says after a few minutes, slipping back into reality. There's an energy humming off her skin, a fresh batch of faith I've never seen on her before.

"It *will* work," I say, reaching out and booping her nose with my dirt-coated finger. It pulls a giggle from her.

"What will we make?" she asks, going back to her pruning.

"The theme is Love in Bloom, right? That's fairly vague and cliché."

We both harvest flowers in quiet contemplation for a few minutes.

"We could make a flower from the flowers?" Pepper throws out.

"That seems a bit . . . on the nose."

Pepper shakes her head. "Ugh. I know. I have trouble not taking things literally."

"What about a couple embracing? Bodies intertwined as they kiss? We could even create a bed of roses or something."

She giggles like a little girl hearing the word *penis* on the playground. "Too daring for the folks at *Something Blue,* I imagine. We could do . . . uh . . . a big heart?" Pepper traces the shape in the air with her fingers.

"Okay. Well. We can keep thinking."

She rips up a few blades of grass and tosses them at me.

"We could re-create various iconic Taylor Swift outfits. Nothing says love like Taylor Swift."

"Aren't a lot of her songs about heartbreak?"

"Absolutely do not get me started, Pepper," I warn, leaning close with a menacing look. Her eyes widen. After a moment, I shoot her a wink.

I move to position myself farther down the row, but I stub my toe on a hidden rock in the process, letting out a tiny *yip* of pain.

"Are you okay?" Pepper says, darting to my side. Her eyes widen as she notices my bare feet. "Where are your shoes?" she scolds, fixing me with a stern look.

"Sorry, Mom," I say, rubbing the joint.

Her scowl deepens. "You should always wear closed-toe shoes while gardening," she says, eyes scouring over me like she's trying to sniff out any other injuries I've suffered picking flowers.

"I'll survive," I tell her, laughing at her over-the-top concern.

After another moment of analysis, she pushes to stand. "Wait here."

Before I can respond, she's marching toward the house, hips swaying. I'll admit it, I admire (ogle) the view.

The organ in my chest that shall not be named squeezes at the pure joy of spending time in the morning sun with Pepper.

Which is ridiculous.

And dangerous.

And not a *thing*.

But as I look at the happy faces of the flowers next me, a silly, Pollyanna impulse has me picking one of the blooms and holding it close to my chest.

I pluck off a petal.

She likes me.

I'm a sucker.

I pluck off another petal.

She likes me not . . .

An absolute fool.

She likes me . . .

I pluck three more . . .

She likes me not . . .

"What are you doing?"

"Nothing!" I shout, shoving my hands behind my back like a child caught at the cookie jar, Pepper looming over me.

She looks at me skeptically. I grimace back from my spot in the dirt, face beet red and green hair curling with sweat at my temples. "What'd you get?" I say, nodding at her full hands.

A tiny burst of color spreads across Pepper's sharp cheekbones. Instead of answering, she plops a navy bucket hat on my head and deposits a pair of yellow Crocs in front of me.

"What's this?" I ask, rolling my head until I can see her under the large bill.

"A hat." She moves back to her spot in the plot.

"Why'd you give it to me?"

"You . . . Your cheeks are getting red," she grumbles, picking up her shears and getting to work. My heart balloons.

"And these lovely things?" I say, grabbing the Crocs by the heels and waving them around.

"Like I said, you can't be working out here without some sort of foot protection."

I notice her own pink pair.

"They're clean," she adds, eyes fixed on the flowers. "I've never worn them. They sent me a size too small. So you can, er, have them. I guess. If they fit. Or whatever."

I slip them on. They're at least two sizes too big. "They're perfect," I say, clacking my toes together.

Pepper glances at them, color darkening on her cheeks, then shoots her gaze back to the flowers.

"Do you wear these during sex?" I ask, poking her for the thrill of seeing more emotion flood her beautiful face.

At this point, she's pure scarlet. "Only with the utility strap activated."

I burst out laughing, watching the resonating twitch at the corner of Pepper's lips. "You're very funny," I say, focusing back on my area of flowers.

Pepper's head whips to me. "You think so?"

I stare at her. "Well, yeah."

"I, um . . . I'm glad. That you think so." She turns back to the flowers, taking a shuddering breath while a smile blooms across her lips. At this point, I can't tell if she's still blushing or if she's just sunburned, but those cheeks are glowing. The effect is minorly devastating, shattering my heart with the surge of emotions.

I look back at the flower clutched in my hand.

There's one petal left.

Chapter 25

PEPPER

The past two weeks have actually gone . . . *well*. I know, I'm shocked too.

Opal and I have developed a sort of routine. She rises early every morning, meeting me in the kitchen with coffee mugs ready, ideas tumbling from those full lips and energy bursting from her seams.

I listen in quiet contemplation as Opal shoots out endless outlandish concepts for our design, our hands moving in sync as we harvest flowers.

Sometimes—when I feel like my chest won't cave in and my voice won't wobble—I talk about Lou. I tell Opal about her skills in the garden, how Lou seemed so in touch with the soil and this land, she could envision an entire season's harvest by March. I talk about how she loved pink tulips but never particularly cared for the white ones. How she gave so much— her flowers, her time, her kindness—to other farms in the area.

We divvy up the yield, about a fourth of the flowers going in Opal's pile to be hung to dry or pressed thin with an iron, a few of the sturdier stems being set aside in the floral cooler to keep them preserved, the rest designated for my wholesale florists.

With Opal's encouragement, I've even started putting together my own bouquets, doing weekly deliveries to various markets and shops around town, and the additional (albeit measly) income stream is nice.

The competition is in three weeks, and we still haven't settled on a design.

"I just don't see why you rejected that so fast." Opal pouts, her mood as gloomy as the thick gray clouds overhead.

"I don't think anyone will get it," I counter. We've been harping on this for a solid fifteen minutes.

"You really think people wouldn't get a life-sized rendering of Jeff motherfucking Goldblum?"

"What does he have to do with love?"

"The man is a sex symbol!"

I bury my head in my hands. "It's not happening, Opal."

She clicks her tongue against her teeth, mumbling something about great artists not being appreciated in their time.

"I still like the Mother Nature idea," I tell her after a few minutes. Opal had sketched up a giant head that we would construct from chicken wire and cover in moss, painting on some features. We'd then have the flowers blooming from the crown of her head like hair.

"It's so safe," Opal says.

"At least it's something."

After we finish pruning, I shake out a row cover, Opal grabbing the opposite end like she did at the plot before as we gently lay it over the plants like a white blanket.

"Not to be dense, but don't flowers kind of need water?" Opal says, tilting her head up to the sky, the clouds swollen and gray with the pressure of the impending storm.

"The row cover still lets some of the rain in," I say, adjusting it so the center rests on the wood stakes scattered through the row and it doesn't crush the delicate tips of the foxglove. "It's the wind I'm worried about. The mountains can tunnel in some heavy gusts."

"Right, and a flimsy piece of plastic is the obvious defense against gale-force winds," she says, giving the setup a dubious glance as I secure the corners with thin metal posts.

I stand, brushing my hands off on my thighs. "It's the best we've got. I'm probably being overly cautious anyway. Flowers survived summer storms long before I came along."

"You? Overly cautious? *Never.*"

I roll my eyes, turning away before she catches my smile. I lead us toward a row of pale pink ranunculi at plot six.

"Why don't we ever harvest from here?" Opal asks, stopping in front of plot four.

My bruised heart sinks to my stomach, pumping a heavy flow of sadness through my limbs as I look at the chaotic patch of land.

Grief is a strange beast. It can lie dormant for weeks. Months. You can go through the motions of life and truly convince yourself you're healed and fine and will actually survive the heartache of loss. And then, like the flip of a switch, it rears its head and snaps its jaws, hungry and ready to devour you whole.

I stare at the tangles of stems and leaves, the plot swollen with flowers ready to be picked, until my vision turns fuzzy. The memories are beautiful but their edges are jagged and sharp, cutting me over and over as they loop through my mind. I want to dissolve into that patch of earth.

"Pepper?" Opal's usually booming voice is soft, gentle, and so is the touch she drops on my arm. "Are you okay?"

I finally pull my eyes away, looking at Opal as panic mounts in my chest. I hate the pain. I hate the memories. I hate the sudden hook of a reminder pulling my chest apart. I search for words, but they're stilted and sharp, too many clogging my throat as I continue to stare at her.

"Sometimes it just hits me," I whisper, voice scratchy and raw.

Then something shifts in those light blue eyes, expression morphing from question to understanding. "Oh, Pepper," she says, reaching out, pulling me close.

I'm not a crier—I swear I'm not—but something about Opal's softness turns me into one. I let her hold me as quiet tears fall from my eyes. She doesn't say anything, just presses even closer, her cheek against my heartbeat, hand rubbing comforting circles along my back.

When I finally feel like I can breathe without crumbling to pieces, I untangle from Opal, turning to the plot. Heart thrumming and hands shaky, I step off the grass and into the foliage, fingertips grazing against the bustling life of this spot.

A few steps bring me to the center, and I push aside the exuberant puffs of a hydrangea to see the small stone marking Lou's final resting spot. As if she knew how much I needed her, Opal appears at my side, taking my hand in hers, letting me lean against her.

"This was the spot Grandma Lou taught me how to grow things. How to nurture them," I whisper. "I think it's the spot we first really connected."

I don't know why I'm telling Opal this, but it feels like something someone other than me should know.

These sweet little seedlings are what make all the hard work worth it, she'd said all those years ago, swinging a pickaxe to dislodge a rock with a radiant smile.

I had stared in wide-eyed observation at the woman I'd only known a few weeks. I couldn't wrap my head around how a person who could break up the hard earth with sturdy swings could also look tender and caring. But that was Grandma Lou, strength wrapped in gentleness.

We give them a home. Their resting place, she'd continued, swiping sweat from her brow with her forearm before getting to her knees. Lou unpacked one of the lily of the valley seedlings from its container, carefully untangling its riot of roots. With something close to reverence, she placed it in the hole she'd dug. *We let them spread their roots. Put down a foundation that makes them strong and glorious. Give them water and TLC when they need it, but, for the most part, we give them space to grow.*

And then cut them down? I'd asked, watching Lou pat the soil around the base of the delicate green stem. It was hard to believe something so fragile could survive.

Grandma Lou had given me a radiant smile. *That's a slightly more morbid way than I tend to look at it, but you're right.* She'd laughed, the sound an echoing whoop that made my perpetually frowning teenage mouth kick up at the sides. *I prefer to think of it as we harvest their beauty. Share it with others. Spread their magic and joy. Then, we do what we can to see them again next season.*

"When she passed," I tell Opal, still leaning against her, "it seemed like the right place to put her to rest."

"It's beautiful," Opal whispers, giving my hand a squeeze.

I snort. "It's an overgrown mess. But I think she would like that." My vision blurs as more tears prick my eyes. "I went a bit rogue and planted one of everything here. But I couldn't decide what would be best."

"From what you've told me about her, it seems perfect."

"She saved me, in a lot of ways," I say, feeling wrung out from all the feelings. I pull away, wrapping my arms around my middle as I carefully step out of the patch and back to the grass.

Opal shoots me a mildly questioning look, but doesn't push for more.

"I didn't stand a chance to be anything but a flower farmer once Grandma Lou taught me," I say, walking back toward the barn, Opal keeping stride, our buckets of flowers sloshing with us.

"These flowers are wrapped around my bones. They're pieces of me . . . The beautiful pieces, at least," I say with a self-deprecating laugh. Opal, always so ready to giggle, doesn't make a sound. I shoot her a sidelong glance.

She stops, staring straight at me. My heart ricochets down to my stomach, then up to my throat with that look.

She sets down one of her buckets, plucking a pale purple anemone from the water. She steps forward and, for a moment, I think—I hope—she's going to kiss me. We haven't touched each other like that since that kiss in the car, the space between us getting wider and wider as each day passes. It's not for lack of want on my part, but all of this is so new, so foreign, I'm following her lead, dancing around the magnetism I feel tugging me toward her.

And I'm scared. Fucking terrified. Because agreeing not to have feelings apparently doesn't stop them from trying to take root. I shouldn't be allowed to like her; even if it weren't against our rules. There's no way in the world anything good can come from it. Trish infused so much rottenness in my DNA, there's no way I can like something without destroying it. Or it will destroy me first. It's the way of life. Break or be broken.

Opal stops an arm's length away, teeth pressed into her lip, the air charged from more than the approaching storm.

In a slow movement, she reaches out, placing the flower into my braid close to my ear, brushing wisps of hair off my temple and dragging the tips of her fingers down my jaw. Her touch lingers at my rioting pulse as she stares at me.

"Every piece of you is beautiful," she whispers, then picks up her bucket and walks away.

Chapter 26

PEPPER

"Absolutely not," I say, scowling at Opal over the rim of my hot toddy before taking a sip. A clash of thunder rumbles through the cabin to emphasize my point. It's been raining for hours now, preventing our evening harvest. I can't say I mind, though. It's been rather . . . nice, spending the night in front of the fireplace with Opal.

"Okay, maybe you aren't getting the vision," she says, sitting forward on the couch to put her mug of tea down on the coffee table. "Let me walk you through it again. It'll be made of lilies, right? And we'll have them forming letters that we'll mount on a wall, following?"

I roll my eyes as a flash of lightning illuminates the room.

"And the letters will spell out . . ." She pauses for dramatic effect. "*Fuck You*. Brilliant, right?"

I flick my wrist, palm up, as I stare at her. "That is the most obscure and unrelated pop-culture reference you could have come up with."

"Lily Allen's iconic song 'Fuck You' is anything but obscure!" Opal squeals, cheeks turning pink. A howl of wind knocks at the windows.

"It's a no," I snap. She's tying my brain up in knots with all her bizarre ideas. I poke at the fire, but it's burned down to a few embers now, ready to snuff out fully any second.

She sulks for a moment, glowering out the rain-soaked window. I close my eyes to the patter of the storm, enjoying the simple quiet.

"Can we at least revisit the Orlando Bloom idea?"

"Goodbye." I stand, marching to the kitchen and rinsing out my mug.

"Listen, grumpy goose, I feel like you're stifling my creative brilliance at this point," she says, following close on my heels.

"Suggesting celebrities with anything even remotely flower-related in their name is not creative brilliance," I say, taking her empty mug and rinsing it out too. "At this point, it doesn't feel like we'll ever land on a winning idea."

"Ye of little faith," she says, leaning against the counter and watching me wash the dishes. "I'll make you see the light one of these days."

"More like you're trying to seduce me to the dark side."

"If that's what it takes," she says with a sniff.

I glance at her, and the tiny menace is grinning at me with more than a little mischief in those big blue eyes. I swallow, fixing my gaze back on the soapy bubbles as I set the clean mugs on the counter. How can someone so cute also be so terrifying?

"Don't waste your energy," I mumble, dragging a towel over the dishes to dry them.

I hear the pop of Opal's lips as she starts to argue, but a booming crash from above rattles the frame of the house, cutting her off.

Our eyes meet for a terrified moment, and then she bolts from the room, feet banging up the stairs.

"Oh shit," she yells, my own legs burning as I sprint after her.

I almost collide into Opal as I enter her room, her short frame stopped inside the doorway. I follow her gaze to a fissure in the ceiling, a steady drip of water falling on her comforter with an audible *plop* every second or so.

"Is that a *leak*?" Opal shrieks as if the ceiling weren't obviously leaking.

The wooden home creaks and groans around us like its bones can't settle into place, the shriek of wind sending a chill down my spine. Another crack of thunder is followed by the dull thud of the large oak tree's branches being blown against the cabin.

I was supposed to get that tree trimmed months ago.

"Um, Opal?" I say, a sense of apprehension coiling at the base of my neck.

Opal ignores me, taking a step farther into the room. "I will *not* tolerate this," she says, as if giving the ceiling a stern talking-to will magically seal it up. She grabs one of the many discarded sweatshirts littering her floor and scrambles to stand on the bed. She balances herself on the squishy mattress, pressing up onto tiptoes to shove the sweatshirt in between the slats.

Another groan.

"Opal. I think—"

"Can anything go *right*?"

Groan. Creak. Thud.

"You need to—"

"Stop telling me what I need to do, Pepper!" Opal says, planting one hand on her hip while the other is stretched to the ceiling, glaring at me all the while. "The roof is leaking! I—"

At the next groan, I give up on trying to gently reason with the oblivious hothead and decide brute force is the way to go.

I take two steps forward and reach out, one hand gripping Opal's hip, the other knotting in the front of her shirt, tugging her toward me with all my strength. Opal pitches forward, losing her balance and collapsing on top of me, both of us bouncing like rubber balls across the floor. Once we land firmly, Opal rears up, hair wild and face furious as she stares down at me.

"What the fu—" Opal's outrage is swallowed by a clash of thunder, then the screech of splintering wood and the clatter of shingles collapsing through the new gaping hole in the roof. The rain seems to pour in forever.

Opal pivots her body slowly, those endless ocean eyes the last thing to turn away from me, to face the avalanche of debris now covering her bed.

She is silent. Piercingly, hauntingly silent. Made all the more terrifying by the howl of the wind and pelting rain.

And then Opal leans her head back and screams.

"Noooooooooo," she bellows. "Oh what the fuck. *What. The. Fuck.*" Opal disentangles herself from me and stands up, and I blame the instant coldness in my chest on the bedroom hurricane and not on the loss of Opal's warmth.

"Why can't anything go right?" Opal cries again. She throws herself against the mountain of flotsam, kicking and clawing at it like she'll unbury her bed.

"Opal, it's okay. It'll be okay," I coo, trying to calm her down. I've never been very good at it. "Don't cry."

"I absolutely *will* cry," Opal says, turning on me. "I will cry and scream and be upset because everything is terrible and there's really nothing else for me to do *but* cry."

"We'll figure something out," I yell over another clap of thunder, stepping cautiously toward Opal. Something about seeing her cry has my chest cracking open like the ceiling moments ago. "Crying won't fix it. We can—"

"No!" Opal shouts, dislodging herself from the wreckage to dramatically stomp her foot. Rain is still pouring in, her hair plastered to her head like seaweed. "Stop talking right now. For once, I'm going to be the grumpy one. I'm going to be the pessimist. And you're going to listen."

I don't say anything, fixing Opal with a wide-eyed stare.

"My bed—my favorite safe spot in the entire world—is now buried under rain and a collapsed roof. The first thing I've ever owned is falling apart, and I'm living with a woman who doesn't want anything to do with me and is so eager to get me out of her life because I'm that much of a burden! So, Pepper, I'm going to cry. I'm going to—"

Without thinking, I reach out, gripping Opal's waist, tugging her close. Then closer still. I squeeze Opal against my chest until part of the ache eases. I can't fix the hole in the ceiling. I can't unbury Opal's bed. I can't do anything but let Opal cry.

Opal is tense for a moment, then sags against me, crying against my chest, resting her forehead on the angle of my collarbone, the rain still coming in droves, soaking us both.

I let her shake and cry and sob until she goes quiet, still holding me close.

After a few minutes, I shift, keeping her tucked against me but angling us toward the door.

"Come." I drag my fingertips down Opal's arm until our fingers twine together.

"Where?" Opal says with a sniffle, eyes red and puffy as she turns her gaze to meet mine.

I tug her through the doorway, shutting her bedroom door, then moving across the hall and pushing open my own.

"Here." I turn her drenched frame, gently pushing her onto the mattress so she lies flat, dragging a throw blanket over her. I shut the door with my foot, the echoing *thud* humming through my chest.

"What are you—"

"I know it's not your bed, but you can use it. Have it.

Whatever you need. You can cry here for as long as you want. I want you to know—to understand—it will be okay. I'll make sure of it."

Opal stares up at me with big, watery eyes and a look so adorably pitiful, I feel my lips twitch in an almost smile. The silence stretches between us, morphing from a quiet moment of kindness to sharp awkwardness.

I clear my throat, smoothing back my wet ponytail and glancing at the door. "I'll, um, leave you to it."

I turn toward the door, but a sudden grip around my wrist holds me locked in place. My eyes dart back to the bed, back at Opal, whose face has ebbed from despair to something softer. Something lovely. And the tiniest bit terrifying.

Opal tugs on my wrist, and my muscles and bones turn wobbly like Jell-O, moving wherever Opal pulls me. Which is how I end up on the bed, curled like half a heart with Opal tucked against my chest, both of us still soaked, a small tremor moving through her body.

I know I should get up and get towels. Go check on the storm in the other room. Take a shower. But I'm so content, so delightfully thrilled to be holding Opal to me, that I, quite simply, don't ever want to move again.

"When the rain comes," I whisper against her neck, my hand moving to tuck her hair behind her ears, "anemones—some of the most beautiful, delicate flowers to ever exist—curl inward and downward to protect their petals from the storm."

Opal doesn't say anything back, snuggling further into me

as the rain keeps pouring down. As she lets out a shuddering breath, the lights flicker, then snuff out.

We're still for a moment, not breathing, then she turns, eyes glinting in the dark. I can't make out her face, but I feel a small shiver of fear run down her spine.

"Well . . . damn."

"That about sums it up," I say, rolling away from her to test my bedside lamp a few times. No luck.

I open the drawer to my nightstand, rummaging around in the pitch black until my hand curls around the small flashlight I keep stored in there. I pull it out, flicking the switch a few times. Nothing happens.

The farm is just far enough outside of Asheville and any other more densely populated areas that the power regularly goes out and stays out for extended periods of time, and Grandma Lou always had flashlights at the ready, but apparently neither of us made it a habit to change the batteries.

"Ugh, I'll be right back," I say, fighting off a chill as the cold rainwater stuck to my skin sinks into my bones.

"You can't leave me!" Opal whisper-yells.

"Are you afraid of the dark?" I ask, squinting at the Opal-shaped lump in the center of my mattress.

"Not a ton of horror movies take place in the sunshine, Pepper," she says in a shrill voice.

I bite back a giggle. "I'll be gone for a minute. Gonna get some flashlights from the kitchen."

Opal whines, but I ignore it, carefully making my way out of the room. The sound of the storm is loud right behind Opal's door, and I can't bring myself to process all the damage that'll be done by the time morning rolls around. I grab a towel from the linen closet, pressing it along the crack to her room like it will make much difference.

With cautious steps, I pad downstairs. The fire is completely out now, whispers of its warmth quickly evaporating in the cool night. In the kitchen, I rummage for a few minutes under the sink before finding two flashlights that actually work.

Back upstairs, I grab some fresh towels from the linen closet and slip back into my bedroom. The sound of Opal's teeth chattering greets me.

"I'm s-so cold," she says, sitting up as I flick on my flashlight and hand her a towel.

"Me too," I say, wringing out my hair, fingers frozen, as a sharp gust of wind bangs at my poorly sealed bedroom windows.

"Should we . . . h-huddle together under the blankets for warmth?" Opal says through blue lips. "This isn't a line, but I d-dead-ass read that removing clothing actually allows you to conserve body heat."

I giggle, but nod, goose bumps prickling along my skin as I shuck off my shirt and jeans. Opal grins before doing the same. We dive under the covers, frozen fingers tickling across warm skin as we reach for each other.

I pull the quilt higher around Opal's cheeks, tucking her in. She lets out a contented sigh against my throat, nuzzling close.

I play with the frayed ends of the blanket, the small tears in the fabric like windows into old memories—teenage me nestled in on snow days, twenty-year-old me sipping something warm and comforting with a book in hand, exploring emotionally complex worlds I never thought would be my own, twenty-one-year-old me being woken up by Grandma Lou, champagne flute in her hand as she sang "Happy Birthday."

We burrow deeper, and I sink into the now adult me lost and confused and somehow comfortable in this moment despite it all. So many happy memories woven into this quilt, another tugging at the fabric.

"I'm sorry about your room," I whisper, my arm cinching tight around Opal's full waist, our bodies pressed together.

She lets out a tiny mumble, arm looping around me too.

Opal is so close and so warm and so soft and I find my throat working, vulnerable words bubbling up, wanting to be said, to be held by her ears.

"I was never supposed to live here," I whisper.

"What do you mean?" she says, shifting so I feel the question against my throat.

I swallow. "This farm. I never even knew it existed until my mom dumped me here when I was seventeen. Thank God Grandma Lou was actually a decent person." I gnaw on my lip, imagining what could have been. "My life could have ended up being so different if she'd been another asshole like my mom."

Opal pulls back, and I feel her eyes on me in the dark room. "Your mother *left* you?"

I let out a scornful laugh, squeezing my eyes tight. "That's not even the worst of it," I mumble, the words like a blade against my heart.

"It's hard to imagine something could be much worse than that."

I gulp, trying to stop the words tumbling out of me. This isn't safe. This isn't smart. I keep talking anyway.

"My mom had a revolving door of boyfriends," I say coolly, ignoring the pang the memory jolts through my chest. "And, like, I don't mean that in a slut-shamey way, or whatever. But they were either guys she was conning or guys she was partnering up with to do a con on someone else. My mother has never interacted with another human unless she thought she could get something from them."

Including me.

"Most of the guys were scumbags at best . . . but there was one. Robert." I suck in another breath as his kind face surfaces in my memory.

"I made the mistake of getting attached to him. He was so . . ." I think back on Robert, how he'd ask me about my day, always bought the cereal I liked.

An angry laugh cracks from my throat. "He was *nice*. He was the first grown-up to be unconditionally nice to me. I latched onto him like a duckling to its mama. Robert wasn't uber rich or anything like that, but he had more money than anyone I'd ever known. I mean, the fact that he had a working dishwasher and garbage disposal and central cooling meant he belonged to the one percent to someone like me."

Opal is quiet, breathing steady, silently encouraging me to keep going.

"I was fifteen when my mom met him. And they were

serious. She'd had 'serious' boyfriends in the past too, but they all crashed and burned sooner rather than later. She swore up and down that things were different with Robert. That she was settling down. No more cons. No more switching schools and moving states and life on the run."

I wanted so badly to believe her, so I did. I entertained the fallacy that life wouldn't be a blur of peers at new schools I'd never have time to connect with, a fresh set of faces and names and places I'd have to memorize, navigating the awkwardness of small talk and social niceties time after time.

"They got engaged pretty quickly. I do think Robert cared about me. He'd talk to me. Try to get to know me. Encourage me with school. And when I started actually doing well in classes after gaining an ounce of stability at home, he opened a small college fund for me. It wasn't anything huge, but it was enough for me to at least get through community college. And, stupid me, I let myself hope. I got these big ideas of getting my associate's, maybe transferring into a four-year program."

Opal is still in the momentary silence. "What would you have studied?"

I snort, pushing away the big hopes of the past that try to hook into my brain. "I had no clue. But that was the allure of it all. For the first time, I'd have a real chance to learn. To explore things. To focus on what the world has to offer and not what my mom could take from it . . ."

I suck in a breath, fighting the what-could-have-been demons as they elbow for space.

"Anyway, my mom left Robert. I guess she was telling the

truth; as far as I know, she didn't actually con him or steal from him or anything. And he wrote to me, letting me know that he had no plans of closing the college fund. That the money was mine to put toward school. He . . . I think he actually believed in me. Isn't that funny?"

Opal doesn't laugh. But that's okay, it makes sense. I'm not sure how anyone could believe in me to reach any higher than the bar my mom set a millimeter above the ground.

"Well, after my mom left me here and made it pretty obvious she wasn't coming back, I started looking into schools in the area. I was all set to apply, and I still had the account information Robert had given me. But when I called, they said the account was empty. Overdrafted, actually. Because the account was in my name, my mom had forged a letter and pretended to be me on the phone. She'd said the money was going toward the SAT, application fees, dorm stuff, all that bullshit."

She'd used it all. Every last cent.

"I was . . . I'm not sure *devastated* is a large enough word for it. I'd clawed my way to that moment, hanging on as best I could to finally reach my future. And she'd burned it all down. Grandma Lou tried so hard to scrounge up the money for me to still go, even offered to take out a loan, but at that point, I was so angry and lost it didn't even seem like a future I could have. It didn't belong to me. So I turned down the offer. Stayed here."

Sometimes I think of that ghost life. That version of me where that one thing worked out. I wonder what she studied. What she knows. What kind of clothes she wears. What city she lives in. Her favorite spot to get coffee. It's so silly, but I'm rooting for her. For the me that never was. I'm sure she'll do better than the me that is.

"I don't talk to my mom anymore. I can't. I tried for a while—a few years after she abandoned me, she'd contact me here and there—but eventually I realized that feeding into her games was like psychological self-harm, setting myself up to hurt over and over again."

Opal is silent, and I squirm at the ugliness of my truth, the way it looms over me, large and dark.

"So . . . yeah. That's my sob story. Pretty pathetic, I know. But it's mine all the same."

Opal squeezes me close, and I feel something hot against my throat—tears or her breath or maybe both.

It feels nice.

But it also feels like too much.

And for the first time since that first night together, I put control in the passenger seat, seeking out her lips. Needing them to touch mine.

Opal indulges me for a moment, her soft mouth and sweet taste—like plums and sin and unwritten words from a pool of ink—flood my mind.

But she pulls back. And an angry phantom of desire takes control of my voice.

"We aren't doing very well with our hooking-up plan," I say, trying not to be too vulnerable as I nestle against her.

"How so?" she whispers, hand trailing from my rib cage down the dip of my waist to the curve of my hip.

"Well, it's been over two weeks since we've agreed to it, and we've only hooked up once. And now we're breaking one of the three rules and sharing a bed." I laugh, but she doesn't join me, and I pull back to see her expression, hopefully read whatever cue I'm missing.

Opal looks at me, then bites her lip, slipping away as she rolls onto her back. "I've been, uh, nervous. To initiate anything, I mean."

"Why?" I ask. I've been terrified to initiate anything either, but I don't know what I'm doing—how I'm supposed to react—if a single night swirled up such a riot of emotions in my chest.

Opal swallows, opens her mouth, then locks it closed, shaking her head. "Because I'm worried it would mean breaking a different rule. And I shouldn't do that. We *can't* do that," she eventually says to the ceiling.

I'm silent as her words sink into my skin. I want to pick at the silence, prod it like a bruise. See how badly I could make it hurt.

"Oh," I eventually whisper.

"Yeah," Opal says back. "Can't go down that road. It would only lead to issues."

Issues. Right. I'd be one big issue. I'd almost let myself forget that I'm only worth being around as long as I'm useful to others.

And, in a sick, perverse way, I'm thankful she just squeezed my heart to a pulp. People usually only pretend to like you with the intent to hurt you. I'm not special, and neither is this. For once, someone is doing me the courtesy of warning me of the con that lies ahead.

I shift my body, shift away from her warmth. "Well . . . we can't have that."

Opal pivots again, turning so her back is to me. "No," she whispers to the wall. Her words become weapons, sharp little daggers slicing me open, mortification dumping salt in the wounds. "We can't have that."

"That's the last thing I would want," I say, staring out the window next to my bed and wishing on a star for the complete opposite. But I'm desperate for the last word, for any upper hand I can find in this sinking ship. "That would be a disaster."

Chapter 27

OPAL

"Well . . ." I say, staring out at the swamp that was once a vibrant flower farm. "Fuck."

Pepper audibly swallows but doesn't say anything.

Thick humidity presses on us like a wall, the resurfaced sun glinting off the pond-sized puddles dotting the land. While not all the plots are destroyed, many are, broken branches and felled trees crushing the plants, the row covers uprooted and wrapped around the damage. Even those that didn't get demolished were still hit hard by the wind, broken stems and ripped petals littering the area.

"What are we going to do?" I ask, a knot of stress ballooning in my gut.

Pepper lets out a slow breath through her lips, and I look at her, shocked by her calmness. She continues staring straight ahead, pale purple circles rimming her eyes. "I really, truly have no clue."

After another minute of hopeless silence, we softly advance across the grass, the tall rain boots Pepper loaned me squelching in the mud. We haul debris away, piling it up in the back of the barn.

"There's not much more we can do but wait," Pepper says when we carry the last branch away, dusting her hands off on her jeans. "Luckily, the farm was designed on a slope, so a lot of the water should drain down the mountain, but only time will tell how long it will take for the soil to fully dry out."

She swallows, eyes hollow as she stares at the field. "But excess rain like this introduces a world of problems. Fungus. Lack of oxygen. Runoff pulling all the nutrients from the dirt . . . Even if we do somehow avoid all that, our blooms for the next two to three weeks are shot to hell. It'll be a while before there's anything viable to sell."

"Let alone use for the competition," I whisper. Pepper nods, slow and disconnected.

"Not sure there's a way out of this one," she says, voice flat.

I open my mouth, trying to think of something encouraging, but she turns before any words come, shoulders slumped and hands shoved in her pockets as she walks away.

•　　•　　•

About an hour later, the contractor shows up to evaluate the damage to my room.

"Y'all got hit hard," Bruce, a big burly man with a stellar mustache, says as he takes a few pictures of the gaping hole in my ceiling. "I've stopped at a few other spots this morning, but this is one of the worst."

"Lucky me," I say, banging my head against the doorway.

"Y'all just a crop farm?" he asks. I appreciate that he thinks I have any fucking clue about agricultural lingo. "Or do ya have some livestock?"

"Specialize in flowers," I say, gesturing at some of the tenacious bundles that still hang from the non-broken part of my ceiling.

"Huh. How'd they fare?"

"About as well as a fish in the desert."

Bruce clucks his tongue and shakes his head.

That rain washed away my purpose, and I feel hollow at the truth of it. No more competition. No more reason to work with Pepper. No more plotting outrageous ideas just to see if I can get her to laugh.

"That's a shame. One of the farms up the road I stopped at earlier had a large flower crop too. Said she lost most of it. Luckily, she has some veggies growing in her greenhouses to help her get over the hump."

"Lucky her." I bang my head a few more times on the door-jamb before helping Bruce hang a tarp over the crater in the roof.

"Y'all need to get you some of those, I reckon," he says, jotting a few notes down before packing up his measuring tools. "Greenhouses, I mean."

Bruce wants to talk about what I need? Let's start with a hope. A prayer. A few extra brain cells, if I'm being greedy.

"You're probably right," I say through numb lips. What's even the point? I've come in here and upended Pepper's life like the storm, and she made it crystal clear last night that she's not interested in opening up her doors for any more.

That would be a disaster, she'd whispered. Because she knows. She knows I'm a mess and she's not interested in cleaning it up. I wish that I still had a chance to show her that I'm good for something, even one thing. Despite her not being interested in my feelings, I still want to do right by Pepper, keep working with her, build something together. I want—

"Wait. Bruce!"

Bruce freezes, one hand paused midstroke of that beautiful mustache.

"You're probably right," I repeat, hopping back and forth on my feet, brain revving up with an idea.

His eyes go wide. "Ma'am?"

I plow forward, grabbing his giant hands in mine. "You, my friend, might just be a genius."

Chapter 28

PEPPER

It's been about a week since the storm, but my mood is as gloomy as ever. I feel so . . . lost. Directionless. Like my tether snapped and I'm floating through space with nothing to grab on to.

Which is probably why I willingly agreed to spend the day running errands with Diksha.

But by the time we get to our fifth stop—the *mall* of all places—I absolutely refuse to get out of the car.

"You need to update your wardrobe," Diksha says through clenched teeth as she puts her entire weight into pulling me out of the passenger seat. "You can't keep wearing the same four pairs of dungarees for the rest of your life and call it a day."

"That's exactly what I can do. I'm an adult, dammit," I say back, propping my foot on the doorframe and pulling against her. "All my clothes are at the perfect sensory texture. I'm not anywhere near stable enough to introduce fresh fabrics."

"Fine!" Diksha releases my arm, and I shoot backward, head landing in the driver's seat, the emergency break digging into my spine. She walks around the car, opening her side and staring down at me. "Dress like Chucky for the rest of your life. See how your girlfriend likes it."

"Opal currently has green hair that's breaking off by the handful, so I highly doubt she'd have anything to say about me wearing overalls and soft T-shirts." It takes me a moment to process Diksha's shit-eating grin. "And she's not my girlfriend!"

"Excellent recovery," Diksha says, scooping her hands below my shoulder blades and pushing me to a sitting position. I slump like a rag doll in my seat.

"She's *not*," I mumble, clicking my seat belt. "I'd hardly even call us friends. We haven't talked much since the storm destroyed all of my hopes, dreams, and prospects."

"You know what I love about you, Pepper? Your muted and undramatic perception of your life. It's a gift." She throws the car in reverse, navigating the crowded parking lot.

I cross my arms over my chest, staring out the window as Diksha drives me home.

"Is the not-talking a mutual thing or are you avoiding Opal like you are your feelings for her?"

"What do you know of my feelings?" I snap back. I hate that she hit the nail on the head with the first part, though. I've been skirting around Opal as best I can. The free fall from excitement to disappointment over the competition hurt way too much for it to be reasonable and safe. Nothing about Opal or her big ideas or her ridiculous jokes or the way she makes my heart race is reasonable and safe.

"I know that every time we've talked or texted over the past few weeks, you've always found a reason to bring her up and go on and on."

"Out of annoyance, primarily," I say with a haughty sniff.

"Right. Talking about how beautiful her art is that you creep on definitely screams that you're annoyed by her and not desperately head over heels."

"I don't creep! I . . . catch a glance here and there."

"Mm-hmm. I also know that you've actively chosen to spend time with her outside of farm work, something which you avoid with every person in your life. Even your best friend, *cough, cough*."

"Do I really have a choice when I was forced into living with her? What am I supposed to do? Hide under my bed?"

"You're getting rather defensive over someone you claim not to have strong feelings for."

"Because I am a defender of the truth in the face of your egregious lies!"

"Calm down, Elle Woods, this isn't a trial. I'm just bringing up a few points."

"Speculation, Your Honor."

Diksha rolls her eyes. "I also know that girl looks at you like she'd move mountains for you. And you look at her the same."

"Can you tell me what this look means?" I say, swiveling my head to shoot daggers at Diksha. She giggles.

"It means you *looooooove* me," she says, taking one hand off the steering wheel and squeezing my cheek between her fingers.

I pull away, sitting in sullen silence for the rest of the drive.

"I know everyone is entitled to an emo phase," Diksha says, putting the car in park. "But I wish you had the courtesy to experience yours when My Chemical Romance was touring. Then you'd at least have an outlet for the moodiness."

"I always feel so validated by our talks, thanks," I deadpan, shouldering my tote bag and opening the car door.

Diksha grabs my wrist and plants a smacking kiss on the back of my hand.

With a sigh, I duck back into the car and do the same to hers. "I hate you."

"Love ya back, babe," she calls as I close the door and walk toward the house, the crunch of gravel as she heads down the driveway echoing around me.

I should probably go check on the plants, see how the different plots are draining, but I'm . . . I'm feeling so damn much—too damn much—I need to take a minute to regroup.

I open the door to the cabin, ready to make a beeline to the couch.

And immediately get a jump scare from Opal, who's standing three inches inside the doorway.

"I have a surprise for you," she says, oblivious to the small heart attack she gave me.

"Wasn't that greeting enough?" I ask, hand on my chest.

Her eyes are wide, burning with energy, as she shakes her head. "I need to blindfold you."

"*What?*"

She moves forward, pulling a bandanna from her back pocket.

"Absolutely *not*," I say, sidestepping her outstretched arms.

Opal's shoulders drop, a hum of nervousness radiating off her. "Can you at least cover your eyes with your hand?" she says, biting her lip.

"Opal, what the hell is going on?"

"Please," she whispers, leg bouncing.

It's not fair how that look of hers unravels me, how after a week of not talking, her radiant energy lights up something in my heart.

With a sigh, I close my eyes and cover them with my hand. I hear her stifled squeal.

"Come with me," she says, looping her fingers through mine, tugging me out of the house. She guides me down the porch steps—I don't think she catches my tiny peek to make sure I don't fall. I'm not about to risk a broken ankle in my attempts to humor her.

Hand firmly back over my eyes, I let her guide me across the grass, the earth still soggy as it bounces back from the storm.

"I'm kind of scared you're going to hate it," she says. "And I probably should have asked you first and I've second-guessed this decision for the past few hours but I went through all the trouble of getting Diksha to take you out all day so I could get them set up and—"

"Wait, what?" My hand pulls away, eyes flashing open,

fixed firmly on her. "Diksha told me she had errands and wanted some company."

Opal yips, diving forward and covering my eyes again.

With a growl, I push her back, using my own hand to do as she wants.

"I'm sorry, but I needed you gone for the surprise to work. I bribed her by promising to design a brand-new logo for her accounting firm and another for Tal's flower shop, along with matching leather totes to get you out of the house by brute force if need be."

That dirty traitor. "Why did you want me gone so badly?"

I don't like being messed with. I still follow where her hand guides me, palm warm against my lower back.

"The surprise," she says like this should be obvious and my questions are ridiculous. "Okay. We're here."

We stop walking. From muscle memory, I can tell we've walked beyond the barn, an area that's generally cleared out, the sun often too harsh and direct to cater to a lot of the flowers I grow. Opal must step in front of the sun, the red glow behind my eyelids replaced with an inky blue. I feel her heat as she leans toward me, angling my body a bit.

She steps away, and I have to check the impulse to pull her back to me.

"Open your eyes."

With a sigh, I slide my palm away from my face, blinking at the sharp sunshine. A bright and glowing reflection makes my eyes water, and I squint at the two large structures standing before me. My eyes skim over and over them, but my brain can't process what I'm actually seeing.

"W-what's this?" I say, turning to Opal. She's staring straight at me.

"For someone that spends ninety percent of her working hours growing things, I really thought you'd be able to identify a greenhouse." She shifts her weight, leg bouncing again.

"No. I mean, what's it doing here?" I spin around to the buildings, then back to her again, blinking rapidly.

"It's a gift." The last word is soft. Breathy. Nervous.

"A gift for who?"

She lets out a rough laugh, takes a step closer, one hand rubbing across the back of her neck. "For you," she says with a shrug. "Or, I guess, us. To grow more flowers. Together."

I'm silent, trying to understand her. This. What it all means.

"Only if you want to, I mean," Opal babbles, moving away. "It turns out Bruce the Contractor's business does greenhouses and hoop houses too. And we got to talking about it and I thought . . . hell, I don't know. I thought it might help."

My jaw dangles open as I continue to stare at her. Slowly, I turn to the large, gorgeous greenhouses placed behind my barn, their pointed roofs reaching toward the sky. "How can you afford this?" I whisper, taking a step toward them.

"Well . . . while I did tie up most of my money in this place, winning the lottery gave me a little bit of disposable income. Plus, Bruce saw some of my shoes and I told him I'd make his wife three pairs, each with their dogs on them, if he'd give me a little discount. Can't pass up an opportunity to put some dogs on some salty dogs."

"I don't know what that means," I say, my throat squeezing tight at the rush of gratitude and longing that floods my system, something like hope ebbing through my veins, creating a subtle ache, soft and shimmering and somehow sweet in the pain.

"There's a bit more," Opal says, cracking her fingers. "Come inside."

She leads the way into the closest greenhouse, and it takes me a few moments to process that it's already filled with blooming flowers. I swallow a gasp, moving in a trance to the center of the space.

Six rows of pallet benches line the building, stretching down about ten feet. They're covered in plants—dahlias and poppies and aster—the joyful blossoms tilting their faces to the light shining in through the glass roof.

"Opal," I whisper, whipping around, needing to see her face in the midst of so much beauty. So many words fight at the tip of my tongue. Beautiful words. Happy words. Thankful words. But all that comes out is "How?"

Opal's smile is slow, hesitant. The prettiest thing on this farm. "I remembered you telling me that Grandma Lou gave a lot of flowers to neighboring farms. So, I called on them. Ones that were already growing flowers in hothouses were more than happy to return the favor and then some. Tal reached out to a few of their contacts too for some of the harder-to-find varieties."

I feel dizzy from the growing pressure behind my eyes, and

a tiny sob is pulled from my throat. I shake my head, trying to find a pinhole of clarity in the fuzziness of emotions.

"Do you hate it?" Opal asks, worry marring her face. "I'm scared you hate it. Was this an awful idea? I'm sorry. I thought it would be a fun surprise. I'll—"

I cross the distance between us in two long strides, one hand reaching out to cradle Opal's jaw, the other diving into her hair and tilting her head so I can press my mouth to hers, swallowing the rest of her words and her nonsense and her overwhelming kindness.

And Opal kisses me back, throwing her arms around my neck, pressing her body against the length of mine.

The kiss isn't gentle. It's frantic and hot, like I can't get close enough fast enough. Like I'll die if my lips stop touching the unbearable softness of Opal's. But there's something peaceful about it too, like every cell in my body can finally sigh in relief at the touch of her mouth to mine. The return of her kiss.

I finally gain a bit more control, taking my time to taste and feel the heat of her, trying to tell her how I could never hate anything she gives me.

"You bought this?" I finally manage, only pulling my lips far enough away to murmur the words against her temple.

Opal shrugs. "I . . . Yeah."

"You bought an *entire* greenhouse?"

"There's actually another one," she mumbles.

I laugh at the absurdity of it. "Opal. My God."

She shrugs again. "I wanted to help you."

"Why? Why would you do this for me?"

And, to my dismay, Opal lets out a frustrated sigh, untangling herself from me and backing up until her legs meet one of the tables, the leaves of the potted plants trembling.

She stares at me with incredulity.

"Because I *like* you, Pepper," she says, throwing her arms up in the air. "Really like you. And dammit, I just want to make you smile."

Her words are huge and terrifying and make my muscles and joints lock up with the shock. Even in the best circumstances, I'm slow to process big moments. Or small ones. Or most moments at all.

But this one?

I'm not sure I'll ever recover. And I'm kind of panicking from the swirl of joy in my chest.

I wish I could take these feelings like a shot. Let them flood my blood and take over my nerves, but only for a little bit. Instead, they're slow. Consuming. Tugging me under until I'm lost to it, any hope of resurfacing gone.

"Could you say something?" Opal whispers, staring at me with a desperate look. "Please?"

I only manage to shake my head, lips parting as if they aren't woefully incapable of saying everything I want to. Need to.

Opal's face falls, and my heart plummets with it. I can't let that stand.

I close the space between us, hands gripping her cheeks, our eyes meeting and locking. I still can't get the words out, my throat constricting, breaths short and sharp. Whatever this is in me, it's bright and terrifying and white hot and I need something—anything—to dull the fire.

I do the only thing I can.

I kiss Opal in a way that I hope says everything my words can't.

She responds immediately, fisting my shirt in her hands, tugging me forward with unexpected force, my body landing flush against hers, the heat of the greenhouse wrapping around us.

The kiss is hot and disorienting, my world folding itself inside out with Opal's soft lips as the center point.

I've loved every kiss Opal has given me, but none of them have ever undone me like this, sending a shiver down my spine while my skin is singed with the heat radiating from the center of my body. It scrambles my thoughts, making me desperate and hungry and reckless. I want more and less and harder and softer. I want hands and lips and tongues and teeth.

I want anything Opal will give.

"Let me touch you here?" Opal whispers against my jaw, her hand resting on the zipper of my jeans.

I should say no, stop this runaway train. This is a bad idea. One of the worst in human history. Because I'm maybe kind of sort of feeling an avalanche of . . . well, *feelings*, and we agreed to none of that nonsense. If a kiss undoes me like this, Opal's fingers probably have the power to ruin me for life right about now.

"What about the rule you were worried about?" I gasp. Her

rejection from the other night is still a raw blister. I'm a fool to pour salt on it.

I'll do it anyway.

"Fuck the rules," Opal says, hands hot and heavy on my hips. She bites my lip. "We can renegotiate them tomorrow. Can. I. Touch. You?" Each word is punctuated by a rough kiss.

"*Yes.*"

My voice is raw, needy, my hips emphasizing the word with an uncontrolled buck against Opal's hand.

Opal doesn't need more than that, fingers quick and efficient as she undoes my pants, pushing the denim low on my hips and dragging her hand across the exposed strip of skin below my T-shirt before diving beneath the elastic of my underwear.

A strangled moan rushes out of me from the heat of the contact, the soft drag of Opal's fingers, the pure delicious torture of that first teasing circle.

"Fuck," Opal grinds out, as if she can feel even an eighth of the pleasure building between my hips. It's not possible. It's sharp and insistent and addicting. Nothing has ever felt this good. But, as my gaze locks with hers—those endless blue eyes filled with heat and want and desire—I can almost believe Opal is getting off on this too.

"I've missed this," she says, teeth grazing against my collarbone. I tilt my head back to give her more. "I've missed *you*. Is that crazy? I feel crazy."

All I can manage is a moan.

"Yeah?" she says, pulling back her face to fix me with a

wicked smirk. Then she's kissing me again, lips on my skin, free hand on my breasts, cupping me and circling my nipple until I'm pressing into her, a whimper tumbling from my lips.

"Let it out, baby," she whispers against my throat, then bites the spot.

The woman is cruel, sending me into this spiral all alone. I'm not going down without taking her with me.

I dig my hand between our tight-pressed bodies, our skin slick, my fingers slipping below the waistband of her shorts. We groan in unison as I feel the wetness already gathering in that sweet spot between her thighs. Opal speeds up her fingers, stars spotting my vision, and I retaliate, plunging two fingers into her, stroking in the way she seemed to like last time.

She apparently likes it this time too, knees buckling as she jerks forward into me. I stumble back, my thighs crashing into the edge of the table behind me. It's a testament to how far gone I am that I don't even bother to check on the pots of flowers that tumble off the other side.

Opal is vicious with the pleasure, building me up and up with every kiss and bite and stroke of her fingers, until I'm crying and frantic, the noise bouncing off the fogged glass of the greenhouse. She collects my desperate moans like ammo, using them to render me helpless. Useless. I willingly surrender, gasping as the first wave of an orgasm pulses through me.

With a ruthless laugh, she pulls her hand back, cutting the pleasure short. I bite back a howl of frustration so hard, I taste blood on my tongue.

"You aren't fighting fair," I whine against her lips, panting and desperate as my hips squirm, trying to regain her touch.

"Neither are you," she says through gritted teeth, head falling forward as I press against her G-spot. "I can't get you out of my head."

I'm on sensory overload. The sweet scent of her. The wetness on my fingers. The press of her hand against my hypersensitive clit as she gives me what I need.

And, somehow, it's still not enough.

I hook my ankle behind hers, pulling her closer. I feel the back of Opal's hand against mine as we stroke each other, every movement small and tight, every sensation magnified and sharp.

My muscles coil with desire as I race toward the peak. I fist my free hand through Opal's short green hair, angling her head to press a deep, dirty kiss to those obscenely full lips. Our tongues tangle, Opal swallowing my moans as I get closer and closer, every cell in my body poised to snap with sensation. I break away only to get air into my too-tight chest, feeling like I'll pass out from the sensations.

And Opal looks at me.

She looks at me like she needs me. Like she'll do anything for another taste of me. The rawness of that look sends me over the edge, the climax rocketing through me.

Opal follows close behind, squeezing around my fingers, her trembles echoing through me.

We stay close through the aftershocks, my head falling

back, Opal pressing her forehead against my heaving chest. I don't ever want to move.

But a nagging, clawing pang of anxiety shoots through me. What did we just do? What does this mean? Because things were *said* that can't really be *unsaid*. Or, if they are unsaid, my heart will be obliterated.

I shift as my pulse kicks into overdrive, and Opal pulls away, hands gentle and delicate as she moves them from between my legs, tracing the curve of my torso, up to my neck. She gives my earlobes a tiny tug, drawing my attention to her.

I look at her precious face and it feels like my heart will explode from every emotion battering it. She presses up to give me a soft kiss, then pulls away, adjusting her clothes.

I do the same, vision fuzzy and throat tight.

The sudden impulse to flee is too alluring to ignore, and I turn, making a beeline for the door. My pulse pounds at my temples, the world swirling. If I run, she can't hurt me. She can't reject me. She can't use all these aching feelings I have for her to crush me. She can't—

"Nice try," Opal says, catching my arm, spinning me to her. She wraps her hands around my wrists, moving me until my back is pressed against the sweating glass of the greenhouse. "I'm not letting you run away," she says, grip loosening, fingers slipping across my palms to tangle with mine.

The sigh I let out is so strong, my body moves to collapse with the release. Opal holds me up, holds me close.

And I let her.

I let her hold me, cuddle me, heart still racing and mind spinning and hope—terrible, wonderful, dangerous hope—swirling through me.

And then I do something I swore I never would. I let myself feel without diluting it with the threat of hurt. A few broken tears slip from the corners of my eyes. Opal doesn't see them, her cheek pressed to my thumping heart.

And, for this moment, I let myself trust she actually wants to stay there.

"That was really fucking amazing," she says after a while. It could be seconds, it could be hours. Time feels rather irrelevant right now. She pulls back enough to smile up at me.

With trembling fingers, I tuck one of the wild strands of her hair behind her ear. It bounces back, sticking straight out. "I didn't know you were also a poet."

Opal giggles, cheeks red and smile wide. She rolls her eyes, taking my hand and leading us outside. The summer sun feels like a relief after the heat of the greenhouse.

"I'm about to compare your vulva to flowers, give me a minute for the haze to clear," she says with a cheeky wink.

"Make sure to throw in a few moon metaphors. Would hate for you to get too cliché."

"Well, duh. All great sapphic poets do." Opal giggles at her own joke.

And I giggle too, punch-drunk and giddy from the sun and the heat and the sex and . . . Opal.

It's all from Opal.

But the giggling is cut short, Opal's eyes shooting wide

and mouth forming a perfect *O*. I jump when she grabs my shoulders. "Wait, Pepper!"

"What?" I say, pressing a hand to my heart. Poor muscle can't take much more.

"The competition! Our design!"

"Yeah?" I say, a tickle of anxiety traveling down my neck at the mention of it. How behind we are. But Opal's grin convinces me any task is possible.

"I have a brilliant idea."

Chapter 29

We've been constructing the base of our competition piece for the last week. All the kudos to Opal; the woman really does have range when it comes to various art mediums.

"If I were a superhero, I'd want my power to be that my hands are built-in nail guns so I wouldn't have to lift this heavy thing," she says at the end of a particularly busy day, dropping the power tool before slumping to the barn floor.

We've been waking up even earlier, doing some building before using the sunlit hours to harvest flowers, then back to construction well into the evening, collapsing into bed in a sore, exhausted heap.

Repairs on Opal's room were finished a few days ago. She still spends every night in my bed.

"I'd want to be needle fingers," I say, sucking on the pad of my thumb that I just stuck. Again.

A garland of dried peonies wraps around me. When we

both discovered I lacked a certain, er, artistic eye when it came to installation construction, Opal kindly assigned me to be the garland-maker. Turns out I'm not particularly good at that job either.

Following competition rules, everything has to be hand-made, but we can pre-make as much as we want before the event. We decided to put together as many of the dried flower components as possible, focusing on stuff that will be easily transportable. We'll be in a mad rush to put together the live flower components on the day of the competition, but it feels good to at least get a few things taken care of.

"What do we still have left to do?" I ask, throwing my needle and fishing line to the side as I prick my finger once more.

The competition is on Saturday, but we head to the Grove Park Inn tomorrow afternoon to begin setup. It feels like my nerves have been wired to a light switch, someone flicking them on every few hours and sending jolts of anxiety through me. It doesn't help that Diksha, lovely, meddling monster that she is, used some of her contacts to garner us a bit of buzz with the *Asheville Citizen-Times* and *Mountain Xpress*. Thank God for Opal because I've clammed up at every interview, the journalists wanting to highlight us since we're the only local team entering this year. Opal navigates their questions beautifully, making them laugh and creating an undercurrent of excitement that's hard not to be swept up in.

Opal groans. "Why are you asking me terrible questions? Do you want the terrible truth, you terrible monster?"

I giggle at the adorable scowl she shoots me. I'm not sure

the exact moment we switched roles, but Opal's grumpiness makes it feel like sunshine is radiating through my veins.

"Come on, my little pessimist," I say, pushing to stand and grabbing the top sheet we have as an extra drop cloth next to me. I reach out my hand to Opal.

"I'm so tired I can't move," she whines, eyes rolling to the back of her head. "Hand me that shovel, I'll bury myself here."

With a smile, I bend down, pressing a kiss to her temple before nipping her earlobe. "I'll make it worth your while if you follow me," I whisper against her skin.

Opal perks up, giving me a mischievous look. "That tone better be a promise for a massage and nothing more. I'm too tired to be of any other use tonight."

I giggle again. As if Opal merely breathing doesn't bring me to my knees on a daily basis.

I tug her to standing, then lead her out of the barn. Night has settled over the mountains, the moon glowing and full. I walk us toward the house, stopping at a level piece of earth and fluffing out the sheet. It settles in a wave on the grass.

Holding Opal's shoulders, I guide her down, gently pushing her so she lies on her back. I plop next to her, our bodies pressed close, the vast expanse of stars shining above us. She sucks in a breath as she stares up.

"It's beautiful," she whispers. "I love it here."

I roll my neck to look at her, and she does the same, the glint of her eyes so bright, it puts the stars to shame. Slowly, she reaches out to me, tracing her fingertips along my cheek. I turn my head so my lips press against her palm.

We stay there for a few priceless moments, Opal's touch warm and safe against my face, my heart held in her hands, my breath catching in my throat. Opal in the moonlight is unlike anything I've seen before. Soft and glowing, pale green hair like gossamer as the wind picks it up.

She lets out a yawn, eyes heavy-lidded as she looks at me.

"Poor Opal. So overworked and tired," I coo, tracing her lips with my fingertip. She scrunches up her face in a half-hearted scowl.

"Don't mock me. I *am* overworked and tired, considering I moved here to sit inside and paint shoes all day."

I give her a pitying look, letting every heated thought rushing through my head play across my growing smile. "You could use a stress reliever."

Opal gives me a questioning look, her gaze flashing across my face, eyes widening a bit at whatever she sees there. "That does sound rather nice," she says slowly, like she's scared to hope for what I'm offering.

I snuggle closer. "Lie on your back," I whisper, nudging her with my chin. She does as I say, eyes hooded and hot. I sit up, squinting at the plot of flowers next to us.

"They say lavender reduces stress," I tell her, plucking off one of the stalks from the plants next to us. I lean over her, trailing the flower head across her bare shoulder and up her neck. Despite the warm night, a shiver runs through her. "Has a substantial calming effect."

"I'm not sure calm is what I'm feeling right now," Opal says, her voice breathy and soft as I continue to slide the stalk across her cheek, my breasts close to her mouth. She presses closer.

"Well, that's no good," I say, trying to bite back my smile at the hiss of breath she lets out when I abruptly move away and pull the soft lavender from her skin.

I straddle her hips, my hands resting on her ribs below the swells of her breasts. "Maybe an aromatherapy massage would be better?" I say, voice dripping with innocence.

Opal gapes up at me.

Pressing my weight into my hips, I sit up fully, crushing the stalk between my palms, dragging my fingers against each other as I slowly grind it up. I can feel Opal's breaths—short and stilted—as her stomach rises and falls against my thighs, an ache building deep in me.

"Relax," I whisper, placing one hand in the center of her chest, her heart hammering against my palm. Opal tilts her head to look at me, eyes glazed and lips parted. After a moment, every muscle releases its building tension, her head still angled slightly up at me.

"Good," I say, letting the crushed leaves fall from my other hand, the sweet lavender musk embedded in my skin. "Now breathe."

I glide my fingers through her hair, rubbing soft circles against her scalp and temples. A small whoosh of breath leaves Opal's lips and dances across my wrists, her eyes half-closed as I continue to work. After a few moments, I give the strands a gentle tug, a gasp pulled from Opal. The quiet sound echoes around us.

I work down her neck to her shoulders, kneading the tight muscles and pulling more sighs of comfort from her. She's so pretty like this, face soft and surrendered. I trace gentle circles across the exposed skin of her arms, down to her palms, tickling my way back up. She smiles and giggles, goose bumps following my touch.

"That's so nice," she whispers on an exhale, eyes fully closed now.

Feeling dangerous, I let my fingers play, slipping under the straps of her tank top, massaging the soft juncture where her chest meets her shoulders. She hums in approval. My fingertips skim lower, a featherlight touch right where the swells of her breasts start, then veering to the side, tracing their curves without touching them. A shiver runs through her.

I drag my fingers back up, knuckles brushing the sensitive skin, and her eyes blink open, fixing on me with a glint. Encouraged, I repeat the circuit until I feel her breaths coming faster and harder beneath me, her chest moving in a jerky rhythm.

With a smile and a wink, I shift, kneeling between her legs, dragging my nails across the warm, soft skin of her parted thighs. I push the seam of her loose cotton shorts and underwear to the side and lean closer, but Opal's hand shoots out, resting on my cheek.

I glance up, seeing her eyes wide and brows crinkled. "What's wrong?" I ask, nuzzling into her palm.

Opal's pupils are blown, nostrils flaring with her rapid breathing while color rushes to her full cheeks. "I . . . Fuck. I, uh, really want this . . ."

After a pause, I grip her thigh with a bit more pressure. "But?" I prompt.

Opal screws up her face. "I'm hot and sweaty," she says, voice a high squeak. "And I don't want you to be grossed out."

I tuck my lips into my mouth, trying not to smile at how absolutely absurd the idea is. I let my gaze lock with hers for a beat longer before taking a slow, leisurely traipse across her face, memorizing the slopes of her cheeks, the lines of her throat, the curves of her shoulders.

I take my time at the swells of her breasts, the way I can see her heart thumping against her chest. With limited self-control left, my eyes skirt down her torso to her hips, then I look between her thighs and lick my lips.

"Opal?"

"Yeah?" she says, voice hesitant. Heartbreakingly shaky.

I look up at her face again. "You're fucking perfect."

Then I lean forward and kiss her to show her just how much I mean it.

I take my time with her tonight, teasing and gentle.

I can't wait, she whispers when the pleasure builds, but I pull away, gentling the tip of my tongue against her in a barely there touch. A delicious torture.

Yes you can, I say against her skin. Her hands grip my hair as a moan breaks from her throat, but my sweet girl endures.

I touch myself as I continue to work her, telling her how beautiful she is. How cute and charming and outrageously wonderful, smiling like an absolute fool at the joy of it all.

When I focus in, letting Opal tip over the edge, she giggles as she comes, her laughter knitting together the delicate, frayed edges of my open wounds.

I crawl back up her body, kissing in reverence until I get to her lips. She presses her mouth to mine, pulling me down on top of her, holding me close. Her kisses are lazy and slow as we both come back to earth. Eventually, I roll to my side, tucking her close, and it isn't long until her breathing evens out, heavy with sleep as the cicadas sing around us.

And right here, right now—under a great big sky, surrounded by flowers and wrapped in the arms of the girl I'm falling for—I know there's no place more special in the world.

Chapter 30

OPAL

The Grove Park Inn stands in front of us like the final boss in a video game: broad and imposing, its redbrick roof glowing in the afternoon sun. I swallow down the lump of nerves in my throat.

"Ready?" I whisper to Pepper, eyes fixed on the giant building.

"No."

I stare at it for another minute, anxiety zipping up my arms. All competing teams were given a complimentary room at the Grove Park Inn for the night before the competition, and it's a shame I won't be able to get any sleep in the bougie-ass beds due to my inevitable panic spiral over tomorrow.

"Ready?" I whisper again.

"Yeah," she says, voice cracking. She leads us inside.

I feel like one classy motherfucker looking around this place. The lobby—if you can even bastardize it with that name;

great hall is more fitting—is massive. The vaulted ceiling is supported by thick pillars of rich wood, and clusters of brown leather chesterfields and chairs create a coziness, the space capped at each end with granite fireplaces, at least ten feet wide.

After stopping at the front desk to get our room keys and a few directions about where competitor materials have been stored, we head to our room.

We take the elevator up, and Pepper reaches out, braiding our fingers together, then tucking our joined hands into the pocket of her sundress as we rise to the tenth floor. As the doors slide open, we look at each other. And grin at the absurdity of our luxurious accommodations.

Zips of electricity spark along my body as we run to our room. I fumble with the key, Pepper's hands traveling over my body, her smile pressed into my neck, her laugh vibrating against my skin until I finally get the door open.

There are two beds, but we don't give the second any attention, giggling and tripping our way to the one closest to the window, tangling on top of the sheets.

"I can't believe we're actually doing this," Pepper whispers, hovering above me. Her smile is broad and electric, and she's looking at me in a way that has me questioning if she means the competition or . . . us.

"I can," I say, straining up to kiss the hollow at the base of her throat. The answer is true regardless of what she meant. That smile of hers somehow grows.

I wiggle out from beneath her, then stand up and jump on the luxe mattress, making Pepper's body bounce and thrash, hair shooting out like ink in water. She squeals in delight, and I jump with all the force I have.

"Stop it," she says, gripping one of my ankles. I crumple down, landing on top of her with an *oof*, and she laughs even harder. "You're ridiculous," she mumbles against my neck.

And it's true. I'm ridiculous and hyper and a fool. All for her. I'd do anything to make her laugh.

She holds me tight against her chest, body shaking with giggles as her hands rub up and down my arms.

The shrill ring of the room's phone slices through our happy haze.

"No!" I shriek, clutching her tighter. No intruders allowed.

With a groan, Pepper slides me off her, keeping me tucked to her side as she reaches for the phone.

"Hello?" Her voice is smooth and smoky like whiskey, and I nuzzle closer to her throat.

I can't make out any words from the tinny voice on the other end, but whatever they say makes Pepper purse her lips. "Oh. Okay. I'll be right down."

She untangles herself to drop the phone back on the receiver, her cheeks flushed and eyes heavy-lidded as she looks at me.

"Who was that?" I ask, wrapping my arm around her waist, sliding her back into my clutches. I'm a greedy thief and I'll rob her of every moment she'll let me have.

"Front desk," she says, giving me a soft kiss on the crown of my head. "Says there's someone needing to talk to us in the lobby. I'm assuming it's about the competition."

"They probably saw our concept proposal and are ready to crown us winners on the spot," I say with a yawn, stretching my arms over my head. It's midday, but our room is so cozy and my limbs feel so languid with lust, I want to curl up here forever.

Pepper sits up and gets out of bed, pulling her long hair into a ponytail. "Wishful thinking," she says, giving me her signature eye roll.

"Maybe," I say, standing and readjusting my clothes. She steps toward the door but I grab her hand, placing a soft kiss to her palm. "Or maybe I just believe in us."

Chapter 31

PEPPER

The problem with letting your guard down for even a moment, is that you find yourself without any weapons the second you need them. And with Trish—her blonde beehive of hair bobbing as she looks at me, hot-pink lips stretched in a slimy grin—I need all the weapons I can get.

"What are you doing here?" I say, stopping in my tracks in the lobby, Opal at my side.

Trish's smile falters for a moment, but she quickly recovers. "Well, hello to you too, doll," she says, high heels clacking as she closes the distance between us, giving me a hug that makes my skin crawl. She holds me a second too long, the smell of nicotine and her vanilla perfume choking me.

"What are you doing here?" I repeat, lips numb, pressure building in my head as I stare at her. I feel Opal touch my hand, but I ignore it, my focus going to survival mode.

"Well, baby, I read about you in the papers, and I had to

see this for myself," Trish says, lifting up her arms and doing a slow circle around the beautiful great hall. "I'm just so proud of you," she says, reaching out and grabbing my hand. I really wish she would stop touching me.

"You read?" I say. I'm not trying to be funny, but Opal snickers at my side.

A flash of anger crosses Trish's makeup-caked face, but she quickly schools her features. "I like to stay abreast of the happenings in my community," she says, voice dripping with honey.

"I thought you were living in Charlotte?"

"Good Lord, what's with the third degree, Pepper? Ain't ya happy to see me?"

"Not particularly, no," I say, my pulse hammering in my ears. My mom's scowl lingers for a bit longer this time.

"Well, I'm happy to see you, honey. So happy. I was up here for a little visit, see, and the second I saw your face in that newspaper, I knew it was fate. Time to reconnect with my girl."

My eyes flick around us, checking the corners like I'm about to be ambushed. Trish tuts.

"You always were so hard to please," she says, voice hushed and solemn. "Here I am, hoping for some grand reunion with my precious daughter, and you're looking at me like I killed someone. It hurts a person's feelings, looks like that. Give me a chance here, Pepper. Please."

I know it's foolish, I know it's reckless, but my heart squeezes because, shit, wouldn't it be nice if that's what she really wants?

"I-I . . . I'm sorry," I say, voice hoarse. "I'm just surprised. You know how it takes me a minute to adjust."

My mom laughs like I'm the funniest person in the world. I flinch at the noise. "Boy, do I," she says looking at Opal. She does a double take. "Well, I'll be damned, you're that sweet thing I sold the farm to! How are ya, honey?"

Opal slants a dubious glance at my mom, lips puckered and arms crossed over her chest. "I'm fine, thank you."

"Ain't ya lovin' the Thistle and Bloom?" she asks, unfazed by Opal's discomfort.

Opal's eyes flick to me, then back to my mom. "It's amazing."

Trish claps her hands in glee. "See! I knew you'd love it. Such a wonderful place. Pepper, I need you to update me on *everything*. I know, how about we get some lunch? This fancy-pants place certainly isn't short on restaurants, I'm sure." She looks around like she's trying to scope out a seat. "Then we can sit and have a nice meal and you tell me all about you and the farm and what's been happening. My treat."

My traitorous heart lurches. Wouldn't that be nice. Wouldn't it feel so damn good for my mom, the person who's supposed to love me unconditionally, to finally want to spend time with me. Know me.

I've convinced myself my heart is hard as stone toward the woman, but even a hint at her affection has it crumbling to dust. I can have all the bravado in the world, but the second she gives me an ounce of attention, I'm a little kid again, eager and bouncing for her approval.

I'm a fool, but I want it. I want to sit with my mom, have

her take me to lunch and listen to stories of my life. I'd tell her about the farm, how it's changed, how it's stayed the same. I'd tell her about Lou and my friends and maybe, if I'm feeling brave, even tell her about some of my feelings for Opal. I open my mouth, about to agree, when I feel a sharp squeeze on my hand.

I glance at Opal, her eyes wide in warning, and I shore up some of my defenses.

"Now's not the best time, Mom," I say, clearing my throat. "We have a lot of setup to do with the competition."

Her lips purse in a pout. "That's a true shame. You can't even spare me an hour? What about half, and we get a coffee?"

I shake my head, pinpricks of unease lifting the hairs at the back of my neck. "I'm sorry, but I really can't."

Her face falls, and it looks so sincere, the next words rush out of me before I can think better. "But maybe after the competition tomorrow? Or Sunday?"

There's a beat, and something in Trish's face shutters, like she's scrounging for what emotion to show. She settles on impotence. She opens her mouth, but I cut her off, a question ballooning in my mind.

"Where are you staying?" I ask, eyes narrowing. "Is it somewhere close?"

Trish's lips part, her lipstick cracking. "Well, that's kind of the thing, sugar. I find myself between accommodations at the moment."

My spine straightens like a joint locking into place, all the pieces clicking together. "You want money," I say, voice low and emotionless as I blink at my mom. She has the decency to look affronted, hand shooting to her chest.

"Oh, God no! What kind of mother do you think I am? It's nothing like that."

"You want money," I repeat.

Trish lets out a fake laugh, her beautiful smile strained and tight. "I've missed my one-track-minded little robot. No, you see, I'm doing better than I've ever been. I have this new beau, Randy, he's actually right over there."

We glance to where she points, seeing a weasely-looking man, tall and thin with sallow skin and a neck tattoo, sulking in the corner, sunken eyes alert as he watches guests roam about the lobby. Trish is truly the world's worst cliché.

"And he's so good to me, sugar, you wouldn't believe it. Building us a beautiful house, ya see. It's going to be huge. A mountain château. And I'm making sure he's adding a whole wing for you, Pep. Because that's what this is really about. I miss you, honey. I wanna make up for lost time. Have a nice house for you to come stay with me."

I stare at her, the icy edge of a knife slicing through my chest.

"But the problem is, the build got delayed. Not by much now, mind you, just a week. Maybe two. But our lease is up on our apartment. Oh my God, this apartment. Wish you'd have seen it. Two thousand square feet. Right in downtown Charlotte. Floor-to-ceiling windows. Living there had me feeling like one of the Real Housewives. Anyway, we didn't renew the lease, obviously, because we thought we'd be able to move into our new mountain mansion. But you know how these things go, delays, delays, delays. So we're in between spots and we sure would appreciate it if you could give us a little help. Maybe let us stay with you until it's done? Or even if you know of a nice hotel in the area." She gestures around at our beautiful surroundings. "I'd love your advice."

There's a beat of silence, my heart sloshing down to my knees, my fingers clawing at the skin of my cuticles. "You want money."

And that does it, her temper sparking, nostrils flaring. That look hooks a chain into the center of my chest and jerks me back, whipping me into the past. Every harsh word. Every broken promise. Every moment of aching loneliness, whether she was next to me or not.

She tries to play it cool, but that always makes the explosion worse. "Pepper," she says through clenched teeth. "I'd like you to shut your silly little mouth and listen to what I'm trying to tell you—"

"I know what you're trying to tell me. I'm terrible at reading people, but I can read you, Mom. You make it so obvious."

That fake smile falls, a deep red rushing up her cheeks and to the tips of her ears. "You better knock it off, young lady. You're being extremely unlikable right now. If you'd—"

"I don't want you to like me, Mom," I yell, throwing my arms up and gaining more than a few looks. "I don't give a fuck if anyone finds me likable. I just want you to care. I want you to care enough about your only child that you have even the tiniest bit of hesitation before hitting me up for money after abandoning me on a random doorstep."

She grips my arm, ripping me into the nearest corner, eyes scanning the room as I garner more attention. "Shut your damn mouth right now, Pepper Anne. I didn't *abandon* you," she spits, face getting close to mine as I shrink under her glare. "You *know* I've always done my best. Have I made mistakes? Sure. Of course. I'm only human. But am I not allowed any grace? Any room for error? What about the mistakes you've made? I never throw your greed in your face. The way you were always putting on airs. I'd never make you feel bad for that."

"All you've ever done in my life is make me feel bad," I say with a choked laugh, tears pricking at my eyes, a few falling down my cheeks. "Do you know how endlessly exhausting it is to be the child of a narcissistic con artist? My entire identity is tangled into this impossible web of your lies and what you want me to be. What role I'm supposed to play. I'm not some piece in your games, Mom."

She leans toward me, eyes on fire, and I feel claustrophobic, like my entire being is shrunk down to the pinpricks of her pupils. Like I'm nothing but a speck, and she's going to wipe me away.

"Some things never change, huh? You'll always be—"

She doesn't get to decide my fate. Instead, Opal squeezes herself between us, pushing my mom closer to the wall and me stumbling a pace backward.

"You better stop talking to her this way before I really cause a scene," Opal says. She's a solid six inches shorter than Trish, but it's obvious who the stronger woman is.

Trish blinks a few times. "Excuse me? Who do you think you are?"

Opal cackles, and I'm filled with warmth at the harsh sound. "I'm your worst nightmare if you keep talking to Pepper that way."

Trish scoffs.

"Don't believe me? Then keep going. Because I know all about you, Trish Boden. I know your aliases and your schemes and all those dusty skeletons in your closet. And I have the means to uncover even more of them if I'm tempted. So, do me a favor. Make my fucking day. Keep talking to Pepper and see how much fun I can have."

I wish I could see Opal's face, read whatever outrageous lie she's going to say next. Because while she may know a bit about my mom's shitty track record, this green-haired devil doesn't have the resources (or, let's face it, the attention span) to dig deeper. But she's putting on quite the convincing performance.

And it's the sweetest thing anyone's ever done for me.

Luckily, Trish has backed herself into enough corners, always trying to squirm out, and she doesn't see through Opal's false bravado.

She lets out a haughty sniff, shouldering her way past Opal. "And here I was, trying to have a civil conversation with my daughter, and she sics a miscreant like you on me. Come on,

Randy, we're leaving," she hollers, snapping her fingers. Randy scuttles over, and they walk to the door. "I'll pray for you both. Bless your hearts," Trish says with venom over her shoulder.

"Fuck you right back, lady," Opal yells.

My mom shakes her head and tuts. Randy, classy man that he is, flicks us off with both hands.

"Might want to take a second to adjust your collar," Opal adds, a vindictive grin snaking across her lips. "Your redneck is showing."

Opal turns to me, her smile falling as she sees the tears pouring out of me at this point.

"Oh, Pepper," she whispers, grabbing both my hands. "Come on."

She whisks me into the elevator, jamming the button for our floor a million times as we ride up. She directs me down the hallway in a blur, my muscles heavy and sagging as sadness churns in my gut. Somehow, she gets me on the bed, my head tucked against her chest as I cry. My heart is battered and bruised like an iris clutched in a fist, but with every soft touch of her hands on my cheeks, my back, my chest, she loosens the grip.

She doesn't tell me to stop crying. She doesn't tell me it'll be okay. Opal doesn't do anything but hold me. Because being held is exactly what I need.

Chapter 32

PEPPER

I wake up hours later with a jolt, my heart thrumming as my mom's sharp voice echoes in my head. It takes me a long time to process that I'm not fighting with her, listening to her smart jabs and cruel words.

I'm in a hotel room with Opal curled against my back, lips against my shoulder, breath soft against my skin.

I'm okay.

Well, that's not exactly true. I'm wrung out and sad and every scabbed-over wound feels cracked open.

But I feel . . . content. Comfortable. Understood by the peculiar woman who's choosing to wrap herself around me. I'm filled with a hope that maybe she'll want to stay there. And that's terrifying. I'm plunged in the middle of an ocean of feelings, wave after wave cresting over my head. All I want is for my feet to touch the ground.

Carefully, I pull away from her warmth and get out of bed.

I look back at Opal, and my breath catches in my throat. She's so lovely—white sheets wrapped around her, cheeks rosy and body relaxed in sleep—and I want nothing more than to crawl back into bed. But I turn instead. That way lies danger and hurt feelings and being let down. It feels too good to be trusted.

Unzipping the outer pocket of my bag, I pull out the small rectangle, dragging the pad of my thumb along the edge as I stare at the painting of me and Grandma Lou that Opal made. It fills me with a sense of peace I'm not sure I deserve.

"You brought that with you?" Opal's voice is soft, and I turn to see her propped up on her elbow, eyes heavy with sleep as she looks at me.

I swallow. She's so beautiful, it's almost painful. "I take it with me everywhere."

"I didn't know that."

I shrug. It's small enough to fit perfectly in the front pocket of my overalls or the back pocket of my jeans. I don't take it out when I'm working—I'd hate to get it dirty—but the light weight of it on my person now feels as vital as breathing.

Opal shifts, sliding off the bed and kneeling beside me on the floor. I fix my eyes on the painting, pressing my fingers into its corners.

"I wish you could have met her." I curl my lips into my mouth, trying to fight the tears steadily rolling down my cheeks.

"Me too." Opal loops her arms around me, gently tucking my head under her chin. "But I'm glad I was lucky enough to meet *you*."

My heart stutters, then beats in double time. I turn in Opal's arms, giving her a look that's painfully, terrifyingly hopeful. "You are?"

Opal grins, threading her fingers through my hair and pressing a kiss to my temple. "If it's not mortifyingly obvious, I really like you, Pepper. Like, massive, draw-your-name-in-hearts-all-over-my-notebook kind of like you. I thought me telling you as much in the greenhouse would kind of solidify the point."

"I . . ." My throat knots up. I want to be brave. I want to be honest. I want to tiptoe out onto that tightrope and join her in the vulnerability. But the risk of it snapping and breaking, that free fall before the crash, makes me shake my head and pull away. "People hyperbolize all the time," I say, plucking at the hem of my T-shirt. "So much of what you're feeling could just be good sex hormones. The high of the moment. It's human nature. It won't last."

Opal shifts, facing me. She reaches for my hands but I pretend not to notice. She leaves hers extended anyway. "I can't predict the future," she says, tilting her head, a soft smile on her lips. "But I don't think that's what this is. Not for me."

I shake my head harder. Her words sound too enticing, too lovely and beautiful and far too good to belong to me. "Don't say that. People wake up every day and decide to leave someone behind; decide you're too much to carry; break promises they swear they'll keep without a second thought."

Opal lurches forward, eyes fierce, hands somehow gentle as she cups my cheeks, tilting my face until I have to look at her.

"Listen to me," she whispers, breath ghosting across my mouth. "You were dealt a shitty hand, Pepper, there's no denying that. And I'll never be able to wipe away that pain. I'll never want to. It's yours to feel as you need. But you've made do for way too long with the person that was supposed to love you hurting you instead. But that stops now. Fuck anything and anyone that made you have to survive instead of live. You deserve a life so peaceful it feels deliciously boring. A life filled with flowers and sunny days and people who show you all the time that you're valued and worthy. You deserve it all."

A sharp sob rips from me, and I fall into her, clutching her close to me. Opal rocks me as I cry and it's too much all at once yet somehow exactly right.

Eventually, I calm down enough to take a breath, and Opal leads me to the bed, lying next to me. She doesn't stop touching me even for a second.

"You scare me," I murmur, my heart aching as it reaches for her.

Opal snorts, nose scrunching. "Pepper, I'm a five-two human disaster with green hair. What part of me could be scary?"

I let out a shuddering breath. "You make me want to hope. And that's terrifying. Because hope lets you down. Hope hurts you."

Opal smooths back my hair, then brushes the tears off my cheeks with her thumbs, fixing me with a devastatingly soft smile.

"Hope doesn't hurt you, Pepper," she whispers. "People do. Hope lightens you and lifts you and expands more room in your heart than you know what to do with. And sharing that hope with someone that will care for it and tend to it like it deserves only lets it grow more and more."

She pulls in a deep breath. Holds it. Lets it trace across my lips with soft warmth.

"I want your hope, Pepper. I'll do everything in my power to protect that hope if you let me. Put it all on me."

I don't answer her with words. I couldn't even if I wanted to; the pang of need that slices through me is so sharp, I have to move. Have to get closer, closer, *closer* to this soft, wonderful woman and her terrifying words and too-big heart. I need her against me and around me and in me and on me.

I need her.

And nothing is going to stop me.

I kiss her so hard, her head rocks back, but it doesn't matter, my palm is there, cradling her to me, my other hand tracing up her stomach, across her breasts, pausing at the beat of her heart, to curl around her throat, feeling her pulse beneath my skin.

Opal's just as desperate.

She undresses us in a blur, hands sure and needy as she strips away every layer until it's skin against skin. We gasp at the contact. Sigh in relief. The want is quick as a flare but steady as a glowing ember. Hot and bright and vital.

Lying side by side, I arch against her body, twisting my hands in her hair and bringing her closer still. I hold her steady as she traces wild paths across my skin—the curve of my hip, the notches of my ribs, the shell of my ear. She makes every inch of me feel stunning.

It's impossible to stop kissing her, feeling those soft lips against mine, catching every moan and whimper in my mouth. Feeding them back to her. Our legs tangle together as we each slip a hand between our bodies, exploring the other, mirroring movements and strokes until we're a closed circuit of pleasure.

Opal nudges me to my back, then hovers over me, smile so radiant, something in my chest cracks. She presses a kiss to the tip of my nose. My temple. My eyelids. My neck. She kisses me like I'm something precious to her, and my throat clogs with so many emotions trying to get out. I bury my face against her chest so she doesn't see, so I don't scare her with every emotion sitting in my eyes.

She laughs softly at something, then sits up, gentling a hand down my thigh. I fall open for her, sucking in a sharp breath as electricity dances across my skin.

"Fuck," Opal mumbles, pinching the fabric of my wet underwear and rubbing it between her fingers. She pulls them down my legs, tossing them behind her, then hums in satisfaction as she touches me some more. I throw my arm over my mouth and bite back a sob.

Kneeling between my legs, she spreads me, holding me open. I look down my body to watch her studying me with hungry desire. She licks her lips and the want radiating from her tense body makes my hips buck in response, greedy for more.

She laughs again.

"I'm not sure what could possibly be funny," I gasp out, trying to twist away as a heavy throb echoes through my center.

She holds me still, smiling. That grin is sugary sweet with

satisfaction, like a lioness sizing up her next meal. "You're just so fucking pretty when you want me."

She drapes my legs over her shoulders as she lies flat against the mattress. Gripping my hips, she jerks me forward, mouth hot and hungry against my clit, pulling a sharp cry from me. I press even closer, gripping her hair at the roots and pulling her against me as my hips thrust in a disjointed rhythm.

"That's it," she says, lifting her head to look up at me, lips wet and full and red. "Show me how much you like it."

My hips grind even harder, and her smile sends a sharp jolt of pleasure straight down my spine.

She bites my hip bone, sucking the skin, then kisses the spot. Her mark leaves a perfect maroon stain, and I have the ridiculous and disarming thought that I never want it to fade. I want to remember Opal's lips on my skin, her head between my thighs, until the day I die.

She returns to my clit with unparalleled focus. My toes curl into the sheets as she licks and sucks me, jaw clenched tight, every muscle poised to snap.

"I'm so close," I pant out, gripping her head, riding her tongue. I feel her hum of encouragement against me, rough and desperate and so fucking excited, it pushes me over the edge, wave after wave crashing through me, and I cry out her name as I come.

She works me through the aftershocks, somehow tender and dirty and so achingly wonderful I'm worried I might do something humiliating like cry or ask her to never leave me. Instead, I tug on her hair again, pulling her up.

Opal comes willingly, kissing me hard and deep as I throw my arms around her neck, pressing our chests together.

After a few more languid kisses, she readjusts our position, back on top of me as she slots her hips against mine. We stay like that for a moment, feeling each other, watching the other breathe. She's so beautiful it almost hurts.

Then she gives a tentative roll of her pelvis.

And I'm absolutely gone.

We both groan, Opal gripping my hips so hard I wonder if I'll bruise, little marks like violet petals along my skin to show how much she owns me.

I watch her face, the way she tilts her head back, eyes closed as she bites down hard into her lip. Color rushes across her cheeks, down her throat, across her chest. I reach out, cupping her full breasts in my hands, rolling her nipples between my fingers, then giving them a sharp tug. She cries out, and I soothe the spot with the pads of my thumbs until she's arching into me, then pinch them again. I feel her pussy clench against mine and I moan.

She's so slick and wet as she grinds against me, crude sounds of flesh against flesh mixing with our pants, kicking my desire higher. She moves faster, harder, little stars dancing in my vision as I stare at her.

"Right there," I gasp out. "Just like that. Don't stop."

"It's so good—you're so good—I *can't* stop."

I come hard and fast, my stomach contracting, my whole body shaking against her.

"Yes," she moans, following me over the edge. With a

hoked sob, she collapses over me, face pressed into my neck, kin slick against mine as we both fight to catch our breath.

And in this moment—with her weight holding my body) the earth, my head floating to the clouds, her heart beating gainst mine—I think that maybe, just maybe, Opal's right.

Hope doesn't have to hurt.

Chapter 33

OPAL

"I want to die," I say to Pepper over the rim of my weak coffe[e] as we survey our competition booth.

Pepper lets out a suffering sigh. "We don't really have tim[e] for the dramatics today."

"I'm sorry, is admitting the truth of my mental state af[-] ter being awoken via hate crime this morning now considere[d] dramatic?"

"Me telling you it's time to get up is not a hate crime," Pep[-] per says, slanting me a sharp look as she pushes a dolly of boxe[s] filled with dried flowers across the space. I wilt against the wal[l.]

"It is when it's four thirty in the morning," I whine.

She lets out another sigh, parking the dolly. Her hands han[g] on her hips as she glares at me, and I push out my bottom lip[,] giving her puppy-dog eyes. Her mouth quirks at the corners.

"We don't have time for this," she says again, glancing a[t] her watch.

"All I need is a quick apology." I drag my toe across the floor, looking up at her through my lashes. She's fully grinning.

Pepper stalks toward me, hands flexing like she's anticipating touching me, and my stomach swoops. I like her so much, it takes everything in me not to jump on her like a koala.

She reaches out like she can't help herself, cupping my face. She leans in, brushing her nose against mine once, twice, then pressing a soft kiss to my lips, little sparks dazzling across my skin.

"I'm sorry for waking you to help me set up for a competition you basically used brute force to get me to do," she murmurs against my mouth.

"Forgiven," I say on the end of a breathy giggle.

With this new wealth of motivation, we get to work on the setup. Pepper moves the various supplies around the space as I start constructing the focal piece, wrestling with chicken wire and fishing nets to drape flowers from.

Not having any misgivings on who's better suited for the task, I put Pepper in charge of stringing the long flower chains across the ceiling and down the back walls. A few of the garlands are suspended straight down to hang, the delicate poms of yellow dahlias looking like stars against the pink-and-purple backdrop reminiscent of early dusk.

After the centerpiece is constructed, I get to work on the finer details—a foxglove to draw the eye, pale pink rose petals to add shade, wispy white anemones to smooth out some edges.

Pepper and I work in focused silence, only pausing to confirm placement or ask if we've added enough flowers to a spot for the right effect. The heavy perfume of the blooms is nice at first, heady and lush, but after a few hours of work, my eyes are itching and my brain feels swollen in my skull from it all.

But I don't stop.

I run down the clock, crawling on my hands and knees, stretching up on my highest tiptoes, building a garden with my bare hands.

It has to be perfect. I *need* it to be perfect. Not for me, but for Pepper. I want to show her I'm good for something—that I can offer her something—even if it's as niche and rather useless as flower art. Something changed between us last night, and Pepper opening up to me is the single greatest gift I've ever received, but it's not lost on me that I keep putting my heart on the line, telling her how much I care about her, and not hearing it echoed back. For all I know, this could still be part of our arrangement to her, and she's letting me bend the no-feelings rule on my part because it means orgasms for her.

It's scary to like someone this much without receiving confirmation that I'm not alone in this consuming feeling.

I walk around the piece again, brow furrowed and gaze sharp, diving at every bud that dares droop out of place. On my fifth lap, I go back in to adjust the top portion, cussing out the yarrow and anemones and chocolate lace flowers for not lying right. I prick my finger on a hidden straight pin holding some stems in place and yelp, a drop of blood welling up on the tip of my finger and dripping onto a white petal.

"I'm a fucking Muppet," I scream, sucking on my finger. "So stupid." With my non-bleeding appendage, I go to adjust the yarrow again (or tear the whole thing out, who's to say?), but Pepper's hand circles my wrist.

"Opal," she whispers, tugging me so I spin to face her. I don't meet her eyes. I don't want to see disappointment or resignation or worry that we won't win. "Opal, look at me."

"Don't think I will, thanks."

Pepper softly grips my chin with her thumb and forefinger, tilting my face up, and I close my eyes at the last second.

She coaxes her hand across my cheek, down my throat, to rest over my thrumming heart. "Please."

Damn woman. I'm pretty sure her touch could make me do anything.

With a sigh, I look at her, bracing for the dismay I'm sure will be etched across her pretty features. But it's not there. Her eyes are soft, crinkled at the corners, mouth stretched in the biggest smile I've ever seen her wear, a steady glow radiating from her skin. Then she hugs me.

"You've done enough," she whispers into my hair, swaying us back and forth.

I go to pull away, to argue, but she holds me tighter.

"There's still things I need to fix," I mumble against her collarbone.

I feel her shake her head, then place a kiss to my temple. "No there aren't. It's perfect."

Shushing any further arguments I try to make, she drags me from the room, and the fresh air makes me light-headed.

Lacing her fingers through mine, she leads us to a refreshment table, shoving a water bottle in my hand and not letting me stop drinking until half of it is gone. I go to speak, but she's too fast, popping three grapes in my mouth.

When I finally swallow them down, she goes to place a cookie in there next, but I dodge her, giggling.

"Okay, okay! I'm resuscitated."

"Phew," she says, pretending to flick sweat off her forehead. "Almost thought I lost you there."

"Hunger takes me to a dark place."

"Yeah, no shit. I'm scared of what will happen if I don't get a full meal in you in the next ten minutes."

"I'll make my final metamorphosis into a cuntosaurus rex and pillage this lovely hotel." I hold up my limp wrists in front of me, making a roaring sound.

Pepper blinks a few times, then throws back her head and laughs. "You're so weird," she says, pulling me into another hug.

"Should we go get changed?" I ask, breathing her in. "Judging starts in about an hour."

Pepper nods, then lets me go. Glancing around for any witnesses, we grab armfuls of snacks from the table and make a mad dash to our room.

After scarfing down some chips and cookies, we take turns rinsing off. For a bougie-ass hotel, the shower is way too small for us to do anything even a tiny bit naughty, and I'll definitely be mentioning this in my Google review.

"Can I do your hair?" I ask, waving my curling iron through the air. I'm having a last-minute realization that incorporating heat tools into the mess on top of my head is asking for trouble. And that's what they call *growth*.

"Um . . ." Pepper eyes my green strands. "We're running a bit behind schedule. I wouldn't want you to be rushed."

With a gasp of not-so-mock outrage, I jump at her, pinning her to the bed and plastering kisses everywhere I can reach.

"Please?" I whine, nuzzling her neck. I feel the vibrations of her laugh against my cheek.

"Fine," she says on a sigh, and I squeal in delight. "But we have to hurry."

I sit her down, curling the back. Her hair is thick and silky between my fingers, and I can't stop playing with it, running my hands through it. Pepper hums in satisfaction while I do, tilting her head back, leaning into my touch. I eventually move in front of her, focusing on the layers around her face.

I try to do a good job, I really do, but Pepper keeps pawing at the tie of my robe, playing with the edges across my chest, and it isn't long until the curling iron is turned off and tossed on the desk and I'm straddling her lap, hands messing up that beautiful hair as I kiss her like I'm starving and she's my first taste of food. We make out like lust-deranged teenagers, giggling and fumbling as we roll across the mattress, fingers clumsy and fast as we sprint toward a shared goal.

"Now we really have to hurry," Pepper says, hair sticking every which way as we lie side by side, panting as sunlight streams through the window.

Grinning like a fool, I jump up and throw on my dress, Pepper following my lead. She pulls on an emerald green jumpsuit that makes her golden skin glow. She's so pretty I think I might die.

Despite her protests, I throw a quick, loose braid in her hair, tucking flowers through the strands. Pepper glances at herself in the mirror, then does a double take, with a smile like a child as she looks at the result.

"Ugh" is all she says, cupping my cheeks and giving me a deep kiss, transferring that smile right to me.

We head downstairs, stopping first in the lobby. The space has been transformed into a buzzing garden to showcase the individual flower entrants. Pepper told me earlier that there are awards for everything from petite blooms to the most giant-ass dahlia someone can grow. She explained it in much more technical terms, but I got distracted by how cute she is when she's excited about a topic.

We weave through a long hallway holding the small-construction bouquets before moving to the lower floor to scope out our direct competition before we're scheduled to be in our booth for judging.

"Opie!" My sisters' voices echo across the room, and a moment later, I'm body-slammed by both, tripping backward as they hug me.

"Hi," I wheeze as they squeeze me tighter.

"Hi, you little superstar," Ophelia says, pinching both my cheeks.

"We're so proud of you," Olivia says, pulling away to greet Pepper with a similar hug.

"You haven't even seen ours yet," I counter.

Olivia waves my words away. "Doesn't matter. I know it's amazing."

My blush is embarrassingly bright. "Are Tal and Diksha here?" I ask, turning to Pepper. She checks her phone.

"Yeah, they're here. Diksha said Tal is deep in florist talk with some colleagues and they'll catch up with us when judging starts."

"Cool."

"No more stalling, let's go quietly heckle the other contestants."

I smack Ophelia on the shoulder.

"I meant *admire*. Gosh, sorry. Freudian slip."

I roll my eyes but follow them into the line of stalls.

The first few stations are nothing special, lots of predictable uses of hearts, a few others that seemed to take the theme as a mere suggestion and used the space to show off their ability to arrange a whimsical-looking flower arch with accompanying bouquets.

"Not sure why we were so nervous," I whisper to Pepper out of the corner of my mouth after staring at a particularly bland display of only roses. She elbows me in the ribs.

"You're going to jinx us."

Pepper appears to be right, because the next row of displays ups the game a bit.

"Shit," she mumbles as we take in a particularly detailed scene.

A man made of flowers holds a standing microphone crafted out of woven pussy-willow branches. He has on hot-pink pants made of ranunculi, and a magenta vest from a variety of blooms. The whole thing creates a vibrant energy that feels somehow familiar. I read the plaque every participant got to draft up for the work and see it's Harry Styles during his Love on Tour tour. After another glance, the resemblance is undeniable.

"I don't mean to be aggressive, but I would make sweet, sweet love to that flower man, no questions asked," Ophelia says, Olivia nodding in agreement.

"I told you the celebrity flower moment is a brilliant idea," I grumble at Pepper.

"I want you to know I'm ignoring you," she says, moving on to the next display.

This one is a giant human heart centered on a wall. It's made of blood-red dahlias and zinnias, rose petals suspended from the ventricles like drops of blood. It's so large and imposing, it almost appears to be expanding and contracting, the effect making me queasy.

"It kind of reminds me of the *Midnight Sun* book cover," Olivia whispers as we step away.

We pass through another unremarkable row, the only standouts being one entry that made tons of different birds and a swarm of bees from blooms, and a second that spelled out *LOVE* from suspended blooms that morphed into a giant flower if you viewed it from a different angle.

One of the flashiest displays in the next row is a replica of a ballroom wedding reception. The floor is in a checkered pattern of tightly packed baby's breath and hyacinth so dark, they're almost black. A similarly deep color was used for a piano in the background, while a couple in wedding attire is placed directly in the center. They've utilized mannequin heads and arms for the newlyweds, but their outfits are created from flowers too, his navy-blue suit appearing fuzzy from the pom-poms of petals, the bride's dress a cascade of white in a stunning silhouette. What's so astonishing is the amount of motion they've infused, creating a sense that the groom just spun the bride close for a kiss, her dress swirling around their ankles.

Well . . . shit.

But a wedding scene is so cliché and heteronormative for the theme . . . right?

The final display in this row reminds me of the scene in *Bambi* before things get traumatizing. Various woodland creatures are scattered throughout the display. A line of fuzzy baby ducks made of daisies are following their mama, with two little bunnies mid-hop in the back corner fashioned from hydrangeas. A family of deer graze in the center, their expressions so animated it takes all my willpower not to let out a wistful *aww*. The surrounding scene is lush with wildflowers. Mother Nature at her happiest and brightest.

"Damn . . . that's really good."

Pepper nods, turning and hustling toward our area. Diksha and Tal wave at us down the hall. "That's enough of that," Pepper says with finality. "No use creating even more doubt for ourselves, right?"

I have to agree.

Some of these are . . . well, really freaking good, and it

creates a sharp bubble of jealousy that hiccups in my chest. Whatever. I can't think about that now because right after we get to our spot, three judges appear, and our moment arrives.

The judges circle our piece—our floral shrine—to one of the greats.

Sappho.

She stands larger than life in the center of our display, a writing tool clutched in one hand, a book in the other. Her body is made from flexible reeds and draped in a Grecian gown of pale pink flowers. Her hair is a mix of fresh and dried blooms, chocolate lace and delicate immortelle, creating the soft full curls.

We fashioned the tablet in her arms by weaving together hardy stems and creating pages of white petals, a cascade of brilliant flowers pouring from her book, spilling to the ground and spreading at her feet in swirls of delicate rainbows, lone petals and blooms sprinkled to the edges of the space, showing just how far her words reach. Ideas sprout around her in the form of flowers, hanging in her line of sight and floating above her head, ready to be plucked and set down to inspire people for thousands of years to come.

The judges circle her like sharks, and I clear my throat, stepping next to her.

"Sappho of Lesbos is not only one of very few poetesses from ancient Greece, but one of the greatest poets in recorded history," I say, voice wobbly as I launch into our allotted five minutes of explanation and inspiration. "Much of her work was

lost for years, and—when it was refound—burned for portray-
ing the sensuality and desire that comes with loving more than
one gender. Like many great women of history, she was scorned
by men who ruled, parodying her memory as overly promis-
cuous and lecherous . . . not too terribly different to how we
shame contemporary women for expressing any sorts of desire."

The eyes of the judges leave Sappho, sticking on me. I
clear my throat again, trying to drum up the courage to keep
speaking.

"We drew inspiration for this piece"—I wave at her tall
form—"from the famous fresco of Sappho. Some historians argue that the iconic painting probably isn't even Sappho, instead
an unidentified woman from Pompeii. I'm not an expert on art
from that era, and I'm certainly not a supporter of revisionist
history or anything like that, but I tend to disagree with them. I
really like the idea that this woman—who's holding her weapons
of pen and paper so close, looking out, lost in thought, some
of the most sacred human experiences waiting in a drop of ink
she'll trace across the page—is Sappho. Plus, I'm evoking the
right of artistic license or whatever."

That earns me a few chuckles from the judges. I pause,
glancing again at Sappho, then to Pepper, who's hovering on
the edges. Her smile is so luminous, it makes my eyes water.

"While so much of her work has been lost to time, what
remains is beautiful. Important. Sappho didn't recite epic tales
or yell at gods." I'm lost to everyone else in the room, unable to
stop staring at Pepper. Her crooked smile and rosy cheeks and

the way she leans forward, like she's hanging on my every word. The next ones come out soft, hoarse. Just for her. "Her poems spoke softly—as intimately as confessions between lovers—about the terrible, wonderful ache of being in love."

Chapter 34

OPAL

"There's no way you aren't going to win," Ophelia says, way too close to my ear. "This other shit is like arts-and-crafts time at a preschool after the kids are all coked up on sugar and recess."

"You have such a horrible way with words," Olivia says, lip curled. "Some things need to stay inside thoughts."

Ophelia gives a haughty sniff. "Oh please. Twitter killed that concept almost two decades ago."

"I think you both should stop talking," I say, one eye twitching as I tear the napkin in my hands to shreds. We've been waiting for close to an hour in the large dining room for the awards ceremony to start.

Pepper and I deflated after the presentation, shrinking in and trailing off while our friends surrounded us and chatted away about how much they loved our design. I know this comedown—this crash—after putting so much of yourself into a piece of art, then releasing it to the public. It's like the tether that holds you to earth snaps, and you float aimlessly into space, having no idea where you'll land. If you'll land. It's terrifyingly lonely.

"If you'd all please take your seats," a woman in a crisp business suit says into a microphone at the front of the room, "we'll get started."

After the room settles into silence, the woman launches into her speech.

"Hello, and welcome to this year's Living Art Festival awards ceremony. I'm Karen Summers, president of the American Flora and Fauna Society, making dreams bloom since 1952."

There's a smattering of applause as Karen smiles at the audience. I'm so nervous I think I might projectile vomit right onto the lilac centerpiece in the middle of our table.

"As you know, our mission at AFAFS is to advocate for farmers and florists across the country, protecting their interests and livelihood, while constantly researching best practices in sustainability for the environment." Karen pauses again, and I do manage to clap my shaky, clammy hands for that one.

But instead of getting on with the damn thing, Karen rambles through an excessively detailed history of the organization and draws out thank-yous to the millions of board members who help make it happen, followed by an equally drawn-out thank-you to the Grove Park Inn for hosting.

"I'd also like to give a special thanks to *Something Blue* magazine for once again sponsoring the grand prize. The exposure you've offered to past winners has launched so many careers, and your championing of the AFAFS keeps our work fertile and in bloom." A tinkle of pity laughter ripples across the room.

"And now," Karen says, clapping her hands, "it's time for the fun part, winner announcements!"

It's mind-boggling (and a tiny bit boring) that there are so many awards for flowers. Purest pink rose. And gerbera daisy. And peony. Cut perennials. Cut annuals. Zinnia solid color. Zinnia bicolor (noice). Dahlia, open center, dark or flame blend, variegated or bicolor (again, noice), three blooms, one cultivar. Dahlia, open center, dark or flame blend, variegated or bicolor, three blooms, three cultivars.

Under the table, I google the majority of words in those last two categories and receive little to no clarity.

And through all of these announcements and rounds of applause, my queasiness grows, nervousness pulsing through my joints. Every few minutes, I can feel Pepper's eyes on me, but I never meet them; the pressure is too intense, too scary. I don't want to see the hope I planted there as the fear we're going to lose shrivels all of mine.

"And now, for our biggest award of the evening." A hush falls over the dining hall and cold sweat prickles across the back of my neck. "The award for best large-scale installation and winner of one hundred thousand dollars goes to . . ."

Karen pops the seal on the envelope, making a show of reading the name and grinning in open-mouthed excitement. She leans in close to the microphone: "May I Have This Dance!"

They project an image of the wedding scene on the screen

behind Karen, the room erupting in applause as a man and woman yelp in excitement, standing and hugging each other before walking to the stage to collect their trophy.

My heart *sinks*.

I don't hear a word of their acceptance speech, the sound of blood rushing in my ears drowning out the noise, my vision going fuzzy as tears gather.

I'm not a gracious loser. Never have been, never will be. Losing fucking sucks—a poignant taunt that your attempt wasn't good enough. Every insecurity gathers in me, small at first, but gaining size and speed as they rush downhill until it's an avalanche of self-doubt threatening to take me out at the knees.

I feel one of my sisters put an arm around me, but I shrug it off. I don't want to be comforted right now. I want to wallow in my misery.

As I turn my face away, my eyes catch Pepper's across the table. And, somehow, my heart sinks further.

Her lips are parted, the corners ticked down, and eyebrows furrowed as she stares at me.

Unable to take the crushing weight of Pepper's expression, I push away from the table, tripping over my feet as I speed to the exit. Embarrassment and failure snag my lungs, stopping me in my tracks in the hall. Not only am I a sore loser, but I'm also a moron making a dramatic exit as if any of it matters. As if I matter.

"Opal?"

Pepper's voice is gasoline on the flames of my messed-up

feelings, every one of her footsteps as she comes toward me an alarm bell blaring that things are about to get so much worse. I wish a trapdoor would open below my feet and swallow me whole. I duck my head, looking to the side as Pepper stops next to me.

"What's going on? Why did you walk out?"

Words dam up in my throat, emotions building into a swollen knot trying to crack through. I want to be the person who lets out a deep breath, calmly turns to Pepper and talks through it all. I wish I could parse out my feelings, lay them at Pepper's feet, ask her to throw me a bone as I sort them into something reasonable.

But that's not me.

Instead, face hot and splotchy, I let out a rude grunt in response, gesturing at the room we vacated, then cross my arms over my chest, staring at Pepper as hurt and embarrassment churns into anger because that's easier than feeling shitty about myself.

And I hate myself for it. I'm a bundle of too-sharp feelings, tangled into knots, and frustrated beyond reason that I can't have a normal reaction for once.

Pepper cocks her head to the side as she looks at me, confusion morphing into cold layers of protection. "What?" she finally spits out, a sharp tone to her voice that makes my angry monster of emotions nod in satisfaction.

"We fucking lost, Pepper."

"Yeah, I noticed."

I scoff. "Well. What do you expect me to say?"

Pepper drags her palm over the crown of her head, smoothing back flyaway hairs, then shrugs. "I don't know. I guess something a bit more substantial than that."

"Ha. You first."

"I mean, obviously it's a less-than-ideal outcome. Complicates things."

Her words squeeze my heart to a bitter pulp. I wonder if anything I ever do, ever try, will wind up as anything other than a complicated mess. "Incredible insight. Thank you for clearing that up."

"Why are you being so mean?" she asks suddenly, shoulders curling as she wraps her arms around her middle. "Are you seriously this upset they didn't like your design?"

Rage lashes through me. "Wow. Real nice, Pepper. What a source of comfort."

"You aren't the only one disappointed here!" Pepper yells, throwing up her hands. "I'm crushed too. So what's the point of all this?" She looks around, as if our mess exists as splattered paint on the walls.

I'm backed into a corner, every insecurity oozing out of my pores, gripping me around the throat.

What's the point.

Fair enough.

While my own pride is battered, under the blaze of Pepper's hurt eyes, I realize how much worse the damage is that I've done to her. I crashed into Pepper's life like a hurricane, disrupting her peace, pushing her limits, then failed her entirely.

I'm the reason for that frown on her face, responsible for

the lines of defeat around her eyes and mouth. I've let her down like everyone else in her life. If she couldn't admit to liking me before, there's no way she'll ever like me now.

Any meaning, any purpose we had, just burned to ash in that dining room. What could either of us hope to rebuild from the soot?

"There is no point," I say, meeting her eyes for half a second before losing my nerve and blinking away. "None at all."

With my head still ducked and tears pricking my eyes, I shoulder past her, leaving yet another mess in my wake.

Chapter 35

PEPPER

Opal and I haven't talked in two days.

And I'm ever so slightly absolutely panicking about it.

Granted, I didn't come close to saying anything even remotely helpful after we lost, but I'm a slow processor; swamped by emotions of my own and trying to understand the ones of others usually leaves me a tangled mess with my head up my ass. What I should have told Opal is that watching her talk about Sappho moved me to tears, that they're wrong for not choosing our design, that I think she's a winner no matter what.

But things derailed so quickly and viciously, I became defensive, Opal's anger feeling personal. Like I hadn't measured up to what she needed me for. Like I hadn't played my role.

It took me back to every tongue-lashing from Trish, every screaming accusation that I'd messed up her plans, screwed up a con. Said the wrong thing, acted the wrong way, and caused her a headache of issues.

I know Opal is not Trish. I know she wasn't using me, but Trish's torture was so acutely personal over the years, it's hard not to assume everyone has the same goal when their emotions run hot.

And I want to tell Opal this. I want to ask her what she was really feeling during our fight, if she's mad at me. I want to apologize that my words hit below the belt, that I hurt her feelings as I navigated my own.

But the silence between us is so vast, growing and growing and, holy hell, growing some more. It's become its own presence, a large blob of a being pressing into the room, squeezing through every crack and doorway and landing on my shoulders, wrapping around my throat so no words can come out.

Opal's slept in her own bed ever since.

I've been trying to carry on with everything else like normal, back to my routine of rising with the sun, picking flowers and bundling them for others to use in amazing creations. But it feels so . . . empty. So hollow without Opal with me, her rosy cheeks and silly comments sharp little memories as I pluck and prune my garden.

I want so badly to make this right. I wish I knew where to start.

I'm not sure how she does it, but Opal always manages to be where I'm not, and I sigh as I watch her duck her head against the sharp, oppressive midday sun and trudge to the shed to work as I stand in the kitchen, washing my lunch dishes. She's going to give herself heatstroke with how much time she's spending in there, door shut tight.

I want to march across the grass and barge into that space. I want to grab her by the shoulders and hug her and shake her and beg her to tell me how to fix this, how to earn those belly laughs and gorgeous smiles of hers.

But I'm not a fighter. I'm not brave or bold or any of those things. I watch life happen around me, getting knocked around by its current, never planting myself firmly enough to push back. I pull the curtains closed against the window and hang my head in shame, tears streaking down my cheeks while my chest is sliced open.

The sensation is disorientingly familiar, and I realize it's grief. Not the rough, calloused-over grief for Grandma Lou I've tucked deep in my chest, never looking at, growing around it until I'm, hopefully, one day big enough that I don't notice its weight.

This grief is fresh and sharp and has teeth that rip me open with fresh wounds.

It's a mourning for the bleak path ahead of me, this empty void where Opal so recently was. She's right there, so close. But, somehow, I've never felt so alone.

Without giving my feet permission to move, I find myself wandering aimlessly through the bottom floor of the house. Stomach curdling, I stop in front of Grandma Lou's bedroom door.

I haven't been inside since she died. The suddenness of her

death—passing peacefully in sleep—too painful, too real, to enter the space that was so entirely her. The preserved little bubble of her last day here. Her last day with me.

When she died and her body was taken away, Diksha went in for me. Made her bed. Opened the blinds like Lou loved in the morning. Grabbed her favorite outfit to be cremated in. Diksha looked for the will too, gathering any documents that seemed important for the management of the farm. There weren't many. She wasn't much of a record keeper, and her room was a designated haven free from work.

And while Diksha gave care to the last pieces of Grandma Lou, I sat like a coward with my back pressed to the closed door, hands shaking as I tucked my feelings away.

I didn't know loss could make you so numb. But the numbness was heavy, sucking all the feeling from my body and leaving me empty. Except for the threat of pain. That lived and grew, making me terrified to even move most days.

It wasn't until Opal showed up that I started to feel again.

With a deep, shaky breath, I raise my hand, and turn the doorknob.

I blink, eyes adjusting to the sunlight streaming in. The room is small, every surface softened by the thin layer of dust that sits upon it. On wobbly legs, I take one step into the room. Then another, standing in the center of her space.

I almost expect to see her perched in her bed, a steaming mug of tea next to her as she reads a book, the way she would smile at me over the edges of it. A knot gathers in my throat, and I look away, eyes landing on her vanity, the small vials of her creams and perfumes, a line of her ceramic trinkets next to the mirror.

Her wardrobe catches my attention next, and I move to it in three strides, pulling the doors open and pressing my face against the familiar, soft fabric of her shirts. I breathe in deeply, a tiny sob rattling out as my tears fall against the worn sleeves. I pull one down from the hanger, sniffing it again and hugging it tight to my chest before I slip it over my arms, wrap it around my torso.

I cry even harder, and it feels so good to let go—to let so many feelings I've held locked in my chest pour out as I wrap myself in her memory.

I miss her. I'll always miss her. But the missing isn't killing me like I thought it would. It's a beautiful ache, a sacred, precious reminder of how much love I hold for her.

I stumble to her mattress, and thousands of late-night conversations, me cross-legged at the end while she was tucked in tight at the top, rush through my head. She talked to me about everything. Flowers and fears and faith and love. She told me stories and listened to mine. She gave me space to grow in that spot at the end of her bed. It was always my favorite.

I curl up tight against her pillow, hugging it to me as more sobs rip through my system, and it's like I can feel her trace a loving hand through my hair, down my back, as she quietly encourages me to feel everything rushing through me.

I cry until my brain goes hazy and the world outside the window is touched with dusk. I cry for this woman I love so much until I can't cry anymore, putting to rest the pain that has eaten at me for so long. And then I lie there, and just breathe.

•   •   •

I stir from sleep a few hours later, rubbing my eyes and stretching with a yawn. I hug the pillow one more time, breathing deep, and I realize that, despite the ache in my chest, I'm smiling.

Sitting up, I click on the lamp next to me, blinking at the light. That's when I notice the intricately carved box on the bedside table, and my smile grows. I'd forgotten this gorgeous thing existed. Picking it up, I roll it between my hands, thumbs tracing over the ornate flowers on the top.

This box held my fascination to no end when I first got to Grandma Lou's house.

All women need a puzzle box to hold their secrets, Grandma Lou had told me one night, sliding it across the table.

What's a puzzle box? I'd asked, trying to pry the lid open without any luck.

Well, exactly what it sounds like, she'd said with a kind-hearted chuckle. *There's a trick to unlocking it.*

She moved to squat beside my seat at the table. With sure fingers, she twisted the three poppies on the top until their longest petals overlapped and a little *click* sounded, a hidden compartment on the side popping open. Grandma Lou fished out the tiny brass key, handing it to me. She slid aside a hidden panel in the shape of a leaf on the back, revealing the keyhole.

Pretty cool, huh?

It's amazing, I said, unlocking the box. She'd had some

letters in there, a few pressed flowers, and a two-dollar bill. *These are your secrets?* I'd asked, twirling the dried tulip between my fingers.

She'd laughed, then poked me on the nose. *Sorry to disappoint, sweets. One day, you can have it and fill it with your much more interesting secrets.*

I'd fiddled with it so often over the years, twisting the flowers on top absentmindedly while I'd listen to Lou talk.

Holding it now with shaky fingers, I unlock it like I've done so many times, the little click creating a familiar echo in my chest. But as I slide open the top, a folded piece of paper tumbles out and onto my lap. It's crisper and newer than the old letters she'd stored in there, and as I pick it up, I see my name scribbled across the front.

There's a pink neon Post-it stuck on the opposite side, Lou's large, rounded letters soft like a hug as I skim what she's written.

TO-DO:

- ~~Rotate dahlia plots for next season~~
- Or trim maple over plot 6 get more light? ✓✓✓
- Consider selling herbs in spring (??)
- Ask Jane Taylor three farms up the hill for sprouts
- Christmas gift for Pepper? → new overalls
- Find lawyer / get estate set up

My choked giggle morphs into a tremble vibrating through me, emotions building behind my eyes. Of course Grandma

Lou would prioritize getting her affairs in order far after her dahlias' well-being.

A few tears roll down my cheeks as I gently place the Post-it on the bedside table. With a deep breath, I unfold the sheets and read.

My dearest Pepper,

Watching you grow is the greatest gift life has given me. I love you now and I'll love you always.

Love,
Grandma Lou

I read it over and over until I hear her soft, lovely voice saying the words to me. When I finally am able to set it down, I look at the second sheet, heart beating up to my throat as I realize what it is.

The will.

Chapter 36

PEPPER

"Why aren't we talking?"

I have Opal cornered. I stayed up all night, pacing around the house until I was dizzy with frustration at how quickly everything crumbled. I've been waiting for her to sneak into the kitchen, standing between her and the coffee machine knowing full well this is a low blow, but I can't go one more day in this silent torture.

Opal's head jerks back, and she blinks a few times, still groggy. I take pity on her, pouring a cup of coffee and heaping sugar in it as she likes, then handing it to her.

Eyes wide and fixed on me, she takes a timid sip. "I don't know what you're talking about," she whispers, gaze falling to the floor.

"Words. Us not using them. I want to know why."

Opal waves her hand. "I could ask you the same thing. I think we both know it's rather obvious."

"Opal, my autistic ass hasn't picked up on something 'obvious' once in my life. So, please, enlighten me."

She frowns, chin lifting in defiance. "I mean, *obviously* I'm mortified about the competition and our . . . our fight after. But you haven't been speaking to me either, Pepper. I've been following your lead."

Now it's my turn to look affronted. "My *lead*? What lead? I didn't lead us here."

"Right, because you've initiated so many conversations since we've been back."

"You're the one who took off," I say, voice rising in a tangled mix of frustration and desperation.

Opal blinks, then looks away, eyes fixed on the ground.

Dammit. This isn't what I want. I don't want more fighting, more confusion. I want to hug this emotional, complicated woman to my chest and hold her there until we figure this out. Maybe hold her there long after that.

"I don't want us not to talk," I finally manage, taking a step toward her. She takes one back. I pretend it doesn't crush me to pieces. "In fact, we *need* to talk."

Her shoulders hunch around her mug, eyes still fixed on the ground. "I know what this is about, and all I can say is I'm sorry."

It takes me a second to realize that she's talking about the competition. "This isn't about that," I say, waving it away. "It's about the farm."

She finally glances at me, face weary and defeated. "Pepper, listen, I'm sorry about all that too. I'm sorry for barging in here and forcing you to live with me and put up with all this bullshit. It was . . . Well, it's been a mess from the start, huh?"

"Huh?" I echo, my chest hollowing out.

She blows out a breath between tight lips, tipping her head back. "And I want you to know that I'm cutting my losses on it. I can't keep torturing you like this, disrupting your life. The farm is yours. We'll call it even."

My head spins, the words she's saying all jumbled up and clanging around up there. "I don't need you to give it to me," I say, lips twisting. "That's what I'm trying to tell you. I found the will."

"You . . . you what?"

"Found the will." I wave the document clutched in my hand. "Lou *did* leave it to me. Left it all to me. Didn't do me a ton of favors in finding the damn thing but . . . yeah."

Opal stares at the paper, lips parted, face pale. Eventually, she nods. "Right. That's great. Even better."

"Better?"

She shrugs, giving me a strained smile that doesn't reach her eyes. "We don't have to go through any official transfer of ownership or whatever legal nonsense. It's yours. Always has been, always will be."

"What's going on?" I whisper, taking another step toward her. Again, she steps back.

It's then that I notice two duffel bags at the foot of the stairs. I stare at them, eyebrows furrowing

"Are you . . . are you leaving?" I say. Panic washes through me, gobbling up every cell as my eyes flick between the bags and Opal's stricken face.

She opens her mouth, shuts it, biting down hard on her lip. She looks at the bags too, then at the door. Eventually, she nods and whispers, "Yeah."

The word scrapes close to the bone, making me grit my teeth from the force of it.

"But . . . why?"

Opal blinks, a few tears slipping out of the corners of her eyes, and I want to go to her. I want to wipe those tears away. Kiss a smile onto her lips. But I can't. I'm rooted to the spot, watching my world fall apart, the pieces slipping away like water through the cracks between my fingers.

"Because I'm sick of being an intruder in your life, Pepper," she says, voice so small, I barely hear her. "I'm sick of barreling through here and screwing things up for you and making messes. So I'm removing myself from the equation." She sets her coffee down on the table and moves toward the bags.

"You don't screw things up." I shout the words. A desperate reach to stop her from disappearing.

Opal lets out a humorless laugh. "Really? Because you've made it pretty clear that this entire summer was one giant disaster."

My head jerks back. "I never said that."

"You not speaking to me got the point across. You might not realize it yet, but I know deep down this is what you want."

"You don't get to assume my feelings for me, Opal," I say,

throwing my arms up. "They're mine to figure out and sort through."

"Well, what else am I supposed to do with your feelings?" she says, voice rising, color high on her cheeks. "It's not like you share them with me. I've opened the vein over and over to tell you how much I like you like a fucking *fool,* while you give me nothing."

"Nothing?" I shout back. "I've given you nothing? I'm an absolute wreck over you."

She opens her mouth, an obstinate twist to her lips, but the sound of a honk and slamming car doors makes us both jump. Our gazes shoot to the window, and we move in sync to see who's here.

"Shit," Opal says, whipping away from the pane and pressing her back to the wall.

"What?" I say, glaring at the strangers in my driveway. The guy has a scraggly, chin-strap beard that he's scratching as he stretches, and the woman is tall and waifish, intimidating in a way that cool people who know they're cool always are. "Do you know them?"

As I say the last part, the woman calls out, *"Opalllllllllllll."*

Opal's white as a ghost, eyes wide and lip clamped between her teeth as she shifts from foot to foot. "That's my, uh, friend, Laney," she says, finally looking at me. "And my ex, Miles."

Chapter 37

OPAL

"Laney," I say, stepping onto the porch. It's the only word I can manage. I clear my throat. "What are you doing here?"

"Well, the prodigal son returns," Laney says, cocking a hip and fixing me with a vicious smile as she slow-claps.

"You came to her," Pepper says from behind me. "That makes no sense."

Laney shoots her a dirty look, but quickly fixes her attention back on me. "What, no love for your best friends, Opal?" she says, gesturing between herself and Miles.

"Hi, Opie," Miles says, giving me a loose wave.

Even from here, I can see how red and glassy his eyes are, and I can tell he's stoned. Well, at least that makes him a bit easier to deal with.

"What are you doing here?" I repeat, moving on wobbly legs to give Laney a stiff hug.

"Well, been so long since we heard from you, we thought

we would surprise you. Started getting worried you'd forgotten all about us now that you have all that big fancy money." She shoots another sharp look at Pepper, but fixes me with a smile. "How ya been, buddy?"

"I've . . . uh . . ."

"Amazing," Laney says. "So, get this. We're finally doing it," she says, gesturing again at Miles.

My eyes flick between them. "Doing what?"

Laney frowns. "Going on tour!"

I literally could not be less impressed. "Oh. Wow. That's great."

"Right?" she says, smirking at me. "Got lined up at a ton of *amazing* venues, dude. Like, you won't believe some of these spots."

"Wow," I repeat, sounding like Owen Wilson. I'm too confused by this surprise and my argument with Pepper and everything colliding together all at damn once to form any coherent sentences.

"I *know*. And here we were, driving to our show in Atlanta, and I was like, *Miles, wait, we can't do this without Opal*."

"Be so bummed to do it without you," Miles says, eyes barely open. I nod at him.

"So I was like, let's go get the bitch and drag her on tour with us!"

"O-on tour? Why?"

Laney cocks her head, looking at me like we're in a play and I'm messing up my lines. "Well, because it's not like you have anything better going on, right?"

"I . . . uh . . . How did you know where I am?" I've made sure to never give her my address, and it's not like my sisters would hand out that information. Especially to Laney.

She waves the question away. "Friend finder," she says, shaking her phone. "Anyway. You in? It'll be so fun. And listen, I know we're in this dinky van, but we can make it work. If not, we're so open to like, whatever you would prefer to travel in and have no problem switching it up. Babe," she says, turning to Miles. "Do you still have that site up with the cool tour buses? Show Opal."

"Dude, some of these are sick," he says, trying to hand me his phone. I kindly slap his arm away.

"And like, listen," Laney continues, as if she ever gives me an opportunity not to listen, "we were totally planning on like, sleeping in the van, doing it old-school like all the greats and shit or whatever but like, if you're more comfortable in a hotel and stuff, we can totally be flexible. We want you to be comfortable, you know?"

Laney looks at me like she's expecting me to say something, and I flap my mouth open and closed a few times. Luckily, Pepper spares me from having to make a comment.

"Excuse me, did you just admit to tracking Opal down on an app?" she says, voice rough and incredulous.

Laney glares at Pepper. "Who are you?"

Pepper places a hand on my shoulder, pulling me to her side. "I'm the owner of this land you're standing on."

"Ew. Property ownership? You should check your privilege."

"Totally," Miles adds, nodding.

I think my head is going to explode. Or Pepper's might first.

"Answer the question." She turns to me. "Opal, did you want them to know you were here?"

Laney rolls her eyes before I can respond. "It's truly not that serious. We're trying to do something nice for Opal."

Pepper steps in front of me now. "No, this is actually massively creepy and fits rather closely to the definition of stalking."

Laney's jaw drops. "Oh my *God*, get over yourself. We're not *stalking* her. I'm her best friend," Laney says, squaring off to Pepper.

"We have a thing," Miles adds dully, giving me a lazy smile.

"*Had* a thing," I whisper with an appalled shudder.

"Tracking down someone's location and forcing them to see you is pretty much the literal definition of stalking," Pepper says, standing to her full height, looking down on both of them. "So I suggest you get the fuck off my property and away from my girlfriend before I act within my rights to remove you myself."

All the air is sucked from the earth, and I stare at Pepper with my mouth hanging open, heart pounding so hard against my chest I'm worried it's going to rip out of there and launch itself at her.

Pepper, at her core, is one of the biggest softies I've ever met. She's the poster child for still waters running deep, nothing but warmth and bubblegum-pink love under that beautiful, but intimidating, exterior. But, as she towers over everyone, her mouth a strict line, jaw set and fists clenched at her sides, she might just be the scariest person on the planet.

I love her so much for it.

"Opal, are you going to let her talk to me like that?" Laney takes a step toward us. "I'm about to—"

It's my turn to move in front of Pepper. I come to Laney's shoulder, but it doesn't matter; no one is going to charge at my girl.

"You listen to me and you listen good, because I'm only going to say it once. If you even breathe in Pepper's general direction again, I will not rest until I have personally and profoundly ruined your life. You've spent the entirety of our friendship walking all over me, and that ends here and now because I'll be damned if you use that foul mouth to threaten her. Now, you better do as you're told and get lost before things get ugly. Understood?"

Laney gapes, blinking at me for a solid thirty seconds.

"Am I understood?" I echo, jabbing my finger against her chest.

She nods, features fixed in a frown as she takes a step back. I follow her until her back is pressed against her van door. I keep my eyes glued to hers as she fumbles with the handle, then squeezes herself inside the driver's seat.

"Same goes for you, Miles," I say, rolling my eyes as he slow-blinks at the scene. He nods and gets in the van.

"You've turned into a real fucking bitch, Opal," Laney says through the protection of the van window.

"Takes one to know one," I spit back. Not my sickest burn by any means, but I have so much adrenaline pumping through me I'm about to pass out if this doesn't wrap up soon. "And lose my number," I add.

Laney flips me off as she peels down the gravel driveway, and I shoot the gesture right back. I giggle as I glance over my shoulder and see Pepper doing the same.

Real classy broads, the pair of us.

Stillness slowly settles back over the farm, and my knees almost buckle as the events of the morning rush into me like a tidal wave.

But Pepper's there, hand on my lower back, pulling me toward her. Hugging me close.

And I hug her right back because it's Pepper and she's perfect and I want to stay here forever.

But I'm not sure I can. Should. I'm taking up space I don't have a right to.

"You okay?" Pepper asks, releasing me and stepping away. I sway toward her, but resist the urge to reach out.

I want to tell her I'm fine. That I'm sorry for one more mess dumped on her doorstep. That if she'll just make this easy, just let me go, I'll stop causing trouble for her. But instead, I say, "You called me your girlfriend."

Pepper lets out a deep, long sigh, digging the heels of her hands against her eyes before dropping them and fixing me with an open stare. "Well . . . duh, Opal."

"W-why?"

Pepper's laugh is fractured and rough, a small shake to her head as she bites her lip. "Because I *love* you."

My mind is wiped clear like a landslide, until shock floods in. "You . . . what?"

"I love you," she repeats, voice hoarse, hands shaking. "I love you in the most basic and complicated and overwhelming and simple and inevitable way possible. I would think that's been obvious for some time now."

I shake my head, a teardrop rolling down my cheek.

"Yes," she says, laughing again, but this time it's soft and bright and painted with a mix of exasperation and joy. "I love you so much I could burst with it."

I look down, dragging my toe through the gravel, something dangerous and beautiful rushing through me.

"The Thistle and Bloom is yours. Fully yours. This is your house," I say, waving at the squat cabin that's become so precious to me that a piece of my heart will always sit right at its door. But I'll walk away. I'll make the stupidest choice possible and take the brutal loss of my money and my dreams and every other fanciful idea I built on this ground if it will make Pepper happy. If it will bring her peace.

Pepper nods, squinting at it, a small smile tugging at her lips. "It is. Are you . . . are you still leaving?"

I rake my hands through my hair, tugging at the ends, an exasperated, desperate feeling swelling in my chest and threatening to crack me open. "Yes? No? Did you mean what you just said? Because I'm giving you an out if it was in the heat of the moment. I know that can happen and the last thing I want is for you to feel trapped or you owe me something. I can't keep screwing up your life. I can't—"

"Opal." She steps forward, placing a finger over my lips. "Please shut up." She says the words softly. Sweetly. Like she placed a heart instead of a period at the end of her sentence. "I want you to stay if you want to stay."

A tiny, frustrated sound comes from the back of my throat, and I back away, putting much-needed distance between us. I can't think clearly with her so close.

"Of course I want to stay," I whisper, looking into her deep brown eyes. "I want to stay so long at the Thistle and Bloom that my veins turn to roots in the soil. I want to walk up and down the rows of flowers until I know the paths in the pitch black, my final destination always being your doorstep. But I'm a mess, Pepper. I came in and upended your life and made a giant disaster of everything. And you don't need that. You don't need the headaches I cause. I mean, look at what just happened. I don't belong here."

Pepper is still as a statue, and I'm scared to even breathe. But, in a flash, she closes the distance between us, reaching out, fingers diving into my hair, tilting my face up to hers.

"You," Pepper says slowly, carefully, so I hang on every word, "are the most chaotic, wild, wonderful person I have ever met. You have upended my life and I don't ever, *ever* want it righted again. If you don't think you belong here, we can talk about that. But all I know is I belong with *you*. We can figure the rest out as it comes. But I love you, Opal. I love you and your messes and your laugh and your hair and the way you say my name with that perfect, exasperated sigh that makes me feel like the word was created just for you to speak it."

My lips part, but no sound comes out, tears rolling down my cheeks. She brushes them away with her thumbs and smiles at me.

"I need you to understand something," she says, voice warm and smoky like a shot of whiskey after being out in the cold. "My house, your house—the details of it don't matter. I want *our* house. Our home. Next to you is my favorite place in the world, and that's the only spot I care about holding on to."

"I love you so much it scares me," I whisper, placing my hands on top of hers. "I'm scared I'm going to screw this up or I'll be too much to deal with and you'll get sick of me. Or that I won't be enough and you'll realize you deserve better."

Pepper laughs, the noise soft and disbelieving. Then she presses forward, kissing me softly, resting her forehead against mine. "You silly, silly woman. We will both screw things up, and that's okay. My love for you exists because you exist. It isn't based on whatever ridiculous standards you hold yourself to. Do you want more than what I have to give you?"

"No," I say, shaking my head. The word is solid, planted and sturdy between us like an oak.

"Do you want someone less? I'm not an easy person either, Opal."

"You're perfect," I say, holding on to her wrists, squeezing them tight. I may never let go.

"And so are you," she says, wiping away a few more of my

tears. "I'm stuck on you and there's no place I'd rather be. So stop trying to talk us both out of it and kiss me already."

And, for once, with no fuss or protest or additional words, I do exactly as she asks. I kiss her until the earth stops spinning, time unspooling around our ankles. I kiss her like it's our first and our last and the promise of every kiss that will come in between.

I kiss her how I love her, deep and steady and a little bit frantic.

And she kisses me right back.

Eventually, we come up for air, giggling and crying, and holding each other so close we sigh at the comfort of it.

As we walk back to our home, I grab her hand. She holds my heart.

And nothing is perfect but everything is right, and that's all that matters.

Epilogue

A few years later

PEPPER

In a world full of endless wonders, the most special place on earth is my spot cuddled next to Opal in front of our fireplace.

"Cheers, to another amazing season," I say, clinking my mug of hot chocolate against hers.

"Cheers, sweetheart," she says, leaning in and giving me a kiss more decadent than chocolate could ever hope to be.

"Couldn't have done it without you."

"Eh, you bring a few skills to the barn," she says, nudging me with her shoulder. I accept the compliment with a scrunch of my nose, turning to watch the first early snowfall of the season dance across the window.

We've finally closed the farm up for the year, and now it's the season of rest until spring rolls around, and I'm borderline giddy at the prospect of gray winter mornings snuggled in bed with Opal, giggling the day away like we did so many times last winter. And the winter before that.

The day Opal chose to stay, it finally felt like life clicked into place. It didn't take long for us to find a rhythm, the energy through the cabin like a heartbeat between us. The way Opal always knows which plot I'm at if I let her sleep in. The unique creak of the floorboards when she gets up from the bed to take a shower. The cadence of her steps through the house when she paces around her studio—Grandma Lou's old bedroom—chasing an idea.

Opal yawns, and I take her mug, setting both on the hearth, then pull her closer to my side, playing with her lavender-colored hair as we watch the fire crackle and pop.

We quickly discovered that one of the best things about having the privilege of disposable income is being able to tap into resources. Like a really dope lawyer.

With the will, it was easy to contest Trish's sale of the property, and while she had spent a big chunk of the money, we got the assets transferred into my name, quickly liquidating them and putting the funds directly into the farm, giving us plenty of room to breathe.

The Thistle and Bloom has been growing wildly ever since.

Opal's added to our success by tying her shoes into the business. The little genius hand-paints gardening clogs—and other various footwear—decking them out with flowers inspired by our gardens. Her online shop got picked up by a few media outlets last holiday season, then a few more, and the demand this past year was so high, she hired two employees to help keep up with orders.

It's hard to believe one person can hold so much beauty within them.

"I have something for you," she says, stirring from my arms and sitting up, a mischievous smile spreading across her mouth.

"Please don't let it be another severed-body-part cake," I say, guard going up. Opal and Diksha have made it a weird bonding ritual to surprise me with a random and highly detailed anatomy cake every few months. Apparently my appalled reactions are "too funny" and "worth every cent." I think they're both evil.

"Not today," Opal says with a giggle. "Here." She reaches around me, rummaging on the low shelf of the coffee table for a moment before dropping a thick envelope in my hands.

She's decorated the outside with doodles, and I hold it close to make out the details in the dim firelight. I feel like I'm going to cry as I realize they're ink vignettes of us—my face scrunched up in laughter, Opal holding me close as we dance in the kitchen, our hands intertwined over a bed of flowers.

I lurch forward, taking her face in my hands and kissing her deeply. "I love it."

Opal laughs, pulling back. "That's not the gift, silly. You have to open it."

"I don't want to rip it," I say in outrage, clutching the envelope to my chest.

Opal laughs again, leaning forward and kissing my forehead. "I'll make you a thousand envelopes, love. But please open this one."

With a resigned sigh, I hook my finger under the seal and pry it open. Glossy magazine paper folded a few times falls out, and I unfurl it, squinting at in confusion. The sheet is divided into a bunch of small boxes, tiny descriptions in each. I look at the second sheet, and it's the same thing.

"Uh . . . thanks," I say, setting them down gently. "I'm always looking for new stuff to read."

Opal snorts. "Oh my *God*, you're hard to give gifts to. Read the note."

I fish into the envelope again, pulling out two more sheets of paper, these crisp and official feeling. I read the one handwritten by Opal first.

Pepper,

You are the brightest person I know and a force of nature. I believe in you to do anything and everything you want, my love. Enjoy every moment of this next journey.

XO,
O

I read it over a few times, eyebrows knitting in confusion. I glance at Opal, and her face is red with excitement, like she's about to explode joy all over me. I look at the next sheet. It's addressed to me, *529 Account Plan* typed across the top in bold letters. I read the first few lines.

Dear Pepper,

Congratulations on opening your 529 Education Savings Plan! Please find your account details below.

My eyes scan over the chart with large numbers multiple times before rolling up to look at Opal.

"Opal . . . what is this?"

"You're going to college!" she shrieks, clapping her hands, then locking them under her chin.

"I'm *what*?"

"Going to college, you gorgeous girl."

"B-but . . . how?"

Opal, grins, grabbing my free hand. "I had a really good year in sales and the farm is in a sturdy spot so I thought about what to do with the extra money, and it was obvious! I set up an education savings plan for you. Now, don't panic, I know it takes you a while to wrap your head around things and that's *fine*. You have all the time in the world. But, when you're ready, the money is there. And it's all yours. I put enough in for the first two years because I didn't want to assume you would do a four-year program or anything like that, but, if you want to, UNC Asheville is right there and I'm ready to deposit the money whenever you need it. And that's what this is," she says, grabbing the magazine sheets. "From UNCA's course catalog. And these are from Blue Ridge Community College. I tore out the ones about agriculture and botany, but obviously you can study whatever you want."

"W-why?" I say, head swimming and heart pounding as I stare at Opal. Lovely, wonderful Opal.

She gives me a look like it should be obvious. "Because you deserve it, silly. Because you wanted to go to school and I want to make every dream you've ever had come true. Because I love you and want to spoil you. Because—"

She doesn't get any other words out; I don't let her. I crash into her with too much force, but my Opal doesn't care, she rolls us onto the floor, giggling as I land on top of her, kissing her lips, her cheeks, her neck, anywhere I can reach.

"Are you surprised?" she asks in a breathless murmur, hands slipping through my hair.

I nod against her chest, emotions clogging my throat.

"Are you happy?" she says, even softer.

I pull back, hovering over her, tears slipping down my cheeks. She reaches up, brushing them away, and I turn my head to kiss her palm. "You make me the happiest person in the world," I whisper against her wrist.

"Right back atcha, my sweet Pepper," she says, pressing up to kiss me.

I sit up, pulling her onto my lap, holding her close in front of the fire as I continue to press kisses to her skin, absorbing her hum of satisfaction.

"Let's look at the classes," she says after a while, grabbing the sheets and holding them to the light. I read them over a hundred times, trying to memorize every word like each one is a door to a new world, one that's mine for the making.

Eventually, Opal slumps against my chest, hand resting

over my heartbeat. "I love you," she murmurs, voice thick with sleepiness. I kiss the top of her head.

"Love you so much," I say back.

I toy with the band on her left ring finger as we sit there, breathing slow and steady.

Opal went through a recent obsession with Victorian times, and now we each wear a gold band with an acrostic rainbow of stones, spelling out the other's name. It's silly and bright and beautiful and makes my heart leap every time the sunlight catches it.

"What comes next?" Opal asks through a yawn.

"Sleep," I say with a laugh, tracing circles along her arm.

"And after that?" She tilts her face to look up at me, a radiant smile on those full lips.

I lean in and kiss her, smiling right back. "Well, I guess we better start planning a wedding."

"Hmm," she says, closing her eyes. "Sounds like a lot of work."

"Yeah, well, at least I know someone that has the flowers covered."

"Tal?" she says, without missing a beat.

I pinch her butt as we both laugh.

And that's how we spend the night, holding each other as we giggle and dream and plan for our future.

Messy and radiant and ours.

Anatomy of a Title

We were about sixteen emails deep in a chain of me throwing around title ideas when my editor finally cut me off on flower puns (that is literally what she wrote in the email, lovingly, of course).

Late Bloomer is my fifth published book, and while each one has presented its own unique challenges and sore spots, one of the hardest parts of bringing *this* book into existence was settling on a title. I'm serious. Writing it was hard, don't get me wrong (there are group texts that show just how annoyingly and obnoxiously I suffered through drafting), but when it came time to officially name Opal and Pepper's story, we spent about five months going back and forth and back again.

Originally, this book was called *Pining*, taking place on a Christmas tree farm—NO ONE STEAL THIS IDEA I STILL CALL DIBS AND WANT TO DO SOMETHING WITH IT—but publishing timelines are their own things (don't get me started on that!), and it was determined that this book couldn't come out for the holiday season as originally intended.

Honestly, I was relieved. While I loved the original idea, early in the drafting process it became obvious to me that Pepper is a flower girlie, and I was ready to stick her in spring sunshine and watch her grow. My Google Doc draft went through some really stellar placeholder titles after that, including GAY, GAYY BOOK, PEPPER + OPAL 5EVA . . . For some reason, none of these were deemed particularly marketable. When I finally turned in the book to my editor, it was called *Lavender Haze*. Now, obviously, I'm an unhinged Taylor Swift fan, but I was really drawn to this title because of the term's importance in queer and sapphic history. Alas, this title was in the running for a while, but apparently, there's some modern curse called SEO (stands for Shit Eater's Organization in my mind) that influences how well something shows up on search engines and social media algorithms that essentially sent me back to the drawing board with titles because there is no way my goofy ass book (affectionate) can compete with the monolith that is Taylor Alison Swift.

When it really came down to brainstorming for launch of this book, I sent lists upon lists of progressively more unhinged title options:

❀ Best Buds → gals just being pals!
❀ More than Buds → lots of talk if the use of "bud" as a euphemism for clitoris was a bit too on the nose

❀ Love in Lavender → must pay homage to that sexy lavender massage moment!

❀ Floral Fixation → so fitting for these two on so many levels

❀ What in Carnation → big discussion on if carnations grow in North Carolina. My research showed that they grow mainly in hardiness zones 7–10, and the Thistle and Bloom is in zone 6b. Important to note that there are over 300 carnation variants, so they can sometimes be grown in zone 6!

❀ Lilac Haze/Gaze/Gays

❀ Late Bloomer

❀ Anemones to Lovers → was told it reads too nautical, so I need someone to write mermaid fanfic of Pepper and Opal and name it this please

❀ I'm So T(horny) → like . . . it's such an obvious, perfect choice.

❀ Doom and Bloom

❀ Nip It in the Bud → again with the nipple/clitoris imagery

❀ In Bloom

❀ Damndelion

❀ These Rose Ain't Loyal

❀ Wild Flowers → I was adamant that if we went with this one—which was a very real possibility for a few days there!—it had to be two words, not one. I thought it looked cooler

❀ Suck My Cockscomb

❀ Golden Shower → in my defense, this is a flower and not just a sex thing!

❀ Every Garden Needs a Ho → my personal favorite, apparently not "appropriate"

❀ Best Laid Plants

❀ Okay, Bloomer → shout-out to Emily Minarik for this one (and honestly so many on this list)

❀ Business Is Blooming → luckily I was able to add this joke in during copyedits

❀ Girls and Roses → my fiancé came up with this one and I would LOVE to see Opal and Pepper put onto a Guns N' Roses poster with this title option

As you can tell, I'm extremely professional and not at all overwhelming to work with! By the time I was cut off, the inside of my brain looked like Florence Pugh at the end of *Midsommar* cry-smiling, enveloped in a mountain of flowers. The chaos was eventually whittled down to *What in Carnation, Love in Lavender, In Bloom,* and *Late Bloomer. Late Bloomer* was always my top choice from those options, but there was a lot of hesitation because of the use of the title and variations in books published some years ago. We—sales, creative, editorial teams—jumped from title to title for months, rotating the option of the day (or hour, at certain points) until I was fairly certain this book would be sent to the printers with [TITLE TK] on the front. Eventually my editor and I were both having dreams about which title we decided on.

Finally, we all came to the agreement that *Late Bloomer* was the one, and I couldn't be happier (unless it was *Every Garden Needs a Ho*) with the result.

Opal and Pepper are my late bloomers. Pepper with her sexual identity, obviously, but more so in how both she and Opal take time to realize their wonderful, beautiful value. It's not an easy thing to admit that you are worthy and deserving of love, prickly thorns and messy roots and all, but it was so special to watch these two discover that in each other, and themselves.

Flowers Mentioned in the Book and Their Symbolic Meanings

As a lifelong flower lover with the astonishing ability to kill every plant I touch, writing about a flower farm allowed me to frolic in my wildest fantasies. One of my favorite parts was researching flowers that grow in Western North Carolina as well as the language of flowers. There is such a rich and dynamic history of what flowers mean and the folklore behind them. I relied quite a bit on Victorian interpretations of flowers and the Greek mythology between the origins of certain species. Below I've outlined some of the most prominent flowers and their meaning within *Late Bloomer*.

❀ Anemone: Pepper's favorite flower, said to symbolize the passing of time and forsaken love. I took some creative liberties with the phrase "forsaken love" and how it represents Pepper. She feels as though the only true love she's known (Grandma Lou) has left/abandoned her, and she is, in turn, abandoning the idea of love. But, in the Victorian language of flowers, pairing anemones with yarrow is said to help heal a broken heart, and this pairing pops up in Sappho's hair at the competition. Also, the self-protection anemones exhibit when they curl in their petals during rainstorms symbolizes Pepper's own disposition of self-preservation.

❀ Aster: Said to have formed when the Greek goddess Astraea wept, her tears falling as stardust to the earth, asters growing where they landed. The flower symbolizes patience and justice. Opal has these flowers in the greenhouse for Pepper. I chose to include this flower as a symbol of Opal's willingness to be patient with Pepper as she figures herself out, and also as foreshadowing for the justice the two women get at the end of the story.

❀ Dahlia: Another one of the flowers Opal has in the greenhouse for Pepper, this flower is a symbol for eternal love. It also symbolizes persistence, which I think is a perfect word for Opal and her unrelenting love for Pepper. Also, they're my personal favorite!

❀ Lilac: First love (aw). Opal harvests lilacs with Diksha while Pepper is recovering from her migraine. I chose this flower because I felt like this moment was one of the first times Opal showed her developing feelings (and eventual love) for Pepper through this act of service.

❀ Poppy: Because of the flower's association with opium, it often is symbolic of sleep. But what comes with sleep? Dreams! This is another flower Opal has for Pepper in the greenhouse, and I wanted it to symbolize Opal's desire for her and Pepper to share their dreams and hopes together.

❀ Rose: This one is rather obvious, but roses symbolize love! They were Grandma Lou's favorite because she is the embodiment of love. In the novel, Pepper states she hates roses because they serve as a reminder of how much love she feels she's lost with Grandma Lou's passing. I like to think that, after a few years, Pepper learns to like roses again as she realizes Grandma Lou's love isn't gone; it just lives within her in a different form. I also like to imagine that she and Opal keep a small vase of fresh roses in Grandma Lou's old room/Opal's new art studio in her memory.

❀ Thistles: Rather harsh in their symbolism, but thistles symbolize general distrust and dislike for humankind, which sums up Pepper when we first meet her. Thistles are also very resilient, able to survive in many environments, much like Pepper. Naming the farm

Thistle and Bloom was a nod to Pepper's growth from prickly and distrusting to opening herself up to others like a blooming flower opens its petals to the sun.

❀ Violets: Tracing back to Sappho, the violet is considered the flower of sapphics. Sappho often referred to violets in her poems about women. The sapphic flag also has a violet in the center. Opal decorates her room with a hand-painted tapestry of violets.

❀ Yarrow: A cure for a broken heart! It is also a flower that symbolizes courage, things both women have in spades. (Get it? Like the gardening tool? I'll see myself out . . .)

Acknowledgments

Despite my many, many group chat texts and chaotic panic emails that express the contrary, writing is my greatest joy, and I can't believe I get to do this job. Although my books are the product of staring (crying) at a blank page alone for hours on end as I try to pull words from my brain, they wouldn't exist without the help of so many wonderful people.

Eileen Rothschild, editor extraordinaire. This is our fifth book together, and I still can't wrap my head around getting to work with you. You are a fearless champion of my work and a powerhouse of a person. Thank you for always giving me the space to try something new, and I'm so excited for all the books our future holds.

Thank you to my spectacular agent, Courtney Miller-Callihan. You somehow manage to put up with my bullshit and never make me feel annoying and I'm so thankful for it. You infuse grace and intention in everything you do, and I'm so lucky to work with you and have you in my corner. Cheyenne Faircloth, you ethereal, wonderful being. Thank you so much for your feedback on early drafts. Your input made all the difference.

Lisa Bonvissuto! You are such a joy to work with, and publishing is so lucky to have you.

I am truly spoiled by my stellar SMP team, and I can never express how thankful I am for your continued support, passion, and love for these goofballs! Lexi Neuville, thank you for being a Canva queen and somehow translating my incoherent emails into beautiful graphics. Alyssa Gammello, you've made so many of my bucket list author event dreams come true. You're a star. Thank you to Brant Janeway and Marissa Sangiacomo for all that you do to get these books out to readers! Huge thank you to Kerri Resnick for designing this cover and to Jenifer Prince for what has to be the most stunning illustration I've ever seen. You both captured Pepper and Opal so perfectly and I want to plaster this image on every surface I see.

Thank you to Ava Wilder for beta-reading this and encouraging me to put down the matches every time I wanted to burn a draft to ash. You're a star. Thank you to Kaitlyn Hill for being eternally encouraging and relatably anxious about how ass the writing process can be.

Katie Holt, you absolute angel. Thank you for being such a bright light. Your joy and love for romance constantly inspires me to keep writing. You're amazing and I admire you endlessly.

Emily Minarik, I don't know why people are so mean to you in restaurants, but I hope you know I always have your back

(I mean . . . I'm too afraid to also get yelled at in a restaurant to hop into the moment in any substantial way, but I will always be there to talk about it after). Also, thanks for beta-reading this book and loving Opal and Pepper as much as I do.

Thank you, Saniya Walawalkar, for always diving headfirst into my atrociously messy first drafts and somehow finding something incredibly kind and encouraging to say. You make me want to bash my head repeatedly on my keyboard a little less during drafting.

My bestie, Megan Stillwell. I don't think you've read this one yet, but you've emotionally supported my neurotic ass through memes and TikToks for years and I literally would not be able to keep pushing through the rough patches of writing without you. I love you.

Thank you to every bookseller, librarian, and reader who has taken the time to recommend my books to someone. You are the backbone of publishing and an author is nothing without book pushers like you!

To my queer found family that has given me the space and love to come into my identity, knowing you has brought me so much comfort.

And to Ben. If everything goes to plan, this book will be coming out forty days before we get married. You have loved, supported, and cheered on every version of me. It's my life's greatest blessing to have you as my best friend and the person I'll be spending the rest of my life with. Thank you for believing in me. I'm so lucky to call you mine.

Ben Eisdorfer

MAZEY EDDINGS is a neurodiverse author, dentist, and (most importantly) stage mom to her cats, Yaya and Zadie. She can most often be found reading romance novels under her weighted blanket and asking her fiancé to bring her snacks. She's made it her personal mission in life to destigmatize mental health issues and write love stories for every brain. With roots in Ohio and Philadelphia, she now calls Asheville, North Carolina, home. She is the author of *A Brush with Love*, *Lizzie Blake's Best Mistake*, *The Plus One*, and *Tilly in Technicolor*.